Guy Bellamy was born in Bristol but has lived mostly in Surrey. After National Service in Germany with the RAF, he went into journalism and has worked on newspapers in Cornwall, Bournemouth, Brighton and Fleet Street. He has written several short stories for *Punch*, and his novels include *The Nudists*, *The Secret Lemonade Drinker*, *In the Midday Sun*, *The Tax Exile*, *The Sinner's Congregation*, *A Village Called Sin* and *The Comedy Hotel*, all published by Penguin. He is married and has a young daughter.

Rave reviews for

The Nudists:
'Whip-crack wit and street-smart prose ... funny, caustic and gloriously readable' – *Evening Standard*

and **The Secret Lemonade Drinker**:
'One of the wittiest books I've read in years' – Erica Jong

and **In the Midday Sun**:
'The blue skies blacken very funnily indeed' – *Mail on Sunday*

and **The Tax Exile**:
'A very funny book' – *Sunday Times*

and **The Sinner's Congregation**:
'High comedy ... high entertainment' – *New Yorker*

and **A Village Called Sin**:
'Boisterous, inventive and funny' – *Observer*

GUY BELLAMY

———

THE COMEDY HOTEL

PENGUIN BOOKS

PENGUIN BOOKS

Published by the Penguin Group
Penguin Books Ltd, 27 Wrights Lane, London W8 5TZ, England
Penguin Books USA Inc., 375 Hudson Street, New York, New York 10014, USA
Penguin Books Australia Ltd, Ringwood, Victoria, Australia
Penguin Books Canada Ltd, 10 Alcorn Avenue, Toronto, Ontario, Canada M4V 3B2
Penguin Books (NZ) Ltd, 182–190 Wairau Road, Auckland 10, New Zealand

Penguin Books Ltd, Registered Offices: Harmondsworth, Middlesex, England

First published by Viking 1992
Published in Penguin Books 1993
1 3 5 7 9 10 8 6 4 2

Printed in England by Clays Ltd, St Ives plc

For Eric and Anne Gilks

For various esoteric phenomena woven seamlessly into this quilt the author is indebted to Miss Lynne Collins and Mr Gordon McKenna.

PART ONE

• A predicament •

Life is not a spectacle or a
feast: it is a predicament.

George Santayana
Articles and Essays

1

Bombshell à la carte

Having secretly endured the painful ordeal of a vasectomy two years earlier, I was surprised to hear my wife telling me over dinner one evening that she was expecting a baby.

She announced it with a pleasure and satisfaction that owed something to the fact that her will had prevailed over mine. I stared at her, understandably lost for words. This was not the sort of news that I expected to come my way over the roast duck when what I enjoyed was gossip – the furtive romances of demure local housewives, the cataclysmic quarrels that were rupturing neighbouring marriages, the awful financial disasters that hovered over the fraught lives of the people we knew. The gossip that I relished lost its piquancy, not to mention the essential ingredient of malice, if I was the blushing, wrong-footed star.

'You're what?' I asked, hoping that deafness had been added to the afflictions which you come to expect at my advanced age. I am thirty-nine.

'I'm pregnant,' said Annette with a pride that glowed.

I poured myself more wine and considered this. The vasectomy had been arranged precisely to avoid this development, although the thought had entered my mind at the time that if an unkind world should uncharacteristically throw an extramarital affair in my direction it could be conducted without complication or consequence.

3

'Golly,' I said.

'I thought you'd be surprised,' replied my voluptuous wife. 'You didn't know you still had it in you, darling.'

The temptation to tell her that I was far more surprised by what she had in her was one that I resisted with a forced smile.

'When do we expect this happy event?' I asked.

The reply was delayed by the amount of food that she had just put in her mouth. Annette is a short, shapely lady with lots of auburn hair, a biggish nose and the slightest squint in her green eyes that adds tremendously to her attractiveness. I should add, too, that her somewhat stocky figure is redeemed by a sexiness that knocks your hat off. Today she was wearing a thick green sweater that didn't conceal her curves.

'Autumn,' she said vaguely. 'Exactly twenty years after Garth.'

We have a nineteen-year-old son, born when we were both twenty, who at this moment was probably drinking tequila slammers in one of those youthful establishments where music has replaced conversation. It was the fact of his growing up that made Annette want another child, and it was the fact of her wanting one and abandoning the Pill that prompted my clandestine operation.

'Well, that's wonderful, darling,' I said. 'I don't know how you did it.' I always choose my words with great care and sometimes think I should have taken up a career where the talent would be useful. Instead I own ten dress shops.

My plate seemed to be empty and I stood up and walked thoughtfully to our huge fireplace. The bricks were the colour of eggshells. Through the window I could see the patio, the pergola and the pond, but it was apparent that the winter had killed my palm tree.

We live beside the Thames, a convenient distance from Windsor, the home of the largest castle and the shortest street in England, the weekend retreat of the Queen, and all because William the Conqueror was attracted to a chalk hill

4

rising steeply beside the Thames. We live amidst history here (Windsor, Eton, Runnymede – the very names have a musty smell) and it is all an unhelpful reminder of the brevity and insignificance of our own short stay on this earth.

When the peacefulness of it all becomes oppressive, escape is available. Our own large house – brightest white with black timbers and a charmingly wonky roof – and the beautiful water meadow landscape in which it stands, are only a fifteen-minute blast on the motorway from our pockmarked capital, a journey I make at least once a week to satisfy the demands of my shops and the orders of the bored housewives who patronize them.

I had reached this stage in my life after what had felt like years of self-sacrifice although there must have been some moments of fun somewhere. Building up my business had in its early period involved eighteen-hour days and many sleepless nights, and bringing up a son had occasionally seemed like a full-time job, too. This was supposed to be the moment when the shops began to run themselves and the dead weight of parental responsibility slipped from my shoulders.

But my wife, who was pouring herself the tiniest Amaretto, evidently had other ideas, and now that the spendthrift eighties had passed into history the future of my shops was beginning to lose its glitter as well.

Standing by the fireplace and considering this I decided that life was a tease, a series of receding targets that were designed to keep you moving, like a laboratory experiment with rats.

'Have you told Garth?' I asked. I could easily imagine the apathy with which my snooze-prone son would greet this piece of domestic drama; when you are nineteen the rest of the world isn't really there.

'Not yet,' said Annette, standing up. She came over to the fireplace and put her arms round me. 'I thought you should be the first to know.'

I kissed her mouth. 'It's tremendous news,' I said. 'But I can't deny that it's a shock.'

5

'It's going to make you young again,' my wife cooed.

'I don't want to be young again,' I said. 'I didn't like it the first time.'

She laughed. 'You're a tall, handsome man with lovely eyes and just a touch of grey hair. But we're going to stop you getting old.'

I kissed her again and she hugged me.

I fancy my wife but I don't trust her.

'I think I need a drink,' I said.

Down by the river, among the weeping willows, the bay willows and the white willows, is a small and prestigious establishment called, predictably, the Willow Hotel. It has twelve superior bedrooms, a restaurant with three Michelin stars, a cosy bar with a log fire, a ballroom that can also be used for small business conferences and a games room where visitors play cards or pool. The predominant sound that emerges from its walls is laughter and for that reason customers who found its name bland have rechristened it the Comedy Hotel.

There was nobody in the bar when I arrived, which suited me: I had a startling domestic revelation to contemplate. I sat at the counter nursing a vodka and watched the river's aloof progress through latticed windows. People could and did arrive by boat but the Thames had other uses, too. A few years ago a businessman, displeased with the accountants' prognosis, had walked out of the bar and into the river and was almost forgotten when his body turned up at Boveney Lock near Windsor racecourse a couple of weeks later.

The odds against a man becoming a father after he has had a vasectomy are one thousand to one. I was familiar enough with the laws of chance, not to mention the gruesome mechanics of male sterilization, to know that I was not the father of Annette's baby, but this was not information that I could pass along to her. She would regard a secret vasectomy as a gross act of disloyalty, a unilateral action intended to deceive her and thwart her wishes. Having reared

6

one fine son, Annette thought it was time to start again and although this girlish idea improved our sex life, it didn't help my peace of mind. I remembered sleepless nights and disrupted days; I remembered demands for attention, requests for money, tours of toyshops and bleak visits to freezing zoos. Obstructive teachers, impatient doctors, barbarous classmates and suicidal au pair girls! And, almost worst of all, I remembered holidays tied to school holidays so that not only did we have to seek relaxation when everybody else did but we had to pay twice as much for the privilege.

I had a vasectomy one lunch hour in London and crept home in pain and triumph, a triumph somewhat tarnished by tonight's news.

Through the window now I could see Laurie Curtis disembarking from his Mitsubishi Shogun with its vulgar personalized number plates.

Laurie Curtis is one of the two men I drink with. He is a wisecracking cockney who has made a little money and moved west in search of peace, space and fresh air. He is a short, plump man with receding red hair, an absurdly drooping moustache and an inferiority complex, but monitoring his erratic progress towards his life's ambition of becoming a millionaire is a hobby of mine. I tell him that with the drop in the value of money being a millionaire no longer has the cachet of even twenty years ago, but it is still a label that he is desperately anxious to hang round his neck and will do almost anything, even work, to obtain. He describes himself as a dealer-entrepreneur which means that he dabbles in anything. His often repeated motto is: You make your profit when you buy. He is always buying and selling things – cars, antiques, sometimes houses – but he produces goods as well if he thinks he has spotted a gap in the market. Not all his ventures in this direction are blessed with success. At some expense he once commissioned a small factory to make two hundred thousand lunch boxes for young children at the very moment when, as if by a secret kindergarten vote, they had all switched to backpacks.

7

He came in wearing his usual brown suit and flowery tie and sat on the stool next to mine.

'I hope you didn't drive home last night,' I said, 'after all that drinking?'

'Of course I drove home, mate. I couldn't walk in that condition, could I?' He beckoned to the barman, a good-looking man named John who did a sideline in home-produced goats' cheeses. 'Double vodka,' he said.

Laurie's drinking is outrageous and so is his post-drinking behaviour. His drunken attempt to impregnate a wheelie bin on one wild Saturday night was an event that still produced a twitch in his wife's cheek if anyone was insensitive enough to recall it.

His wife is a formidable lady called Judy who at forty is two years younger than Laurie. Their marriage is a battle-ground. Flying plates and mousetraps in bed are only the half of it, but the violence is all one way. It is Laurie who sports the black eye or the fat lip, and I thought that it was only a matter of time before he left home in the Shogun to find that the brakes had been seriously tampered with.

I remember that Annette once complained to me that Judy kept hitting her black labrador Baron, and I said: 'It's all right when she hits her husband, but it upsets you when she hits the dog.' But months later when people were being shot up, shot down, bombed, tortured and maimed in Iraq, public opinion remained resolutely dumb until pictures began to appear of distraught cormorants dying in an oil slick in the Gulf, and I realized that the English really do prefer animals to people and my wife wasn't in the warped minority to which I had assigned her.

Why Laurie put up with it and how they stayed together was only a mystery until you saw their beautiful daughter Helen, the glue that bound them.

'What's the news?' I asked him when he had a hand on a glass.

'We're buying a place in France,' he told me.

'Oh good,' I said. 'Judy will enjoy that.'

8

He drank his vodka and thought about this. 'My wife is to enjoyment what a heatwave is to a ski resort,' he said, 'but I wasn't going to buy it if she wasn't going to use it.'

'And she likes France?'

'She thought it would be good for Helen.'

Helen, their pride and joy, is sixteen. Laurie worries about her education, her health, her prospects, her friends. He broods over her chaste infatuations. Judy watches her endlessly, worried about what undesirable characteristics she may have inherited from her father.

'Where will this be?' I asked. 'Cannes? Fréjus? Menton?'

'Wrong coast, mate,' said Laurie. 'We're looking at Normandy and Brittany so we can zap through the tunnel for the weekend. Fancy a game of pool?'

And so we took our drinks into the immaculate games room next door. Pool was the current craze, not American pool and striped balls with numbers on, but seven yellow ones and seven red ones with a black ball to finish: snooker for the man in a hurry. All you had to do was pot your seven balls and then the black, and so many people were now gripped by this challenge that there was usually a row of coins on the side of the table, a reservation placed there by people who were waiting to play.

There was something so simple about knocking these little phenolic resin balls into the pockets that a failure to do so always seemed like a piece of bad luck that couldn't possibly happen again. This certainty that things will improve – the same kind of irrational optimism that sustains golfers – prolonged many a career that deserved to be abandoned.

I broke the balls with such force that the white ball jumped off the table and rolled across the floor's red carpet.

'Do you want twenty on it?' Laurie asked, seeing my poor start.

I looked in my wallet and found unusually that there was less than twenty there.

'You're gambling mad,' I said. 'You probably give Judy five to one she doesn't have an orgasm.'

'Twenty to one, actually. Are you on or not?'

9

'I don't have twenty.'

'Letters of credit? Tsarist bonds?'

'Make it a fiver.'

My game didn't improve and as a hotel guest came in to challenge the winner I returned to the bar alone.

I don't drink in public houses any more. The part-time staff and the sloppy service have convinced me that they don't really want customers, and their eager adherence to our antisocial drinking hours is a discouragement to a serious drinker. Just as you are getting into your stride they start asking for your glass and inquiring whimsically whether you have a home to go to. There is also these days the constant possibility of sudden violence, with the concomitant risk of spilt blood or, worse, drink.

In the Comedy Hotel the bar doesn't close until the last drinker has zigzagged to the door, voices and fists are never raised, and the contingency of a civilized conversation lies all round you. I climbed back on my stool and asked John for another vodka. There was a new drink on the optic called *SWWId*, and I was wondering whether to try it when Alec Benson came in.

Alec Benson is the other man I drink with. He is a tall, lugubrious man, just a few years older than me, who is the headmaster of the local school. He is good company over a drink but not entirely free from the latent personality disorders that are inseparable from the teaching profession, some of them created by the simmering resentment at their permanent shortage of folding money.

But Alec is a born pedagogue and his desire to teach is not confined to the classroom; it seems sometimes to spring from a desire to air his knowledge. 'Do you know how they make those?' he'd ask, or 'Do you know the origin of that?' I always said 'Yes' very quickly, preferring the bliss of ignorance to the prospect of a lecture.

Tall, thin, ascetic Alec and short, fat, earthy Laurie – they would probably have never got together if I had not been here to serve as a catalyst.

10

'Where's Laurie?' Alec whispered now in a strangely confidential manner. He had black curly hair that was grey at the temples and thick black-rimmed spectacles which he now pushed up a little with his right thumb.

'He's playing pool,' I told him.

'Good. I want to talk to you in private.'

'What will you drink?' I asked.

He wanted lager. More expensive drinks were something that he usually avoided. He had been married for eighteen years to a very bright lady called Kitty who disapproved of drink and quite a lot of other things as well. She was a sparky, bird-like creature, a political activist who had made several unsuccessful attempts to win a seat on the county council. She was currently campaigning for more lead-free petrol. You had to admire her but she made me nervous. Once when we invited them round to dinner she cast a pall over the whole proceedings by announcing: 'This meal would feed a family in Addis Ababa for a week.' She had emotional links with Africa although she had never been there. The previous Christmas she had invited a charming black professor called Oliver to spend the holiday with them and we had introduced him to the intoxicating night life of the Comedy Hotel. Kitty was thirty-nine but looked younger. Sometimes, in stretch jeans tucked into high-heel boots, she looked ten years younger.

I pushed the lager towards Alec and realized that the new drink on the optic was not called *SWWId* at all; it was upside down, of course, and the label said PIMMS. I was so fascinated by this discovery that I wasn't really concentrating when Alec said: 'I'm going to get married.'

'You're what?' I asked, giving him all my attention.

'I'm getting married.'

'I don't believe you.'

'Suspend your disbelief, Max.'

'What about Kitty?'

'Well, naturally she's delighted. Look, this is very confidential.'

11

'Confidential? It's bloody mystifying,' I told him, picking up my vodka.

'It's quite straightforward,' said Alec. 'Walter is dead.'

'I'm sorry to hear that.'

'Don't be. The grief that followed his death was – how shall I put it? Imperceptible.'

'In fact there wasn't any?' I suggested.

'None.'

'Who's Walter?'

'Who *was* Walter. Walter was the neo-fascist who married Kitty twenty years ago.'

'I didn't know that.'

'It isn't something that a person in my position cares to shout about. We've been living in sin for eighteen years. He refused to divorce her and we had no option.'

'But now the spiteful old twat has expired?'

Alec nodded enthusiastically. 'A heart seizure, apparently. That's quite painful, isn't it?'

'I've no idea.'

'I wouldn't like to think that his departure went smoothly.'

He was looking unusually cheerful. His normal demeanour was that of a man with many burdens. Even his jokes were on the acidulous side. A weight had clearly been removed by Walter's abrupt departure.

'The important thing is that Walter's dead,' I said.

'As a doornail. So Kitty and I plan a quick secret wedding at some obscure register office as soon as possible and we'd like you to be there as a witness.' He waved a hand in the air. 'Apparently I need a witness.'

'Is this a good idea?' I asked.

'Is what a good idea?'

'Very few relationships between a man and a woman are enhanced by marriage. Are you sure you aren't better to leave things as they are?'

'Don't talk cobblers, Max. We've been as good as married for eighteen years.'

'But the crucial fact is that you *weren't*.'

12

He looked at me as if I had switched the conversation into a foreign language with which he was only barely familiar.

'What are you talking about, Max? I'm forty-four, for Christ's sake. Anyway, there's Steven.'

Steven is their seventeen-year-old son.

'Steven?' I said. 'Unmarried parents don't worry kids any more.'

'*Au contraire*. It unsettles them. We've had some cases at school. That's why this is so hush-hush. I've got to get married without my son finding out.'

He looked at me, his partner in this conspiracy, as if he wanted my approval as much as my co-operation in the register office. He wore an old grey suit that bore the marks of chalk dust, and worry lines criss-crossed his face.

'Count on me,' I said. 'Weddings are great fun so long as you don't have one of the leading roles.'

'This one will be on the quiet side,' he said. 'We don't want crowds throwing confetti.'

Laurie returned from the games room looking only slightly put out by a comprehensive defeat on the pool table, and lit his customary Hamlet cigar.

'Alec, baby,' he said. 'Tell me again how brilliant my daughter is.'

'Helen is a very clever girl, Laurie. You can be proud of her.'

'Is she heading for Oxford?'

'Quite possibly. I'm making her head girl next term.'

'And Steven will be head boy?'

'He deserves to be,' said Alec, 'but nepotism forbids it.'

We were apt to sit in the Comedy Hotel in a glow of achievement and self-satisfaction at the way we had each brought up our only child. Think what you like about us, we seemed to be saying, and then cast an envious eye at our wonderful offspring.

'The key is to have only one child,' Laurie said. 'You can give it your undivided attention.'

The remark gave me a jolt.

'I forgot to tell you,' I said. 'Annette is pregnant.'

There was no point in concealing the fact; it would be apparent soon enough. Luckily I had told nobody about my vasectomy.

'*Enceinte?*' said Alec. '*Gravid?*'

'The pudding club?' said Laurie. 'I thought we'd finished with that old caper?'

'So did I,' I confessed.

'A mouth to feed, a bum to wipe, an obstacle to contentment,' Laurie said. 'Haven't you heard about the rhythm and blues method of birth control?'

'I think she must have done something when I was asleep,' I said weakly.

My son Garth was sprawled on the sofa drinking beer from a can and watching television when I reached home, and I remembered that he had asked for a talk. He is a tall, slim young man with a lot of unruly blond hair and a cheerful face. At nineteen he had reached an age, I was well aware, when parents get quietly airbrushed from the picture. I was glad to talk to him.

I fetched myself a coffee and joined him on the sofa.

'Who's winning?' I asked. There seemed to be a soccer match on the box.

'Villa,' he said, without looking round.

A few abortive forays into the world of full-time employment had bounced him straight back home again, sometimes for weeks, as he struggled to resign himself to life's pitiless equation: work equals money. A brief flirtation with the trendy world of computers had been his most recent assault on normality, an exercise which ended sooner than most. I wasn't surprised. I can't tell a computer from a refrigerator myself.

I sometimes think that Garth and I are victims of Britain's strange educational system that has you leaving school knowing that the Indian Mutiny was in 1857 but not knowing what caused the First World War. Eventually I had him sent to one of those private schools where children with famous names studied origami, acting, canoe making and how to be forthright about sex. But in the end the child is the handiwork of the parents and flaws reflect on the father too. Not that I regarded Garth as flawed: it was just a question of finding him the right career.

'You wanted to talk,' I said.

His eyes briefly left the screen as he looked at my end of the sofa and nodded.

'About me,' he said.

'About your future?'

'My immediate future. I want to go to Spain.'

My heart sank a little at this. I liked having Garth around and people grew up too quickly. I was more conscious than most of the fleeting years and they were really flying now. It is no longer a question of people remembering what they were doing when President Kennedy was assassinated. These days it was becoming harder to find somebody who was alive when it happened. Already men who will never see sixty again were too young to have fought in the war, the pop stars of my youth were going bald and the women whose glamorous photographs had first aroused my interest in the female form had been transformed at depressing speed into plump and benevolent grannies, sometimes with zimmer frames.

'Is this instead of a job?' I asked.

'No, it's in search of a job.'

'It's difficult to imagine the long-term benefits of getting a job in Spain,' I said. 'What sort of work could you get? Barman?'

'Only dead fish swim with the current, Dad,' he said, crushing his now empty can of beer.

'Nevertheless some people choose a career and stay with it.'

'What awful regrets some people must have.'

He gave me a sidelong glance which did not encourage me to pursue this line. He had my eyes, but the thick hair and

15

the evasive manner were Annette's. They both seemed to carry a cargo of secrets that I would never unwrap.

'It's a test of character for them now,' intoned the soccer commentator. 'They've got to dig in and believe in themselves.'

Garth switched the television off with the remote control. There were more important things on his mind.

'I need five hundred pounds,' he said with the ingenuousness of the young. 'Air fares and keep until I find a job.' He was still crushing the beer can which had now assumed a strange shape. 'I'll pay you back.'

I drank some coffee. 'I wondered what fathers were for,' I said.

'To like provide, Dad.'

'To guide, to advise. To instruct.'

'That's the theory.'

'What's wrong with it?'

'Look at the fathers! Thigh deep in cack, most of them. What qualifications do they have to advise or instruct? Why would anyone listen to their advice? It's a joke, Dad. Most of the kids I know are trying to straighten out their old men.'

'They don't feel, perhaps, that their fathers having lived longer know more?' I asked hopefully. Communicating with young people had become more challenging lately, another sign of *tempus fugit*.

'If you're travelling in the wrong direction, time only makes it worse.'

He discarded the beer can and leaned back on the sofa, hugging his knees. He was wearing an old blue sweater with nothing underneath, dirty jeans and trainers.

'It's funny,' I said, 'how the lousiest education system we've ever had has managed to produce the omniscient teenager.'

'We're talking about life, Dad, not Archimedes' Principle.'

'If you'd like to give a short lecture on hydrostatics I'd be delighted to listen.'

But he was not to be distracted. 'If these fathers are so well placed to tell their sons how to live their lives why have they made such a mega mess of their own?'

It is little questions like this that occasionally make being a parent feel like wading through treacle. 'Perhaps their mistakes enable them to point out life's hazards,' I suggested, but I knew that I was on the ropes. I could remember delivering Garth's speech myself.

'Where's your mother?' I asked.

'In bed.'

'I think I'll join her.'

'What about the money?'

'It's a loan,' I said.

He unwrapped his lanky frame from the sofa, stood up and punched the air. 'That's really nice of you, Dad.'

'Enjoy it,' I said sadly. 'You're dead a long time.'

2

Wedding belle

Yesterday I was thirty-nine. Today I am forty. This may sound like a mundane trek across twenty-four hours to those who weren't there to welcome the Beatles, but my battered contemporaries, struggling to get their second wind, bridge this momentous chasm with a chill in their hearts, knowing it to be one of life's more sinister journeys. Yesterday I was not long out of my twenties; today I am on a cresta run to my half century, if I ever make it, with no prospect of remission for good conduct. Goodbye cradle, hallo grave.

I bought champagne, a selfless enough act for a man who regards the stuff as achromatic cider, and to acknowledge my mournful milestone Mrs Hadfield, Mrs Curtis and Mrs Benson joined their husbands amid the darkened timbers and the brass ornaments of the Comedy Hotel.

Annette's pregnancy had elbowed aside my birthday as a subject of conversation before the first cork had been removed. Judy Curtis and Kitty Benson studied the expectant mother with something that looked suspiciously like disbelief.

'Was it *planned?*' asked Judy Curtis, a formidable lady both physically and mentally, who spent some time in one of the proliferating fitness clubs, building and tuning her muscles so that she could chastise her intemperate spouse. She had an impressive amount of blonde hair swept back from her broad forehead but her handsomeness was almost masculine. If I were ever to get into a fight myself, I should prefer to confront Laurie.

'Of course,' said Annette, challenging me to deny it with a look that would have frozen salt water. 'We've raised one fine child. Why not another?'

'I think it's wonderful,' said Kitty Benson, who was ignoring my champagne and drinking fruit juice. She was a sexy little creature in a white trouser suit, lots of black curly hair and huge spectacles. On another occasion I would have expected her to deliver a stern lecture on rising populations and diminishing food supplies but this wasn't the right moment. Instead, she recalled the painful birth of her son Steven, beginning with the joys of morning sickness and leading us, for all I knew, to the facts and the myths surrounding post-natal depression.

Laurie, Alec and I did a sideways shuffle in the face of this womanly chat and embarked on a conversation of our own. It was sad that when women came out with their husbands they usually ended up ignoring them and talking among themselves.

'I'm surprised that you celebrate your birthday,' Alec said, 'being so sensitive about the vanishing years.'

'Any excuse for a drink,' I said. 'It'll be the wedding anniversary next.'

'I never remind Judy when it's our wedding anniversary,' said Laurie. 'It seems to depress her.'

'It looks as if she's going to take her O levels in karate,' I said.

'I know,' said Laurie. 'I need an anti-missile missile system.'

A whiff of cordite seemed to surround their relationship and yet their meeting had been romantic enough. He had spotted her statuesque figure in a card shop and instantly followed her down the street. Lusting forlornly after the curve of her buttocks he had stepped in front of a London taxi and been knocked ten yards across the road. Judy was among those who bent concerned over his prostrate body and eventually, at his request, joined him in the ambulance. The rest, as they say, is mystery, but there must have been something attractive about the indomitable little man with his constant energy and his endless supply of money-making ideas. They were married quickly and Helen was born on the anniversary of the contretemps with the cab.

When the women drifted back in our direction I tried to tempt Kitty with a bottle of Louis Roederer.

'Don't be naughty, Max,' she said. 'You know that I'm teetotal.'

'Kitty believes in everything odd, from acupuncture to Zoroastrianism,' said Alec.

'We're learning slowly,' said Kitty. 'Twenty years ago everybody smoked and we got our drinking water from the tap. Now nobody smokes and we buy our water in bottles in supermarkets. There's a quiet revolution going on and it's going to reach you drinkers one day.'

Judy, I discovered, had brought me a present, a video devoted to the year of my birth: the Festival of Britain, the abdication of King Leopold, the triumphant return to Downing Street of Winston S. Churchill at the age of seventy-seven. And Kitty, spotting the appearance of gifts, produced from nowhere a colossal book, the biography of some long-dead politician. I could see at a glance that it was so huge and so detailed that it was going to take a hundred pages to get the recalcitrant subject out of his nappies.

I ordered more champagne and reflected that if Clement Attlee was Prime Minister when I was born I was even older than I thought. My expectant wife arrived by my side.

'Should you be drinking in your condition?' I asked.

'I slurped my way through Garth's pregnancy and it didn't seem to do him any harm.' She was wearing something that hadn't come from any of my shops, a neat suit with a bell skirt that she had found in a more expensive outlet.

'Where is our son, by the way?' I asked. 'Why isn't he celebrating his father's birthday?'

'He said he doesn't drink with wrinklies. Isn't he sweet?'

'All our children are lovely,' said Judy. 'It's adults I can't stand, particularly male ones.'

Laurie winked at me. 'If you can't say something nice about somebody, say something nasty.'

'He's a money earner though,' I said to Judy with a smile.

'I should hope he is,' she said, 'otherwise he'd be no more than a supine adjunct.'

The adversarial nature of their marriage almost made them a cabaret act. If they had begun to club each other like Punch and Judy it would have been entirely in character. The tension and the violence seemed to suit them both.

Alec came over and took me to one side.

'It's Friday,' he said. 'At Maidenhead. They don't do them at Windsor. You'd think we two were getting a bit old for births and marriages, wouldn't you?'

'Old enough to get them in the right order,' I said.

'We're having lunch afterwards, tell Annette.'

Just after this Laurie began to sing. I think it was a birthday song for me. It is everybody's illusion that they can carry a tune but in Laurie's case the belief was particularly ill-founded.

That night, while Laurie dreamed of adventurous projects and financial coups, Judy cut off his moustache. She couldn't remove it entirely for fear of waking him, but she lopped off enough with her little nail scissors to make what was left look ridiculous. The grown article had always looked slightly silly, having a droopy and woebegone aspect that did nothing for his face, but when Judy had completed her midnight pruning he looked like a rhesus monkey. There was nothing cosmetic about her intentions: this was an assault.

I hadn't realized that there was something more ferocious than the usual implacable hostility in the air until I got home from the party and Annette regaled me with an account of her conversation with Mrs Curtis.

'Perhaps if he keeps on drinking and driving he'll crash

21

and be killed,' said Judy, betraying a rare glimpse of optimism. 'But knowing my luck he'd probably survive and become a vegetable. More than he is already, I mean. Or he'd end up on one of those life-support systems and I'd have to dust him every day.'

I found this sort of conversation quite shocking and was slightly alarmed at the way Annette regarded it as no more than the usual female tête-à-tête.

'Judy went through his credit card bills and found that he kept using a petrol station at Henley,' said Annette. 'So she went over and toured the area and found his Shogun parked outside a flat. So she thinks he's got a woman.'

'I don't think so,' I said. 'I'd have heard. Anyway, Judy seems more interested in bedding plants than bedding him.'

The following morning I was in the newsagent's when the Shogun pulled up outside. Laurie ambled in, searching for cigars.

'You look different,' I said.

He pointed at his upper lip and I realized that the moustache was missing.

'I'm glad you've taken it off,' I said. 'I always thought it made you look sad.'

'I am sad,' he said. 'And I didn't take it off.'

When we were outside and could talk in some privacy on the pavement he told me what had happened. 'You're not even safe when you're asleep,' he said.

'She thinks you've got a woman,' I said. 'You're lucky it was only your moustache she cut off.'

He winced at the picture this evoked. The business with the scissors seemed to have taken the spring out of his stride.

'I wish I'd time for women,' he complained.

'Henley? A flat?'

'She thinks it's a woman? It's an artist, male. Well, sort of male. We're working on a children's wall-frieze, a continuing story that kids can add to and stick on their bedroom wall.'

'You're full of ideas.'

'So's my wife. When she broke a bottle over my head last

22

summer I thought it was just the nuts and bolts of domestic bliss. But scissors are different. They cut bits off you.' He opened the door of the Shogun and produced a mournful smile. 'I could start disappearing, bit by bit.'

It was difficult to reassure him with any conviction. If Judy was checking his credit card bills and touring Henley in search of his parked car she had introduced an element of espionage into their marriage which made slumber perilous.

'If I notice any bits missing I'll have a word with your wife,' I assured him.

On Friday, feeling like a couple of undercover agents who suspect that their mission has been blown, Annette and I climbed into Kitty Benson's Vauxhall Viva and headed for the register office with Alec and his bride-to-be. Packing the four of us into the smallest car available was part of Kitty's security precautions; she felt that there were enough pupils and former pupils around for Alec's battered Escort to be recognized by somebody as it was parked outside the big event.

The Viva was a car rich with stickers. FREE TIBET and I USE UNLEADED it said on the rear window next to a label proclaiming THE WILDFOWL TRUST. Inside was another unequivocal communiqué: NO SMOKING. Herded too close together for comfort in the Vauxhall's confined space, we moved like conspirators towards our secret appointment.

Alec had discarded the teacher's grey for a new shantung suit, brown shot through with red. It seemed to glisten in the light. Kitty had overhauled her image, too. 'I won't be a second,' she had announced in the chilly hallway of her semi-detached, and she wasn't. She was twenty minutes. Her knee-length white silk dress bordered on the virginal.

'You look lovely,' said Annette, kissing her on the cheek. To my romantic wife today's proceedings represented passion, colour, glamour and excitement, a midweek fairy tale to lighten the burden of household chores. 'You should be flying to Venice tonight.'

23

'I always fancied a honeymoon in Rotterdam listening to Pavarotti,' Kitty said.

The idea of a honeymoon had never occurred to me. It was difficult to imagine these newlyweds rogering the socks off each other in some peeling guest house or, indeed, anywhere else.

'Of course,' said Kitty when we were in the car, 'most women who get married a second time marry a younger man.'

Alec, it emerged immediately, had been at the sauce – a brandy or two to fortify him through the coming solemnities. 'I always thought I would marry Mavis Jones,' he said.

'Who the hell is Mavis Jones?' I asked.

'His first love,' said Kitty over her shoulder as she drove down Windsor Road. 'He's never forgotten her.'

'I think it's time he did,' said Annette. 'When did he last see her?'

'Twenty-four and a half years ago,' replied Alec with an unwelcome preciseness. 'I got edged out. Ike and Tina Turner became Tina Turner. Sonny and Cher became Cher. Alec and Mavis became Mavis. The auguries aren't good. Men seem to get mislaid.'

'Why didn't he marry her?' Annette asked. She seemed to have decided to address all questions to Kitty, as if Alec had been downgraded.

'Oh, that would have been much too daring,' said Kitty. 'He's not a man who lives dangerously. In fact cutting his toenails without putting his glasses on is as reckless as he gets.'

Ignoring this taunt, Alec peered glumly ahead at the busy traffic. It was difficult to believe that we were going to a wedding. The mood in the car was suited to a quite different ceremony.

When we arrived at the register office the English sun was doing its normal sixty-watt bulb performance, light without heat, and to add to the jollifications an Irish wolfhound was laboriously voiding its bowels on the confetti-strewn steps.

Inside there were other couples waiting in a flush of anticipation to tie the knot. One pair wore identical clothes, a sure sign, so far as I was concerned, that their lift didn't reach the top floor. They both had white suits with red edging and could have been refugees from a circus. Another couple looked as if natural caution would have persuaded them to have an alert midwife in attendance at the nuptials.

It was marriage by conveyor belt and we waited our turn.

'I feel boggy at the queats,' said Alec, 'whatever that means.'

'Have a mint,' said Kitty. 'I can smell the brandy.'

A tall, thin man with sleepy eyes beckoned us into a room that was full of chairs. There was accommodation for many guests but our wedding party, unlike some riotous gatherings in this austere room, was only a subdued quartet. Alec and Kitty sat together in the front row and Annette and I sat on either side of them. The formalities of what followed passed me by but I had the distinct impression that the tall, thin man didn't believe a word he was hearing and was on the verge of producing a polygraph to flush out the lies. Alec stood awkwardly, sweating golf balls and looking deeply uneasy, while Kitty took it all calmly, having been through it all before.

'Walter must be whirling in his sarcophagus,' she said as we left the room. There was a tremendous relief on her face and a slight smile at the thought of an old enemy finally thwarted. Alec seemed restored to normal now that the ordeal was behind him. 'That wasn't so bad,' he said, as if he'd been given an unexpectedly easy ride at the dentist. 'Mrs Benson and I will now buy you lunch.'

'Mrs Benson,' said Annette. 'Your partnership is now official. Isn't that wonderful?'

'Eat your heart out, Mavis Jones,' said Kitty, and she planted a lingering kiss on her husband's pale cheek.

3

A girl gone wrong

I rise at seven, driven from my bed by the pungent gabbling of Brian Redhead, and, via lengthy ablutions in the bathroom, head for a lonely breakfast in the kitchen where the radio is replaced by my morning newspaper. Annette, always a late riser, seems now after her disturbed nights reluctant to get up at all.

Over the Alpen I search between the surrealistic advertisements for cigarettes for the sort of news item that will set a man up for the day and send him out to do the world's work with something approaching a smile on his face. Today there were two:

> *Author of 'How*
> *to Live For Ever'*
> *dies at 29*

and, which was even better:

WOMEN 'WOULD PAY FOR SEX'

One in eight women would pay for sexual intercourse, according to a survey conducted among 400 women for BSB's TV series Sex, Lies and Love. They would offer up to £200 for 'passionate sex and fulfilment of all their fantasies', £100 for 'something to remember – a bloody good time' and £60 for 'absolute ecstasy'.

This was not information that you would guess from studying women's faces in the street and I left the house feeling strangely encouraged. Only the rumble of a newly emptied wheelie bin being returned to its cubbyhole broke the blissful silence.

My shops – called, with all available modesty, MAX HADFIELD – had spread through the Thames Valley like a dose of non-specific urethritis before running into the formidable antibiotic of Mr Major's recession. Recessions were supposed to hit steelworks, engineering and shipbuilding, but this one was crippling travel firms, airlines and hotels. It was hurting shops. Having killed my ambitious plan to open new ones, it was now raising the awful possibility of closing some old ones. I decided on a tour of my estate.

All towns look alike today and half the time I didn't know which one I was in until I studied the accounts in my shop. The multi-storey car park, the graffiti-covered lift, the indoor shopping mall – Smith's, Boots, Argos, Burtons – and the halls alive to the sound of musak. My own humble enterprise was usually found among these giants where I had to balance extortionate rents against the amount of business generated by my popular neighbours.

Our target was the average woman. It is a sign of the optimism that I brought to this venture that I hoped to get such an elusive creature in my sights but, on the whole, we succeeded well enough. Between the downmarket stores that specialized in seconds, and the scented salons of *haute couture* there had to be something for the averagely smart lady who had access to a credit card. And we had it – not just dresses and blouses and trousers but fichus and dirndls and gilets and guimpes. Say what you like about the feminist revolution, it certainly put money into women's handbags.

When I had parked my Rover and descended in the malodorous lift with one of the world's losers who shuffled off at the ground floor on his heels with his mouth hanging open (clearly in the new classless society a future member of the Tory Cabinet), I realized as I walked past the lottery kiosk beneath the atrium that I couldn't remember who managed this particular shop. I regarded this as an ominous sign: somebody who had the correct grip on his business wouldn't have had to think twice about who was in charge of their money.

It was Charlotte, in a barium-yellow cashmere sweater and maroon culottes.

'Good morning, Mr Hadfield,' she said respectfully as I breezed in. 'Would you like a coffee?'

'Please,' I said. 'How's business?'

'Quiet,' said Charlotte looking embarrassed. 'There is also a spate of shoplifting.'

I went through to the tiny office at the back of the shop and sat down at the only desk. I found the cash book, the invoice book, the order book, the VAT file and the petty cash pad and spent half an hour absorbing their gloomy message.

I was halfway through this depressing exercise when Charlotte brought in my coffee. She was a skinny creature who, you were surprised to discover when you got her from the right angle, had enormous breasts. It was like discovering mountains in Norfolk or legs on a fish. She had told me when she arrived in the shop two years ago with her cerulean eyes and her startling, secret accessories that she would not be staying long as she and her husband intended to start a family. Later, as no family appeared, she became girlishly confidential about their failure in this department. Her husband, a college lecturer, had become increasingly jaded and now found the necessary stimulation only in travel. They had made love on trains, planes and taxis and, once, on a bus. If he kept his strength up he was destined to create a first in the Channel tunnel.

'I don't know why high interest rates should hurt us, but there's no question that people have less to spend,' she said as I took the coffee.

'They need their money to pay bigger mortgages, Charlotte,' I said. 'You were some way below target last month.'

28

'This month is worse,' she told me.

I considered this news as she went back to the shop. If my other nine little goldmines were going to produce figures like these, I was staring a crisis in the face. I had borrowed fairly extensively myself. More shops, larger orders, bigger discounts was the guiding philosophy here; it was a strategy that would be badly damaged if I started closing branches.

Just as I was transferring the harsh facts to my briefcase a commotion broke out in the shop. Over the chipboard partition I heard a girl shout: 'Sod off!' and then Charlotte's raised voice declaring: 'They're in your bag. I watched you put them there.'

The girl's voice came back very calmly: 'You'll be hearing from my father's solicitors' and then there was a crash, the sound, I subsequently discovered, of one of the dummies going over.

'You're not going anywhere, girl,' Charlotte now said. 'Oh, what a piece of luck. There's Mr Plod.'

I thought that it was about time I intruded on this scene and I locked my briefcase and went out. Helen Curtis stood white faced in the middle of the shop clutching a large green bag with both hands.

'Helen,' I said. 'What's going on?'

She looked at me, shrugged sadly, and said nothing. She didn't even acknowledge that she knew me. She was a short, pretty girl with blonde shoulder-length hair and a pale face. She was only sixteen but looked a couple of years older.

At the door Charlotte had intercepted a passing policeman who now came in.

'Shoplifting,' Charlotte told him. 'You'll find skirts in her bag.'

The policeman, a young man who seemed unhappy about this interruption of his quiet stroll, took the bag from Helen and pulled out three eighty-pound skirts.

'I was going to pay for them,' said Helen.

'The hell you were,' Charlotte said. 'You were leaving the shop.'

The policeman looked at the name on the bag. It said 'Harrods, Knightsbridge'.

'If you were going to pay for them,' he asked, 'why had you put them in the bag? Have you got two hundred and forty pounds on you?'

It was a question that Helen declined to answer.

'You'll have to come with me, young lady,' said the policeman. 'You can ring your parents from the station.'

I couldn't begin to imagine how Laurie and Judy would react to the news that their beloved daughter, the repository of all their hopes, had been arrested for shoplifting. I was much too surprised to think about that.

'Helen, what were you playing at?' I asked, confused.

Charlotte looked at me, surprised. 'Do you know her?'

'She's the daughter of a friend,' I said. 'This is pretty embarrassing.'

But Helen wasn't embarrassed. She had looked slightly shaken at first, but her manner now was defiant. She stared straight at me as if I were the architect of her misfortune. She had only spoken once since I appeared and she wasn't going to speak again. She left the shop in the company of the policeman without looking back.

'They've still got our skirts,' I pointed out.

'Exhibit A,' said Charlotte.

'What am I going to tell her father?'

'That he's reared a thief,' said Charlotte.

Women are unforgiving creatures, particularly when they are dealing with other women. As I drove to my second appointment I went over and over the strange scene in the shop and wondered how the damage could be repaired or reduced. I began to see myself, as the owner of the shop, as Helen's accuser. It wouldn't look too friendly to Laurie and Judy.

The second shop, in an almost identical arcade ten miles away, had red SALE signs in the window, a matter that was left to the manageress's discretion when stock was slow to move. It seemed to be working. Both the manageress, a stout

30

middle-aged lady I had pinched from Marks and Spencer, and her surly teenage assistant, were dealing with customers when I went in. I hurried past the rails of beautiful clothes to an annexe at the back. There was no desk here, but a small white table with a phone.

I rang the police station to which Helen Curtis had been reluctantly escorted and after about ten minutes was put through to the officer in charge of the case. He came at me with a nasal inflection so strong that it sounded as if his mouth had retired for the day and left his nose to complete the shift. When I told him that the father of Helen Curtis was a personal friend of mine I got the impression that my intervention was far from welcome.

'So?' said the nose.

'I don't want to press any charges,' I said.

There was a pause at the other end as if what I had said was too shocking for him to take in. Then I heard the shuffling of papers before the querulous gendarme was whispering triumphantly in my ear again.

'It's not entirely up to you,' he said happily. 'She's done Boots, Laura Ashley, Woolworth, Our Price, Next, Hammick's, Dixon's, Freeman Hardy and Willis, Currys, Smith's and seven other boutiques. They don't all take so lenient a view.'

'Blimey,' I said.

There is something peculiarly depressing about an airport if you're not actually travelling. The excitement that is there for the traveller is just chaos for those who are merely one of life's chauffeurs.

Annette and I drove Garth to Gatwick with mixed feelings. We were happy that he was happy about what lay ahead of him, but worried about what he was going to do on the Costa del Sol which was not, as far as I could tell, the launching ground for spectacularly successful careers based on industry and application. At the same time my wife and I had agreed long ago that we would not be the type of parents who won't let go.

31

'You could have got a job in London and saved on air fares,' I said when we arrived on the crowded concourse.

'I'd sooner have root canal work,' said Garth, cheerfully lugging a huge holdall that contained everything he would evidently need for the next few months.

I followed him through the jostle of casually dressed families, hyperactive now at the prospect of a fortnight's holiday in the sun, phlegmatic blacks in immaculate suits awaiting a flight to Gabon, German businessmen with locked briefcases heading morosely for Frankfurt, and a whole gaggle of grinning Japanese who could have been going anywhere in the world to preach their profitable message while opening another ten car factories.

When Garth had checked in his holdall and collected his boarding pass we went to find a cup of tea, or what passed for tea at a British airport.

'No more schlepping around in old clothes,' said Annette when we had found a table. 'We want to hear that you have a job.'

'Don't you worry, Mum,' he said.

'All I can remember about Spain,' I said, 'is dogs barking on balconies.'

'It's a nocturnal society,' said Garth. 'You get up late and have a siesta.' His young face, full of vitality, grinned at this leisurely prospect and I wondered whether he intended to seek work at all. There was something evasive about him now as if he had not learned the lesson of the past few weeks, that problems intensify if you're not working. As he sat there running one hand through his unruly blond hair and clutching his boarding card with the other, I realized that the missing element which might have kept his life on more conventional lines was a woman, but he had an unfortunate taste in girls, being helplessly won over by a face or a figure, quite regardless of their owner's qualities. Many other girls who could have enhanced his life had despaired of arousing his interest. Given his tastes, the affairs were predictably short lived and he could leave the country now without the disruption of a tearful farewell.

32

'Well, I must fly,' he said, standing up.

We stood up, too, and he kissed his mother. I went to shake his hand but he bent his arm with his hand held high as if we were about to indulge in some arm wrestling. It turned out we had to slap hands. I hadn't realized that his generation, which had changed so much, had also disposed of the customary handshake.

When his lanky frame disappeared with a final wave I suddenly envied the freedom he had to vanish for a few months of sunshine while we were left to fend off rain and bills. Travel had not been so simple when I was his age.

Annette and I walked back in silence to the multi-storey car park. As usual when I left Garth I feared that I would never see him again, a melancholy presentiment that had accompanied most of our partings since he was a small boy. But whether it was his death or mine that was supposed to prevent our reunion was never clear.

What was clear to me now was that these forebodings had acquired an extra bite since my vasectomy, because there could never be another Garth. The lady in south London had been very anxious that I should appreciate that.

I had delayed having a vasectomy for many months, imagining that it involved a couple of nights in hospital which would have been difficult to arrange if Annette was not to know. But then I discovered by accident, listening to some freshly neutered accountant in the Comedy Hotel (who had so many children that his distracted wife was reputed to dip her elbow in the soup to test its temperature) that the whole thing could be done in the lunch hour. It was like going out to post a letter or buy some cigarettes. You didn't even go into hospital.

Two weeks later I arrived, minus my customary aplomb, at a Doctor Mortimer's surgery in south London, where nobody would know either me or my wife, and sat in a small white waiting room listening for cries of pain or, conceivably, bricks being banged together. Words like geld and emasculate came to my mind.

33

Doctor Mortimer turned out to be a woman of about thirty-five called Rebecca, a discovery I made with mixed feelings given that she would be brandishing a scalpel. Suppose she, like so many of her sisters these days, hated men?

Her first job, I found, was to try to talk me out of it. She asked where my wife was, because 'this step has to be a joint decision', and when I assured her that I was single she wanted to know what I would do if I got married and had to tell my fertile bride that there could be no children. It began to dawn on me that this small operation was one that she could easily refuse if the candidate seemed unsuitable, and I quickly invented a divorced wife and five expensive children who were slowly dragging me to the bankruptcy court. She looked at me in a funny way and I could see that her darkest suspicion was that many men availed themselves of her services not to exercise an intelligent control over the size of their families, but to enable them to pursue a trouble-free life of wild sexual promiscuity.

'More than anything else,' she said eventually, 'you must accept that this is irreversible.'

'Oh, I do,' I said fervently.

She stood up and led me into the next room. It was sparsely furnished, a portable couch in the centre of its lino floor being the main item on view. Nearby on a glass-topped table there was an array of medical equipment that I didn't care to look at. It was being arranged in a certain order by a young blonde nurse who didn't bother to look up when we came in. The room's one window gave a cheerless view of high-rise flats with their balconies covered by drying washing, an advertisement hoarding featuring an Italian car and turbid clouds drifting across the capital's lowering sky.

'Undress behind the screen and put this gown on,' said Doctor Mortimer. She handed me a green gown and I looked round for a screen which I now saw in the corner of the room.

'I have a very low pain threshold,' I said. 'I get jumpy when I need a haircut.'

'Perhaps I should give you a general anaesthetic. Then you could get your hair cut at the same time,' said Doctor Mortimer.

The prospect of being looked after by two women filled my head with prurient notions, a development that was abruptly forestalled when the doctor casually numbed my equipment with a swift injection in the scrotum. They made me lie back then while we waited for it to take effect.

'Not much chance of a hard-on now then?' I joked but they both pretended that they hadn't heard.

Lying back, my head was lower than the rest of me so that I couldn't see what they were doing. This was probably just as well. Snip, snip.

Of course I had read about it in *Pears*. 'The tube on each side is cut and a small piece is removed. This is to leave a gap to prevent the cut ends from reuniting. The cut ends are sealed and the skin cut closed.' Reading about it was one thing, but lying on this rickety couch with a scalpel hovering above your private parts was quite different. I tried to raise my head but could see only theirs.

Doctor Mortimer had a round, friendly face that looked as if she was kind to animals and children (probably in that order) and yet she spent her working life poring over the genitals of men with a pair of scissors. How did you go home to dinner after a day like that? And what about the nurse, a cool, embarrassment-free number who couldn't have been older than nineteen? What crooked career path had deposited her in this macabre situation, and what effect would it have on her sex life that had, presumably, barely begun?

I lay there worrying about the two of them with their grave expressions and their lethal weapons and suddenly the whole thing was over. It hadn't taken ten minutes.

'I've put in two stitches,' said Doctor Mortimer, straightening up.

'Only two?'

'It was a very small cut.'

I got off the couch and walked with infinite care to the screen in the corner.

35

'Tea or coffee?' the nurse asked. It was the first time that she had spoken to me.

'I ought to be going,' I said.

'Not for twenty minutes,' said Doctor Mortimer. 'You can't leave for twenty minutes.'

When I had dressed she took me back into her office and the nurse brought me a coffee.

'We need a sample,' said Doctor Mortimer.

'A sample?'

'Of your sperm. For tests. Not now, of course, but after six weeks or so to make sure it's worked.' I nodded. 'The sperm beyond the cut end will still go into the seminal fluid and it may be three months before they have all been ejected. We have to check again then, too.'

'Right,' I said.

'Use a condom and transfer it to this bottle. You didn't drive here, did you?'

'Of course not,' I said, foreseeing difficulties.

A quarter of an hour later I walked gingerly to my car and drove home. I felt like the footballer who forgot to make the right protective shield with his hands before the free kick.

And now my wife was pregnant!

'I'm writing a book,' said Kitty Benson. 'It's called *God is a Woman*.' She flitted round the room with a cloth, redistributing the dust.

'It's come to something,' said Alec, 'when your wife takes up feminism at thirty-nine.'

Annette and I had dropped round on a Sunday morning to deliver a belated wedding present. The ceremony itself had arrived so suddenly that there wasn't time to get the particular music centre that they had wanted. But it had arrived now from some tireless factory on the other side of the world and Alec was busily installing it in a corner of their sitting room.

'What music would you like, dear?' he asked.

'Something by that chap who writes all the musicals,' said

Kitty. 'Looks as if he's got a stocking over his head.' She put down her duster. 'We're going to have a spring clean. There's a man coming to do the carpets.'

Alec grimaced. 'When we were single we used to put the carpets over the washing line and beat the dust out of them. Now expensive men are coming with magical shampoos.'

'It's all part of the liberation of women, dear,' said Kitty, sitting down. The small room was conventionally if unimaginatively furnished: a sofa on which Annette and I were sitting, two armchairs and a small coffee table on which stood a bottle of sherry that all of us except Kitty were drinking. The old-fashioned fireplace was now, in April, a barren centrepiece to the room. From the new wedding present there came a song from *Aspects of Love*.

'When did you get interested in all this?' asked Annette, helping herself to more sherry. 'The liberation of women, I mean.'

'My dear, I've *always* been interested in it,' said Kitty. She looked like a little bird, perched on the edge of her chair, turning this way and that and almost twitching with energy. 'It's a British problem, I've concluded. Do you realize that universal suffrage got here later than most places? Even Russia had it before us.'

'We jumped ahead, though,' I said, 'with a woman in Downing Street.'

'Tokenism,' said Kitty, 'and where is she now? More importantly, where are her successors? There's not a woman in the Cabinet.'

Alec, his music duties accomplished, took the other armchair. 'Whose fault is that?' he asked. 'She practically picked it. Women don't like working with women.' He poured himself a huge sherry.

I noticed now a picture, hanging over the fireplace, of their son Steven. He was sitting on an upturned milk crate, his thumbs in the belt of his stone-washed jeans, glowering at the camera like a young film star who was trying to project a trendy image of moodiness and menace. It was

37

evidently a picture that somebody in the family enjoyed, but I found it thoroughly intimidating.

Kitty said: 'In many ways this is the worst country for women. We're a tradition-bound, class-ridden society that only has one new idea every hundred years. In America all wives are called Honey and blow the family funds on breast implants, tummy tucks and lip injections. They have fun.'

'And that's what you want, is it?' Alec asked. 'A tummy tuck?' This was a more serious conversation than he wanted on a Sunday morning and its tone made him restless.

'What we want,' said Annette, woozy with sherry, 'is straitjackets for men.'

'Alec doesn't move enough to need a straitjacket,' said Kitty gaily. 'He's the only person to stand still in a strobe light.'

I poured my wife another drink. She was fun after a sherry or two.

'Women don't know what they want,' I said. 'That's the whole point.'

'A Gucci handbag, a Pucci dress and a Shiatsu massage,' said Annette. 'That'd do for a start.'

'I have a title ready for my second book,' said Kitty. 'I find the titles come easier than the books.'

'What is it?' asked Alec warily.

'*Orchids in the Cesspit*. It's a sort of history of women and their achievements.'

'How many pages will that make?' asked Alec, winking at me.

'My husband resents my ambitions. Those who can, do. Those who can't, teach.'

I put down my sherry. 'You two used to get along fine,' I said, 'before you were married.'

'Alec would feel happier if I was writing a monograph on tiddlywinks,' Kitty said. 'He wouldn't feel threatened.'

Alec was casually tapping his knee to the music. 'I don't feel threatened, dear. I wish you every success. If I had the time I'd write a book myself but I have to go out and earn a living.'

38

'He only has thirteen weeks' holiday a year,' said Kitty. 'Jeffrey Archer would write two books in that time.' She said it with a big smile that she flashed at all of us. She was such a happy, bouncy little thing that I wondered if the rest of us would share her sparkle if, like her, we gave up alcohol. She was a gleaming advertisement for abstinence.

But this was evidently not an idea that had occurred to Alec because he suggested that the two of us should adjourn to the Comedy Hotel for a pint before lunch while our wives returned to their respective kitchens. Given what had gone before I thought this was a brave proposal, but the expected opposition never appeared and half an hour later we were sitting at the bar with pints of Whitbread.

'She's changed,' he hissed. 'You saw it, didn't you?'

'Changed?' I said.

'It's bloody amazing. We live together in perfect peace for eighteen years, then we get married and all hell breaks loose.'

'She's more confident now,' I said. 'She's expressing herself. She's got security.'

'What happened to my security? I need a flak jacket back there. She's hitting me with ideas I didn't even know she had.'

He peered at me through his thick-rimmed spectacles as if I had the answer to this sinister shift in his domestic arrangements and I had to laugh. The truth was that my admiration for Kitty was somewhat greater than my admiration for Alec. Kitty was a dynamo, a cauldron of ideas and energy who worried about wildlife, denounced racism, eschewed tobacco and drink, battled endlessly to win a council seat and now, at thirty-nine, had decided to try to write a book. While these little explosions – or signs of life – were going on all round him, Alec had found neither the drive nor the confidence to escape from the mundane shackles of the schoolroom where, no doubt, he said the same things year after year. The poet and the pedagogue – if they hadn't given it an exhaustive eighteen-year trial I would never have expected them to wed.

39

I said: 'I'm a great admirer of Kitty, though perhaps Mavis Jones would have been easier.'

'Oh, I don't want a doormat,' he said, picking up his beer. 'I want Kitty. The old version, the mark one model. Do you know, the day we got home from the wedding she moved all the furniture around? "I've always wanted to do that," she said. "Well, why didn't you?" I asked. But you're right. She had felt insecure.'

At this moment Laurie Curtis came in and sat on the next vacant stool. I hadn't seen him since Helen's arrest although he had rung me that evening in some distress to apologize. I don't know which of us was more embarrassed. His arrival, which was normally a very verbal business, took place this morning in complete silence. It was apparent that he was trying to re-grow his moustache.

'Good morning, Laurie,' I said, hinting that common politeness demanded a word or two.

'Morning,' he muttered. He stared at the bar, not looking at us, and suddenly the words poured out. 'They're going to do her. They're going to take her to court. I can't understand it. What got into her? She wasn't short of money. In fact she'd been spoilt rotten. It's broken my heart, I can tell you.'

'I'm very sorry,' I told him. 'I tried to get them to drop it but her activities were so widespread that my vote didn't count.'

'That's another thing,' he said. 'Why did she choose *your* shop? Was she trying to humiliate me? All those shops and she had to get arrested in yours.'

'What is this?' Alec asked, stirring from dark thoughts about his wife's new prescriptive message. 'What are we talking about?'

'I think Laurie had better tell you,' I said. I had refrained from mentioning the subject to him or to anybody.

Alec's face was a picture. After all, Helen was one of his star pupils, his potential head girl. He couldn't have looked more surprised if Laurie had been telling him that Judy had opened a bordello and invited Kitty to join the team.

40

'She needs counselling,' he said immediately when Laurie had stopped.

Laurie's voice had choked and I thought he was going to shed a tear. 'She needs a good hiding,' he managed to reply.

'That's the last thing she needs, Laurie. We're talking about psychology here.'

'Bollocks,' said Laurie. 'Head doctors? Leave it out.'

His reaction, which evidently annoyed Alec, summed up Laurie rather well. The cultural influences in his life had been *A Fistful of Dollars*, *Top of the Pops*, Majorca and the thrusting intellect of Alistair Maclean.

'It's a cry for help,' said Alec. 'She's trying to tell us something.'

This tired approach didn't impress his listener, who said: 'I could understand it if she was a boy. Boys are villains. But a girl!'

'If only you'd read *King Lear* you'd realize that daughters can be difficult, too,' I said.

'What does Judy say?' asked Alec.

'What do you think she says? It's in the genes. Mine.'

'She could have a point there,' I said. 'Have you got any previous?'

'Don't take the piss, Max. I've never robbed anybody in my life. Well, not as such.'

It became necessary to cheer him up. His daughter's experiments with *laissez-faire* capitalism had aged him a little and removed his natural exuberance. He hadn't even ordered a drink. I bought him a pint and said: 'What you need to cheer yourself up is a fresh money-making idea, and I've got one for you.'

'What?' he asked when he had made deep inroads on his pint.

'Boys' pyjamas. They're boring.'

'So?'

'We need new exciting designs. Alcatraz markings or traditional arrows showing that the little prisoner is being banged up for the night. Soccer strip jim-jams. A-team.

41

Ultimate Warrior. You could organize all that with your connections and I'll sell them to doting mothers in my shops.'

A money-making idea to Laurie was like a fix to a junkie, but today he just said sadly: 'It sounds good, Max. I'll look into it.' He sat slumped on his stool in a posture of utter defeat.

The customary atmosphere in this bar of quiet professional satisfaction, of peaks having been conquered and rivals quashed, had dissipated in the gloom that emanated from the wounded father.

'She was such a wonderful girl,' he said, more to himself than anyone else. 'I taught her everything I know.'

'Then they brought her home from the maternity ward,' I said, but no jokes would lift his spirits now.

'Would it help if I talked to her?' Alec asked. 'After all, I am her headmaster.'

'Would you do that, Alec?' Laurie said, reviving a little. 'I can't seem to reach her. I can't get her to explain at all.'

'I'll be glad to, Laurie. I'll talk to her like an uncle. I can't bear to see a bright girl like that throwing it all away.' He produced some change from his teacher's stipend. 'Let me buy you a drink as well.'

4

Kitty's thesis

Annette's pregnancy went unremarked for days on end. It was a subject rich with traps that I was anxious to avoid. But there was something triumphal about her behaviour, suggesting that her condition had been achieved in the teeth of fierce opposition (as, indeed, it had). She was looking forward to a scan that would tell her the birth date and possibly the sex of her eagerly awaited package – the complex world of childbirth had moved on since the arrival of Garth.

In the meantime she curled up lazily on the sofa with fat books and glossy magazines that were aimed at the minds and purses of productive mums. She learned that more male babies are born than female ones but higher male mortality sets about correcting this imbalance. Women start to outnumber men at fifty, apparently, and by eighty there are twice as many of them. This information slightly dampened her hopes of having a daughter.

'You don't seem very interested in this baby,' she said once.

'Of course I am,' I told her. 'But it isn't a baby yet.'

My problem was that I couldn't tell her I had had a vasectomy; and inquiries I had made suggested that there was still a very outside chance that I was the father. So I kept *schtum*, unsure of my ground, and contemplated dramatic blood tests later. But the constant thought in my head was: If I'm not the father, who is?

One evening I returned from another unpromising day at work, searching for a sign of hope among the sombre account sheets of my endangered empire, to find that Annette had stripped the wallpaper from the downstairs toilet and was now painting the walls white with a huge roller. The paint in her tray looked edible, like ice cream. She had these urges and splurges, suddenly and without warning changing the shape or colour of some neglected corner of the house. I saw it now as some sort of nesting instinct. The rejected wallpaper, featuring hundreds of little brown birds, lay in shreds on the floor. I was glad to see it go but could only wonder at the effort that had gone into this small improvement. Wasn't there something more important that needed doing?

'Hiya,' she said cheerfully. 'What do you think?'

'Big improvement,' I said, 'but is it work for a pregnant woman?'

'Pregnant's not ill,' she replied, adjusting the shower cap she was wearing to keep flecks of paint from her beautiful hair.

I went into the kitchen in search of the smell that would give me a clue about tonight's menu and found that a card had arrived from Garth. It showed *una calle* in Marbella, a narrow street that no vehicle could invade, with brightly tiled pavement and open-fronted shops. The tiny stretch of sky that could be seen at the top of the white buildings was all blue.

I turned it over. 'Guess what?' it said, in his hasty handwriting. 'I'm earning! Also swimming, dancing, drinking and playing. Couldn't you get them to tow Britain south a bit? The climate is different here. Love, G.'

After my initial pleasure at hearing from him, I was consumed by envy. I don't remember swimming, drinking and dancing in some sun-baked Mediterranean playground when I was nineteen. I was studying the retail trade as an underpaid but ambitious shop assistant in a benighted corner of Kilburn.

44

Annette came in.

'That's a strange card,' she said.

I put it down. 'What's strange about it?'

'Notable for its omissions, I'd say. What job is he actually doing? Where's he living? He hasn't even given us an address.'

'On all known form he'll be in touch as soon as he needs something,' I replied.

I took a bottle of wine into the dining room. The house was a lot emptier since Garth had left. It felt as if about six people had moved out. I sat down and poured myself a glass.

If I'm not the father, who is? Because I have always suspected that my wife is immoral or would be if the opportunity presented itself, I have taken some care to keep those opportunities to a minimum. Good-looking men with a certain glint in their eye have not been invited home. Alec Benson and Laurie Curtis, the men who loom largest in what we call our social life, are not the stuff that sex symbols are made of. Women can spend hours in their company without thinking about sex at all.

I met Annette in 1971 on the day that Khrushchev died. I was twenty and she was nineteen. It was at one of those Saturday night parties of booze and music that you keep going to at that age in search of youthful pleasures. The host was usually somebody you didn't even know. I spotted her across the room, a shapely little thing with lots of red hair, a biggish nose and green eyes with their slight squint. The combined effect of these unpromising particulars was the most sexually provocative girl I had ever seen.

I stared, entranced, and she came straight over.

'Annette Hamilton,' she said.

An hour later we were making love in the broom cupboard.

She had just come back from Greece where she had been working as a travel courier, shepherding homesick package holidaymakers from one exciting outing to the next. Before that she had been a nanny in London to the two children of

45

a satirical comedian. She had never had what people call 'a proper job'.

I married her quickly, scared that she would escape. A sexually exhausting few months produced Garth the following year. We make love all the time except when she's pregnant. She won't do it when she's pregnant. She won't do it now.

But, as I said, I have always suspected her of infidelity. I have always nursed the private conviction that she was quite capable of fellating the milkman or surprising the gardener with a hand-job. The sexuality is there, brimming behind her secretive smile and waiting to be unleashed.

I should have been alerted by her eager attitude to sex at our first meeting. If I could have her in the broom cupboard within an hour, what exciting prospects were there for the rest of mankind? But of course vanity discounts their chances.

She came in now with the food trolley and began to lay the table. I got up to help. It was casserole, a real toothpick job.

'I'm beginning to miss him,' she said, when we were eating.

'Who?' For one mad moment I thought she was about to reveal the name of a secret lover.

'Garth. I'm used to three sitting here.'

'Are you worried about him?' I asked. I could see that this was a sober moment for her. The young bird had flown the nest.

'Not at all,' she said firmly. 'He's gone abroad to have fun. I did the same thing myself.'

'But he's a man. He'll need a career.'

'What the hell,' said Annette. 'In seventy years we'll all be dust. Including Garth.'

My wife has a cheerful way of consigning us all, somewhat prematurely, to the dustbin and then building some kind of philosophy on it. I don't know whether it was hedonism, nihilism, fatalism or positivism, but I found it rather depressing.

I told her: 'You often say that, or something similar, but it isn't clear to me how it's supposed to affect our behaviour. I mean, it's not my fault, our going to be dust. What am I supposed to do about it?'

'Enjoy yourself. Make the most of things.'

'Short-term happiness often leads to long-term misery, in my experience.'

'It depends what you mean by long-term. In seventy years –'

'Yes,' I said. 'I know.'

'I hope Garth has fun. I hope he has a hell of a wonderful time.' She put her hand on her tummy. 'I hope this one does, too.'

Alec Benson sat at the bar in the Comedy Hotel cleaning his spectacles with his handkerchief.

'I have spoken to Miss Helen Curtis,' he said.

'And?' I asked.

'I've found out what the problem is. But I don't see how I can tell Laurie.'

'What is the problem?'

'*Entre nous*, she hates her parents. I mean, really hates them. She says she'd like to kill them.'

'Any particular reason?'

'Oh yes, she's quite specific. She says they've turned her home into a battleground for the last sixteen years. Verbal violence, physical violence, flying missiles. She said she had been living in a war zone. At one time she sympathized with one, at another time the other. But eventually she gave up on both of them for poisoning the atmosphere in which she lives. She's quite a sensitive girl, actually.'

She had been sent to Alec's study that afternoon by her form-master – a man known as Beans because his name is Harry Coe – having no idea why he wanted to see her. For Alec the confrontation was tinged with embarrassment: he was always uneasy, he said, with the children of his friends. It was difficult to establish a headmaster's remote and

47

omnipotent persona with an errant pupil if the child knew that you were getting joyously drunk with her father the previous evening.

She stood at the door and said: 'You wanted to see me, Mr Benson?' She was one of the prettiest girls in the school with her thoughtful, pale face and blonde hair, and in her school uniform of blue blouse and grey tunic an appropriate subject for the sexual fantasies of the perverts who specialized in that kind of thing.

'Come in, Helen,' he said. 'Sit down.'

She sat upright in the chair with her hands in her lap and looked at him steadily. There was no shortage of confidence.

'You're in a spot of trouble, I gather,' he said.

'Oh,' she said, realizing now why she was here. 'Have the police been to see you, to find out what sort of girl I am?'

'The police? Not yet.'

'But you're worried about the good name of the school?'

It was a measure of Alec's uneasiness at this situation that he had allowed himself to become the victim of the interrogation.

'Helen, I want to help you,' he protested.

'It was my father then,' she said. 'I'm a great worry to him.'

'Most people are a great worry to somebody else, whether they know it or not,' Alec told her. 'But naturally your parents are worried. Your father has the highest possible hopes for you and doesn't want to see you throw it all away.'

'I don't really care what my father wants, Mr Benson. Or my mother, come to that. She's a cow and he's a pig.'

'My, my, we are into animal imagery,' he said, seeing that the heavy hand would be no use here. 'Why do you say that?'

And then she told him about the noxious atmosphere at home, the low-pitched violence and the occasional flesh wounds, and Alec was slowly exposed to a child's vision of hell. There were no tears. There was a hard streak beneath the demure exterior, developed perhaps by her reluctant ringside seat at countless domestic battles.

48

'And so you stole to hurt them?' he said.

She nodded her complete agreement.

'Well, sod them,' said Alec, trying to strike the right note. 'The real casualty is you. Can't you see that?'

'That's what hurts them, Mr Benson,' she replied with chilling accuracy. 'Actually, I'd like to kill them for the pain they've caused.'

'To you?'

'And to each other.'

In the Comedy Hotel Alec put on his newly cleaned glasses and asked: 'How do I tell Laurie this?'

'I don't know,' I said. 'But I think you should.'

When Laurie shuffled in half an hour later, however, neither Alec nor I felt like broaching the subject.

'Your daughter despises you' was not the sort of conversational gambit that guaranteed a pleasant evening, and Laurie clearly regarded this place as his sanctuary from his problems at work, his angry wife, his angry daughter.

We played pool. I beat Alec and Alec beat Laurie and Laurie beat me. Honours even, we returned to the bar.

'Your moustache is coming along,' I said.

'Slowly, mate. Very slowly.'

'Perhaps you could insure against it happening again?'

'I don't believe that terrorism is susceptible to actuarial analysis,' said Alec. 'How is Helen?'

'We don't seem to be talking,' said Laurie.

In the absence of the correct donor, I bought for my wife on Mother's Day a German grill-stone. It promised to 'spoil guests with some really fine meals' so Annette decided to invite friends in.

It was a natural ollare stone from the southern Alps and it had to be heated in the oven for twenty minutes. You then placed it on your dining room table with spluttering burners beneath, and cooked your steak or your fish or vegetables when you were ready to eat them. Being a slow eater myself, I was quite used to picking my way through food that had already cooled to an unacceptable degree, and I was looking forward to a non-stop supply of hot steak and a bottle of wine. My only concern was the company.

Alec and Kitty could be expected to behave with decorum, neither hurling plates nor boring their hosts; but the Curtis marriage was now such a potent mix of violence and rancour that to invite them into your home was to expose yourself to the risk of damage to something precious that was inadequately insured.

In the event they all arrived smiling, as if promises of best behaviour had been demanded and given, and we rushed them into the dining room where the grill-stone was now a searing three hundred degrees centigrade.

'Grapes on the sideboard when nobody's ill!' exclaimed Kitty. 'Posh!' Annette had made dozens of mandarin pancakes from flour and water and you wrapped your sizzling biscuit-sized slice of fillet steak in one with bits of carrot, celery and onion and ate it without needing knives and forks. (This was just as well, as most of our best cutlery was in the Bermuda Triangle of the dishwasher where favourite cups and plates could languish for days until my wife thought there was enough material to justify switching the thing on.)

'A most unusual meal,' said Kitty Benson, 'but quite delicious.'

'How clever of you, Annette,' said Judy Curtis. 'Dinner parties will never be the same again.'

They were both wearing blue dresses, as if some suburban guide had designated this as the correct wear for dining out this month.

'How's the book coming along, Kitty?' I asked.

'Wonderfully. Did you see that the first Briton in space is going to be a woman? It's very helpful to my general thesis.'

'What is that exactly?' I asked. 'Your general thesis?'

She picked up her orange juice and sipped it. She alone was ignoring my wine.

'I suppose, basically, it's that women are practical and men are dreamers.'

50

'That's why women never invent anything,' I said.

'Did you know,' she said, ignoring this shaft, 'that one in seven women are raped by their husbands? One, in the north-west, was raped every night for twenty months.'

'What was she feeding him on?' Alec asked. 'Raw meat?'

'We're concussed by your wit, darling,' Kitty told him with a look through her large spectacles which suggested that silence would be his safest option. 'What Alec needs is a compliant houri.'

I poured the others more wine. 'I hope the book launch party will have more than orange juice,' I said. 'We want it to go with a swing.'

'Champagne, of course,' said Kitty. 'I'm quite accustomed to watching other people drinking.'

'She sits there at parties watching everything disintegrate around her, including me,' said Alec. 'She even used alcohol-free baby wipes on Steven when he was born.'

I took a freshly cooked piece of steak from the stone and wrapped it in a pancake with some celery. I thought that with food like this I would soon be as fat as Laurie. He was sitting, unusually quiet, on my left and eating pretty steadily himself.

'How *is* Steven?' he asked now. 'You people are bloody lucky with your kids. God knows where we went wrong.'

'The Helen business must be very disturbing for you,' Annette said sympathetically.

Judy Curtis stared mistily down at her wine as if we were discussing a daughter who had died.

'I remember when she was a little girl,' she said. 'She came into the kitchen and said: "Mummy, I know the Lord's Prayer." I can't remember it all but it began "Our father who farts in heaven" and ended up "deliver us from the eagles". She was four years old and wasn't trying to be funny.'

'What will happen to her?' Annette asked.

Neither parent seemed capable of answering this and so Alec spoke up.

51

'A *mauvais quart d'heure* in court,' he said. 'She'll get probation. It's lucky she's only sixteen. If she was seventeen she could get something harsher.'

'How do you know?' Laurie asked.

'They've been in touch with me. The court needs a report on the home life, the school record and a medical history before they can put a child on probation. I've told them she's an exemplary pupil and that the shoplifting is quite out of character.'

'What is probation, anyway?' Judy asked.

'It's a supervision order. It doesn't amount to much. She'd have to keep in touch with the probation officer and they'd keep an eye on what she was up to. But if they thought that she was unrepentant or wilful they could fine her or make a supervision order with conditions. This would mean that she would be given a few little jobs to do every week for however long the order lasts.'

'You know a lot about it,' said Annette.

'I'm a headmaster. Occasionally one of our little lambs falls by the wayside, but none has ever surprised me as much as Helen.'

'We were pretty surprised ourselves,' said Judy who, I could now see, had been totally dispirited by the whole business.

'Which reminds me,' said Laurie, lighting up a cigar, 'we have a favour to ask you. You and Annette,' he said, looking at me.

'Of course,' said my wife, somewhat incautiously to my mind.

'The thing is,' said Judy, 'we've got to go to France to look at this house.'

'And we can't take Helen out of school because of her O levels,' said Laurie. 'Baron we can put in kennels.'

'I see,' said Annette. 'You'd like us to put Helen up?'

'It's only three days. She can hardly stay with her headmaster,' Judy said, smiling at Alec.

'That's fine,' I said. 'Send her round. I'll lock up my valuables.'

52

My continual attempts to be humorous aren't always successful and this one produced the sort of silence that breaks a comedian's heart. I was obviously the only person who thought it odd that they should ask us to provide Helen with hospitality after she had robbed my shop, but then I'm used to being in a minority.

5

Winning bid

The following week, as rain swept in to postpone our hopes of summer, I bought a girl in an auction on a riverboat. It was the last thing I expected to happen.

The occasion was a charity evening organized by one of those vehemently male associations, membership of which provides a boys' night out for housebound husbands who justify their guilty absence by raising money for deserving causes. I belong to the Chamber of Commerce myself, an organization with more selfish objectives, but Laurie, who had acquired a couple of tickets to the event, thought that an evening drifting down the Thames and getting drunk would make a welcome change from marital fisticuffs.

I always imagine that in years to come when clouds are dispersed by planes spraying chemicals and the weather is controlled by governments, people won't believe the rain we had to put up with, but once we were in the boat, and seated for dinner in a surprisingly large room, there was something cosy about the pitter patter on the river beyond our window.

It was one of those evenings where a lot of eating and drinking is accompanied by tedious speeches replete with vulgar jokes some of which I probably invented myself when I was sixteen and have heard twenty times since. The speeches give way to an interminable charity auction when the main fund raising takes place – footballs signed by Bobby

Moore or even a more recent soccer hero, cricket bats signed by brilliant batsmen, obviously not English, and, for all I know, the discarded jockstraps of forgotten pugilists. After that there is a cabaret.

You might have thought that such an occasion would attract as big a crowd as an open air rally for agoraphobics, but there was something about the charity label that pulled in men who were usually at home. I was only there myself as a kindness to Laurie who, depressed now almost beyond hope, implored me to go with him.

The champagne certainly cheered him up. 'I'm going to liquidate some capital,' he announced as he toyed with his chicken roulades.

'You mean spend money?' I asked.

'That's it,' he said, wiping his mouth. 'If this place in France is anything like the picture I'm going in with both feet.'

He was wearing his usual brown suit which I idly studied for bloodstains. His moustache was beginning to look like a moustache again.

'Does Judy like it?' I asked.

'Loves it. I think she'd sooner live there than here. Since the Helen business her priorities seem to have changed.'

'How do you mean?'

'She talks about France more than she talks about her daughter.'

For a couple whose marriage was as fragile as theirs to even contemplate a joint venture like this struck me as odd, but then people strike me as odd. They don't even conform to their proclaimed pattern.

'Don't talk about liquidating capital,' said a man who was sitting on Laurie's other side. 'Things are so bad I had to sell a vineyard last week.'

I leaned forward to take a look at this impoverished guest. He was a fat, red-faced man of about fifty who didn't appear to be suffering unduly from his financial reverses. For no apparent reason perspiration coursed down his cheeks.

'We're all walking on eggs, mate,' Laurie told him. 'But I've got a feeling that things are going to improve.'

The man looked at him keenly. 'What gives you that idea?' he asked.

But before Laurie could deliver an upbeat view of the nation's economy there was a banging on the top table – a spoon on a plate, by the sound of it – and gradually everybody stopped talking. One of those bright young men who always seem to have more energy than you was on his feet and delivering some sort of speech, which was a suitable moment for me to allow my mind to drift off to the problem of my shops. I have never liked people making speeches at me – it seems so antisocial. After all, I have things to say too.

We were cruising under Maidenhead Bridge when I gathered from his tone that the end was in sight. This year, he declared, charity begins at home. People were dying in Asia, starving in Africa and vanishing in their thousands in the sinister ghettos of South America, but tonight's effort was directed at London where a thousand people slept rough in the streets. This piece of commercial chauvinism attracted tremendous applause.

And then the auction began. A bewildering collection of prizes, most of them donated by philanthropic traders, were dangled before the drunken bidders. Alongside the inscribed baubles of showbiz and sporting heroes were such material delights as a crate of wine, a set of bagpipes, a flight in a balloon, a week in Mauritania, a Rolls-Royce for a month, a weekend in the Alps, a home computer, a chaise longue, an octagonal greenhouse and a hang glider.

Lot 38 was Sadie Beck.

The murmurs of approbation that greeted her appearance seemed to put bagpipes and hang gliders into perspective. What I noticed first were her creamy shoulders protruding from a silk black dress. A matching black bow in her fair hair held it in a ponytail, and she had one of those pert faces that the papers used to describe as gamin – wide eyes, snub nose and small round mouth. I took my wallet out.

56

'What is on offer here exactly?' I asked Laurie.

'Dunno, but I suggest you sit on your hands,' he said.

What was on offer, the auctioneer announced with only the barest hint of innuendo, was a night out with Sadie Beck – theatre tickets and free five-star dinner afterwards. The proposition was sufficiently ambiguous to produce predictable guffaws and it seemed to me, from some distance away, that Sadie Beck had blushed. From that moment, of course, it was merely a question of saving her from these unworthy animals.

I was just considering what sort of opening offer would sound reasonable when a shout of 'One hundred pounds' came from Laurie's choleric neighbour.

'One fifty,' I said immediately.

'What are you doing?' asked Laurie. 'You've got a wife at home.'

'I'm giving to charity,' I said. 'I'm like that.'

From a table at the other end of the room there came a call of two hundred pounds and it was followed immediately by another of two fifty.

'Three hundred,' shouted Laurie's neighbour after a long consultation with his wallet.

'Three fifty,' I said.

The auctioneer was beaming triumphantly now at the interest being shown at Lot 38. Greenhouses and home computers had a limited appeal in comparison.

Sadie Beck was looking at me, her most determined supporter. I tried to indicate, with a reassuring smile, that her future was safe with me.

Somebody called four hundred. He didn't look like the sort of person Sadie Beck would care to spend an evening with, being both corpulent and unkempt, and I called four fifty.

'Where do you think this is going to end?' I asked Laurie. I had rather expected to have won the prize by now.

'It could go four figures,' Laurie said. 'They're showing off, aren't they? Half of them have never been out with a pretty woman, and they've had enough drinks to go for it.'

A new voice from the top table called five hundred and I wondered if he was there to push the price up. I looked at Sadie Beck's creamy shoulders and thought of the homeless poor sleeping on the Embankment.

'Six hundred,' I said.

'I thought you were going up in fifties?' Laurie asked.

'I've thrown in a sixty-second lap,' I told him. 'I've got to shake the others off.'

I thought it had had the desired effect because it was some time before anybody said anything.

'Come along, gentlemen,' cried the auctioneer. 'Have you all done at six hundred?'

'Seven hundred,' said the fat man, but not with much enthusiasm.

'Eight hundred,' I replied in a tone of voice that was intended to convey that any other bidding would be quite hopeless and produce only frustration, defeat and humiliation. This time the silence was eloquent. The auctioneer scanned the room, seeking out those who had been bidding and inquiring, with raised eyebrows and hands, whether they had retired from the battle.

'Sold to Mr Hadfield,' he announced. 'Now, Lot thirty-nine.'

I winced at the mention of my name and was modestly surprised that he knew it. I had imagined myself to be incognito among these drunken do-gooders: now I could see stories in the local press (Shops Owner Buys Girl) or even something punchier in the national tabloids (Knickers Tycoon in Charity Leg-over Shock).

A member of the organizing committee headed in my direction and with him came Sadie Beck. Some girls, lovely at a distance, are not improved by proximity: discouraging flaws emerge on the approaching beauty. This was not the case with my prize who seemed to get better the closer she came. Her blue eyes and her limpid complexion temporarily deprived me of the power of speech. I stood up.

'This is Sadie Beck,' said the committee man. 'A bargain at eight hundred pounds.'

58

I passed him the wodge of fifty-pound notes that he was indirectly asking for and he gave me an envelope containing theatre tickets and restaurant vouchers. I smiled at Sadie Beck.

'You didn't fancy the bagpipes then?' she asked. She had a husky voice that was intensely sensuous.

'You can't take bagpipes out to dinner. You'd look silly,' I said. 'What do we do now?'

'I think I give you my phone number,' she whispered. 'A snip at eight hundred pounds.'

'It sounds like a bargain to me,' I said. 'Write it on the menu.'

She sat in my seat to write down her phone number while Laurie gaped. Shoulders had not previously struck me as one of nature's erogenous areas but hers, seemingly sculpted in ivory, were made to be kissed. I nobly resisted the temptation and nervously put the menu in my pocket hoping that Annette wouldn't find it there. Central heating had made it difficult to destroy embarrassing literature.

Sadie Beck stood up and held out her hand very formally.

'Are you going?' I said. 'You only just got here.'

'I'm helping out tonight, Mr Hadfield,' she said. 'Our date is for May twenty-five.'

I shook her hand and let it go reluctantly. She seemed quite stunning to me.

'I'm looking forward to it,' I said. 'Do you enjoy the theatre?'

'I love it,' she replied and gave me a smile into which I could read all the things I wanted: her helpless desire for me, her deep gratitude that I had made it happen, her passionate hopes for our future relationship. And then she was gone.

'Well,' said Laurie, 'you're well buggered.'

'What?' I said, sitting down. I was feeling both elated and confused.

'Buying a girl in front of all these people? What will Annette say?'

'Annette's not here, is she?'

'But a lot of people are.'

59

'My wife has always been in favour of charitable works,' I said. 'It's something she likes to encourage.'

'I doubt whether she'll be too happy if you go poncing off to the theatre with a bird like that, mate.'

A young man clutching a notebook came up to our table.

'Local paper,' he said to me. 'You won the date with Sadie Beck? Could I have your name?'

'Peter Huntley,' I said.

'I thought the auctioneer said Hadfield?'

'Yes,' I said. 'I noticed that mistake myself.'

Our temporary guest arrived with enough baggage to stay a lot longer than the three days her parents had mentioned. By the time she had unpacked in her room it was littered with hair dryer, compact disc player, a pile of cassettes, curling tongs, an armoury of cosmetics including hair spray and a cream for dealing with spots, a bottle of vodka (for her hosts?), a dozen videos and a pile of lurid-looking paperbacks. I thought she was going to ask for her own personal television and recorder.

When she came downstairs for dinner Annette was still busy in the kitchen and so it fell to me to offer her a drink and generally exhibit a hospitable streak which in the circumstances did not come easily.

We sat down and talked about her, both carefully avoiding the vexed subject of larceny. I am now an authority on sixteen-year-old girls. What do you want to know?

I suppose the biggest surprise is that they don't call their teachers 'sir' any more. In fact they feel closer to their teachers than they do to their parents, partly because their teachers are younger and partly because their parents 'don't really know what's going on'.

Their heroes are good-looking men, usually in adverts. They want to go to college purely because they can't make up their minds about a career. Their favourite activity is listening to very loud music and drinking (the vodka wasn't for her hosts, and Helen was now sipping a sweet sherry).

But – I have to admit it – they work hard. Helen Curtis is

studying home economics, German, French, sociology, biology, chemistry, physics, maths, English and English literature and will take all ten subjects in her O level exams this summer. For the last two she has to write five essays each.

She sat in the chair and told me all this as if she hadn't recently found time in her crowded schedule to rob my shops. But she's a pretty little thing with her long blonde hair and it is not difficult to listen to her. She is the sort of girl who, if she was serving you over a shop counter, you would establish eye contact with, which was not always something that seemed necessary when you were out shopping.

When we sat down to dinner Annette tried to draw her out on the subject of her parents. The look in Helen's eyes told me that we were exploring unwelcome territory.

'My father was always bent,' she announced as if she was revealing a fondness for golf.

'Bent?' said Annette.

'A busy little word, bent,' I said. 'It has at least five quite different meanings.'

'I meant dishonest,' said Helen Curtis, the student of English. 'When he was about twenty he switched the numbers on the front doors of two houses so the survey would get him a mortgage.'

'He told you that?' Annette asked.

'He's very proud of it.'

'He's very proud of you,' I said, feeling that somebody should speak up for the absent father.

'Well, I can't say I'm proud of him.'

'And what do you think of your headmaster, Mr Benson?' Annette asked.

'Weak,' said Helen briefly.

She had an inner confidence that was unnerving in one so young, and she behaved as if the thieving spree had been the work of a quite different girl.

'A tough nut,' said Annette, when Helen had gone into the hall to make a phone call. 'What happened to the carefree days of childhood?'

'They don't have them any more,' I said. 'They study sociology.'

Helen's phone call was shorter than I had feared. An hour and a half's chat to someone in Alice Springs was the sort of thing that I had expected.

'Why did anyone buy the first telephone when there was no one to speak to?' she asked when she came back.

'That's something that I've always wondered about,' I said. I was afraid that she was going to sit around now so that we felt obliged to entertain her or submit to her choice of viewing on television, but she said that she was going upstairs to do her homework.

'What is it?' I asked, interested.

'An essay on poetry.'

She disappeared upstairs, Annette vanished into the kitchen, and twenty minutes later when I seemed to have been reduced to watching a chat show on television, the front door bell rang for rather longer than was necessary. I got up to answer it.

Standing on the doorstep, a Sony Walkman clamped to both ears, was Steven Benson. He was wearing black jeans, black T-shirt and Chelsea boots. His dark hair, cut in a fashionable style which meant that the bottom inch was very short and the rest not cut at all, looked as if it hadn't seen a comb for some time. His face looked tired and had no colour.

It was months since I had seen him and I was surprised at how tall he was.

I said: 'Hallo Steven. What can I do for you?'

It was apparent that he couldn't hear me and it occurred to him eventually to remove the Walkman from his head.

He didn't meet my eye, but seemed to be studying my shoes as he announced: 'I've like come to see Helen. She rang me.'

Whom do you blame for what children become? What turns the cheerful, hopeful ten-year-old into a rude, rebellious and ungrateful teenager? What malignant ingredient poisons the mix?

62

I ask these questions as if I don't know the answer, but I do. The papers and the pundits witter on about our unruly schools or the baleful effects of television; psychologists, summoned to the fray, discuss the destructive influence of the child's already wayward contemporaries, or 'peer group' as they like to call them. But it's the parents, first, second and last. They alone have had the child from birth. They have controlled its behaviour, guided its thoughts, fed its ideas, encouraged its talents, provided its ideals and been responsible finally for the person. The mature teenager is their handiwork. Its character stands before them to say: You were an excellent parent. Or: You should have been shot before you had me.

So Steven Benson, aged seventeen, was a considerable surprise. His father had devoted his life to training children and it might have been expected that he had some expertise in this field. Perhaps in handling thousands over the years he had failed to pay enough attention to the one. Maybe it was all a question of the time available. After all, the children of the famous – politicians, television personalities and all the other monstrous ego-trippers – provide a shameful procession to the courts, even while their preoccupied fathers rise ever higher in their own glittering and exalted circles.

I couldn't help thinking, too, that Kitty, with her unaffected concern for leaded petrol, hungry Africans, vanishing wildlife and demoralized women, had overlooked a primary cause for attention in her own home.

'You've come to see Helen?' I repeated. I hadn't thought, when we agreed to put her up, that we were going to have a party and nor did I want one. 'I believe she's doing her homework.'

'I said like I'd come round,' he answered in a dreary monotone without looking at me. He swung the now disconnected Walkman to and fro.

For a moment I wondered what to do. The single unassailable fact that this was my home and not Helen's had obviously not even occurred to my surly visitor, and I felt vaguely that the subject had a moral dimension somewhere. Should girls of sixteen entertain boys in their room? Would I be neglecting my obligations to Mr and Mrs Curtis if I allowed it to happen?

On the other hand, there was a limit to how rude I could be to the sons of my closest friends, however unattractive I found them.

'Come in and wait in the hall,' I said. 'I'll tell her you're here.'

'That would be really nice,' he said, walking past me into the house.

Helen Curtis was sitting at the small table in her bedroom writing on large sheets of paper.

'Would you describe Beckett as a poet of metaphysical poverty?' she asked to my astonishment.

'I wouldn't describe him that way myself,' I said, 'mainly because I have no idea what it means. Listen, you have a visitor.'

She looked up guiltily. 'Who?'

'Steven.'

'Oh, mega!' she said, putting down her pen.

'Will you come down, or should he come up?'

'Send him up. Then we won't disturb you and Mrs Hadfield.'

This seemed the worst possible option to me but it had the evident approval of the visitor who produced a broad grin when I went down to tell him that Helen would see him upstairs. He didn't produce any words, though. He brushed past me and demolished the stairs in huge, ungainly strides, leaving me standing in the hall as if I were the humble factotum.

I went into the kitchen to find Annette.

'Who was that at the door?' she asked.

'Steven.'

'What did he want?'

'Helen, apparently.'

'Is he still here?'

64

'They're both upstairs.'

'Is that wise?'

'No,' I said. I went over to the table where she was making some cakes. 'What was I supposed to do?'

'If she was your sixteen-year-old daughter would you let her have a young man in her bedroom?'

'If she was my daughter she'd know how to behave,' I replied.

I returned to the sitting room and the television on which the chat show had given way to an assessment of the steam-powered car. I turned it off and was aware immediately of a tremendous din upstairs. The room that we had given Helen was directly above my head and from it now came the sound of her compact disc player at full blast, the thumping noise of a modern pop group with what they mysteriously regarded as music. In the brief respite between tracks there was wild, uninhibited laughter.

I began to feel like a man who, with the best will in the world, has microwaved the cat. Presumably I used to be seventeen myself. At any rate I could well imagine what the cagey Steven Benson had in mind. There is still one way in which each generation resembles the last.

Annette came in.

'I've got it,' she said.

'Good,' I replied.

'Make them coffees. Take them up. Interrupt them. Hint that it's time for bed.'

'They're probably already in it,' I said. 'But it's a good idea.'

I went out to the kitchen and put the kettle on. It was an electric kettle which, as the water heated up, made a noise like an approaching train. In the end I couldn't even hear the racket above. I gave them Gold Blend and cream, put the cups on a tray and headed upstairs.

I wondered what sort of reception I was going to get. Was I the geriatric intruder, thoughtlessly invading their pleasure, or the considerate host catering to my guests' needs? Could these two between them find a smile?

At the top of the stairs I became aware of a different noise that was definitely not coming from the CD player: the rhythmic banging of the bed's headboard against a wall, the throbbing tempo of copulation. I stood frozen with my tray, hoping I was wrong, but some subsidiary sounds – gasps, little yells, grunts – persuaded me otherwise. This was not a scene I was anxious to behold.

I put the tray on the floor, knocked on their door and shouted 'Coffee!'

Then I fled downstairs.

It was hard to associate the demure schoolgirl who ate up her Shreddies at the breakfast table the following morning with the breathless cries of sexual gratification I had heard the previous evening. We learn to wear a mask at an early age.

She sat in the kitchen in her grey and blue school uniform looking as if the process of human reproduction was a recondite subject that she hadn't yet been told about, let alone indulged in. By not so much as a look in the eye did she betray the fact that her homework had been laid aside last night for frantic sexual games.

'How did it go?' I asked, pouring her tea.

She looked at me quizzically.

'The essay,' I said. 'The poet of metaphysical poverty.'

'I didn't manage to finish it,' she said. 'I'll do it in the lunch break.' She smiled at me ruefully as if the burden of homework was an injustice that I would remember and share.

Out of deference to our young guest, Annette had abandoned her morning lie-in and she came up now carrying poached eggs.

'I have to go to hospital today,' she said, 'for a five-month scan.'

'What's a scan?' Helen asked.

'Something magic if you're pregnant,' Annette said. 'You see your unborn baby on a screen, and they can tell you its

66

weight and date of birth. Sometimes they can even tell you the sex.'

'Can they tell you the father?' I wanted to ask but didn't. Instead I said: 'I'll come with you. It'll be an interesting experience.'

'What about work?'

'It's beginning to depress me.'

We saw Helen off on her pink bicycle, with her stirring memories of the night before and her unfinished homework, and later we drove to the hospital in the Rover.

'I have every reason to believe that they were at it last night,' I said. It was something that I couldn't quite bring myself to tell her the previous evening, feeling in some way responsible.

'What do you mean "at it"?' Annette asked.

'Coitus, coition, coupling, congress, copulation,' I said. 'And that's just the Cs.'

'I don't believe you,' she said, looking shocked.

'It sounded like it to me. Of course I speak from memory. But if they were playing Scrabble they were getting pretty excited about it.'

The previous evening I had shown Steven to the door directly I heard his footsteps on the stairs. Sexual fulfilment had failed to liberate his tongue and he made a soundless exit.

'Come again when you've got less time,' I told him.

'I daren't tell Judy – she'd go bananas,' Annette said in the car. 'But perhaps you should speak to Steven's father.'

This was not a prospect that I relished. There were several aspects to last night's developments in the guest's bedroom that dismayed me. Apart from the event itself, which was appalling enough, I had the sheepish feeling that nobody should be having sex in my house if I wasn't. But mainly I felt a degree of blame for what had occurred, a guilt that would not make an inquest with Alec the sort of conversation that I enjoyed.

At the hospital we waited in a cheerless corridor with several pregnant women. There are nearly five and a half

67

billion people on this planet and ninety million new arrivals every year; I was not convinced that the frenzied productivity I saw all round me was absolutely necessary. I had the lofty sense of responsibility of the recently vasectomized, an incongruous feeling to sustain as I escorted my pregnant wife into the nurse's room with its ultrasound scan equipment.

Annette lay on a bed and bared her stomach. The nurse, a cheerful, middle-aged lady, rubbed oil on it and then passed the scanner backwards and forwards over her skin. High-intensity sound was beamed through Annette's abdomen into the womb, and the sound was reflected back to create a picture on a screen in front of us. The wonders of modern science! I seemed to be looking at a baby gorilla eating an orange, the scene having been shot through six layers of gauze.

'Are you one of those who wants to know the sex?' asked the nurse. 'A lot don't. They can get over any disappointment in the excitement of the birth but not now with months to think about it.'

'I'd love to know,' said Annette, staring at the screen.

'It's a question of spotting its thingummy,' said the nurse. 'The baby's fine, by the way. It weighs half a kilo and should arrive on September twenty-six.'

To have inferred this from the strange picture on the screen seemed little less than a miracle to me. When the nurse drew our attention to what she said were arms and legs I felt as if I had been to one of those art movies and then read a review which demonstrated humiliatingly that I had missed the whole point.

'What about its thingummy?' I asked.

'Can't see it,' said the nurse, peering at the screen. 'I think you can be pretty sure it's a girl. It could be a boy who is shy but I think it's a girl.'

'That would be lovely,' said Annette as the nurse removed the oil from her stomach. 'Would you like a daughter, dear?'

Yesterday's events with Helen had not persuaded me that

68

having a daughter was all joy and laughter, but I murmured my enthusiasm for the idea and we went out to the car.

'That was very informative,' Annette said as I drove into the street. 'We learned a lot.'

But what I did not know was that the most important single fact about this baby was the one thing that the scan had failed to reveal.

The day after they came back from France, Judy Curtis served Laurie with a dog-food omelette.

Seething with hate in the kitchen after a routine fracas, she abandoned the ham omelette she had intended and opened a can of Pedigree Chum that should rightfully have ended up in the bowl of Baron, their black labrador.

The dish was delivered to her husband in a stony silence and he devoured it happily while reading a newspaper.

'That was delicious,' he declared when his plate was empty.

Judy Curtis watched him scoff the lot with mounting frustration. Her intention was to cause discomfort, if not nausea, and he had reacted as if a cordon bleu chef had produced a delicacy in his kitchen.

She wanted to shout at him and tell him what a pig he was, so undiscerning where food was concerned that he couldn't even tell good food from dog food. But there was a trace of shame at what she had done, and the realization that he might never trust her cooking again, and so she retreated to the kitchen to think of other less subtle ways of lowering the quality of his life.

She told this story to my wife in the supermarket where the strangest confidences are exchanged beside the shelves of baked beans. Annette couldn't stop laughing.

'Did you give Baron the ham?' she asked.

'Yes, I did, and he wouldn't eat it. Perhaps dogs really are getting the best food.'

When Annette told me this I felt a wave of the nausea that Laurie had so conspicuously avoided. I also felt a sense of betrayal that actually shocked me. Cooking food for somebody else is a matter of trust. We all hope that the chef doesn't spit in the soup, but how do we *know*?

'I think it's disgraceful,' I said.

'Don't worry,' said Annette. 'We don't have dog food.'

Playing pool with Laurie later I asked him how he felt. He seemed surprised at the question.

'I'm fit as a butcher's dog,' he pronounced.

The appropriately canine nature of the simile made my smile of approval seem somewhat overdone.

He tried to pot an easy red and missed by inches.

'I'd throw my cue to the floor but I'd probably miss,' he said. 'Why do you ask about my health?'

'I don't know whether it's the strain of your job or the stress of your marriage, but I'm always rather surprised to see you in one piece,' I told him.

'My marriage is the same as it has always been. Bit of an altercation last night, but that's par for the course, mate.'

'What happened?'

'She said she needed a hobby. I suggested she take up alligator wrestling and things went rapidly downhill after that. But in France everything was wonderful. We've bought a house at Beuzeville, by the way. I sent the money across today and I'm now a French property owner.'

'How much?' I asked enviously.

'Works out at about thirty-five grand. Things are cheaper there. Thanks for looking after Helen. Did she behave herself?'

'She behaved like an adult,' I told him.

6

Money talks

On a beautiful May evening I sat at the bar of the Comedy Hotel engaged in the harmless sport of eavesdropping and brooding over a visit to the bank which had left me profoundly uneasy. I ordered a pint of his strongest lager from John the barman and glanced round at his other customers.

They included tonight a couple of homosexuals who owned a local antique shop and who were discussing the dangers of the 'apple chop' which I gathered was the removal of the Adam's apple in a transsexual operation; a fat man called Robin, who was known as Round Robin, and who arrived by boat although his enthusiasm for alcohol was such that he often had to return by taxi; a couple I didn't know who were paying too much attention to each other to be married; a new receptionist from the hotel who had come in for a quick bacardi; and a rather glamorous blonde called Drusilla, freshly back from a Tunisian honeymoon, and now sipping fancy drinks with the bookmaker and football club director who had, after a reputedly virginal courtship, become her husband. Her smile had lost its romantic sheen and the look in her eyes was that of a woman who had seen more than enough of that sort of thing.

Several years earlier, emboldened by drink, I had tried in my charming way to crack her myself.

71

'Would you sleep with me tonight,' I asked, 'if I gave you a million pounds?'

She looked at me and thought about it very hard.

'Yes, I would,' she answered finally.

'Well,' I said, 'I wouldn't insult you by offering money.'

This seemed to get right under her cuticles and I thought she was about to throw drinks. Instead, she asked me to leave her company in language which surprised me.

'You'd sleep with a man for money, but not for pleasure?' I asked.

'What makes you think,' she replied scornfully, 'that sleeping with you would be a pleasure?'

We nodded at each other across the room now like a couple of old warriors who years ago had fought an honourable draw, and I resumed my eavesdropping. A good one floated in from my left.

'I was watching a video of *Towering Inferno* last night and I thought "This is bloody realistic. I can smell the smoke,"' said the new receptionist. 'Then I discovered that the kitchen was on fire.'

John came over to see how I was.

'How's the goats' cheese?' I asked.

He sold the goats' cheese he made to London restaurants, taking one day off a week to provide a personal delivery service. At one time, seeing an empire growing before him, he had kept and milked the goats himself, but this had proved too ambitious and now he bought the goats' milk and confined himself to making the cheese.

'There's a recession,' he said.

'I don't think the others have noticed,' I said. 'Why does everyone in here smile so much?'

'They're demented,' he said miserably.

He was called away by the newlyweds and I downed a good third of my pint.

I needed the drink. That afternoon, in a mood of some foreboding, I had been to my bank in the city to discuss a few harsh realities with Mr Fleming.

72

I left the Rover at Hammersmith and caught the Tube across London with the usual yawning, white-faced multitude who, now that they were denied cigarettes on the Underground, looked more suicidal than ever.

Mr Fleming, a dome-headed gentleman who looks as if he is suffering from irritable bowel syndrome, was hardly more cheerful. He was hearing my story, or something very similar, ten times a day.

In 1987 I had five shops with expanding profits. That year they made £240,000. It was boom time with Mr Lawson, a plump somewhat saturnine gentleman who said he was Chancellor of the Exchequer. People talked about expansion and a 'rush for growth'.

I went to see Mr Fleming who in those days wore a quite different expression. Over one of his black coffees and in less time than it takes to get fifty quid out of his cash dispensing machine, I got my hands on half a million pounds. Two hundred thousand was a business development loan over five years and the rest was on overdraft.

It was the money that I needed to buy the leasehold on five more shops and stock them with garments that cash-happy housewives would find irresistible. On the basis of the profits of the first five shops I confidently expected the second five to push up my income to half a million a year. It was early in 1988.

The roof began to fall in that year although not everybody immediately heard the sundering of oak beams and the cascading plaster.

I am paying £15,500 every quarter in interest on my overdraft, including bank charges. The BDL, as we failed tycoons call a business development loan, is costing me £13,800 a month.

This is no longer money that I can afford.

I explained this to Mr Fleming who had greeted me with all the enthusiasm of a tired prostitute who finds another forty men queuing outside her door when she thought it was time for cocoa and slippers.

I told him about takings and costs, wages and debts. I discussed predictions and projections, cash flow and interest rates, absent customers and income that was no longer disposable.

The gruesome scenario produced such a conflicting array of expressions on Mr Fleming's face that I half expected him to round off the performance by pulling his bottom lip over the top of his head.

'You're skint,' he said.

'Is that the technical term?' I asked.

'It's not good,' he said wanly.

We drank black coffee. He blew his nose.

'If you give up smoking you get colds all the time,' he told me, as if he would prefer to talk about anything except the matter in hand. 'Have you considered workforce imbalance correction?'

'I don't think sacking people would scratch the surface of the problem,' I said, 'quite apart from the fact that I'm operating on minimum staff already.'

'Well, the debts are there,' he said, 'or rather here.'

I wanted to coax time not money out of him on this visit but, of course, to a bank they are the same thing. It was my weakness but also my strength that the shops weren't worth very much at the moment; if the bank decided to foreclose on me they would get only pennies.

The thought had certainly occurred to Mr Fleming who now rested one hand on his head and said: 'We don't want to pull the plug on you, Mr Hadfield. What we need is some restructuring.'

I nodded and tried to look impressed. Bank managers address you with the dubious authority of a bald trichologist; if they're so financially knowledgeable, why aren't they rich?

'What did you have in mind?' I asked.

'As you see it, it's a question of weathering the recession? You see light at the end of the tunnel?'

'Absolutely,' I told him with such conviction as I could muster. 'Recessions end. Things improve. Governments have got to get themselves re-elected.'

'You're talking about hanging in there?'

'That sort of thing.'

He started to sketch some figures with his finger on his glass-topped desk. He looked up.

'You have a house,' he said.

'Yes,' I replied. 'We live in it.'

'Thames-side mansion, isn't it? What's it worth?'

I shrugged. 'Who knows these days? The last valuation was eight hundred thousand.'

I discerned the first flicker of relief on his mobile face.

'You'll have to pledge it,' he said. 'We need collateral that's separate from the business. In this climate the bank needs some security.'

'I'm quite prepared to do that,' I said, 'in return for a temporary reduction in payments.'

His fingers resumed their calculations on the top of his desk. 'I think we can come to some arrangement.'

Ten minutes later he stood up, shook my hand and showed me to the door. I wandered down the green carpets of the bank's corridor and, moved by the diuretic effect of the black coffee, slipped into an immaculate toilet for a pee. From one of the three spotless cubicles there came the noise of a barrage balloon being painfully deflated. This was followed almost immediately by the sound of a dustbin full of cold porridge being emptied into a swimming pool from a great height.

It seemed an apt comment on my colloquy with Mr Fleming and I hurried out to find a train.

Thinking about all this in the Comedy Hotel I discovered that I had finished my drink and was ordering another when Alec came in and so I bought him one too.

'How's your hyperactive missus?' I asked. 'Still worrying about vanishing pandas and topsoil erosion?'

'She's standing for the bloody council again,' he said. 'But I'm more worried about Steven.'

An unpleasant memory returned to disturb me.

'What's the matter with him?' I asked.

'He's acting odd. Withdrawn. Unfriendly. I can't work it out.'

'It's called puberty,' I said.

'He's seventeen, for God's sake. Allow me to know about these things, Max. I teach hundreds of the bastards.'

'He came round to see us when Helen was staying,' I told him. 'I hope that was okay?'

'He what?' said Alec, turning to face me.

'Came round to see Helen. Was that unusual?'

'What did you do?'

'I let him in. I could hardly turn your son away, could I?'

'Yes, you could,' he said. 'What happened?'

I tried to assemble an edited version of that horrendous evening. I had to tell him something because if news of Steven's visit ever came out Alec would rightly berate me for keeping it from him.

'They played records by the sound of it,' I said.

'And what else, I wonder?' he snarled. 'Jesus, Max!'

'Don't shoot the messenger,' I said evenly.

'It sounds as if you were the impresario.'

I disguised my anger at this suggestion with my usual skill. I could see that Alec was upset and had no doubt that he would soon be apologizing.

'You know what I think?' he said.

'What do you think, Alec?'

'I think he's found out that his parents have just got married. He's found out that he's been illegitimate for most of his life and it's unsettled him.'

'How could he have found that out?'

'God knows. Perhaps somebody saw us and told him. Perhaps he went through a drawer and found some document. You haven't told anybody?'

'Certainly not.'

'He might have overheard something at home when we thought he was out of earshot.' He picked up his drink for the first time but was too preoccupied to sip any. 'It's bloody embarrassing, actually. How do you explain it to a kid?'

'He's got ears,' I said. 'There's brain in there somewhere, I assume. Try words.'

'I do it for a living,' he said. 'You spend your life transmitting, but is their set switched on?'

He picked up his pint at last and drank copiously.

'I'm sorry I got cross,' he said. 'It looks as if I've got a problem child just like Laurie and Judy.'

Helen appeared in court looking the picture of aggrieved innocence, a blue bow in her hair and her school uniform freshly ironed. She sat at the front with her mortified parents and listened expressionlessly as a civilian from the Crown Prosecution Service told the three lady magistrates what had brought Helen Curtis to this unhappy appointment. It was a story that took some time.

The blouses that vanished from Laura Ashley, the pills and potions from Boots, the lavish volumes from Hammick's, the videos from Woolworth, not to mention the depredations at Max Hadfield's excellent chain of shops. The three magistrates listened to this protracted saga of purloined pens and stolen shirts with an awe that bordered on admiration. Not many youngsters were that *busy*. The Viking pirates who looted and pillaged their way round Europe in the tenth century would have recognized Helen Curtis as one of their own.

When the magistrates withdrew to study a report from the probation officer, Laurie looked across at his wife to see how she was taking this public humiliation and was surprised to see a solitary tear running down her cheek. Laurie's reaction was less tender, a quiet fury that his daughter had exposed him to this embarrassment.

They were told to stand when the magistrates filed back. Their chairman, a large woman of advanced years with one black hair sprouting from her chin, now addressed the unrepentant defendant.

'Helen, we have been told that you come from a very good home and although there may have been difficulties between you and your parents they are really no excuse for such behaviour. You went into a dozen shops clearly intending to steal. It is no good saying that you succumbed to temptation.

It was a premeditated decision to take things that did not belong to you. Although we accept that it might have been a cry for help, shoplifting is stealing and is viewed therefore as a very serious offence by this court.'

All this was delivered in a gentle tone of voice as if the magistrates couldn't quite reconcile the clever, hard-working schoolgirl in front of them with the string of offences that were attached to her name.

'We think you would benefit from a term of probation, Helen,' she said. 'But we can only put you on probation if you agree?'

Helen Curtis, gazing at the floor, raised her head to nod once.

'Two years' probation then,' said the magistrate, but she hadn't quite finished. 'Being put on probation for two years does not mean that you are getting away with it. You will be under the supervision of a probation officer for that period of time, during which you are to lead an honest life, keep regular hours and do as you're told. You are to visit the probation officer when told to do so, and allow him to visit you in your home. You are to notify him if, for any reason, you want to be away from your normal address. If you fail to do as you are told and do not meet the terms of this order you will be brought back to court and could be sentenced again for these offences. And you could find that the court sitting on that day would deprive you of your liberty. Go away now and try to be sensible. And try to respect the parents who have shown to this court that they both care very much what happens to you.'

When the Curtis family, each locked in their own thoughts, emerged from this ordeal and climbed into the Shogun parked outside, it occurred to the father that his daughter had not uttered a word since she left home.

I am indebted to Laurie for this account of that morning. I wasn't there myself, despite being what the police called a loser in the case, having been to London on another desperate mission to save my business.

78

'Not one word,' said Laurie. 'Is it dumb insolence? Does she hate us? Is she worried about something? What's it all about, Max? You're a success at this parent business.'

We were sitting in the Comedy Hotel drinking Czechoslovakian Budweiser, a big improvement on the American version. Neither of us had the energy to stand up and play pool. In fact Laurie looked as if the day's events had taken something out of him that he would never quite regain.

'You taught her silence,' I said. 'You don't talk to her enough, but most parents are like that. After a while they seem to be wondering who these young people are who keep coming home and occupying the furniture.'

He was low enough without my revealing the depth of his daughter's contempt for him, and I was still preoccupied anyway with an extraordinary episode that had taken place earlier that day.

I had taken the train to London as the Rover was being serviced. My destination was a supplier in Covent Garden with whom, in the current depressed climate, I wanted to discuss some extended credit. It wasn't the sort of conversation that you could conduct on the phone.

As I was walking along Neal Street I became aware of a beggar with a black beard who was sitting against a wall with his legs sprawled out on the pavement. Beggars were on the increase in London and, mysteriously, they all carried the same handwritten message on their piece of cardboard: HOMELESS AND HUNGRY. PLEASE HELP. This one was resting on a large leather holdall, and by his feet was a biscuit tin into which people dropped coins.

Feeling perhaps that if I was kind now my supplier might be generous with me later on I bent down and put a pound coin in the tin. The beggar was wearing a bright pair of red and yellow socks which protruded incongruously from his torn and dirty trousers.

I turned to look at him to see whether any thanks were coming my way, and he stared at me sadly with an

79

extraordinarily piercing pair of eyes. I was somewhat thrown by this and almost defensively I took another pound coin from my pocket and dropped that into the tin too.

He nodded now as if I had come up with the correct answer, and I continued along Neal Street wondering whether, if the recession got any worse, there would soon be more beggars than pedestrians on the streets of London.

My little deal with the Fates paid off because my supplier, a Sephardic Jew who was one of my favourite people, greeted me with grave courtesy, sympathized with the size of my problem, and extended my credit from three months to six. Of course, a couple of years earlier I had been one of his principal customers.

I left his office feeling suitably relieved and took a taxi across town to Harrods. We shop owners like to keep an eye on the opposition. The latest little gewgaw in the toy department was a kids' hovercraft, a full-scale working model that cost three and a half thousand pounds.

I caught the five o'clock train home in the hope that I would avoid the clammy rush of knackered commuters. I was lucky in this because there was only one other person in my first-class compartment, a distinguished-looking gentleman in a smart suit who was studying the financial pages of the *Evening Standard*. The first-class compartment was all very well, but when you had the full complement of six in there, snoring and farting their way home, it could get to be a mite too cosy.

We had been going about twenty minutes when the inevitable ticket inspector slid open the door. I took out my wallet to find my ticket and a loose credit card fell to the floor. I bent down to pick it up and found myself staring at a bright pair of red and yellow socks.

For a moment they rang only a distant bell and it wasn't until the ticket inspector had gone that I remembered where I had seen them before. I stared at my travelling companion, engrossed in his newspaper, and recognized the piercing eyes. The beard had gone but I now saw that the leather holdall was on the rack above his head.

The idea that beggars travelled first class and no doubt had a house in the country with Tang dynasty porcelain in the loft shouldn't have surprised me. It's an upside-down world, after all. But I still felt vaguely shocked. I was a victim of the recession myself.

I said: 'I want my two quid back.'

For a moment he didn't answer, as if he imagined that I was talking to somebody else. But there wasn't anyone else and he lowered his newspaper and looked at me.

'Terribly sorry?' he said, meaning 'pardon?'

His accent was straight from the upper reaches of the Conservative Party.

'I want my two quid back,' I repeated.

He stared at me with his piercing eyes and then produced a surprisingly gracious smile.

'Sorry, not following you, old boy,' he said.

'The two quid,' I said, 'that I gave you in Neal Street.'

This didn't leave him a lot of room for manoeuvre, although I was quite prepared to grab and open his leather bag, revealing, no doubt, some very old clothes, a biscuit tin and a theatrical beard.

He continued looking at me, but the gracious smile had gone. He seemed to be considering his options.

'You want two quid, d'you say?'

I nodded. 'That's it.'

He put his hand in his trouser pocket, pulled out two pound coins and gave them to me. He evidently regarded this as an end to the affair for he returned now to the financial columns of his evening newspaper.

This wasn't quite what I wanted. There were a hundred questions I would like to have asked. How much did he make? Where did he change? Did his family know? How did he occupy his mind all day? How long had he been doing it? What job did he once have?

But it was clear that I wouldn't be getting any answers today because the train was slowing down and my companion was standing up. He pulled the holdall off the rack and started to open the door as the train stopped at Wraysbury.

Just before he got out he turned back to me.

'Matter of interest, old boy. How did you recognize me?'

'The socks,' I told him.

'Thought so,' he said. 'Forgot to bring a change.'

I told Laurie this story and I thought he was going to have an apoplectic fit.

'What about the income tax?' he asked.

I must admit that this was not an aspect that had occurred to me.

'He's probably on social security,' I said. 'Too old to hire, too young to retire.'

'Well, isn't that bloody marvellous?' Laurie said indignantly. 'My daughter dragged through the courts while some toff makes a fat living cheating people.'

'People aren't honest any more,' I said. 'It's the system. Dishonesty is rewarded.'

It was true. Nobody was innocent. In today's murky atmosphere it was the unscrupulous who prospered. Bogus tax returns, offshore nest eggs, artificial bankruptcies, adroit name changes. Do unto others before they do unto you. A small shoplifting expedition was in tune with the times.

'You're honest,' said Laurie, obviously not feeling quite able to make the claim on behalf of himself.

'That's why I'm going broke, Laurie,' I said. 'My prospects are black.'

'People have always got to buy clothes,' he suggested.

'No, they haven't,' I said. 'They've already got them. When did you last see a nude lady in the street?'

'Not recently enough, Max, but I live in hope.'

I ordered another Budweiser. 'What are you doing on the money-making front at the moment?' I asked.

'The royal wedding,' he replied.

'My God, is there going to be another one? I suppose that now they've decided divorce is okay the weddings will be never-ending.'

'It's an anniversary, actually. Charles and Diana. Ten years. I'm doing mugs, posters and souvenir place mats. I'll have made fifty grand before it's all through.'

'Good lord,' I said, feeling thoroughly depressed at the way that everybody (including beggars) still had the talent that had deserted me, the talent to make money.

The following morning Kitty Benson rang.

'What are you doing today, Max?' she asked.

'The best I can,' I told her.

'You're not one of those nine-till-five wage slaves, you're a free spirit. I need a pair of hands.'

It has always been difficult for the self-employed to convince the rest of the world that they work quite hard because they are spotted relaxing at unconventional hours, and Kitty Benson's assumption that my day was empty and waiting for some kind soul to fill it was no more than the normal reaction to my situation.

'What is it, Mrs Benson?' I asked.

She wanted me to help her deliver her election address to five hundred homes in the area, she covering one side of the street and me the other. I had helped her once before on an earlier, abortive attempt to get herself elected to some council or another and she clearly regarded me now as the unpaid assistant whose services she could call upon.

I didn't mind. I was quite interested. This was as near the soil as grass roots democracy got.

We set off on foot in the back streets of a town nearby, each clasping a pile of her election leaflets. A glance at this revealed that Kitty was ignoring the political heavyweights in this contest and running as the Environment candidate. It was hard to see the connection between tropical rainforests, coral reefs, mangrove swamps, coastal wetlands and other threatened areas, and the soporific security of the Thames valley, but I didn't care to raise the matter. The election address was printed on green paper and bore a large picture of Kitty smiling very seriously behind her big glasses.

83

'Every time a plant species becomes extinct, thirty dependent animal and insect species could die out with it,' she told me briskly. 'Where's that leading us?'

'Fewer insects?' I tried.

'Sometimes I think you don't take these things seriously, Max,' she said.

'Does Alec?' I asked.

'I'm afraid my political ambitions have him chewing the carpet.'

'And what about your book?'

'I've got a joke in it. Every book should have a joke.'

'I meant is Alec interested?'

'The only thing that interests him at the moment is Steven, who's rapidly turning into the sort of lout that other parents have. Do you want to hear the joke?'

'Hit me with it.'

'What's the difference between a clitoris and a pub?'

'You've got me there, Kitty,' I said, slightly surprised.

'Most men can find the pub.'

She went across the road chortling, leaving me to my side of the street, and I started to slide her green message into some highly polished letter boxes.

On the doorstep of a house called Nuestro Casa I met an elegant lady who had emerged coincidentally as I arrived at her door, and so I relayed a little of Kitty's message, with special reference to ozone layers, chlorofluorocarbons and the Montreal Protocol.

She held up one flat hand. 'I'm afraid you've exceeded my attention span for that sort of thing,' she said.

I met Kitty at the corner.

'Do you think that there's a correlation between intelligence and baldness?' she asked. 'Why do the truly moronic always have a full thatch?'

I wondered what doorstep contretemps had produced this thought.

'It obviously isn't going to be necessary to use finger dye to stop multiple voting,' I said.

'That reminds me,' she said. 'I heard from Oliver this morning.'

Oliver was the black charmer who had been her guest at Christmas. 'How is he?' I asked. 'Also, where is he?'

'Freetown, wherever that is.'

'Sierra Leone.'

'As to how he is, it's difficult to tell. When the leader of a country wears a uniform, the people are in trouble. That's one thing that history teaches us.'

When blacks are good-looking they look better than any white, and Oliver was sensationally handsome. His features seemed to have been chiselled by an artist who had an idealistic picture of what the human face really looked like. And with the looks there was the charm, the inner warmth and the gallantry. He kissed the women that he met on both cheeks and made their men feel neglectful. He stood up, offered seats, fetched drinks, listened attentively to the tedious problems of others, and made Annette, Kitty and Judy smile in a way that their husbands hadn't managed recently. He had a sly sense of humour, too.

'Laurie talks about his offshore money,' he said once. 'I think he has a bank account in the Isle of Wight.'

He always wore a blue sleeveless sweater with a white shirt and red bow tie. 'You should have been an actor, Oliver,' I told him. 'There are producers in Hollywood screaming out for someone like you.'

But he was a professor in African history and serious about his work. What political activities he was involved in we never knew but he had a vision for his continent which was focused largely on the organization of food supplies and the wild hope that haunting pictures of pot-bellied children would vanish from the world's television screens.

'He's frightened of being arrested,' said Kitty as we trudged the streets of what she hoped would become her constituency. 'Being arrested is part of normal political life there. You don't lose elections, you get shot.'

'Well, they're strange people,' I said. 'The former Liberian president, Samuel Doe, used to feed starving people to his two pet lions.'

Kitty stopped in the street and looked at me as if I had hit her.

'And what did Saddam Hussein do to the Kurds, or Hitler to the Jews? The whites are pretty strange people, too.'

'I'm not talking about their colour, I'm talking about races,' I said. 'Some are odd, even if it does offend your liberal principles. Take the Chinese. They're a century behind everybody else. They ignore human rights. They steal, torture and kill. They don't drink beer and play pool. They're not proper people.'

'Jesus, Max,' said Kitty, 'if you're the silent majority thank God you stay silent.'

We split up then and took opposite sides of a long street of terraced houses. There were six steps up to each front door and six steps down again, and today's mission began to be more a question of physical stamina than political ambition. The people I met managed to conceal their enthusiasm for Kitty's message, but accepted her leaflet politely as if they could find a use for it. I imagined them jamming it under the short fourth leg of a wonky table, entertaining the children with a paper plane, making comic hats or, in these affluent acres, rolling it up and snorting coke. Nobody went so far as to promise a vote.

But Kitty was far from discouraged when we met up again at the end of the street. She seemed to be carried along by the impetus of her own enthusiasm.

'They're getting the message,' she said. 'They can see that there is no point in making plans today if there isn't going to be a tomorrow. It's a revolution.'

'Who is getting this message exactly?' I asked.

'The old lady with the walking frame was very sympathetic,' she said, pointing up the street.

'Let's hope she lives long enough to get to the polling booth.'

I returned home two hours later, invigorated by my incur-

86

sion into the world of real politics, and poured myself a whisky. Then I went out to see whether the revolution had begun but there was only an old man in a cardigan mowing his lawn.

I dialled seven digits and held my breath. It had been a long time since I last did this sort of thing.

The husky voice said: 'Sadie Beck.'

'This is your auction winner speaking,' I said. 'How is my prize?'

'Your prize is fine, Mr Hadfield. Where shall we meet?'

'You'd better call me Max,' I said. 'Where do you live?'

'Strawberry Hill.'

Sadie Beck of Strawberry Hill! It sounded too good to be true.

'Is there really a place called Strawberry Hill?' I asked.

'Well, there's a railway station. It's just after Hampton Wick and Teddington if you're coming from London.'

'I seem to have a car,' I told her.

'So much more comfortable,' the husky voice agreed. 'Just tell me where you want me. The conditions of this deal are that I put myself at your disposal.'

'It sounds good,' I said.

Chamoising the Rover later, I allowed myself to catalogue the many enjoyable ways in which she could put herself at my disposal, and to ponder optimistically on which of them she might agree to.

But on Saturday evening when I cruised into the forecourt of an expensive-looking block of flats, the Sadie Beck who appeared immediately, as if she had been waiting in the hall, had shed the flirtatious facade of auction night and adopted the intimidating demeanour of a successful and dynamic career woman. I stood, flunkey like, holding the car door open.

Nevertheless I detected a certain nervousness as we drove towards London and she found herself closeted with a man she didn't know who could conceivably possess some or all

87

of those unfriendly characteristics which got my sex regularly on to the lurid pages of the Sunday newspapers. I tried to allay her fears by inquiring politely about her job. It was difficult to concentrate. The navy-blue two-piece she was wearing was sober enough, but she had used some powder to darken her eyelids and the kohl-eyed effect was sufficiently sexy to produce a physical rearrangement in my underpants that would, in the street, have alarmed a myopic nun at two hundred metres.

Sadie Beck, I learned, was twenty-eight, and held a dauntingly responsible position in BBC television where she was called a production assistant. One day she might even be a producer. Her name, she told me with just a hint of reproach, did regularly float up-screen during the endless credits that acknowledged the assistance of absolutely everybody except possibly the tea lady at the end of today's programmes. I promised to watch out for it.

We parked off the Strand and walked sedately towards the theatre. There was a strong feeling of unbroken ice, of the proprieties being correctly observed and bottoms remaining untouched.

The message of the play, set in an unspecified breeze-block city, was that countries who once fought over oil, will one day fight over water. It was written by a rising star in the opaque world of 'alternative comedians'. Its title was *Water*.

In the crowded interval bar I kneed several old ladies in the perinea to get at a large gin. Sadie Beck drank sherry.

'It isn't Stoppard,' she said.

'Stoppard's got a sense of humour,' I agreed.

'We don't have to go back. It's not compulsory.'

'That's right,' I said. 'It's a prize, not penance.'

With only minimal feelings of guilt we fled into the street, and it was only when we reached the restaurant and had been shown to our reserved table that I was able to get a good look at her. Up until now she had spent the evening sitting beside me while I stared doggedly ahead at the traffic or the troupers.

Her fair hair was no longer in a Bardot ponytail but had a loose, abandoned look that made me think of rumpled beds. I gazed at her magic eyes and snub nose and they made me think of rumpled beds as well.

'You must have an army of fans,' I said.

'He fished.'

'She parried. Anyway, you're very beautiful, if it isn't sexist these days to say so.'

'All compliments are gratefully received round here,' she said. 'I was immensely flattered by your hard-on in the car.'

'That's about as sincere as flattery can get,' I said, refusing to be thrown by her candid approach.

'I suppose it is,' she said, laughing. 'There's no such thing as a dishonest erection.'

This plunge into the philosophical aspects of sexual tumescence struck me as a profitable step in our relationship. After all, we could have been engaged on an arid discussion of the London theatre, which was less likely to promote closeness.

'There was a man,' she said, 'but now there isn't.' Lips pressed together told of an opportunity lost.

'Who was he?' I asked.

'A news reader. One of those self-adoring prats who think that the ability to read simple English sentences puts them on a higher plane than everyone else. He bored me boss-eyed in the end. Well, in the beginning, actually.'

A waiter arrived with menus and the offer of drinks while I considered this. I had met few women who were so neatly dismissive.

It wasn't one of those restaurants where the waiters made you feel that you should be sitting at attention. It was an efficient, noisy place. I stared uneasily at a menu which offered me a starter of rabbit terrine, Baltic herring or lobster and mango salad.

'Drink?' I said.

'Let's get on to the wine.'

The wine relaxed us both and the conversation swiftly

took on a warmer, more intimate quality; but surprisingly she didn't ask whether I was married.

'You own shops,' she said in a tone of voice which suggested that, when I had the odd moment, I also buggered goats.

'Dismal, isn't it?' I agreed.

'How many are there?'

'Ten.'

'Ah, that's different. You're a tycoon – a magnate, even.'

'I've stretched my resources until they twang,' I told her. 'I could soon be an ex-tycoon.'

'But good-looking with it.'

She sipped her wine and looked at me over the glass. This was the first compliment she had paid me.

'I did a maximum-money minimum-effort graph,' I told her, 'greed and laziness being my two most deeply ingrained traits. The answer was shops – the more the better, with other people running them.'

'I should say your most deeply ingrained trait was honesty then,' she said. 'You're also more enterprising than most people.'

The multiplying compliments did wonders for my self-esteem. Recently I had begun to wonder whether my best years were already behind me.

The waiter brought her dinner. At the heart of it was chicken but it had been packaged in such an exotic way that the dish was unrecognizable to me. I sliced my lamb and told her: 'As I am both honest and enterprising I have to tell you that it is absolutely essential that I make love to you tonight.'

She stopped eating and smiled. 'Essential to what?'

'Sanity, vanity, happiness, health.'

'Where? When?'

'Here? Now?'

'In an African hut they do it in front of the others but I don't like an audience.'

'So you work for BBC television,' I joked.

'Our viewing figures are going up, actually.'

'Don't say going up. It has associations.'

It only dawned on me that she was as enthusiastic as I was about my suggestion when she refused pudding.

'We ought to be getting along,' she said. 'I'll just have a coffee.'

We left the restaurant holding hands and I was relieved to discover in today's disorderly capital that the Rover still had four wheels. As we crossed the river at Putney, she said: 'I think it's only fair that you get your money's worth.'

I had forgotten about the eight hundred pounds and I was sorry that she had mentioned it. We had moved on since then and the money seemed to move us back. But I reached her flat in a ferment of expectation. It was a spotless, well-furnished place on the third floor, two bedrooms and a large living room with two television sets, a necessary accessory, I imagined, of the job.

Sadie Beck removed the top half of her two-piece outfit to reveal a white silk blouse that she immediately began to unbutton.

'Let's go to bed,' she said. 'Have you got a willy-wellie?'

'The language of young people is a constant mystery to me,' I said, kicking off my shoes. 'However, I have had a vasectomy.'

'That's the best news I've heard all week,' she said, taking my hand and leading me into a large bedroom that smelt of flowers. By the time I had removed my shirt she was standing before me naked and it was only then that we kissed for the first time.

Satyriasis – meet nymphomania.

PART TWO

· A maze ·

Life is a maze in which we take the
wrong turning before we have learned
to walk.

Cyril Connolly
The Unquiet Grave

7

A boy gone wrong

June is the cruellest month (*pace* Mr Eliot) because it brings
with it such sunny hopes and then grimly rains on you.
Cloudless skies are supposed to link the Derby at the beginning of the month with Wimbledon at the end but the reality
is usually more moist.

Two phone calls on the first day, a Saturday, told me not
to expect too much from this particular thirty days. One was
from the husband of Mrs Tibbott, one of my shop managers,
telling me that she had succumbed to an obscure brand of
summer flu and would be unable to open the shop for a few
days. The other was from my skinny yet busty star Charlotte
saying that somebody had smashed the shop window
overnight. I got into the Rover, bunged the *Celts* by Enya
into the stereo, and headed for work.

Having got out of the multi-storey car park without being
mugged, I threaded my way through the usual Saturday
morning collection of eczematous youths, belching pensioners
and malevolent traffic wardens, past Papa Luigi's pizzeria
and the Indian's card shop.

I decided that a 'get well soon' card for Mrs Tibbott
would be worth a couple of Brownie points and went in. The
sad, dark-skinned Indian watched me approach.

'Munning,' he said.

He always said 'Munning' to me and at first I wondered

95

whether he thought I was a late British painter of horses who had made a sensational and posthumous switch to commerce, but once I realized that 'Munning' was foreign for good morning I entered into the spirit of things.

'Munning,' I said.

'They broke your window,' he told me.

I nodded. 'This is an uncivilized country.'

There wasn't much left of the window, only a few jagged pieces round the edge. Charlotte was still gingerly picking the fragments from her window display and dropping them into a cardboard box.

'They've done Burnham as well,' she said. 'June rang up.'

The news that two of my shop windows had been destroyed set an alarm bell jangling in my mind. One was the luck of the draw, the price we pay for the way we rear our kids. Two sounded like a campaign.

I went into the tiny office at the back of Charlotte's shop and made a series of phone calls, to June at Burnham, to the insurance company and to a local glazier.

Charlotte appeared with a box of tinkling glass.

'The police looked in. Said there's nothing they can do.'

'Thanks,' I said. 'The glazier will mend it this afternoon. Was anything stolen?'

'Nothing was touched.'

'Mindless hooliganism,' I said. 'I could almost respect them more if they had taken something.'

'Nothing was taken at Burnham either,' said Charlotte.

'And no other shops had their windows broken?'

'Not that I've heard.'

She took the glass out to the back and I wrote in Mrs Tibbott's card. (It worried me. Get well soon? Why 'soon'? Why not 'now'? Why do people who supposedly wish you well want to see your illness prolonged?) I addressed the envelope, found a stamp and then went out to look at my broken window. A pair of huge breasts went past, followed eventually by a woman, but I had other things to think about.

That morning I had an appointment at a factory in Whitechapel with a man called Keith. Keith was a typical East Ender, tall and grey haired although still in his thirties, whose proudest boast was that he didn't see a tree until he was sixteen.

Keith owned the factory, which wasn't much more than a small Nissen hut, and filled it with strange women of various ethnic origins who sat at machines all day producing clothes. Keith knew how to make others work for him. I always imagined that somewhere else he had another Nissen hut in which fifty monkeys attached to fifty typewriters churned out television scripts.

A lady I knew, who had once designed elegant clothes before marriage to a building tycoon and the demands of five children had swept her into luxurious obscurity near Ascot racecourse, did the occasional design for me, as much for her own self-respect as for the niggardly cheque that I sent her, and these designs I rushed to Keith and his morose team of performing machinists. Today's gem was a short shift dress, a sexy little number in cotton that I had failed to obtain elsewhere.

Keith produced roll after roll of fabric.

'What colour are we talking about here, Maxie?' he said. 'Amber, apricot, coral, flamingo, peach, salmon, tea rose? What about blue? Azure, cyan, gentian, indigo, lapis lazuli, sapphire, ultramarine? Polka dots are in this year.'

'Nobody has improved on white as a colour,' I said. 'I want six dozen in cotton, half of them bigger than size fourteen. Big girls can't get into modern things. The fashion business thinks all women are wraiths.'

He wrote down my instructions obediently.

'How's business?' he asked.

'I can't tell you how bad, Keith,' I said. 'You should be asking for cash up front.'

'You made a mistake, Maxie boy,' he said. 'Ten shops is no good. You either want one good one or fifty. If you had fifty you could get everything specially made for you instead of the odd shift dress, and you'd cut your costs.'

'Thanks,' I said. 'Cheer me up some more.'

'With ten shops you should have specialized in one thing – socks, jeans. The Pantie Shop. The Hankie Shop. That's the way it goes these days. Your little empire's all over the place, the worst of all worlds.'

'It's a real pleasure to come here and chat with you, Keith,' I said. 'You really buck a chap up.'

'Why don't you specialize in stuff for the health clubs in the light of all this get-fit mania that seems to have gripped the birds? Stretch Lycra leggings, leotards, sweatshirts, headbands, wristbands? That's where it's at, Maxie.'

'A bit late now,' I told him, feeling even more downcast than when I arrived. 'I'm several miles down a quite different road that is beginning to look like a cul-de-sac.'

He stopped talking now and looked at me seriously.

'You were joking when you mentioned money, weren't you? You're not about to go belly up?'

'I'm at the mercy of the economy like everyone else,' I said. 'I have to take it a week at a time. However, I have noticed a dearth of customers.'

'Perhaps I'd better send my bill with the goods.'

'You'll be paid quickly,' I promised. 'And you'd be paid even quicker if you stopped calling me Maxie.'

I fled from the dinginess of the East End, with its ugly streets and its ugly names, and wondered how long it would be before the world brought me something to smile about.

The following morning I had a phone call from the police. Two more of my windows had been broken. The news, which was bad enough, was particularly unwelcome on a Sunday when I was reluctant to discard my slippers before the Comedy Hotel opened its doors for business, and was quite happy to be left alone with the Sunday papers. The headlines that appeared on Sunday were unlike those that were published in papers during the rest of the week; the Sunday newspaper journalists seemed to have their eyes on a different, infinitely more bizarre, world and their headlines jumped out and knocked you back. *Siamese twin kills brother in bungled suicide attempt* – they'd never tell you that on a Monday when they were more concerned with earthquakes in India, bush fires in America, train disasters in France and explosions in the Lebanon.

After protracted negotiations with the telephone switchboard I found the glazier's home number.

'I want cash,' he said. 'If you're becoming a regular customer I don't want to wait for the insurance money.'

'I'll pay you this morning,' I told him. 'I'll meet you at the shop.'

He was already well on his way to replacing the first window when I got there.

'What's going on?' he asked. 'Have you sacked somebody?'

He was one of those bright young men in their late twenties who will work all hours if there's tax-free money in it.

'Nobody,' I told him.

'Well, somebody doesn't like you.'

'Yes, I got that feeling myself.'

'It's usually money,' he said, without looking up from his work. 'Money or sex, but money usually.'

'Well, I might owe the government a few bob but they wouldn't send someone round to smash my windows, would they?'

'With this government nothing'd surprise me.'

I went into the shop and started to clear up the glass. The idea that I had an unknown enemy out there began to disturb me. Four windows in two days wasn't the mindless hooliganism that I had mentioned to Charlotte. There was something sinister about it.

An hour or so later in the Comedy Hotel Alec bought me a pint and tried to cheer me up.

'I blame you,' I said, not entirely playfully. 'These are the kids you prepared for the world.'

It was apparent that Alec was not the most suitable person this morning to cheer anyone up.

'Perhaps I should have chosen another career, but it's too

99

late now,' he said. 'Frankly, I'm becoming disillusioned with the whole business. The Helen affair depressed me more than I realized. If a girl like that takes up shoplifting, what hope is there? I'm sick of classrooms, parents' visits, examinations and school dinners.'

'That's another thing,' I said. 'Why do you teach them to call their midday meal dinners? Why don't you call them school lunches and save them social embarrassment later?'

'You *are* in a bad mood, Max,' he said, and I was. I drank my beer and looked out at the Thames which flowed soberly past the bar. A motor launch hauled up to the jetty and Laurie climbed out. He was wearing, unusually, jeans and a white T-shirt.

'A friend took me for a little ride,' he said when he came in. 'You've got to do something on a Sunday morning once you've read your *Sunday Sport* and discovered which TV star has been knobbing some alien.'

'It's nice to see somebody cheerful come in,' said Alec. 'What will you drink?'

'A civilized pint,' said Laurie. 'What else would an Englishman drink on a Sunday morning?'

'Hemlock?' I suggested.

'Max isn't in the best of humour this morning,' Alec said. 'Somebody is breaking his shop windows.'

'The world is full of vandals,' said Laurie, 'but I've got a money idea for you, Max, so you can start smiling.'

'Tell me,' I said.

'Fly buttons.'

'What?'

'Have you ever considered how awkward it is for a left-handed man to do up his fly buttons? They suffer in silence. The market for trousers with fly buttons arranged for the left-handed man must be vast, mate.'

'Any more ideas you want to delight us with, Laurie?' I asked. 'I've still got half a pint left.'

'You don't like it?' he asked, surprised.

'We don't have fly buttons any more, Laurie. They went out with cigarette cases and hair cream.'

100

'What, none? I bet the upper classes still use buttons. In fact, I bet they still use cigarette cases and hair cream. It takes years for a new idea to penetrate those reactionary minds.'

'Let them suffer in silence,' I said. 'I'm not here to help them.'

'You're right,' said Laurie. 'He is in a bad mood.'

'You don't understand,' I said. 'Nobody else's windows are being broken.'

But few things are more boring then other people's problems, and Laurie had more interesting things to discuss.

'Judy and I have had an idea,' he said. 'Why don't you all come and stay in our home in France for a summer holiday?'

There was something about Sunday mornings that transformed people: they wore a different personality along with the change of clothes. Laurie, who on another day might have been mournfully immersed in black thoughts about his turbulent marriage, his disgraced daughter and his endlessly imaginative business gambles, was this morning a determined fun-seeker. The prospect of an away-from-it-all break began to brighten my mood and I decided to grab a little of this Sunday gaiety myself.

'Gorge ourselves in some gastronomic temple?' I said. 'Why not?'

Even Alec, who was a comparative stranger to the foreign holiday, looked enthusiastic.

'It'll have to wait until the end of term,' he said.

'We thought the end of July,' Laurie said. 'Fix the kids up with a holiday somewhere else.'

But the following morning reality returned. Two more windows had been shattered on Sunday night. Once again nothing had been stolen. There was only a carefully arranged window display littered with shards of glass, and a cool breeze blowing through the shop.

I looked at the wreckage and felt an intense anger. Was I supposed to sit back and allow this systematic damage to continue?

I decided to ring the police and persuade them to show

more interest in my misfortune. This was trivial everyday stuff to them, but I was beginning to feel victimized.

After two hours and four phone calls I managed to get an appointment with an officer in the Thames Valley police force, and early that afternoon I was shown into his office. It was surprisingly bare in this technological age. There was an area map on the wall behind him and a lonely telephone on his green desk.

'I can understand your concern, Mr Hadfield,' he said after standing up to shake hands.

'But?' It sounded as if he was going to say 'but there's little we can do'.

'But there's little we can do,' he said. 'We get this kind of thing all the time, but your vandal doesn't leave fingerprints. He does the damage and vanishes into the night. You're insured, I take it?'

He was a big, elderly man with boyish black hair and a wandering left eye. He did not inspire confidence.

'This is a vandal you could catch,' I said and he smiled tolerantly at the absurdity.

'Would that we could,' he said. 'Vandalism is the modern plague.'

I leaned across his desk. 'I think I discern a pattern,' I said, spelling it out. 'I have ten shops. On the first night they break the windows in two of them. On the second night they break the next two. On the third night they do two more. I have four more shops whose windows haven't been broken yet.' I looked at him to see whether he was following this. The right eye seemed to be concentrating.

'I see what you're driving at. The trouble is it would tie up four policemen and our staffing levels are nowhere near adequate at the moment. The government boasts about law and order but won't put its money where its mouth is.'

'Perhaps we should wait until two more windows have been destroyed, then you'll only need two policemen.'

He looked at me with both eyes this time and drummed his fingers on his desk.

'There are people out there committing real crimes,' he said. 'Rape, burglary, car thefts. Arson seems to be in fashion this summer for some reason.'

'Catching anybody?' I asked.

'Not yet.'

I gave him a look which seemed to have some effect.

'Write down the names and addresses of the other four shops,' he said. 'We'll see what we can do.'

'I'm very grateful,' I told him.

Depression saps your energy and that evening I couldn't find enough of it to go looking for an outbreak of merriment in the Comedy Hotel. Six months of pregnancy had produced in my wife an urge to splurge, fits of extravagance that were quite at odds with our present financial situation.

She had been out herself and I came home to find a Gucci handbag in golden suede with matching loafers, and a pair of Armani sunglasses. The total bill could not have been less than a thousand pounds. Packaging this green-eyed treasure cost more than I could ever have imagined.

'Loafers are just what you need when you're pregnant,' she said, when I hinted that this was a spending spree we could have done without. 'And the sun has been troubling my eyes.'

'But *Gucci* loafers? *Armani* sunglasses?'

'You always told me we were well off.'

'I don't think that's something you have heard me say lately,' I told her.

'There's a card from the golden boy on the mantelpiece,' she said, eager to change the subject.

I went off and picked it up. The picture was of Seville. 'You'll be glad to hear I'm still earning money,' said the message on the back. 'Hope you are both well. See you soon. Love, Garth.'

'What does he mean "see you soon"?' I asked.

'Search me,' said Annette, and went out to the garden.

I sat in an armchair and picked up a newspaper. If I was

103

going to stay in I might as well check the evening's television. I'd heard that the new game for stay-at-home couples was to prop the camcorder beside the bed and videotape your lovemaking, but there wasn't any of that to film at the moment in the Hadfield home and Annette, a zealot for straightforward sex when she wasn't pregnant, had never been one for the frills that more jaded appetites required. It looked as if I would have to settle for a journey down the old Sahara Salt Road where, apparently, camel caravans still drew pillars of salt out of the fiery depths of the Tenere Desert.

But Annette had other ideas.

'I've lit the barbecue,' she returned to announce.

We had built a barbecue and bar in the corner of the patio where on a summer's evening my wife could sometimes be found sipping champagne while I opened a can of lager. The view from here was of our pond and our long lawn which dropped down to a vegetable garden at the bottom that was tended by our ancient but effective twice-a-week gardener, and beyond that was the river.

The metropolitan estuary that crept through London's grime and crime, past its sky-rise slums and its Victorian riverside warehouses, had escaped into the placid beauty of the countryside here and seemed a much more attractive stretch of water. Its neighbours were trees, not bricks and mortar, and the craft that floated on its shimmering surface were devoted to idle pleasure and not the relentless demands of work; brightly coloured pleasure boats replaced the grimly laden barges and swimmers ventured into the river's clear shallows without the prospect of a stomach pump later.

This evening as I went out two pleasure boats drifted past, and drifting up from the boats I heard cries of 'Lucky bastards' and 'I'd like to live there'.

In this privileged enclave money ruled. But who ruled if you didn't have any money?

I went to the bar and distributed cutlery, then I went in and opened some wine. Annette was preparing a salad to accompany the steaks. Even six months pregnant she moved like a lewd dream. Her body seemed to invite male attention and the broad beam couldn't sabotage the effect of her seductive eyes. There was always to me something whorish about her, although my private picture lacked priapic men bearing banknotes. Her stocky little hands would never have taken money, being far too busy administering secret pleasures.

It was, for once, one of those lovely June evenings that you remember when you are scraping ice off your car's windscreen only a few months later. The sun looked as if it was going to hang in the sky for ever. I watched my wife, with her mysterious cargo in her womb, turning steaks and singing a song about the sea. I would have paid a lot to have known what was going on inside her head.

Sitting at our little bar beneath the pergola of vines, roses and clematis, I thought that this would be the life if I could afford it. I poured some wine and a sizzling fillet steak was placed in front of me.

'I suppose that in view of this new-found poverty we can't afford a holiday this year,' Annette said, pushing a bottle of French dressing in my direction.

The bottle's origin reminded me. 'I forgot to tell you that Mr and Mrs Curtis have invited us and Alec and Kitty to their holiday home in France next month,' I told her.

Annette grimaced. Her earlier incarnation as a travel courier had curbed her desire to go abroad, although she had occasionally been prevailed upon to languish for a couple of weeks in five-star comfort on the Côte d'Azur. My own tastes were for somewhere warmer and further south.

'You're making a face,' I said. 'Don't tell me you'd prefer Margate.'

'How can *he* afford a place in France, anyway?' she asked. 'Some people would borrow to the hilt rather than pull their belts in.'

My relief that she was beginning to think seriously about the cost of things was tempered by a suspicion that she would refuse to join our friends in France.

'We all borrow,' I said. 'It keeps the wheels of commerce turning. But I do get the idea that Laurie has managed to stash away a few quid over the years, mostly in Guernsey or Jersey.'

'People are pretty disgusting,' said my pouting wife. 'I'd sooner have been an elephant.'

I pondered this as I drank my Vina Real. I have never pretended to understand women's minds, anyway, but I supposed that what I was dealing with here was naked envy.

'Ride the wave, kid,' I said. 'Take his hospitality.'

'I'm not flying when I'm nearly eight months pregnant,' she said. 'Funny things can happen.'

'We'll go by boat,' I promised.

The telephone rang before I could pour my Alpen on the plate. Its shrill yell filled me with dread: the news brought by early morning calls was always bad, usually involving burglary, broken windows, staff sickness or some other disaster which would give the day a nasty flavour even before it had begun.

'It's Fielding, Mr Hadfield,' said the voice of an elderly man. I knew nobody called Fielding and the slight hangover produced by too much wine at last night's barbecue meant that my fuzzy head would never place the voice which sounded familiar.

'Hallo,' I said noncommittally. 'What can I do for you?'

'No, no,' said Fielding. 'It's what we've done for you. We caught him red-handed. I had an idea after you left. As he'd broken six of your windows why didn't we stake out the other four shops? His movements, after all, were getting a bit predictable.'

'That was a clever idea,' I said. 'And he turned up?'

'On a bicycle. He's only a kid. He took an axe out of a bag he was carrying on his handlebars and our man jumped him.'

'Before he broke the window, I hope?'

'Oh, yes. But he's admitted that he did the others. We've got him in custody now.'

'Well, congratulations,' I said. 'It's a big relief. He didn't happen to mention why he was doing it, I suppose?'

'He's said very little. An extremely unpleasant youth from what I've seen of him. We're waiting now for his father to arrive. The boy wouldn't give us his name for six hours so the parents must have been frantic.'

My chief emotion was a desire for revenge. The youth would no doubt be taken to court, gently chastised by a deranged beak who was notoriously familiar with the agonies of adolescence, and invited to take two sweets out of the tin. I wanted to loosen his teeth.

'I wouldn't waste too much sympathy on the parents,' I said. 'It's a pity you can't charge them, too.'

'Our experience is that kids these days lead their parents a dance,' Fielding said. 'Discipline died twenty years ago. It's the flower power kids of the sixties who now have their own teenagers.'

I wasn't really up to a debate on parental discipline, or the lack of it, before breakfast, and tried to break the call. But Fielding, already at work, was evidently finding like many people in an office that a conversation on the telephone shielded him from harsher duties.

'It's funny that you should touch on the subject of parents and their responsibility,' he went on, 'because this kid with the axe is the son of a headmaster. You'd think he'd be better behaved than most.'

'Really?' I said, feeling a slight shiver. 'What's his name?'

'Benson, I think it is. Yes, Steven Benson.'

'I know him,' I said with a heavy heart. 'I know his father.'

'Ah, well now perhaps we'll come to a motive.'

'He's got nothing against me that I'm aware of,' I said defensively. 'I find the whole thing mystifying.'

But when I took a cup of tea up to my sleeping wife I could only wonder at the extraordinary coincidence of both Laurie's and Alec's children attacking my business.

'Who was that on the phone?' Annette asked from the depths of her pillow.

'The police,' I said. The reply brought her to full wakefulness. 'My shop windows were broken by Steven Benson.'

'No,' she said, staring wide-eyed from her pillow.

'Yes,' I told her. 'Do you think my friends' kids have got a grievance against me?'

'They've got a grievance against their parents,' Annette said. 'They're getting at them through you.'

'How come I got chosen as conduit?'

'You were there.'

I sat on the bed.

'In the end it's embarrassing,' I said. 'What am I supposed to say to Alec?'

'I should have thought the onus was on Alec to say something to you. Thank God we brought our son up properly.'

'Of course,' I said, 'we didn't send him to Alec's school.'

I left this atmosphere of mutual congratulation and went down to look at the post. As it happened, there was another card from Garth, this one posted in Barcelona.

'He seems to be travelling around a bit,' I said when I took the card upstairs. 'What's he up to?'

'That's what young people do,' Annette said sleepily. 'They travel around a bit.' I realized that I had woken her up for a second time and decided to go to work.

The manageress at the first shop I visited was one of those tense, beautiful women in their late thirties who wants a man but is frightened by them. Today she seemed to be frightened by something else.

'Did you see that Marks and Spencer made hundreds of people redundant?' she asked me. 'If they're finding it hard, what hope is there?'

'I saw that, Hannah,' I said. 'What sort of week did you have here?'

'The worst ever, I'm afraid. Where has all the money gone?'

I spent most of the rest of the day looking for it. I don't know where it had gone, but it wasn't finding its way to my empty tills. Six shops had failed to cover their on-site costs – wages, rent, electricity, business rates, phone calls – never mind the interest on the loans that had enabled me to open them in the first place.

I arrived home in my now customary depression and was trying to revive myself with a whisky when Alec arrived. Annette had opened the door to him and he came into the room looking as if a pack of rottweilers were in close pursuit.

'What can I say?' he said and sat down. It turned out that he couldn't say anything. He seemed to be suffering from expressive dysphasia. He took off his spectacles and sat there shaking his head.

'Would a whisky help?' I asked.

He indicated with the slightest nod that this was an idea that was worth a try and I poured him a glass of J. and B. He emptied half of it very quickly and said: 'This is a blow to my *amour-propre*, Max. I'm a headmaster and I can't even handle my own son.'

This struck me as such an accurate summary of the situation that I could think of nothing to say that would console him. He took another swig of the whisky and the power of speech gradually returned.

'I've come round to apologize, Max, of course, and that I do. I shall get Steven to come round and apologize to you personally as well, but it still leaves me wondering why the hell it happened.'

'What got into him?' I asked.

'God knows. We're not talking about a brain surgeon here, but I never believed he was that stupid. In fact I've always been quite hopeful about him. As Anthony Burgess said, no teacher can be a pessimist.'

'Have they had him in court?'

Alec nodded. 'Remanded for reports. It's the Helen thing all over again. And a couple of months ago we were all congratulating ourselves on the way we had brought up our wonderful children.'

'I remember,' I said. 'Another drink?'

He was brandishing an empty glass.

'Kitty's shattered,' he announced. 'I suppose it won't pull in any votes.'

This struck me as slightly unkind, but he seemed too distressed for me to mention it. I poured him another whisky and sat down.

'She's bound to be upset,' I said. 'He hasn't done his career prospects any good.'

'If he's got any career prospects. He's gone so strange lately that I don't know what'll become of him.'

'Did you find out whether he knows about the wedding?' I asked. 'You thought it would unsettle him.'

'How can I find out? I can hardly ask him.'

'My wife, who is an astute student of human nature, thinks that both Helen and Steven were getting at their parents through me. I must say that if she's right I don't much appreciate the role I've been assigned.'

Alec looked astonished. 'Why would he do that? Why would he want to hurt me? I've spoilt him rotten.'

'Perhaps that's the trouble,' I said.

Alec stared at our carpet as if his house didn't have one. 'I'm too kind,' he said. 'Too kind to be a father and too kind to be a teacher. That's what Mavis Jones used to say. That I was too kind.'

I wanted to tell him that bringing up children wasn't simply a question of kindness or cruelty, or discipline or laxity, but depended on more subtle reactions that were far from black or white. But children were his field and I wouldn't expect him to tell me how to run my shops.

So I said: 'How about a game of pool? Take your mind off things.'

'You're very kind, Max,' he said and stood up.

I didn't tell him that his hit-and-hope brand of pool was just what I needed to get my mind off my own problems.

8

Money to burn

I held a crisp new fifty-pound note high up in my left hand
and introduced a lighted match to it. It was one of the most
painful things I have ever done.

At first the high-quality paper refused to burn and the
flame licked ineffectually at its bottom corner. But then the
note began to change colour and the new dark colour had a
flame dancing on it.

I felt sick. It wasn't only the thought of what that note
could have bought me; I was thinking as well of old folk
barely surviving on beggarly pensions and enjoying a decent
piece of meat once a month if at all.

'What the hell are you doing?' asked Annette.

'I'm doing what you do,' I told her. 'I'm burning money.'

She looked at me icily. 'You're not going mad, are you?'

'But this is what you do, Annette! You burn money. You
don't respect it. You spend it like a drunken sailor. Look!
Watch! This is you in action. Oh dear, another fifty quid
gone.'

My dramatic lesson did not have the effect that I intended.

'If you can afford to burn fifty-pound notes I am obviously
spending less than I should be,' she said. 'This is the
behaviour of a rich man.'

I dropped the charred remains of my money in the grate
before they burned my fingers.

'It's the behaviour of a desperate man,' I corrected. 'We're staring ruin in the face and you carry on spending as if we printed our own money. You buy clothes you don't need, food we don't eat and baubles we don't want. You go to the supermarket without a list then impulse-buy your way round the store so that you spend a hundred pounds instead of fifty, and still manage to come home without the coffee that we've run out of . . .'

It was a speech she had heard before so now that I needed her to listen she ignored it.

This little crisis had been precipitated by her purchase that day of a skirt in some fancy boutique whose prices made my own shops look like a street market. But upstairs her clothes occupied ninety per cent of our huge wardrobe.

'Did you really need it?' I asked.

'Not now. I'm pregnant. But I'll need it when the baby arrives.'

I sat down. 'Annette, you've got more clothes than any of my shops.'

She looked at me as if there was small hope of my ever understanding the requirements of women. 'I went out today looking like this. Five years ago I wouldn't have gone into the back garden looking like this.'

She was wearing a rather sexy yellow track suit. (The thing about her body had always been its *accessibility*. It was seldom constrained by jackets and belts that frustrated the friendly wanderings of a man's hand.)

'I like track suits,' I said. 'They're sexy.'

'Not with a six-month pregnant woman inside they're not. What is this? Are we going broke?'

'Yes,' I said.

'It's going to be wine in a can and Tesco champagne, is it?'

'I doubt whether champagne will figure in the shopping list at all.'

She turned back to the television and I realized that she was trying to watch a programme. But evidently what I said had troubled her because after a suitable pause she asked:

112

'What has gone wrong exactly, Max? What's gnawing at you?'

I sat on the sofa beside her and I could still smell the burnt fifty-pound note. I looked at what was left in the grate and wondered if the bank would replace it if the number was still readable.

'There's a shortage of customers,' I said. 'Women don't have much money to spend this year apart from somebody I could touch with a very short stick and she's not one of my customers.'

'I do read the newspapers,' she said. Her tone of voice suggested that this was not a conversation that she was enjoying. 'I'm aware that we have a recession. I know that interest rates are putting firms out of business because they borrowed to start up. So you're having a thin time. But it's no more serious than that, is it?'

'I borrowed,' I said. 'Or have you forgotten my expansionist phase?'

'And you're not taking enough in the shops to pay the interest on the loans?'

'I'll make an economist out of you yet,' I said. 'We're heading for a one-room flat in Brixton.'

'I've always rather liked Devon.'

'That's Brixham,' I said, but she indicated that she knew with an expression that commented sadly on my obtuseness.

Weary of arguing, I closed my eyes. A normal man lives on his income. A man in trouble lives on his capital. A man in serious trouble lives on an overdraft. There were happier scenarios at the other end of the spectrum, the end to which I vainly aspired. A rich man lives on his interest. A very rich man lives on the interest on his interest. It had once taken generations for a family to reach that sort of affluence but today, paradoxically, young men from nowhere were transforming themselves into multi-millionaires before they were out of their thirties, and then buying islands and football clubs, or starting airlines or film companies. It had obviously not occurred to them during their soaring ascent to riches to open ten dress shops.

Strident music told me that the television programme Annette had been watching was over. I opened my eyes to see four words moving slowly up the screen: Production Assistant – Sadie Beck.

The telephone rang at work the following morning.

'Sadie Beck,' said a familiar voice.

'How extraordinary,' I said. 'I had a dream about you last night after seeing your name on my electric television machine.'

'Pleasant, I trust?'

I told her modestly: 'It must have been. I woke up with an erection like a baseball bat.'

'Oh dear, it sounds as if the bases are loaded.'

'Don't pursue the baseball analogy too far. I know very little about the game.'

'I'm a New York Mets fan myself. Have you never been to Shea Stadium?'

'Only via a Beatles video, I'm afraid. What can I do for you, Sadie, I hope?'

She was not a girl to prevaricate. 'I didn't think a passion like ours should be allowed to wither on the vine. Particularly with this baseball bat business. In fact I half expected you to ring.'

'My head is duly bowed,' I told her. My attitude to Sadie Beck was that my life had quite enough problems already without adding to them unnecessarily; when you're in a hole, stop digging. But the sound of her husky voice brought back memories of the wide eyes and the pretty mouth and it was suddenly as if she was in the room beside me.

'I know,' she went on. 'You can't come out to play because the dog's got a migraine. I've heard all the excuses.'

'I don't have a dog,' I said. 'You put money in one end and turds come out the other. I can turn my cash into something better than that, like bottles of stuff that you can drink.'

'How is business, by the way? You sounded a little gloomy about it in the days when you had time for me.'

114

'It's worse now than it was then. Disaster looms. The trouble is that I've got used to certain luxuries, like living indoors.'

'Okay, a cheap date. Why don't you come up and have a look round the TV studios? It's bloody fascinating, apparently, if you don't actually work here.'

'You don't think I'm a little old for you?' I asked.

'If that worries you, why don't you go in for cryonics?'

'Cry what?'

'Get yourself deep frozen and wait for me to catch you up.'

I looked round into the shop that she had caught me in – after several calls elsewhere, I subsequently learned. Charlotte was safely removed from earshot and was actually dealing with a real customer.

'Okay,' I said. 'Give me the conducted tour of the studios.'

I used one of our six bedrooms as an office for the clerical work that my faltering venture requires (I can claim heating and lighting against tax), and I was wrestling with the accounts that evening and trying to brighten their ominous message when the front door bell rang. When it rang again I realized that Annette was in the garden, and I went down.

I always tried to open the front door with an expression that would convey immediately and beyond any possibility of misinterpretation how unwelcome the visitor was. It was easy enough to amend the performance in the unlikely event that the caller was somebody you actually wanted to see, an eventuality that did not arise in this case.

Steven Benson stood on the step, apparently in the same black jeans, black T-shirt and Chelsea boots that he had worn on his previous visit. The bottom inch or so of his hair had been freshly cut so that what was left looked like a beret.

He gave me a lazy man's smile which involved lifting one side of his mouth while the rest of his features remained immobile.

'Dad sent me,' he said.

I stood back. 'Come in, Steven.'

'The guilt trip that parents lay on you,' he said as he walked in. This was the language of youth and I had no idea what he was talking about.

'What can I do for you, Steven?' I asked when I had sat him on the sofa.

'It's about the windows,' he said, scratching a pale cheek.

'Ah, the windows.'

'You see, you told Dad that I came round here to see Helen.'

'Yes, I did,' I said.

'That was kind of cruddy.'

'It was?'

He nodded and stared at the floor.

'Mega cruddy.'

I didn't say anything.

'Did you know my parents only got married this year? For most of my life I've been a bastard.'

'So what?' I asked.

'It's not a great thing to find out,' he replied, still staring at the floor.

But I was impatient now to hear the promised apology. There was work to be done and I didn't have time to waste entertaining this louche jerk.

'I get the feeling that you don't like me, Steven,' I said. 'This conversation doesn't seem to have much point.'

He looked up at last. 'You're the bourgeois, Mr Hadfield. You buy cheap and sell dear. You're fuck-all use to anyone.'

I chew people like this up for breakfast but the prize didn't seem to be worth the effort.

'What are you going to be if you grow up?' I asked. 'A social worker?'

'It wouldn't be a bad idea. Ten million people can't afford adequate housing. Five million people don't eat properly. Perhaps I'll be an MP.'

I had once wanted to become an MP myself, but time lays bare such fanciful notions and pretty silly they look in retrospect.

116

'The fact that you're irrevocably mediocre will be no handicap,' I assured him. 'You think you can find twenty thousand people to vote for you?'

'You live in the dark ages, Mr Hadfield. Most people in Britain are younger than you. They've got like different ideas and needs.'

'Are you what they call the wave of the future?'

'I'm the present. You're the past.'

'I'm only forty.'

'Five hundred years ago you were dead at forty.'

I wondered how this strange, half-educated youth passed his time when he wasn't breaking windows. I remembered Alec telling me that Steven had once figured in an insect-eating competition – moths, worms, spiders. He had been defeated by a slug. He had obviously found the time, though, to sift through a few political tracts.

'If you're so interested in politics,' I said, 'why don't you help your mother get elected to the council?'

His lip curled in what was meant to be a smile. 'Mum's playing at it,' he said. 'Fucking whales.'

'How did you find out about the wedding?'

'Friend of mine's dad works at the register office.'

'And you hold it against your parents, do you?'

'Couldn't give a fuck.'

This was so transparent a lie that I would have begun to feel sorry for him if he hadn't been so thoroughly unpleasant. Sons of headmasters usually emerged more civilized than this and I couldn't help but blame Alec for the job he had done here. It made me ask: 'Do you think your father's in the wrong career?'

'He's on the wrong planet,' said Steven Benson.

'I bet he didn't break windows as a kid.'

'All he could break is wind.'

To listen to this demolition job on his father, bumbling and unsuccessful though the father may have been, almost made me weep. The sacrifices that Alec had made for his son, including most recently a late wedding to legitimize him, counted for nothing in the face of his awful offspring's smouldering animosities and festering resentments.

'You can fuck off now,' I said. 'I'm talking to you in your own language so that you can like understand.'

He stood up and looked round the room.

'It's all right for you, Mr Hadfield,' he said. 'You've made your wedge.'

I didn't move and he let himself out.

That night in the Comedy Hotel Alec asked: 'Did Steven come round and apologize?'

'Well,' I said, 'he came round.'

'Good,' said Alec. 'That'll be good for him.'

The ballroom at the Comedy Hotel was crowded on two nights of the year: New Year's Eve, and the evening in June when they held their Midsummer Ball.

For reasons which owed more to a recently created tradition than to the personal preferences of any one of us, we and our friends appeared regularly at these functions as if there was no question of our doing anything else on evenings of such significance.

We didn't go so far as to wear dinner jackets although there were those who did. I wore a fairly sporty suit with a pink shirt, Alec wore the sedate grey which he thought suited a headmaster, and Laurie was in his habitual brown with a green tie. His ensemble was considerably enhanced by what looked like the beginnings of a black eye.

As we made our way to our table in the corner, he muttered to me: 'A cruise missile can hit a garage door from eight hundred miles. That's spitting in the wind beside my missus.'

Judy was indeed sailing towards our table like a fast-rising light-heavyweight who had recently decked the leading contender and now had the champion in her sights. She looked as if it would be no surprise to her if she were waylaid by a fawning autograph hunter. Her long white dress accentuated the power that lay beneath its silky material. Annette

118

wore a flowery dress designed to conceal her pregnancy, and Kitty was her normal perky self in the white trouser suit we had all seen before.

'How is our campaign going?' I asked when we had sat down. Laurie was pouring champagne but Kitty was demanding orange juice.

'I do believe I'm going to win,' she said, winking at me from behind her large spectacles. 'They've had enough of the other lots.'

'Really?' I said. 'Kitty Benson, county councillor?'

'Our time has come, Max. Be sure you're there for the count. You mustn't miss the expressions on the faces of the losers.'

'I'll be there,' I promised. 'What about the book?'

She pushed out her bottom lip in a manner that was meant to tell me that here the news was not so good.

'It's been sorely disrupted by the Steven thing,' she said. 'He's shot my concentration to ribbons. He found out, you know, about ...' She looked at Laurie and Judy to see whether they were listening. 'About that morning at Maidenhead.'

'I know,' I said.

'It's had a bad effect on him. I didn't think he'd give a damn.'

'I'd have thought he'd be grateful,' I said.

'They don't think like that, do they? They seem to *want* an excuse for a grievance. It allows them to behave badly.'

'If you ask me,' said Laurie, 'this parenthood caper isn't all it's cracked up to be.'

'Unless you have a good son like Max and Annette,' said Judy Curtis. 'How is Garth, by the way?'

'Sunning himself in Spain,' Annette told her. 'It sounds as if he is actually doing some work.'

'You're the right couple to have another kid,' said Kitty. 'I've decided I don't understand children. Bored at five, irritable at seven, rebellious at nine and out of control by the time they're fourteen. Who needs it?'

Alec had nothing to say on this subject and it seemed to me that this son's behaviour had had a seriously dispiriting effect on him. It wasn't even clear that he was listening to the conversation. This was all the more odd because the predominant sound in the Comedy Hotel now was laughter. At every table people seemed to be telling jokes or relating experiences that each had a hilarious outcome. Our little table, with its differing problems, seemed more sober than most.

A clutch of waiters swooped round the large room taking orders and soon reappeared with trays of food. Like many a fan of the bottle, I preferred drinking to eating. Drinking was so much easier: no knives and forks and condiments and serviettes, no remorseless chewing and searching and cutting and forking. Just gulp, gulp, gulp. You could do it standing up. You could do it playing pool. But tonight, although food featured on the programme, the emphasis leant towards the drinks and the dance, and it was my hope to concentrate on the former. Terpsichorean frolics aren't exactly up my alley, having wasted valuable drinking hours in my youth learning the foxtrot, the quickstep, the rumba and tango only to discover that what girls wanted was an adept partner at the bop, the jive, the frug and the twist.

And now it was the lambada, an imported gyration which had gripped the trendy hearts and limbs of the younger generation, and which was much in evidence once the food had been cleared away and the band had lured resplendent couples to the circular dance floor in the middle of the room.

As Annette had decided that dancing in her condition was ill-advised, I thought that I would be able to concentrate on the bottles of wine that had appeared on our table. But Kitty, determined to ignore her worried spouse, dragged me on to the floor.

We hadn't been there long when a man who knew Kitty from her political activities took her away from me and I found myself dancing with a young woman called June, Jean, Jane or Joan who was no doubt constantly misheard because she leaned backwards when she spoke as if she thought that she, or knew that you, suffered from halitosis. Attempting to grasp the rudiments of the lambada and the fundament of Miss J., I spotted Judy Curtis cavorting with a young man who was blissfully unaware of the potent realities of his partner's left hook.

'Who's Judy dancing with?' I asked Laurie when I got back to the table.

'Peter.' He made a series of oblique gestures with one hand, one arm and the side of his head which led me to believe that Peter was the star drummer in a successful dance band. Soon afterwards it became clear that the information he was attempting to convey was that Peter masturbated with a frequency and dedication that would jeopardize his prospects of a podium place in the next Olympics, if any such prospect existed. Or Laurie thought he did or thought that he behaved as if he did or looked like the sort of person who probably did and, anyway, Laurie didn't like him.

I looked round at the people who came to the Midsummer Ball. It was astonishing how many couples emerged from their luxurious riverside retreats where, for most of the year, they stayed decently hidden. Several had arrived by boat. There was a hatchet-faced financier who had been cleared at the Old Bailey the previous year of a scam involving shareholders' money. He kept a boat on the Thames and rarely spoke to anybody. There was a Yorkshireman with psoriasis who moved in the political world or, rather, outside it. His unsuccessful attempts to get himself selected for a safe parliamentary seat had now reached an embarrassing level of failure and when you talked to him you discussed any subject but that. There was the clerk of one of the local councils who always hovered uncomfortably at social occasions like this, with his unhappy, overweight wife. He was a neurotic and resentful man who obviously felt that life should have dealt him better cards but it was hard to discern, when you met him, why life should have been so generous. There was also the owner of the Comedy Hotel, a startlingly good-looking chap called Giles who had inherited this little business from an indulgent aunt and who constantly invested the profits in airline tickets to faraway places so that postcards kept arriving from Cagliari and Cape Town, Lima and Astrakhan, each urging the staff to work harder.

Seeing me looking at him now he waved across the ballroom. His latest tan was being admired by the Brimble sisters, two girls in their early twenties whose sexual exploits had filled many a conversational void. The one to whom Giles was paying particular attention was reputed to have a wild sexual appetite that required three in a bed. Her flabby and promiscuous sister had once been described by Laurie, with his fine sensitivity and delicate turn of phrase, as a mobile knocking shop.

But none of these people aroused the interest of Alec who stared into his wine as if there were fish in it. His trance was eventually broken by Judy Curtis who had returned from her whirl with the toy boy to strong-arm Alec to a reluctant perpendicular and propel him to the dance floor with hardly any physical effort from him.

Kitty watched him go. 'He's taking the Steven business very badly,' she said. 'He blames himself. He's quite right to, of course. It's in the blood.'

'I see,' I said. 'Steven gets his virtues from you and his faults from his father?'

This feminine thesis was familiar to me. My wife routinely attributes any little flaws she spots in Garth to me. She has always regarded it, for instance, as one of my eccentricities that I stir my tea anti-clockwise, and she was noisily triumphant when she first discovered that he did the same thing.

'It's there for all to see,' said Kitty, shrugging. 'Which one's fighting an election, writing a book and making things happen? And which one is slumped in a stupor of defeat and making excuses?'

'Are you implying that your husband has a criminal record?' I asked.

'I'm talking about backbone,' said Kitty. 'Grit, fortitude, moral fibre, tenacity, mettle, character, courage, determination. Or, in today's disgusting argot, bottle.'

'Blimey,' I said. 'You ought to write a book knowing all them words.'

Alec's experience on the dance floor had stirred his brain because when he returned, or was delivered parcel-like by Judy, he sat down and announced: 'Steven despises me.'

'Surely not,' said Annette, who had listened to Kitty's summary of the Benson family's problems with little expressions of concern. 'You mustn't let it get to you, Alec. He broke a few windows. He's not the Yorkshire Ripper.'

'I did a few naughty things when I was his age,' said Laurie, an admission that produced no cries of disbelief. 'We used to have gate-stealing competitions.'

Alec was listening to none of this. 'It's not that he hates me, or feels that I've been unfair to him in some way. He *despises* me. He holds me in contempt.'

'Why?' Annette asked. 'Or what makes you think he does?'

Alec had resumed staring at his wine. 'It's difficult to earn a son's respect if you're his headmaster. I expect he hears the other kids tear me apart. Who knows? They all want Gary Lineker to be their dad.'

'Who is he?' Kitty asked.

'He's a football person,' I told her. 'A little young to be Steven's father.'

'How do you know he despises you?' Annette persisted.

'He told me,' said Alec. 'He said: "I despise you." '

'A simple declarative sentence,' I said. 'My compliments to his English teacher.'

'You should have belted him,' said Laurie.

'Oh yes,' said Alec, laughing bitterly. 'That would have helped a lot.'

I disturbed this maudlin symposium by calling for more wine. It was going to take more than words to restore Alec's *joie de vivre*.

'Did you hit Helen when she robbed my shops?' I asked Laurie as he filled our glasses.

'I never hit women,' he said, lighting one of his small cigars. 'Unfortunately this is not a reciprocal arrangement.' He fingered his eye which everyone was tactfully ignoring.

'Dance, Max?' said Judy.

I stood up. 'No violence, mind.'

'My old man's a squalid little squirt,' was her opening remark when we reached the dance floor. Feeling her muscles beneath her white silk dress I had to think twice before offering mild disagreement.

'He's an inventive and hard-working man, Judy,' I said. 'How many people have homes in France?'

'Quite a lot of French people have. How many people have shoplifting daughters?'

'You blame him?' I asked. It sounded familiar.

'Of course I do. Where's the discipline? Where's the affection?'

I wanted to tell her that her own violent behaviour was a contributory factor in her daughter's estrangement, but thought better of it. Getting flattened by a woman on a public dance floor would be bad for my image.

By the time we got back to our little party it was clear that the evening was breaking up. A man at the next table whose shoulders seemed to start at his ears had begun, with no noticeable encouragement, to sing 'Flower of Scotland', and my pregnant wife was indicating that she was ready for bed. Kitty, too, seemed anxious to escort her disconsolate husband home.

'I hate going to bed late,' she said. 'I feel so pessimistic next day.'

But for everybody else, it seemed, pessimism arrived no matter what time they retired.

The more I think about death the more selfish I become. The obligation to enjoy what's left becomes more pressing every day. And so I went off to meet Sadie Beck without a flicker of guilt.

I had never thought much about death but lately it had become a recurring subject in my mind. I had taken to checking the ages of the recently departed who are featured in obituary columns and become alarmed at how many of them, even without the helpful shove of Aids, are in their forties and fifties. It confronted me with this question: How am I going to make my own inelegant exit? Would it be in a late-night car crash in the Rover, with my pain-racked body transferred in agony from a wet road to a stretcher and my life prolonged for a dazed week or two in the intensive care ward? Was a disease already establishing itself in some unregarded corner of my body, before treating me to a six-month nightmare of terminal pain and drugs? Or would I keel over one day and find instant and painless oblivion? Only a year or two ago death was something that happened to other people, but now the thought of it had moved in like a lodger to play a disquieting role in my teeming imagination.

It was a field of thought that heightened your awareness of the passing days, the lost opportunities and the missed pleasures, and having dallied in that field during the drive to London I arrived at the Television Centre like a panic-stricken drunk who had heard somebody call last orders.

I presented Sadie's name to a uniformed flunkey at the reception desk and after studying me closely he waved me away to a chair and picked up a phone.

She came out of a lift in a tight maroon dress that stopped well above the knee and was slashed up one side in a thigh-revealing mode. I don't remember any woman ever looking quite so pleased to see me.

'Hallo, lover,' she said with reckless indiscretion.

I kissed each cheek in the conventionally platonic manner, but she took my hand and led me back to the lift. Her fair hair was in a ponytail again and her wide eyes looked up at me as if she couldn't really believe I was here.

'Sadie Beck of Strawberry Hill,' I said. 'Where are you taking me?'

'Into the entrails of TVC,' she said. 'I'm going to show you what a clever girl I am.'

The Television Centre, or TVC as I had to learn to call it, is built like a wedding cake. The corridors on each floor are circular so that even when you are lost it looks familiar. The idea that this could cause whole segments of stuff to arrive at the wrong destination amused me and also explained much about the building's electronic output.

We stopped at one of a hundred doors and entered a darkened room where two men were watching a piece of film. They ran it and stopped it and re-ran it and made notes all the while on a clipboard.

'This is Max,' said Sadie Beck. I was impressed that she carried sufficient weight to interrupt them with an outsider.

'Hi,' said one of the men, looking up. The other just smiled and I realized that he was a woman.

'Hallo,' I said. I have a certain sympathy with lesbians because men are, after all, pretty horrible.

'We're making a documentary about teenagers,' Sadie said. 'Know anything about them?'

'I've got one at home,' I said.

'Each generation is supposed to be cleverer than the last, but it's hard to believe it, listening to some of this lot,' said the man with the clipboard.

'Who says they're supposed to be cleverer?' I asked. 'I haven't seen a Shakespeare or an Einstein lately.'

'It's like your sport, innit?' he said, resorting for some reason to a working-class south London accent. 'In any sport you can measure with a stopwatch or a tape measure we get better and better, so it's logical to assume that in sports we can't measure in that way, like football or tennis, we are also getting better.'

'What's that got to do with teenagers?' I asked.

'Same thing. It's your evolution, innit?'

A youth on the screen with a mohican haircut and a ring in one ear was talking about Dostoyevsky's spell in Siberia and so I shut up.

'This is the boy,' said the clipboard man. 'I'm going to make him a star.' He fast-forwarded the film and the student

126

of Russian literature was replaced by a young girl who talked about refugees in Kurdistan and cyclone victims in Bangladesh.

'Listen to that,' the man said. 'It's the compassionate generation.'

Sadie glanced at me. 'You look doubtful,' she said. 'Isn't this a picture of teenagers that you recognize?'

'The ones I know rob my shops and break my windows,' I said. 'But it's good to know there are others.'

'These are they,' said the lesbian. 'This is an encomium, or it will be when we weed out the yobs.'

'It's the yobs you should be doing,' I said, 'and then cut to the parents and let everyone see who is to blame.'

'Your own teenager is a perfect example of the species?' Sadie said with a smile.

'Well, of course. Reared with loving care.'

'I thought he might be.'

It was half an hour before she was able to take a break from this twilit conference and we went to the bar for a drink. Famous faces drifted in and out, grabbing liquid refreshment between more onerous duties.

'I had hoped that I would be able to leave with you,' said Sadie, looking cross. 'But we've got to wrap this up tonight.'

'I can go home alone. I'm a big boy now.' But I struggled to disguise my disappointment.

She put her hand on my knee. 'If you ever want me, you only have to ring.'

'Ring, ring,' I said, looking at the piece of thigh revealed by her slashed skirt.

'Would you like to come down and watch them reading the news before I go back? Come and see the secrets of the autocue.'

So I followed her to a studio and watched the news. It needed two people to read it and what they read took the gilt off my secret meeting with Sadie Beck. The recession was getting worse.

127

9

Return of the prodigal

One lunchtime towards the end of June I arrived home to find a blue Range Rover parked outside our front door. We have two front gates and I always sweep in one and out of the other, parking right outside the front door on the few feet that the Range Rover now occupied. I parked behind it and walked the last ten yards.

Annette opened the door before I could find my key.

'Look who's here!' she said delightedly. 'The wanderer returns!'

Behind her was Garth. The golden boy, as she liked to call him, was genuinely golden now with the deepest tan he had ever had. But his face looked thinner as if a few meals had been missed during this exposure to the sun, and he looked tired.

'Hallo, Dad,' he said. 'I've got something for you.'

As I gave him a hug he slipped me a handful of fifty-pound notes. It was the five hundred pounds that I had lent him to go to Spain.

'Well,' I said, 'I didn't expect it back so quickly. Whose vehicle is that outside?'

'My employer's,' said Garth, as we went in. 'I've just driven up from Marbella.'

He said it as if he had just cruised down the motorway from London and not completed a marathon, thousand-mile journey over the indifferent roads of three countries. The thought made me feel old.

'Doesn't he look well?' said Annette. 'Doesn't he look fine?' She held his hand with both of hers and didn't want to let go. Garth smiled wearily, the warrior home from the war.

'How about a salad on the patio?' suggested Annette.

'That would be really nice, Mum,' Garth said.

The two of us went out to arrange the furniture while Annette went to the kitchen. My son was wearing ragged jeans, an old white shirt and white beach shoes with no socks. He was in serious need of a haircut.

'It's lovely to see you,' I said when we sat down. 'What the hell have you been doing? Not playing table football, evidently.'

Garth had once been a table football champion, a fascinating talent which I had to remind him repeatedly did not lead to wealth.

'I'm a driver,' he said immediately, and I looked at him.

'You're well paid for a driver,' I said, 'if you can afford to return five hundred pounds so quickly.'

'It's surprising what you can earn if you're prepared to do long distances and sleep in the vehicle. I've been to Marseilles, Paris, Lisbon. We're talking thousands of miles, Dad. I even went to Amsterdam.'

The idea of my son careering around Europe in a Range Rover took some time to assimilate. At home, although he had passed his driving test at the first opportunity, he had never owned a car and rarely borrowed mine. Questions rose in my mind, but Annette appeared with food. It was probably just as well: there are few things young people detest more than an inquisition, and it would have seemed less than welcoming when you have just crossed Europe to get home.

Plates of smoked salmon were laid before us, along with lettuce, tomatoes, asparagus and prawns. Annette opened a bottle of white wine and said: 'Well, this is lovely. The family together again. We've missed you, Garth.'

He drank the wine as if it were beer. 'Come down, Mum. Come and see some real sun.'

129

Annette laughed. 'I think I'll have the baby first.' She turned to me. 'He brought me an early birthday present.'

I made a mental note that her fortieth birthday was coming up any minute and asked: 'What was it?' She stood up and went into the house, returning with a short, expensive leather jacket. Then, from inside it, she produced a crocodile handbag. The two together, even in Spain, could not have cost less than six hundred pounds. On her birthday last year he had bought her a bottle of perfume that perhaps cost twenty.

'Very nice,' I said. 'I don't think we stock anything like that.'

'How *are* the shops, Dad?' Garth asked.

There had been a time when he would have delighted me by showing an interest in my business. I had proudly imagined him inheriting a thriving concern, building on what he had been given and passing on an even larger enterprise to the next generation. That was how the rich handled it.

But the shops had never interested him much and with the alarming drop in takings this year it was probably just as well.

'They're doing very badly, son,' I told him. 'In fact struggling to survive. No doubt you've heard about the recession as you hurtle about Europe?'

'I can't say I have.'

'It's managed notwithstanding that to exist.'

It was impossible not to envy somebody who could blithely ignore the harsh realities that were harming so many others. Fun in the sun was a happier prospect than pain in the rain, and what really hurt me was that the same freedom for the single teenager had not existed when I was Garth's age or had not, at any rate, existed for me. I was in my late twenties before I had enough money to open a bank account without attracting the ridicule of the bank manager, and seven days abroad was a rare extravagance that was preceded or followed by weeks of miserable economies.

'There must be easier ways to make money, Dad,' said

Garth as he ate his smoked salmon. 'Some men earn more in a year than others do in a lifetime.'

'And you're going to be one of them?'

I had the awful feeling for the first time in my life that my son was judging me and had found me wanting. I had failed to measure up to some new financial criteria – six months ago he didn't give a damn about money.

'Earning just enough to live on is a real bore,' he said. 'The hand-to-mouth existence takes all the pleasure out of life.'

He finished the smoked salmon and took a hefty swig from his wine.

'What are we doing this afternoon?' he asked, looking first at Annette and then at me.

'I have to go to Windsor,' I told him, 'to look at my shaky business. What about tomorrow?'

'Let's have lunch at the Waterside,' he said. 'I'll pay.'

The Waterside Inn at Bray is supposed to be one of the two or three best restaurants in Britain.

My son was becoming a big spender.

I opened my first shop in Peascod Street, Windsor. I had the whimsical idea that a young Royal would come trotting down the hill from the castle and buy a pair of culottes. A plaque announcing 'By Royal Appointment' would be over the door within a week, and the Rolls-Royce and a home in the West Indies would follow soon afterwards.

Today Windsor depressed me. The grey brick castle squatted in the centre of the town like a medieval prison, and excitable Japanese tourists filed round the windy streets buying picture postcards of Coldstream Guards. Nell Gwynne's Restaurant still offered afternoon tea in the room used by Charles II and Nell Gwynne, but elsewhere history had been usurped by more modern tastes: Burger Kings, Pizza-Huts and Southern Fried Chicken. Peascod Street itself, now crammed with exactly the same shops as filled other high streets, was hardly the most elegant thoroughfare. It would have fitted easily into the grubbiest town in Britain. The town's commemorative blue pillar box and ancient well, neither in use, were not so much incongruous as ignored.

But Windsor, with its Great Park and its Long Walk, its pigeon-infested Guildhall and its formidable statue of Queen Victoria, probably depressed me most today because it represented the start of my folly. The empire began here. It was the success of Windsor which precipitated the expansion that I now regretted. Other towns were not crowded with money-laden tourists, a point I overlooked in my surge for growth.

But the news now was that even Windsor was doing badly. It wasn't losing money like some of my branches, but the profits had halved in the last six months and were still going down.

Mrs Spalding greeted me as if I were the guest of honour at a wake. She had been in charge of the shop ever since it opened and was my longest-serving employee. She was around fifty, a plump usually cheerful woman whose husband worked on the railway.

I took one look at her face and said: 'Is there *any* good news?'

'Those shift dresses you got Keith to make in Whitechapel have all gone. We could have sold twice as many.'

'I can still do something right then.'

'Not really,' said Mrs Spalding. 'You under-ordered.'

'I couldn't afford any more,' I said. 'Shall we re-order?'

'By the time we get them the moment may have passed.'

I looked round the shop and wondered how much capital was tied up here in clothes that nobody was buying.

'What we needed,' said Mrs Spalding, 'was a June election. They always create a boom to win an election. Now they don't have to bother.'

'If Mr Major went to the country now he'd get his head cut off,' I said. 'Liquidations and bankruptcies at record levels, and these are the people who put him in. They're predicting that twenty thousand companies could fail this year and who are the worst affected?'

132

Mrs Spalding looked at me and raised her eyebrows as she waited for the answer.

'Firms with high borrowings who are under-capitalized. In a word, us.'

Mrs Spalding sat down on one of the chairs that were used by customers who were waiting to be served in the days when there were customers who were waiting to be served.

'Why don't you sell half the shops and concentrate on the best, Mr Hadfield?' she asked.

'Sell them? I can't give them away. The only shops opening now are charity shops. Oxfam, cancer, Africa. Soon the high streets will consist entirely of charity shops and building societies, and where will the ladies buy their clothes then?'

I went into the office at the back. It was larger than the others because at first I had thought that it was an important part of the business. In my later shops the offices got smaller and smaller to leave more room for the shop, and I did much of the paperwork at home.

I sat at Mrs Spalding's desk and studied the figures, the orders, the invoices and the VAT book. It was a horror story that would have made a gruesome movie. On the wall was a certificate that Mrs Spalding had won for a window display soon after we opened. It was hard to recall the enthusiasm and energy that had set us off on an exciting journey that was intended to take us to the pot of gold at the end of the rainbow.

Perhaps in this temple of tourism we should have gone wholeheartedly for the visitors' market and sold T-shirts with castles on the front and Nell Gwynne bonnets. But all my products were duplicated in the other shops and the banausic trash that was unloaded on the foreign visitor here would have looked out of place in my other nine outlets.

The sad decline in Windsor's business was an augury that not even Mrs Spalding's optimism could ignore. When she came in to find me poring over the figures she suggested a cup of tea.

'What have you learned?' she asked.

133

'I have seen the future and it doesn't work,' I told her.

'My husband is quite certain that I'm going to lose my job.'

I looked up at her. 'If you lose your job, Mrs Spalding, I shall lose my house.'

'I think I'd better make that cup of tea.'

When she brought it in we sat down and discussed the good old days when every line sold and every customer spent. But our attempts to cheer each other up were fatally undermined by the crucial but unmentioned fact that our conversation was not interrupted by a single customer.

At five o'clock, feeling more than usually in need of a drink, I got in the Rover and drove direct to the Comedy Hotel.

Laurie Curtis prowled round the pool table in search of a ball that he could pot. His bulky waistline and his flowery tie threatened constantly to illegally move one of the balls, and when he saw one that he thought he could dispatch to a pocket he found he was handicapped by his shortness and had to use a rest. An additional impediment was the smoke in his eyes which curled up from the cigar in his mouth, but his play was so erratic that it sometimes seemed to be irrelevant whether his eyes were open or shut.

I examined his face for signs of combat but no fresh wounds were visible. He looked tired, though, as if the strain of hunting for money-making ideas or the disappointment of his daughter were beginning to tell. I waited until he had missed his shot before asking: 'How's business?'

He sat down and picked up a pint of new weak lager that the Comedy Hotel was trying out. They called it a 'session lager' which meant that you could drink it all evening and go home more or less sober, which seemed a strange idea to me.

'I'm thinking millennium,' said Laurie.

I looked at him blankly.

'We're coming to the end of it, aren't we?' he said. 'There's a lot of money to be made.'

134

I potted a red, missed another, and sat down myself.

'How?' I asked.

'Do you know that all the hotels in London are booked up for December 31 1999? Concorde's going to take you to London, Paris, Moscow and New York so you can see the new century in in four cities on the same night.'

'And where do you fit in,' I asked, 'supposing you last that long?'

'That's what I'm thinking about. The story of the twentieth century, its wars and murders, its heroes and villains. The whole hundred years, summed up for your grandchildren.'

'What are you talking about? A film, a book, a video, an ice show?'

'I haven't got that far yet,' he said and went across to study the pool table. The pattern of the balls did not please him. The yellow ones, which were now his, clung to the cushions so that the pockets were inaccessible.

He said: 'What about bantams?'

'Is this another money-making idea?' I asked as he bent over the table and tried to move a yellow to a better position.

'They breed like rabbits and soon you've got hundreds. They also look after the partridges.'

'You haven't got any partridges.'

'Well, somebody has and what they need are bantams. I could also sell bantam eggs.'

I walked across to the table and potted three reds. 'How many bantam eggs do you need to make an omelette?' I asked.

'I'd paint them and sell them as quail eggs.' He picked up his lager. 'During prohibition this beer would have been legal.'

'Why don't you stop this fund of ideas and go and live in France?' I asked. 'You've been slaving your guts out for too long.' His receding red hair seemed to have moved back at least an inch since the start of the year.

'How can I answer that?' he said. 'I'm married. I don't even know where my next orgasm is coming from.'

135

'How is Judy the bruiser, anyway? You don't seem to have any new injuries.'

'We're pretty close at the moment, as it happens.'

'So are boxers in a clinch.'

He bent over the table again and tried to pot a yellow but it missed the pocket. I got up and got rid of my last red and then missed on the black. There were now seven yellow balls on the table and one black. Laurie delightedly laid snooker after snooker so that I could never hit the black. Meanwhile he slowly got rid of his yellow balls.

When I had lost we returned to the bar. Victory seemed to have done Laurie good.

'What about a series of monthly magazines that tell the story of the century? We sell 'em a binder and they have to collect the lot. I could find a hack who would knock it together. The printing costs would be the only thing that mattered and I could buy that at the right price.'

'You make your profit when you buy,' I told him.

'Exactly,' he said, as if I had neatly encapsulated a maxim that he had been groping towards for years. He pushed his half-full lager glass away and asked John for a whisky. 'I haven't done too badly,' he said, 'for a boy from humble origins, but it's making the money that damages the marriage.'

'How's that?' I asked.

'Business,' he said, sipping his whisky. 'You think of it every hour of the day. How to turn a penny. No time for the wife, see?'

'And you attribute the odd holocaust with Judy to this, do you?'

'Certainly,' he said.

So far as I was concerned the Curtis marriage, like prewar Russia, was a riddle wrapped in a mystery inside an enigma, and I had long since despaired of understanding how a relationship which veered so alarmingly from tenderness to terrorism could survive so long.

'A man has to ask himself – which is more important, money or marriage?' Laurie said.

'And which is?' I asked.

He looked at me as if I was trying to catch him out. 'You're a cynical bugger, Max. I don't know how Annette puts up with you. How's Garth, by the way? I hear he's home.'

'Happy and prosperous,' I said.

'You're a lucky man with your child. You've heard about Alec, I suppose?'

'No. What?'

'He's taken to his bed and won't get up.'

Kitty Benson greeted me with a green rosette. She was making it herself and it was about eight inches in diameter and thick with folds.

'What do you think?' she asked. 'Put the others in the shade, won't it?'

'Is this in preparation for your coming triumph?' I asked.

'Absolutely. The press picture after the votes have been counted. Kitty among the vanquished.'

When I asked her if Alec was about she had to drag herself back from her victorious dream to think for a moment about whom I was talking.

'Alec?' She dropped her voice. 'He's in bed. He won't get up.'

'Can't or won't?'

'Won't.'

I had called in on my way home from my chat with Laurie. I naturally hoped that I might cheer Alec up in some way, although a demoralized headmaster taking to his bed without good reason was a fascinating prospect in itself.

'Will he see me?' I asked.

'I'll find out.' She disappeared, forgetfully leaving me on the step. It only occurred to me then that I hadn't seen Alec since the Midsummer Ball and he had seemed low enough on that night. My own disturbing preoccupations had prevented my noticing his absence from the Comedy Hotel. Your friends could wander off and die these days and the demands of the world left you unaware of it.

Kitty reappeared, still clutching her verdant rosette. 'He'd like to see you, Max,' she said. 'Go on up.'

I ascended the narrow staircase with an excited curiosity. This wasn't like visiting the sick. Even his wife didn't take his problem seriously.

Only one room upstairs had a light on and I went in. Alec lay on his back in pink pyjamas in the dead centre of the small double bed. He looked like a dubious but deceased political hero whose followers, reluctant to let him go, had opted for embalmment, but he opened one eye and said: 'Max. Kind of you to come.'

'What are you doing in bed?' I asked. 'You can't drink beer lying down.'

He answered without opening either eye. 'I've no wish to get up.'

'Oh really?' I said, sitting on the edge of the bed. 'Why's that?'

'I'm too depressed.'

I looked at him but the eyes stayed shut. By the side of his bed was a glass of water, his spectacles and a book, but I couldn't see what it was.

'Depressed people don't take to their beds,' I said. 'They drink arsenic or cut their throats with a breadknife. Something constructive.'

'Depression debilitates. I'm a destroyed man, Max.'

'It looks more like a terminal sulk to me, Alec,' I said. 'Why don't you come down to the Comedy Hotel and let me wallop you at pool? At least it will cheer me up.'

He behaved as if he hadn't heard this and said: 'What Steven did would have shattered any father, but if you're a headmaster it's a thousand times worse. Turning hundreds of kids off the production line is what I do. *Mens sana in corpore sano*. But who can have any faith in me now? I can't even control my own son. I can't even turn him into a respectable human being.'

'He's a bright boy,' I said doubtfully. Defending Steven Benson to help revive his father would stretch my talent for dissembling.

'The window thing, the Helen thing, the Kitty thing.'

'What's the Kitty thing?' I asked.

'The Steven disaster hardly touched her. Her mind's on other things. It's certainly not on me or her son.'

'Well, she's a busy lady,' I said. 'What do you want – some fat old biddy peeling potatoes and muttering in the corner?'

'Do you know what she said? She said she's devoted her life to Steven and me and it's time that she devoted some to herself.'

This struck me as so incontestable that I felt like dragging him from his bed and putting a bucket over his head.

'Good for her,' I said. 'When the book royalties come in you'll be proud that she's your wife.'

'They say too long a courtship spoils the marriage. Last night I had a dream about Mavis Jones.'

'Mavis bloody Jones?' I said. 'Is she still drifting around in what you call your mind?'

'She was a wonderful girl, Max. I remember her still.'

'You're married to a wonderful girl, in my opinion,' I said, 'but if you prolong this caper you'll end up sleeping in a bus shelter. What does the school say?'

'Kitty told them I'm ill.'

'What a dutiful wife. Where's your son and heir?'

'Christ knows. Dismantling Buckingham Palace, I expect.'

'Well, there you are then,' I said. 'Like Kitty, you've got your own life to lead. Forget them. Get up.'

He stared at me as if I was going to attack him. Perhaps I had raised my voice a little.

'And what will that achieve?' he asked.

'We don't know that,' I said. 'But what we do know is that continuing to lie in bed will achieve sod all. I'm going downstairs now while you dress. I shall then take you for a drink.'

I walked out of the room without waiting for a reply.

Downstairs Kitty was still at work on her rosette. 'And how is my recumbent husband?' she asked, but her attention reverted immediately to the flowery artefact in her hand as if she was only making conversation and could happily continue with her work if no answer appeared.

'Shush!' I said and pointed at the ceiling. The creaking of floorboards told us that a man was on the move.

Driving to the Waterside Inn at Bray the following day I told Annette and Garth about Alec's prostrate protest.

'Now we know where Steven's flawed personality comes from,' announced my wife briskly. 'I knew he couldn't have got it from Kitty. She's much too bright.'

'So behave yourself, Garth,' I said. 'You can see who will get the blame for any of your shortcomings.'

I watched him smiling in the rear-view mirror. It wasn't one of these smiles that the smiler is entirely happy with: there was something at the back of it – anxiety, uncertainty, concern.

I imagined that he was worried about his future, which made two of us, and thinking then of the painful transition from schoolboy to man, a transmutation that some never manage at all, I was reminded of my last visit to the Waterside Inn.

Three years earlier I had succumbed to a virulent bout of nostalgia on discovering that it was exactly twenty years since I had left school. I became filled with curiosity about what had happened to some of the boys who had sat beside me during those long miserable years, nurturing dreams that seemed to our young minds to need only patience to come true. One quiet afternoon I ransacked a dozen telephone directories and within a few days had located three about whom I was especially curious.

I invited them to lunch at the Waterside. I was richer then. I took the trouble to get there early and arrived in a mood of high expectation. Having a son who was then sixteen, I was keen to see what had happened to these ex-schoolboys, to find out what the world had done with their vulnerable ambitions.

Davis was the most talented of the three, a brilliant violinist

140

who awaited the day when he would join the London Symphony Orchestra. Cheney was a dour fellow, as people with a scientific bent often are. It was his intention to become part of Britain's nuclear programme, if we still had one. The most effete was Johns who lived for the theatre and only really came alive on stage. While still at school he formed his own amateur dramatic society and once a month staged a short play – *Fumed Oak*, *Box and Cox* – in his local village hall. Some boys from the form were conscripted into this venture which apparently they welcomed because they met girls with rabid sexual curiosities whom Johns had also enlisted from a neighbouring convent school.

They arrived in their separate and uniformly humble cars and each of them looked much older than the thirty-seven or thirty-eight they must have been. Davis was greying and Cheney was bald. Johns wore glasses which magnified his eyes in a peculiar way. I took them to the bar for a pre-lunch slurp and asked what they had been up to. So far as I was concerned their answers made me regret my impulsive invitation.

Davis, the youthful prodigy with a violin, had got no nearer the London Symphony Orchestra than the tenth row of the audience at the Royal Albert Hall. He was a nurse in a mental hospital where he seemed to spend a lot of his time fending off the wild attacks of his unhappy patients. Cheney, who had coveted a career in nuclear physics, was an engineer who specialized in drains; and Johns, the Laurence Olivier of our day, was a restaurant manager in Putney. The chill wind of reality which blew through our little group seemed to effect only me. None of them betrayed the slightest hint of remorse or disappointment.

'School meant bugger all,' said Johns when we were eating our lunch and attempting to recapture the old days. 'The Archbishop of Canterbury failed his eleven-plus and left school with no qualifications. Now he reads the Bible in Greek.'

Cheney finished eating, lit a pipe, and started to tell us

141

about the years he had spent in Africa with a wife he had met when she was spot welding in a components factory. His main talent at school had been making rude noises with his bottom and his subsequent preoccupation with drains was entirely appropriate.

'How did you get on with the blacks?' I asked, fearing the worst.

'They didn't even invent the wheel,' said the Pétomane of the lower fifth.

'God, I thought that old settlers' cliché was dead and buried,' I said. 'You're living in a time warp, Cheney.'

He was a very aggressive youngster, but I told myself that blokes with pipes didn't hit people.

'If you haven't been there, you don't know,' he said.

'Yes, I do. I read books, see films, watch television.'

Davis, who was rescuing a piece of roast beef from his teeth, said: 'What's this all about, Hadfield, anyway? What's happened to us isn't interesting.'

'No,' I said sadly, 'it isn't.'

And so, as I drove Annette and Garth back to the Waterside, I could only wonder what the world had planned for my son.

He had had a short haircut, administered apparently by a girlfriend, and no doubt suitable for his return to the Iberian sun. To me it looked a botched job. Hair that would otherwise have laid on his head was now too short to relax and stood upright at a variety of angles. But he had, out of deference to his surroundings, discarded his jeans and slipped into a pair of brown slacks that actually had creases down the front. His pink shirt was smart, too, but there was no tie.

Our host led us through the beautiful restaurant to the terrace where we sat at a small white table beneath a weeping willow and drank gin and tonics. Hot canapés arrived with the drinks, arranged around a rose that had been made from a beetroot.

'It's a classy joint you've brought us to, darling,' said Annette. 'And what a lovely setting.'

142

'It's got three stars from Michelin and Egon Ronay,' said Garth. 'This is where the rich eat.'

'I'm delighted you can afford it,' I said, looking at swans on the river. 'I can remember when you thought that money was something rather grubby that obsessed your inferiors.'

'I'm well into it now,' Garth said, smiling. 'I'm going to get as much of the stuff as I can lay my hands on. Truckloads. Boatloads. I think money's really nice.'

A launch throbbed past, frightening the ducks. A man was sunbathing on the cabin roof. The Thames was surprisingly narrow at this point and the opposite bank was all grass and trees with no sign of human encroachment.

Eventually we were summoned to our table inside. A room which had once been octagonal had had its shape altered by a riverside extension which had doubled the size of the restaurant. The decor was green and pink – green chairs, pink tablecloths and pink and green curtains and carpets. Pink artificial flowers loomed over the eaters' heads. Wedgwood china plates bearing a picture of the Waterside Inn were in place on our table when we sat down, along with fresh roses and freesias. There was obviously something deeply gratifying for Annette in being taken to one of the best restaurants in England by a son whose start in life had been, to say the least of it, uncertain. Her husband had always led her appetite to less exotic locations.

In London a restaurant as expensive as this would have been crammed with tedious robots on expenses, but the Waterside was patronized by people who actually had money: young men impressing beautiful girls; old ladies, sometimes four at a table, spending what their rich husbands had left them; retired couples on a treat and sometimes whole families. There was a lovely lady in a silk suit and floppy hat who looked as if she should have been at Ascot, and in contrast at another table, a man with huge arm muscles that were amply revealed by a grubby short-sleeve shirt. He seemed to be rather out of place but then I saw who he was eating with and realized that he was a pop star's minder.

It was over lunch that the conversation took a rather depressing turn. Garth, having imbibed generously from what he described as the *vino tinto*, although that was not how it was designated on the Waterside's wine list, adopted a rather truculent attitude in the face of questions about his future.

It had seemed to me to be a good opportunity for a serious talk: we had his attention for an hour. At home he was curiously elusive, forever on the move, and now that he was apparently domiciled in Spain there could be no conversation at all.

I found myself discussing aptitudes and attitudes, application and ambition, career paths and CVs and the long-term satisfaction to be derived from the slow, determined climb to success and prosperity. I don't know why I went on in this vein because I don't believe the crap myself. Sometimes when talking to your son you go on to automatic pilot and hear yourself mouthing paternal homilies that you've listened to somewhere, perhaps from your own parents, and didn't believe when you heard them but still felt, without examining the subject too closely, that this was the sort of thing that parents *should* say to their children.

When I had finished, Garth said: 'You mustn't expect too much, Dad. You paid for a private education, but that mustn't put me in your debt.'

'Of course not.'

'In a way, it was to satisfy you.'

I didn't say anything.

'You see,' said Garth, 'parents bring you into the world without asking whether it's what you want, and then lay burdens on you. It's really boring. I mean, when do I have my say?'

I could see what he meant but I still felt that my generosity and concern were being shoved back in my face.

'I suppose we thought that the best education would help you,' said Annette, looking at me.

'That was probably true thirty years ago,' Garth said. 'Today it's a meritocracy. Kids shoot into Oxford from comprehensives. The Prime Minister left school at sixteen and it didn't cost his parents a penny. There are wily buggers out there who were too busy dreaming about their future to listen to the rubbish that teachers spout. I know three young millionaires and they haven't got an O level between them.' He picked up his wine and drank a lot of it. 'I'm not complaining about the education, but don't expect too much from it. Don't think it's an investment that's going to produce a dividend, because that puts a burden on me that you're not entitled to dump there.'

He looked at me now and held my gaze.

'There's no burden, Garth,' I said.

'Just be happy, Garth. That's all we want,' said Annette, who didn't like the serious tone of this conversation.

'If only it was that easy, Mum,' he said.

The food that had arrived while this was going on was slowly disappearing. Annette and I were eating lamb; Garth had chosen poached salmon. But wonderful though the meal was, my enjoyment had been marred by my son's little declaration of independence.

There seemed to be something portentous in the way that he had sought to dampen our high hopes for his future.

10

The beggar's tale

The day before Garth was due to return to Spain I decided to skip work and spend some time in his company. It wasn't at all clear from anything he had told his parents when he would see us again so I thought that I would grab a day with him before he nonchalantly deserted us. This was natural enough in itself, but an additional motive for me was that I had detected changes in him which, if not monitored stage by stage, would eventually turn him into a complete stranger.

I took him for a lunch drink at the Comedy Hotel where I inveigled him into our first ever game of pool. After lecturing me on the virtues of the maple cue as against the ash cue, he resoundingly beat me three times, a humiliation which I attempted unsuccessfully to endure with good grace.

'Come for a ride in the Range Rover,' he said, as if I needed consoling. 'I've got to pick up some cassettes from my girlfriend.'

'I didn't know you had a girlfriend,' I said.

'Well, she's one of my girlfriends, and she's going to lend me some music.'

Music was what filled the Range Rover as we drove off, although it was hardly what I recognize as music. Somebody who couldn't sing was shouting words I couldn't hear against a noise I didn't like. My son tried to remove my

146

expression of distaste by telling me that this performer earned two million pounds a year.

'Lonnie Donegan was paid three pounds ten shillings to record "Rock Island Line",' I said. 'Now people who can't sing become instant millionaires.'

'What are shillings?' said Garth. 'Come to that, who's Lonnie Donegan?'

I could feel the icy wind of the passing years on the back of my neck again, but I fought back.

'There hasn't been a good pop song for twenty years,' I said. 'Where are songs like "Ruby Tuesday", "Whiter Shade of Pale" or "Where do You go to My Lovely"?'

'You're showing your age, Dad. You'll be saying you don't like pubs next.'

'Well, I don't. I drink in hotels. Bring back the half crown and the ten-bob note, big cinemas and proper plays on television by Rattigan, Priestley and Shaw. All changes are for the worse, that's my conclusion.'

Perhaps envying his freedom of movement, I was feeling magnificently grumpy.

'You have a problem with recent developments, Dad? VCRs, CDs and DATs?'

'Only an initial problem,' I said. 'Where are we going?'

'Wraysbury. The girl's called Annabel Henderson.'

'What does she do?'

'As little as possible.'

It was a sunny afternoon for once and we turned into a quiet avenue of larch trees where imposing detached houses were separated from the road by large immaculate lawns.

'Her father must work slightly harder,' I said.

'I gather he works in the Foreign Office,' Garth said. 'He's an Arabist who used to work for the Levant Consular Service.'

'It sounds impressive,' I said, impressed.

We turned into a drive and cruised up to a large white house that had a balcony running round the upstairs floor. A small blonde girl appeared immediately at the front door.

147

'That's Annabel,' said Garth, switching off his engine. We got out.

'This is my father,' said Garth. 'He's come for the ride.'

'Hi,' said Annabel. She had panda-like eye make-up but lacked the panda's shyness. There was a message on her pink T-shirt that said DON'T JUST STAND THERE DROOLING. CHARM THE HELL OUT OF ME. Pert pectorals loomed beneath this nonsense and I found it necessary to study the words as if they had come from the pen of Shakespeare himself. Her thin wrists looked as if they would snap like a stick of grissino.

'Come in,' she said. 'I'll find the tapes.'

We followed her into a hall that was as big as a room. Gold-framed prints of horses and fields hung on the walls, and a curving staircase that was at least ten feet wide led up to a balcony that was strewn with flowers. But the influence of youth was here too: pop music blared from a distant room. Rod Stewart's sore throat didn't seem to be getting any better.

We were led into a sitting room that made our own lounge (tastefully furnished by my wife) look seriously underfunded. On the other hand, the armchairs and sofas that seemed to be in abundant supply had that classic gilt-edged build that looked good in glossy photographs but were hell to sit on. I sat on one and Annabel, who had taken to holding my son's hand, led him to a music centre in a corner where he worked his way through a pile of audio cassettes, selecting some of them. It was clear that my presence wasn't necessary for this operation and I was left on my own to admire my opulent surroundings.

A youth came in then, no doubt the Rod Stewart fan, with black hair held in a tail at the back by an elastic band.

'Hi,' he said to me.

'That's my brother, Bobby,' Annabel called from her consultation in the corner. 'It's Garth's dad.'

'Hallo,' I said. His face reminded me of somebody and trying to remember who it was I could think of nothing to say to him.

'Dad's coming in to vet your boyfriend,' Bobby announced, and I sat back amused at the prospect of Garth finding himself subjected to some sort of parental scrutiny. It didn't seem to concern him, however, and he continued studying and separating the cassettes.

There were footsteps in the hall and I looked forward to meeting the owner of these palatial premises. When they reached the door I saw that it was not only Annabel's father but also her mother and I stood up.

There have been very few truly surprising moments in my life – surprises that open the mouth and deprive you of the ability to blink – but this was one of them. I was looking at the Neal Street beggar.

He came in smiling and asked loudly: 'Where's Garth?' The piercing eyes were what I had noticed in his son, and they focused now on Garth who abandoned the cassettes to come over and shake hands.

'How do you do, sir?' he said, and then turned to be introduced to Annabel's mother. His good manners and impeccable behaviour would have been a pleasant surprise if I hadn't just exhausted all capacity in that direction.

'So you're the young man who wants to run off with my daughter,' he said, still smiling. His dialogue seemed strangely stilted in this domestic situation, as if he had remembered it from a very old film.

'If only he did,' said Annabel, and it was quite clear to me that her father was putting rather more weight on their relationship than it would stand.

'This is my father,' said Garth, neatly avoiding his host's question.

I shook his hand and looked at him and he looked at me and I saw that something was troubling him, something that he couldn't pin down.

'Mr Hadfield,' he said. 'A pleasure to meet you.'

I bowed to his wife. 'What a lovely home you have, Mrs Henderson,' I said.

'Isn't it gorgeous?' she said, giggling. She turned to Garth, studying him from head to foot as if he were prime beef in a cattle market, and laughed some more.

There was a certain drunken hilarity about her which suggested private drinking. I wondered whether she was privy to the secret life of her mendicant spouse, or did she imagine that he spent each day in the salubrious portals of the Foreign Office, looking after Her Majesty's diminishing interests in the Middle East?

I was hypnotized by the beggar myself and couldn't take my eyes off him. The metamorphosis from London tramp to country squire was so complete that I could only stare in disbelieving admiration. But I could see by the look in his eyes that he was no longer entirely happy with this family scene which had developed a worrying aspect that he couldn't quite identify. The smile that he had brought into the room had faded, and the occasional frown flickered across his handsome face as he tried to remember who I was or where he had met me.

He was talking distractedly to Garth about Spain and how fortunate he was to be able to spend 'more than the statutory fourteen days' there, and then I saw the truth dawn. He looked round thoughtfully at me, temporarily forgot what he was going to say and then began a slow withdrawal from the room. He flicked back the cuff of his fawn suit to consult a Tissot gold watch.

'I'm so sorry, I have a couple of phone calls to make,' he said. 'Have a good time in Spain, Garth. Nice to have met you, Mr Hadfield. Don't let my wife spend too much in your shops.'

He made a cool exit, leaving his wife in the room. For one mad moment I had the idea that his phone calls were to be to certain muscular and retarded gentlemen who would ensure that my journey home terminated in a nasty accident. Secret survives but Hadfield doesn't! Why else would he have to make the calls before I left? But I dragged myself back to the real world (where beggars lived in mansions) and engaged his wife in the sort of banal chat that social occasions like this make inevitable.

After a while I decided to lift the conversation to a more meaningful level, and asked: 'What does your husband do?'

'Oh, he's a boring civil servant,' she giggled. 'The FO.'

I studied her closely and saw that she believed it. The burden of the beggar's secret was even bigger than I had imagined. What agonies and fears he must have had to carry every day.

As Garth drove me home with his hoard of cassettes, I said: 'Mr Henderson seems to think you want to marry his daughter.'

Garth laughed. 'Who knows?'

I thought: My son to marry a beggar's daughter?

In the event this was the least of my worries.

Garth left the next morning while the world slept. He had to be at Newhaven for the Dieppe ferry by seven and I found myself stumbling round at five o'clock making him tea.

'It would be much nicer if you stayed here,' I said. I didn't want to see him leave.

'Who was the man who criticized parents who wouldn't let go?' he said, patting me on the back.

'That was me,' I agreed. 'It was before I knew that you were going to drive the length of France and Spain where road accidents are just about the highest in the world.'

'That's Kuwait,' he told me. 'More crashes per passenger mile than anywhere else.'

I handed him the tea and he sat down.

'When will you be back?' I asked.

'September?' he said. 'October? I don't know. I'm trying to make enough money to keep myself next winter. It would be really nice to come home and take things easy for a while, and Mum will want some help with the baby.'

'You're good with babies, are you?' I teased.

'I meant shopping.'

We went out to the Range Rover with his cases. As usual at that early hour there was a bright sun that few would see; by the time that most people had opened their eyes the clouds would have returned to their customary position overhead. I helped Garth put his luggage into the Range Rover and gave him a hug.

'Look after Mum,' he said, and then saw that she had stirred from her bed and was waving from an upstairs window.

'For God's sake drive carefully,' I said, and watched as he drove out on to the road as quietly as possible. When he had gone I went upstairs to Annette and got back into bed but I couldn't sleep. I lay there worrying and wondering about Garth and then I imagined horrendous road accidents involving French lorries and upside down Range Rovers with their wheels spinning in the air.

After an hour of this I got up. I went into the room that I used as an office and picked up my diary to see what else a day that had started so early had in store for me.

I had made a note that this was the morning that Steven Benson was due to appear in juvenile court and decided to go along. After all, they were my windows that they were talking about, and I was curious about how the world would punish him.

As I arrived in the car park, the star of the show was climbing out of the Bensons' Ford Escort. He was wearing a grey flannel suit that I had not seen before, and a genius with a pair of scissors had evidently been hired to restore some normality to his hairstyle.

Kitty waved and I went over to join them. Alec, now fully restored to the vertical, looked like a man who, due to some titanic chronological cock-up, was a guest at his own funeral.

'*Le grand moment*,' he said. 'Are you here as a witness? I don't think the public are allowed into juvenile courts.'

'I'm what you might call an interested party,' I told him. 'They were my *fenêtres*.'

Kitty smiled and said: 'What a dismal way to spend a morning.' Steven glowered like a cat in a basket who had every reason to believe that his prospects of sexual happiness were about to be seriously tampered with.

'I hope this isn't going to damage the election campaign,' I said to Kitty.

'You don't know much, Max,' she said. 'The papers aren't allowed to name defendants in a juvenile court.'

We waited in a corridor, sitting on wooden forms that I had last seen at school. Young policemen strode past, ready to give evidence in one court or another. A man shouted Steven Benson's name, and the four of us filed into a large, musty-smelling room with high windows and a lot of chairs that faced a table at one end. Here sat three magistrates who were all men and who examined us as we came in as if we might be carrying firearms.

A stern-looking lady in a grey two-piece came in another door with a man. She went to a desk at the front and began to relate the story of Steven Benson's mindless rampage. She delivered her account in clipped, brittle tones, as if she was reluctant to let the words go.

It was a depressing story. Steven Benson's lawbreaking spree had been less imaginative than Helen Curtis's and ultimately less rewarding: at least she had ended up with some cosmetics and a few books and videos.

The chairman of the magistrates, a large, bald man who could quite easily at one time have dabbled in a little Sumo wrestling, listened to this tale with eyebrows that were permanently raised. When the account of Steven's mis-demeanours drew to its close, he leaned forward and said: 'I can't help noticing that although these offences took place in different towns the owner of the windows is always the same man. Is Mr Hadfield by any chance in court?'

I stood up.

'I wonder whether you can help us, Mr Hadfield?'

I stared at him, wondering how I could.

'There is the element of a vendetta here, you see,' he said. 'Why always your windows?'

'I wish I knew,' I said.

'But you know Steven Benson?'

'I've been a friend of his parents for many years.'

'Ah.' This one syllable was followed by a wave of the hand which I took to mean that I could sit down. The chairman was now receiving the thoughts of the colleagues on either side of him simultaneously in each ear but this was not causing any confusion as he was obviously listening to neither of them.

'Steven Benson,' he said, and Steven stood up. 'These offences are not denied?'

'No, sir.'

'Is there anything that you would like to tell us, by way of explanation?'

'I'd like to say I'm sorry,' he replied in a firm voice that seemed to me to be a little short on sincerity.

The man who had come in with the woman now stood up and delivered a glowing testimonial about Steven, as he called him. The man, who I gathered was the probation officer, described my wild window-breaker as a gifted and hard-working boy who had never been in trouble before and who was, in addition, the son of a much-respected local headmaster. This last piece of information came as a pleasant surprise to the magistrates who then took a keen interest in Alec. But Alec sat there glumly enduring his humiliation and not wanting to exchange glances with the three men who sat in judgement.

'This is all very well,' said the chairman when the probation officer had sat down. 'But it rather leaves open the question of motive and, with it, the possibility of repetition. The bill for this damage, apparently, is getting on for ten thousand pounds. It's hardly something we can ask a schoolboy to pay, which makes it all the more important that it doesn't happen again.'

The probation officer stood up. 'Quite so, sir,' he said. 'I'm quite confident that this will never happen again. I've spoken to Steven on several occasions. It was an isolated event precipitated by an imagined grievance and there is genuine remorse. I would not expect to see this boy in court again, and I hope that you will take the view that everybody is entitled to one mistake.' He sat down.

'Who paid for the windows, anyway?' Alec asked when we were outside. 'There was a time when I thought I might have to.'

'The insurance paid,' I said, 'and then they upped my premium.'

Predictably, Steven had received two years' probation exactly as Helen had. It was a sentence that cheered his parents up. Kitty had been worried that he would be sent away for a few months; Alec was more concerned about the possibility of a fine.

Steven Benson didn't react in any way. He appeared to me to be neither contrite nor embarrassed. He walked to the Ford Escort, got in the back and waited to be driven home.

Kitty raised her cheek to me for a goodbye kiss. She seemed to have gone through the morning's sad proceedings with her mind on something else.

'Two down, one to go,' she said.

'What do you mean?' I asked, baffled.

'Garth is now the only one *not* on probation.'

I was sitting at the bar in the Comedy Hotel that evening, musing on the waywardness of youth and the ingratitude of teenagers, and marvelling at the wonderful way in which so many people rushed into the awesome role of parenthood when they were so ill-suited for it.

A man climbed on to the stool next to me, so close that our elbows touched. I turned, confident that it was Alec, in need of verbal and liquid comfort, but it was my beggar from Neal Street (or a former Arabist in the Levant Consular Service, now resident in Wraysbury).

'Good evening, Mr Hadfield,' he said. The accent which had seemed so classy on the train and merely well-off middle class in his splendid sitting room, was now your run-of-the-mill south London: he was clearly a man of many parts. He was wearing a brown check suit that looked like suitable garb for an exclusive golf club.

'Hallo,' I said cautiously, not wanting to encourage his company. I was looking forward to a game of pool.

155

'Garth told Annabel that you could always be found here,' he said, holding up a five-pound note to attract John's attention. 'What will you have?'

My pint glass was only two thirds empty, an embarrassment I quickly rectified. Getting something off this man felt like an achievement when the public's funds normally flowed so generously in the opposite direction.

'I wanted to have a quiet word with you,' he said when the drinks had been served. 'An astonishing coincidence has put me in an awkward situation.'

'I can imagine,' I said.

'You were the first person to recognize me after hours, and for you to then turn up coincidentally at my house – well, it must be a million to one.'

'I can see that it was difficult,' I said. 'I was fairly surprised myself.'

He picked up his drink, a large gin and tonic, and took out the ice which he dropped in an ashtray where it started to melt. I was trying to remember his name in case I needed to use it.

'The thing is,' he said, after a large sip from his glass, 'have you told Garth?'

'Garth? No,' I said. 'It didn't seem necessary. He's returned to Spain now, anyway.'

'Well, that's a relief.' He took another sip. 'I've no doubt you think me evasive, but I'm concerned about my daughter's happiness. I would do anything for her, anything at all.'

'She doesn't know?'

'None of my family knows.' He pressed his lips together and raised his eyebrows as if to say 'Strange, but that's the way it is.'

'I must congratulate you,' I said. 'Keeping a secret like that must be some feat.'

'It hasn't been easy, but I've been lucky. At least,' he said smiling, 'until I met you.'

I took a drink from my lager and wondered when Alec

156

would come in. If this conversation survived until I had to buy the beggar a drink it would nullify my little triumph.

He was studying me carefully with his fierce eyes. 'Do I gather that I can count on your discretion?' he asked.

'I won't tell anyone,' I said. 'I've got my own problems to worry about.'

'Business bad?'

'Terrible.'

A wallet packed with fifty-pound notes was suddenly produced from his inside pocket. I knew my fortunes were plummeting, but had I now reached the stage when I could be bribed by a beggar?

'I'm in your debt,' he said, 'and I'd like to give you a little present.'

'Pay for another drink, Mr Henderson,' I said, suddenly remembering his name, 'and we'll call it quits.'

This he gladly did, but the open wallet remained on the counter like an invitation. He stared at it and said: 'It's not only my family. There are other considerations.'

'What are those?' I asked.

'The government runs a cowboy organization called the Inland Revenue.'

'Really?' I said. 'What do they do?'

'They take your money away.'

'Surely they don't send a notice of assessment to beggars?'

'They send them to anybody who makes money if they can find them. Whores, burglars, mobsters, racketeers. All they want is cash. They leave the law to the police.'

He looked genuinely aggrieved at this as if the world was being less than fair to him.

'Tell me something, Mr Henderson,' I said, 'seeing that you're in my debt. How much do you make from this begging game? Enough to travel first class, evidently.'

'Between you and me?' he asked.

I nodded.

'Around two hundred a day. That's the target I aim for.

157

Some days it takes longer than others. The weather's a factor. Some days I never reach it, other days I get more.'

I whistled in surprise. 'A tax-free thousand a week? Fifty grand a year?'

'That's it,' he said, nodding. 'Hence my concern about the Revenue.'

'And you never were in the Foreign Office.'

'Oh, I was. I'm an Arabist. But our influence in the Gulf isn't what it was and they cut staff and gave me early retirement. That was ten years ago and I've made more money since than I ever did then. Begging is an Arabic talent.'

The connection had not occurred to me and suddenly it all made sense. 'And your family never knew about this change of career?'

'They thought I'd been promoted. There was more money about and I started work later. I have my pension, too, you see.'

He stood up and finished his drink. I had the impression that he felt he had been talking too much. 'I have to go,' he said. 'We're going out to dinner. I throw myself on your mercy, Mr Hadfield, but if there is ever anything I can do for you, only ask.'

At the door he passed Alec who was looking just as sombre as I had expected. Not as sombre as I was, though.

I was now poorer than a beggar.

I have never pretended that I understand women. Their behaviour and reactions have baffled me for two decades. But when Annette sank into Bunyan's Slough of Despond I felt able to have a couple of guesses about what was troubling her. Oddly, the pregnancy wasn't one of them; she was cruising through that like a lady born to breed.

The first thing that was upsetting her was Garth's departure. The second, looming like Father Time with his scythe, was her fortieth birthday.

'Let's go away for a couple of days,' I said. 'Have your birthday in Cornwall.'

For once I seemed to have come up with the right answer.

'That would be lovely, Max,' she said.

I made a few phone calls to my underworked staff and another to a grand hotel that we knew in Cornwall. Well before lunch we were on the road.

Driving to Cornwall used to be a journey of great visual pleasure. It took six hours or so, but you were continually passing through or stopping at attractive places that made you envy the locals: Shaftesbury, Sherborne, Chard, Honiton, Launceston, Bodmin and Redruth. And on the way you climbed through the red hills of Devon and saw views that belonged on picture postcards.

That's all changed today. You join a motorway not far from your front door and the next thing you know you're at Land's End. You've saved a lot of hours, but what have you missed?

We left the main highway after only a three-hour drive, and headed down country lanes to the south coast. There, surrounded by hundreds of blue hydrangeas the size of party balloons, was the Carlyon Bay Hotel which the Hadfield family knew was the best in Cornwall.

It was a huge, grey, ivy-covered building that stood in flower-filled grounds a few yards up a hill from a long sandy beach. It had two pools, indoor and outdoor, two tennis courts and its own golf course. The rooms were wonderful.

By the time we went down to the bar that evening for what my extravagant wife referred to as an aperitif and I, more commonly, called a pre-nosh snort, she had cheered up enormously and I knew that this was money well spent. We sat in comfortable armchairs with our drinks and looked out at the evening sun on St Austell Bay.

A couple befriended us at this point, always an ominous development. If they were boring each other, what were they going to do to us? They took the other two chairs at our table and asked if we were here for long. She was a rather attractive brunette in her mid-thirties; he was a mournful-looking chap a few years older. She talked, he listened. I

159

think that people talk too much socially because they think that others expect them to, but if they shut their teeth and tried to look vaguely attractive that would be quite enough effort on their part for me. Anyway, she went on for some time about the days in the eighteenth century when smuggling was a minor Cornish industry. She had just returned from Jamaica Inn which had been a centre for this sort of thing and wanted to tell us about it. Her husband sat picking his teeth with a distant expression on his face and I thought that if she had ever fancied him, I could never fancy her.

Suddenly he leaned across to me and, speaking over his wife, asked: 'Have you ever been to Docklands?'

'A strange shift in the conversation,' I said. 'Have you ever read Virgil?'

He looked at me, utterly confused, and it was no consolation to him that I regarded it as my wittiest riposte for a long time. Even Annette, no great fan of my unkind humour, began to giggle.

I took this to mean that she was still in a good mood and suggested that we go to eat. We left our lonely couple to their smuggling memories or, more likely, a prolonged silence, and swept into the dining room.

We had stayed in this hotel eight or nine years earlier and had fond memories of the place. Then, as now, the idea had been to cheer Annette up, an objective which the friendly staff and lovely surroundings had achieved without a hitch. Annette's parents had been killed in a gliding accident in Christchurch, New Zealand, and finding herself an orphan at thirty-two had temporarily knocked the shine off her.

My own father had died at about the same time, his final terminal illness being regarded by him as a triumphant vindication of his lifelong pessimism. We took my mother (who has since died) and had a splendid time drinking cocktails round the pool. Only Garth was bored. Like a lot of ten-year-olds, he sat around not saying very much and you wondered what revenge he was planning for when he was old enough to take it.

160

It was Garth who occupied Annette's mind over dinner. 'We all used to think that we were wonderful parents with wonderful kids and now look what's happened to Helen and Steven.'

'It hasn't happened to Garth,' I said. 'He's working hard for a living.'

'Doing what, I'd like to know? Why can't he get a proper job?'

To Annette a proper job was one in which you wore a tie and suit and were marooned in somebody else's premises for eight hours a day, five days a week.

'He doesn't want the dribble, dribble of the weekly wage,' I said. 'He sincerely wants to be rich.'

'That's another thing,' said Annette. 'This obsession with money. I can remember when money meant nothing to him.'

'Then he grew up. I was always fairly partial to loot myself.'

'He talked about money at the Waterside as if it was a woman or a drug or something. It turned him on.'

'It happens to young men of nineteen,' I said. 'They suddenly realize that it's the only thing that stands between them and everything they want.'

'No, Max,' said Annette. 'It was an end in itself. He doesn't want anything. Only money.'

There was a noise outside and we saw that a helicopter had landed on the hotel lawn. A naval pilot climbed out.

'It's hit a bird,' the waiter explained. 'It happens all the time.'

Annette demolished a trifle and said: 'I hope we can still afford this sort of thing.'

She looked particularly attractive tonight in a maroon silk dress she had acquired from somewhere. It went well with the hair that had received at least two hours' attention in a local salon. Not for her the unwashed hair of a complacent wife. If she hadn't been seven months pregnant we would have been rolling around on the floor.

161

'You're married to an economic basket case, dear,' I said. 'I'll end up making widgets.'

'However, you still have credit cards.'

'Several,' I said.

Schmaltzy music greeted us in the lounge afterwards; there were people dancing and for a while we joined them. But Annette tired quickly and we sat down and ordered coffee.

'We could always economize,' she said. 'My mother used to darn holes in socks. Now we just throw them away.'

'It'll take more than you darning my socks to save us from the consequences of this recession,' I said. But I was so touched by her offer that the following morning, her birthday, I drove her to Truro – through Cornish villages with strange names like Grampound and Probus – and bought her a Chanel shoulder bag in quilted leather with a chain strap.

Annette squealed with delight, but my credit card groaned.

11

A testing time

The human mind has an infinite capacity for avoiding the truth, and my own had remained happily shut off from the subject of Annette's pregnancy: the reality was growing in front of me but my brain managed to shun the issue for weeks at a time.

One morning in July I was studying the London telephone directory in search of the number of a customer called Morton, who was showing a marked reluctance to settle his account, when the name Doctor Rebecca Mortimer jumped out at me from the page and, without pausing to think, I rang her.

'My name is Max Hadfield,' I said. 'A couple of years ago you did a vasectomy on me.'

'Oh, yes?' she said.

'I wondered if I could come and talk to you.'

There was a pause at the other end of the line and I heard papers being shuffled. 'I could fit you in at three this afternoon.'

This was obviously not the quick chat that I had intended but a professional consultation that was followed by a bill.

'I'll be there,' I said.

She had evidently come on a bit since she assaulted me with a scalpel because she now lived in a large house in Ladbroke Grove that had three floors above ground and one below. There was money in mutilating men.

She opened the door herself.

'Ah, yes. I remember you,' she said, smiling.

'You never forget a –' I couldn't bring myself to finish the sentence, and followed her into a rambling house where the furniture mixed rustic with antique and one room led on to another seemingly for ever. Eventually we reached one that was used as an office, and she sat me in an armchair and herself in a prim upright job on the other side of an antique desk.

'How can I help you?' she asked. Her round, friendly face had aged a little and now she seemed nearer forty than thirty-five. 'Has the snip been causing you any trouble?'

'Only in one respect,' I told her.

'And what's that?'

'My wife,' I said, 'is pregnant.'

I thought this would knock her for a loop but doctors seem to be incapable of surprise. She turned to a screen, an incongruous modern invasion beside her antique desk, and began to read whatever was on it.

'I have your details here. You provided us with the necessary samples afterwards. The operation was a complete success.'

'Which leaves the question of my wife.'

She pressed a key which evidently blanked the screen and turned back to me. 'They say there's one chance in a thousand but I've never encountered one and I do two thousand a year.'

'Two thousand?' I said. It sounded a lot.

'It's only eight a day. We're not even very successful when the odd customer comes back and asks for it to be reversed. Of course they're conducting trials on a new technique now in China.'

'A bit late, I'd have thought, for China to start worrying about vasectomies.'

'I'm talking about reversing them. They inject the sperm ducts with liquid silicone rubber which hardens into a plug. The plug is easily removed through a puncture in the skin that doesn't even require a stitch. Fertility returns within a month.'

'Yes, well,' I said, implying that fascinating though this no doubt was, it had little relevance to my predicament.

'Is it possible,' said Doctor Mortimer, looking slightly uncomfortable, 'that the father-to-be is someone else?'

'The thought flits across one's mind,' I conceded.

'And how would you view that?'

'I wouldn't be all that delighted.'

'No, of course. Well what I suggest is that you provide us with another up-to-date sample so that we can see if there had been any leakage.'

I considered this request with a sinking heart as she handed me a bottle. 'The trouble is that my wife won't make love now that she's seven months pregnant.'

'Masturbate into a condom,' said Doctor Mortimer briskly. 'You can do it here, if you like. We have a small room with the appropriate literature.'

'Literature?'

'*Playboy*. That sort of thing.'

'A topless nurse might do it,' I said, not entirely light-heartedly, but this was clearly not part of Doctor Rebecca Mortimer's service.

'I've known some go to Soho,' she said as I stood up. 'It always seemed an unnecessary expense to me.'

I had reached the door when she said suddenly: 'So you decided on a second marriage?'

'Pardon?' I said, turning.

'The screen said you were divorced with five children.'

'Ah, yes,' I said, retreating from the room.

A liar needs a good memory.

'To make love to a man who not only has had a vasectomy, but is also wearing a condom, lifts sensible precaution to the realms of paranoia,' said Sadie Beck. 'Are you sure we shouldn't be in separate rooms, just to be on the safe side.'

'We don't want your soaring career to crash-land in the nursery,' I said, running my hand up the outside of her naked leg. 'A tasty career girl can't be too careful.'

She was lying naked on the pink duvet in her bedroom with its fragrance of flowers. One awkward phone call had delivered us to this enchanted rendezvous. She had taken the call at TVC with considerable aplomb.

'You said if I want you I only have to ring,' I said.

'Yes, sir, I remember that,' said her husky voice, and I realized that she was not alone.

'I have a problem and I thought how nice it would be if you could help.'

'I would like to think that I could. What's the nature of the problem?'

'I have to provide a sperm sample to make sure my vasectomy is still sound.'

'I think I follow you, sir,' she said.

'You can't just shoot off into the air and catch it in a cup.'

'Indeed not. That would be quite the wrong approach.'

'You need a condom which ideally requires a partner.'

'We're talking about controlled emissions?'

'Emission control? Isn't that part of the American space programme?'

'The space programme. I'm glad you mentioned that, sir,' she said. 'We're talking logistics and receptacles here, I think. I'd like to help.'

'When do you think blast-off could take place?'

'Thursday, twenty-one hundred hours?'

'Strawberry Hill?'

'Yes, sir. Thanks for ringing.'

She hung up. It turned out that the call had found her in the office of the head of the channel, a man in whose company rising stars did not make romantic dates on the office phone if they wanted to be taken seriously.

But now, in the privacy of her flat, she was a different person.

'How many condoms did you bring?' she asked. 'Roughly.' Her blue eyes sparkled.

'Just the one.'

'Meanie.'

'We only have to use a condom once. The other times –'

166

'I thought the efficiency of the vasectomy was in question?'

'Yes – my wife's pregnant.'

'Well, that's not the sort of thing to inspire confidence in a single girl.'

'My suspicion,' I said, 'is that there is a man.'

'I hope so,' said Sadie. 'Unless this is the Second Coming.'

'I mean some man other than this man.'

'This story gets better and better,' she said, pulling me down to her. 'I thought your marriage was rock solid.'

'Talking about rock solid,' I said, 'where did I put the condom?'

The condom was not a device that I was overly familiar with; by the time I had reached an age to enjoy the games that people play, bright young girls were taking the Pill. But now that the health risks had made sexual intercourse slightly more dangerous than mountaineering, and girls, anyway, were becoming wary of the Pill, the huge displays of differing condoms hit you in the eye directly you walked into a chemist's.

'I know what you're going to say,' said Sadie. '"How do you put these things on?"'

'How do you put these things on?' I asked.

'You roll them like this.'

'Look,' I said. 'It's just my size.'

'I suppose you got the girl to measure you in the shop?'

We made love then and the inhibiting effect of the condom seemed to prolong it. My climax was delayed by the cooling grasp of my rubber overcoat, a disincentive that did not affect my eager partner who went from one orgasm to another with a fervour that I thought might damage her health. When I finally reached my objective we lay there for some time hardly able to talk.

'I never realized a clinical project could be such fun,' she murmured eventually. 'Anyone else want a sample?'

'Mmm,' I said.

'Why don't you join a sperm bank? It's one bank you could be in credit at, and making the deposits would be so enjoyable.'

167

'Customers with a vasectomy aren't what they want.'

'I wasn't really thinking of them,' said Sadie, swinging her legs to the floor. She put on a white housecoat and stood up. Her wide eyes gazed down at me.

'Drink, sir?'

'I'd love a coffee,' I said.

We went into her spotless kitchen.

'The trouble with condoms is that you don't feel it trickling down your legs afterwards,' she said.

'That's an important aspect of it, is it?'

'Oh, absolutely.'

When she had made the coffee we sat on tall stools in the kitchen and held hands.

'Tell me about your wife, Max,' she said.

'She's pregnant.'

'And this came as a surprise?'

'Just a bit,' I said.

'I can't wait to hear the results from the lab.'

I leaned across and kissed her. 'I'm pretty curious myself,' I told her.

Ten minutes later I went out into the warm summer evening and drove my pleasurably acquired consignment to Ladbroke Grove.

The following morning I had a phone call from Mr Fleming.

'It's about your house, Mr Hadfield,' he said.

'My house?' I said, temporarily nonplussed. Calls from Mr Fleming were unwelcome at any time, but if they settled on the subject on my house they induced feelings not far removed from panic.

'You are pledging it against our various arrangements,' he said.

'Yes, I remember,' I told him. 'So what's new?'

'I want to get it valued. It's written in here at eight hundred thousand pounds which I think was a figure you mentioned, but you can't give houses away at the moment. A more up-to-date assessment is needed for our books.'

A slight chill came over me at this. You pledged your house and received a loan, and then you repaid the loan and everyone forgot about your house.. For a bank to start demanding updated valuations produced a picture in my mind of circling creditors and escape routes closing.

'It must be at least half a million,' I said, 'but it will go up again. Today's figure is irrelevant, because no one in their right mind would sell a house now.'

'Nevertheless we need a realistic valuation to keep our books tidy,' said Mr Fleming. 'We can always shift it upwards if things improve.'

'I hope you're not planning to sell my house, Mr Fleming,' I said. 'I keep all my stuff here.'

'I hope not, Mr Hadfield. I earnestly hope not. Now when can I send a valuer round? That's why I'm ringing.'

'When would you like to send one?' I asked. 'I'll make sure I'm here.'

'Tomorrow morning? Eleven?'

'Fine,' I said, and replaced the phone.

'Who was it?' Annette asked.

'A bird of prey. It's amazing what they can train birds to do these days.'

A few days later I drove up to Ladbroke Grove. The recession was now hitting London's traffic and I cruised along Goldhawk Road and Holland Park Avenue without the usual halts and jams. Empty taxis glided about; I had read that their drivers were now getting an average of only one fare an hour.

Doctor Rebecca Mortimer was engaged when I arrived slightly early, and I was admitted by a young nurse with buck-teeth who showed me into a small room littered with magazines. I shuffled through them in search of *Playboy* but it was presumably doing duty in a room that served a different purpose.

When I was ushered into the doctor's presence, she was holding a report.

169

'They've checked your sample, Mr Hadfield,' she said, 'and I'm afraid you're definitely sterile.'

'Afraid?'

'Well, normally it would be an occasion for me to congratulate myself, but if your wife is pregnant I can see that the news creates difficulties.'

I sat down. 'Is this absolutely definite?' I asked. 'I mean, can I be sure –'

She laid the report on her desk. 'It's definite as of now. I suppose there's an outside chance six months ago or whenever it was that something got through, but it's a lot less than one in a thousand. More like one in a million.'

'Right,' I said.

She looked at me. 'What do you propose to do?'

'I don't know,' I replied, shaking my head.

She leaned forward and laid both hands on her desk. 'My advice, given that million to one chance, would be not to make a song and dance about it now. Why don't you wait until the child is born and then arrange a blood test?'

On Saturday evening of that week I was driven in Kitty Benson's Vauxhall Viva to a dreary town hall where discoloured cream paint peeled from the walls and the windows were badly in need of sponge and water. At one end there was a stage but in the middle of the hall about forty people sat at trestle tables counting votes.

It had been polling day in the election for a county councillor and I had spent much of it with Kitty knocking on doors and suggesting to the astonished inhabitants that the quality of their lives would be improved if they toddled along to their local polling station and cast a vote on behalf of Mrs K. Benson.

It was a bad year to be doing it. Public opinion, that ever-fluctuating morass, was increasingly lining up behind the idea that all politicians belonged to the walking wounded, the seriously demented or the certifiably loopy, and that anybody who had anything to do with them was exposing their equanimity to serious risk.

170

Most treated me as if I had escaped from somewhere. Others grabbed the opportunity for a little doorstep altercation. A gangling youth with waxy face and drooping moustache told me: 'Lenin said that democracy was subjecting the minority to the majority.'

'Whereas he wanted it the other way round,' I said. 'What a turd.'

An old lady, who seemed glad to have a visitor, asked: 'What does she stand for?'

'Well,' I said, having very little idea, 'she doesn't stand for any nonsense.' And I pushed some leaflets into her hand and hurried away.

It was a by-election, the incumbent Tory having forestalled a terminal illness by consuming a pint of carbolic acid after leaving a note which said: 'There are no Socialists where I'm going.' There was a lot of correspondence in the local papers about this afterwards from people who were infuriated by his cryptic farewell. He could hardly have imagined that Jesus was a Conservative. Perhaps he meant that he was going to hell? The argument rumbled on for weeks.

When we arrived at the town hall to see who would replace him, our driver was the outsider, Mrs Benson herself, who had packed husband, son and unpaid help into her small car because it was covered with all the right stickers. Her simple platform of environment, pollution and conservation would not have sat easily with my gas-guzzling Rover.

She proved to be an assertive parker, edging out the Mayor's Jaguar in a race for the last space in front of the town hall. We climbed out and went in.

Votes were still arriving from distant village halls where officials had sat all day watching democracy in action. When the boxes were unlocked and emptied on to the trestle tables it became clear that nobody had been injured in the rush as the British public exercised its right to choose the people whose decisions would sour their lives. From one box fewer than thirty votes fluttered out.

I was glad to see Steven come with us, much as I disliked

171

him. I thought that it was an encouraging sign that he was showing some interest in his mother's brave sortie into local politics. Not that his appearance would have won her any votes, but the polling booths were closed now. Beneath torn jeans he wore the large white shoes that all youngsters seemed to wear today. They looked like boats.

'Is she going to win?' I asked him, to make conversation.

'Now I've seen the others I think she might,' he said, feeling obliged in the presence of his father to be civil.

'She'd make a good councillor,' I said.

'Are you sure?' said Alec. 'I think she'd blow the rates on an institute for destitute prostitutes and call it compassion.'

'And then she'd cut the defence bill by covering everybody with woad and hoping it frightens the foreigners away,' Steven suggested.

'I don't think county councils handle the defence bill,' I said.

Kitty had drifted away to chat to her opponents in this largely ignored battle. The Tory candidate, a smooth thirty-year-old with greased hair and the eyes of an assassin, had the relaxed air of a man who had generously agreed to go through this ludicrous charade before taking his rightful place on the county council. The Labour candidate, a bearded polytechnic lecturer, looked as if he were several cards short of a deck, and the Liberal or Social Democrat, or whatever the centre party were calling themselves this week, was a small, humble little man who looked as if he was waiting for instructions from his wife who stood beside him in an ankle-length burnouse.

Confronted by this opposition, I began to wonder whether Steven was right and whether a discerning public might not prefer a transparently good woman like Kitty Benson to this grisly trio of morons on the make.

I went over to her.

'It's looking good,' she whispered. 'Watch the piles over there.'

I looked at where the votes were ending up in four piles.

'Which one is yours?' I asked.

'The nearest one. You can see they thought I'd come fourth.'

The nearest pile was slightly higher than any of the others, a fact which had now caught the attention of the Tory candidate who was staring at the piles of votes with knitted brows.

'If only Oliver were here. He'd love this,' said Kitty. 'I don't know why he went back to Africa.'

'He's African,' I said. 'Could have something to do with it.'

But she was in a nostalgic mood and would have liked him to be here for her triumph. 'I remember him telling me how they had to get their water from a dam when he was a child. It had living things in it and they had to sieve it through their clothes.'

'We'll be doing that in the Thames valley soon,' I said.

'Not if I get on the council we won't.'

She was wearing her white trouser suit on which was pinned her green home-made rosette, and she had paid a rare visit to the hairdresser's. A reporter came over to her, a tall young man with a lot of prematurely grey hair.

'They seem to think back there that you might sneak this,' he said. 'Can you give me a few biographical details, Mrs Benson?'

'Sneak it?' said Kitty. 'I hope that's not the way you're going to describe it in your newspaper?'

'Earth-first Kitty shatters the Tories?' said the reporter.

'That's better, young man.'

I left Kitty to handle her first press interview and joined Alec and Steven who were now sitting down at the side of the hall.

'We might be on the verge of a sensation,' I told them enthusiastically, but neither seemed very interested.

'It's a protest about interest rates,' Steven said. 'What the hell do the people who live round here care for pandas and pollution?'

'It looks as if they do,' I said, disappointed at their reaction.

173

'Trouble is, I can't get interested in politics,' Alec said. 'Series of five-minute wonders, and all forgotten in a day or two. The plight of the Kurds, the aspirations of Montenegro, the rolling bandwagon of Hindu fundamentalism, the daily explosions in Belfast or Beirut . . .'

'But this election concerns you,' I said. 'It's about schools and hospitals and street lighting and roads and new supermarkets and lovely old town centres that suddenly disappear to be replaced by something hideous.'

'It's about me coming home to dinner and finding that my wife's at some committee meeting,' he said.

There was a perceptible shift in the mood in the hall now, and looking across I saw that the vote counters had stopped work. They sat back, their jobs done, and turned their seats so that they were facing the stage.

At the centre of it stood the returning officer who was waiting for the candidates to join him. The Tory, looking a lot less haughty than an hour ago, was first up the steps. He took his place beside the returning officer and waved in a subdued fashion to a yelping bunch of Young Conservatives. The bearded Socialist, thwarted in his gormless quest for public office, looked as if he wondered where the late councillor had bought his carbolic acid. The third man looked, as he had all along, as if he wondered what was going on.

Kitty, detained by the press, was the last to climb the steps and was obviously surprised by the cheer that she received. She was waved into line by the returning officer, impatient to impart his news. The results were announced alphabetically, and the Tory, who was called Acheson, had obtained 3607 votes, an amount which temporarily convinced a group of purblind loyalists that he had won. Their cheers died on the smoky air as the news quickly followed that Benson, Kitty, had collected 4240 votes. There were 701 for the Labour candidate and the Liberal Democrat (as they were apparently now known) had received 1560.

It took a moment for the size of this upset to sink in. This was not the result that people had come here to hear. But once the news had been absorbed, or confirmed by those nearest, tremendous applause and shouts filled the hall. It looked to me as if Labour and Liberal Democrat supporters were joining in this demonstration of joy, moved more by the defeat of the hated Tory than by Kitty's remarkable success.

She came down the steps looking dazed, a disorientation not helped by the flashguns of the photographers. One of them wanted a picture of her kissing her husband and I could see Alec warming to the idea of his wife's political career.

'That was mega, Mum,' said Steven. 'Totally fantastic.'

'Thank you, darling,' said Kitty. 'I'm sure you'll be a great help with all the work that this is going to bring.'

Steven nodded doubtfully at this and I could see that the little four-letter word had upset him.

'Thank you, Max,' said Kitty, 'my loyal supporter and unpaid campaign manager.'

'Is that what I was?' I asked. 'You look knackered.'

'Let's go and get a drink,' said Alec. 'This needs celebrating.'

'You can drink a toast to me in orange juice,' said Kitty, turning to wave to the people who were still cheering her from the public gallery. 'You're right, Max. I'm worn out. What I need now is our holiday in France.'

12

A desertion in France

Judy Curtis sat in the stern of the channel ferry *Pride of Le Havre* with a look in her eye that did not bode well. She sipped nervously at a cup of coffee and stared at the foam track of the boat which seemed to stretch like a motorway all the way back to England.

'Frenchmen are different, Max,' she said. 'They appreciate women. To them the act of love is an art.'

We had left the others upstairs in the observation lounge where passengers could sprawl on comfortable seats and read or sleep. I wanted to walk round and look at the ship: six hours on a channel ferry was a prospect of terrifying boredom. Judy was restless for quite different reasons, and after a gin at the bar, a walk on the deck and a tour of the duty free shop, she was talking to me about sex.

'I know very little about the French,' I said. 'France is a place that I usually fly over.'

'I suppose you think it's all Gauloise and garlic with men in funny berets carrying strings of onions round their necks?'

'And it isn't?'

'The Frenchman is the most civilized man in Europe,' said Judy Curtis firmly. 'You only have to look at the clothes they design, the food that they cook, the art and the architecture.'

I drank my coffee and looked at her. 'Why this panegyric about the froggie?' I asked.

'I'm in love with one,' she replied promptly.

I put my cup down. 'You're what?'

'Didn't you wonder why I encouraged Laurie to buy a place there? Didn't it surprise you?'

'It did,' I admitted.

'I went on the first trip for something to do. But then I met Jean-Paul. You must keep quiet about it. Laurie doesn't know.'

'And Jean-Paul? Is he in love with you?'

'I believe he is.'

I sat there in mute amazement. Frenchmen, with their mysterious talents for *boules*, ballads and sexual intercourse, became an even more impenetrable species if among their number was a masochistic stud who was seriously contemplating a romantic entwinement with Judy the bruiser.

'Blimey,' I said eventually.

She looked at me coldly. 'You find it surprising that he would fancy me?'

'Not at all,' I said quickly. 'I was thinking of Laurie.'

'That's something I never do,' said Judy, finishing her coffee. 'I worry about Helen – at least I did until she turned her back on us. But Laurie? People like that don't deserve thinking about.'

The Curtises and the Bensons had effectively dumped their troublesome teenagers, plus one dog, and all four seemed both proud and relieved at the achievement. Helen had gone to stay with an aunt and uncle in the Cotswolds, and Steven was camping with friends a few miles up the Thames. But now it was beginning to sound as if Judy would not be there to welcome Helen home.

'What are you going to do,' I asked, 'about Jean-Paul?'

'That,' she said, putting her cup on the table, 'is up to Jean-Paul.'

I wanted to ask her what he did for a living and how they had met but she was ready to move. When she stood up and looked down at me it was like a vulture rising on a thermal. I hoped Jean-Paul could handle himself.

'We should join the others,' she said. 'I wanted you to know this now because you're going to know it soon anyway.'

'I wish I knew what you have in mind,' I said, but she was already threading her way through the ferry's human cargo, teenagers lying on the floor with cans of Coke, babies in pushchairs, weary men carrying mugs of beer and women studying road maps of France.

Upstairs my wife was reading a travel book about Normandy, Kitty Benson was looking at some council documents, and both Alec and Laurie were noisily asleep. We had risen at six to catch this 8.30 ferry and my Rover had chased Laurie's Shogun all the way to Portsmouth through rain which only stopped when the *Pride of Le Havre* edged its way out of the harbour.

I sat next to Kitty. 'You're on holiday, councillor,' I said. 'Put those papers away and relax. Follow the excellent example of your husband.'

She lowered her papers and glanced at Alec. 'He seems to have gone from premature ejaculation to premature senility without any intervening period of masculine normality.'

Annette laughed. 'That's telling them, Kitty. Thank God I voted for you.'

'Debates in the council chamber are about to reach a new level of interest,' I said. 'Remind me to attend.'

'Shall we wake these bastards up and have lunch?' she asked.

It took no more than a quarter of an hour to get our little party up and moving. We descended precipitous steps and made our way to the restaurant where a buffet lunch was being served. Sitting here and drinking wine made the tedium of the crossing seem bearable.

'You're going to love France,' said Laurie, now assuming the role of host. He had at last forsaken his brown suit, and was wearing light blue slacks, a white shirt and a black sweater. 'They wash their bums in the duvet, you know.'

'Bidet,' said Judy.

178

'Whatever.'

'It's a long time since Alec and I went abroad, isn't it dear?' Kitty said.

Alec nodded. 'Greece, wasn't it?'

'My God, that awful taverna,' said Kitty, laughing. 'They took us upstairs to show us the rooms in the hope that we would stay there. The first door they opened there was a drunk asleep on the floor. "Wrong room," said the man. Then he opened the door of another room and there was a naked couple making love.'

'Did you learn anything?' I asked.

'Well,' said Kitty, looking at her husband, 'I noticed the man was on top.'

We all laughed at this except Alec who stared frostily at his egg mayonnaise.

We were in mid-channel now and people were lurching around with plates of food. This was the posh restaurant with tablecloths and serviettes and I wondered who we were travelling with. There was a tatty cafeteria next door where backpacked youths queued for chips, but in here the customers could include almost anybody. After all, if you were taking the Roller to the south of France how else could you get there?

Marooned in this floating diner, I could only wonder why I was here myself. This was not my sort of holiday at all. When the chance came for escape I wanted to stroll in shirt sleeves with the sun on my face and a sky that stayed eternally blue.

I'd had my fill of English resorts in my younger days when money was not plentiful, and I had seen more than enough of their tawdry attractions: pebble beaches that broke your feet, windbreakers to keep out the wind, umbrellas to keep out the rain, and poorly stocked snack bars that were usually closed and invariably dirty. Tacky Torquay, poxy Weymouth, bloody Bognor. Bingo and chips. No style, sun, grace or charm. They didn't even reflect England. When I chose a holiday now I rejected any destination north of the 40th

179

parallel which cuts into Europe in the middle of Portugal, misses Madrid, bisects Sardinia, and clips the toe off Italy before separating Greece from Albania.

But today, almost without thinking about it, I was being transported to a coast that was no further away than Manchester. The clouds would be just as low; only the prices would be high.

Eventually I remembered how I came to be included in this expedition: pregnant Annette wouldn't fly, and we both shared a mild curiosity about Laurie's *Maison Normande*. I resolved that if the heavens were going to pour liquid on my head, I would pour much more down my throat.

It would be hyperbolical to describe Laurie's house in France as having the appeal of a condemned bus shelter, but it is in that direction that you looked for the words that would do it justice. It was like him to have found the most expensive place on the north coast of France and then bought a shack. On the one hand it looked as if it might fall over; on the other, it had been there so long that there was no reason to expect it to collapse now.

It seemed to be a bungalow, but rickety wooden steps at one end led to a first-floor door as if the two floors were not internally connected. The bottom yard of it was stone, but above that were the timbers which we came to see were an intrinsic part of the Normandy builder's craft.

The journey from Le Havre had taken less than an hour. Once we were out of the port the roads were mercifully empty and the only hold-up had been at the huge suspension bridge at Tancarville where we had to pay a pound to cross the mouth of the Seine and head west. The weather was predictable: roses may have been blooming in Picardy next door, but here in Normandy the rain was coming down like *les stair-rods*.

I can't pretend that the sight of Laurie's continental investment did much to lift the prevailing gloom.

'Is that it?' Annette asked when we got out of the car and,

to be sure, my initial thought was that this was some sort of out-house, servicing the needs of the main building that was not yet in view.

'Wonderful, isn't it?' said Laurie. 'A steal at three hundred and forty-five thousand francs. You make your profit when you buy.'

The idea that the channel tunnel bestowed on this shanty the status of an investment struck me as particularly optimistic even if it had cost only £35,000, but I didn't say anything. We followed him indoors.

There were two rooms downstairs, a living room that was sparsely furnished, and a kitchen, and two small bedrooms upstairs. A tiny bathroom had been built on at ground-floor level at the back. There was one toilet.

It was difficult to see how Laurie was going to play the munificent host against this backdrop; when he was at home he felt his hospitality had been exposed as deficient and his reputation for generosity damaged if guests didn't leave his home on all fours.

We carried our luggage in and Annette flashed me a look which said that this was a highly unsuitable destination for her Louis Vuitton suitcases. I pretended to miss it, feeling a surge of embarrassment at our situation. I could hardly tell Laurie, now that we had got here, that his pride and joy was not good enough for us.

The Hadfields and the Bensons were allotted the two small bedrooms upstairs. Laurie said that he and his wife could make up a bed in the living room downstairs. Judy Curtis took this news with the genial equability of someone who had other plans.

Upstairs Annette tried to arrange her extensive wardrobe in what looked like a broom cupboard.

'Where are we, anyway?' she asked, picking up a map.

'Place called Beuzeville.'

'It makes you wonder what third world countries are like.'

'What can we do?' I asked. 'You can't hurt their feelings.'

'They don't seem to mind hurting mine.'

181

I had hoped to see a bit of France but when we went downstairs I gathered that everybody felt they had travelled enough for one day and Judy was preparing a salad that she had brought with her. Quantities of drink had been installed here on earlier visits and we had, anyway, all spent some credit card money in the ferry's duty free shop.

Soon we were all sitting round a white marble table that looked more Spanish than French, munching lettuce and quaffing *vins du pays*. Alec and Kitty obviously found the situation wonderfully exciting – one cheap trip and here they were in the real France on a free holiday.

'*Voulez-vous prendre un verre?*' Alec asked, waving a bottle in front of Laurie.

'Don't start that old caper,' said our host. '*Je suis anglais.*'

My own mood at this inaugural supper was one of darkest foreboding, and it was not helped by the occasional glance at my wife who, depressed by her surroundings and no longer able to drink like the rest of us, looked like someone who had an appointment with the guillotine before breakfast tomorrow. But as it turned out she had nothing to worry about.

We awoke next morning to bellows from below. I heard Laurie's voice shouting but I couldn't catch the words. I put on my dressing gown and went to the door

'What's up?' I called.

'The bitch has gone,' he shouted. 'She's left me.'

I went downstairs.

Laurie was holding a sheet of paper torn from a pad. I took it from him and read 'Goodbye'. As an epitaph on seventeen years of marriage it struck me as a trifle laconic but I could see that Judy's nocturnal exit would have been conducted at a speed which precluded literary composition.

'Where is she?' I asked stupidly. I hadn't really woken up from what, against all the odds, had been a very comfortable night's sleep.

'How the fuck do I know?' asked Laurie irritably. 'She's buggered off, hasn't she? The devious cow.'

Mr and Mrs Benson, disturbed by the noise, now arrived

downstairs wearing, respectively, some blue Marks and Spencer pyjamas and a full-length pink nightdress.

'What's going on?' asked Kitty sleepily.

'It's Judy,' I said. 'She's left.'

This was a much bigger surprise to them than it was to me; they hadn't had the benefit of a seminar on the ferry on the sexiness of the French male.

'Left?' said Alec.

'Right,' said Laurie, 'leaving a farewell note.'

'What did it say?' asked Kitty.

'Goodbye,' said Laurie.

'She's gone then,' said Alec.

'That seems to be the gist of it,' I said.

By the time we had all dressed and gathered at the marble table for a continental breakfast, each of us had had time to consider the significance of Judy's defection.

'There has to be a man,' Laurie said, serving coffee. 'She fancies Frenchmen. She's always raving about that singer Henri Leconte.'

'I think he's a tennis player,' I said.

'The bugger with the big nose.'

'De Gaulle?' said Alec. 'If he was a vocalist it was very much a second string to his bow.'

'Whoever,' said Laurie. 'She fancies the sods. She says they like women. Spend their lives slobbering over them. Probably why the Germans took Paris. Difficult to repel Jerry when you've got your leg over.'

This breathtaking insight into the recent bloodstained history of the world reduced us all to a thoughtful silence: French and Germans, each rampant in their own way.

'Had she met anyone?' I asked.

'Yeah, there was a barman we got to know. Nice chap. She was all over him.'

'What was his name?'

'Jean-Paul.' He rhymed 'Jean' with 'teen'.

I looked out of the window. All you could see were fields and trees. It wasn't raining but it was promising to.

'I just can't understand it,' said Kitty. 'Was she planning it, or was it a spur-of-the-moment thing? It seems so –'

'Devious,' said Laurie.

'And what about Helen?'

Laurie looked like a man who had suffered a severe personal catastrophe. The flesh around his eyebrows had sunk so that you could no longer see his eyelids. Today's crisis had obviously taken him by surprise.

'Do you know where this chap lives?' Alec asked.

'No idea. He didn't even work in the bar where we met him.' He looked up at us. 'I've been had over.'

We sat in silence for some time, trying to think of something to say that would comfort our host, but nothing sprang to four desperate minds. What emerged instead was the discovery that Annette's thoughts about Judy's disappearance had followed a rather different path to those of the rest of us.

Without any consultation with her spouse, she announced: 'We'll have to move into a hotel.'

'Oh?' I said.

'I can see the way it's going to be, Max,' she said. 'Kitty and me shopping, cooking, washing up. Well, that's not my idea of a holiday.'

There was a look of triumph in her eyes; she had seen her opportunity and grabbed it. I didn't blame her. Twelve hours in Laurie's foreign property had produced a yearning in me for a little comfort, not to mention attentive waiters, deep carpets and unlimited service just a phone call away. I looked at Laurie, to see how he was taking the suggestion. He had every reason for feeling hurt.

But he was nodding, and even looking relieved. Of course the disappearance of his wife would have meant that he alone shouldered the burden of keeping the guests happy.

Only Alec demurred. 'It's a question of cost,' he said frankly, but Laurie jumped in quickly to deal with this.

'As I'm supposed to be your host I'd be glad if you'd let me pick up the bill,' he said, and this time Alec did not demur.

184

After some communal washing up we all departed to our various quarters to pack. My wife's mood had changed completely and she quietly sang to herself as she retrieved her expensive dresses from the broom cupboard.

When the Bensons were ensconced in the back of the Rover, Annette called out to Laurie in the Shogun: 'Follow us!'

There was only one direction to take from here and Annette, my glamorous opponent of thrift and student of guide books, knew where it would bring us: Deauville – with its luxurious casino and its glittering shops, its races and its film festival. Deauville – the 21st arrondissement of Paris!

Annette was hell-bent on luxury now and the rest of us were dragged in her wake.

The Hôtel Normandy, with its bell-turrets, cob-walls and marble columns, was not like Laurie's place at all. It had three hundred rooms, three restaurants, two swimming pools and twenty-one tennis courts. It was the best hotel in Deauville, a fact which Annette pretended to be surprised by when she had guided us unerringly to its Norman courtyard.

Our journey, past a patchwork of fields and thousands of groaning apple trees that were striving to support the local production of Calvados, took less than half an hour. Deauville, with its clean, cobbled streets and beautiful shops, was a picturesque surprise. The Hôtel Normandy's ornate entrance faced the town, and its back faced the sea.

Our room was really four rooms if you counted the bathroom and the toilet. There was a living room with tables, desk, armchairs, television and fridge filled with drinks and, on the other side of some expensive pink curtains, the bedroom. Both had glittering chandeliers and the walls in both were in pink and white fabric which matched the curtains and the canopy over the bed.

'Better than Beuzeville,' said Annette, running a finger over the antique furniture.

'Beuzeville was free,' I reminded her.

185

'You can't stay in a place like this if you're going to worry about money,' I was told. 'You'll be carried out a gibbering wreck.'

I tried not to worry about money an hour later when I took the lift downstairs to look at the sumptuous premises. (My most recent bad news before leaving England had been that the bank had valued my house at only £450,000.) In the cocktail bar, a small dark panelled room in which the walls were enlivened by colourful paintings of the local horse racing, I paid sixty-four francs for two small bottles of beer, which was nearer seven pounds than six, and we were surrounded by encouragements to spend. In the lovely reception hall, which was full of blue marble columns, there were gold cabinets offering the wares of Chanel, Nina Ricci, Estée Lauder, Cartier and Ralph Lauren. I resolved to steer my wife past them.

That afternoon our depleted party took a walk along les Planches, the famous wooden promenade that ran along the top of the white sandy beach. If you believed the gossip columns this strange walkway was the very centre of fashionable weekends in Deauville, the spot where you would suddenly be confronted by a face you had only seen before in a film.

There may have been some of those but our preoccupation with the absent Mrs Curtis diminished our powers of observation.

'So bloody devious,' Laurie said. He seemed to have taken a liking to the word and he emphasized it by waving a colourful umbrella that he had wisely bought.

'Well, people *are* devious,' said Kitty. 'We all know that. When you see a tearful husband on television appealing for help in the search for his wife's killer, you know immediately that he is the man who buried the meat-axe in her neck.'

'Do you see how she illustrates a story that reflects badly on a woman with a story that reflects badly on a man?' Alec asked. 'Neat.'

But nobody was willing to explore this sidetrack.

'What happens if Judy returns to the house and finds it empty?' Annette asked.

'I hope she does,' said Laurie. 'I hope she has to hitchhike back to England.'

'No, you don't,' Kitty said. 'You must go back to the house and leave a note telling her where we are.'

Early that evening I left Annette soaking in the bath and went out for a stroll on my own, having arranged to meet the others for dinner. It was a pretty town. The four- and five-storey buildings with their brown timbers and white balconies looked like something out of Toytown. It was the cleanliness of the streets that struck you first if you came from England: the pavements weren't just swept but sprayed with high-pressure hoses which astonishingly didn't always shift the copious quantities of canine excrement which is such a feature of France. The centre of the town was the Place Morny where fountains splashed below half a dozen flags. A statue at one side seemed to be of Harold Macmillan, but the French didn't like us that much. It was the Duc de Morny, whoever he was.

I walked down the street to Le Drakkar bistrot and ordered a pint of beer. The man offered me English but I told him that I had come here to get away from that. The bistrot is one of those civilized institutions that the British are not quite ready for yet: a wonderful bar with comfortable stools all round in the middle of the room, and tables laid out beyond it for dinner. Alcohol meets food, a conjunction that we haven't made at home yet. Through the window I watched a party of Japanese tourists I was certain I had seen in Windsor. They wandered around not with a Pentax but with a video camera. Photo albums had no future in Tokyo.

It was a good place for people-watching. I had never seen so much kissing and hand-shaking in my life. The men kissed each other on the cheek and they all shook hands with the barman when they came in. The stylish French women all looked a bit confused as if somebody had been making love

187

to them for an unreasonable period of time, like a couple of days, and they were no longer sure what month it was. The French, I decided, were an affectionate race.

But the affection did not extend to me. I detected a distinct feeling of coolness towards the only Englishman in the bar, and found it difficult to understand why. I could see why quite a lot of other countries might dislike us – Germans, Spanish, Italians, a dozen newly named states in Africa – but the patent dislike of the French seemed unreasonable. We bought their wine, shared Concorde and let them play rugby with us. What more did they want?

We ate that evening in La Potinière, the hotel's *restaurant gastronomique*. By the time we arrived at the grand marnier soufflé we were all beginning to see Judy's disappearance as a fortunate development which had manifestly improved the quality of our holiday: at Beuzeville it would have been *tarte aux pommes*.

'I drove out to the house this evening,' Laurie told us when we had reached the coffee. 'She hasn't been back.'

'You left a note, I hope?' said Kitty.

'Just saying where we are,' Laurie said. 'She'd have a nerve to show up here now.'

'Nerve is what Judy's got,' said Kitty. 'Running off with a Frenchman? Your average English housewife wishes she had the guts.'

'You make deserting her family sound laudable,' Alec said.

'We only have one life,' said Kitty. 'And we have a duty to enjoy it. Do you argue with that?' She glared at her husband through her large spectacles; it was a look that defied contradiction.

'I've always put responsibility first myself,' he said. 'I suppose that sounds wimpish today. The new thing is to put yourself first.'

'Judy put responsibility first for sixteen years and what did it get her? Helen. We've done the same and produced Steven. All that sacrifice to produce a couple of rogues. I've finished with it. It's my turn now.'

'Oh come on, Kitty,' said Annette. 'That's a bit hard. All kids go off the rails once in their life.'

'Yours didn't,' Kitty said. 'Perhaps we should all have come round to you and Max for lessons. Judy took Helen's stealing very badly, you know. She felt she had wasted most of her adult life. I'm sure she'd be here now if it hadn't happened.'

'What did she say to you?' Laurie asked.

'She coined a rather good word, actually,' Kitty told him. 'She said she was beginning to think that she supported youthanasia. Killing teenagers.'

I wanted to speak up here and deliver my little speech about parents being to blame, but I didn't think it would contribute much to the total of human happiness in my immediate vicinity. I would have told them how I used to go to football matches with Garth on Saturdays, treat him as an equal, talk to him incessantly and imagine that I was opening his mind. At the same time I never put any pressure on him. My own parents had never been satisfied. If I got seventy-eight in an exam they asked why I hadn't got eighty. So I always said to Garth: 'You can do it.' And I left it there.

But I didn't deliver this speech and later, of course, I was glad that I had kept my mouth shut.

I was up first the following morning. I put on my dressing gown and went into the grey-tiled bathroom for a shower.

As I took my dressing gown off I became aware that unusually there was a sheet of paper in the pocket and I pulled it out. It said 'Goodbye', the valedictory bulletin from Judy the bruiser which I had evidently stuffed in my dressing gown twenty-four hours earlier. Looking at it in the bathroom's bright light I could see the outline of other words on the paper, words that had been written quite forcefully on the previous sheet in the pad. Holding it up to the light I read *Le Cheval Blanc, Quai des Passagers, Honfleur*.

My wife was sitting on the side of the bed when I came out – my wife, with her seductive smile, her dishonest eyes and her auburn chignon. (I think she's very attractive sexually. (The trouble is I am not the only one.))

'Seven months pregnant and you still look good for a tumble,' I said.

'Don't mention it,' she answered, standing up. 'Getting round all these expensive shops is going to be a real effort.'

'Why not skip that part of the holiday?'

'That *is* the holiday,' she said. 'Why are you holding a piece of paper?'

'Judy's at Honfleur. Look.'

She took the paper and studied it. 'Somebody must go and talk to her,' she said, 'but not me in my condition. Where's Honfleur, anyway?'

'It's around here somewhere,' I said.

Breakfast was served round the pool. It was a beautiful indoor pool with a vast glass roof that slid open on those rare occasions when the sun appeared over Normandy's genteel resorts and grand hotels. Mostly it was shut.

The others were already sitting at a table for six beside the pool. An old lady was swimming the length of it in her spectacles; the water didn't touch her chin.

'Why is it that the French who cook the best meals in the world can't boil an egg?' Kitty asked.

'Thanks for the tip,' I said and went over to the buffet to get myself some scrambled egg and ham. When we were sitting down I produced the sheet of paper.

'Honfleur?' said Laurie. 'That's where we met Jean-Paul.'

'I thought it might be,' I said. 'Annette thinks somebody should go and talk to her.'

'Well, she won't want to see me,' said Laurie.

I thought that Kitty might volunteer for this diplomatic mission but she held back. I think that secretly she admired what Judy had done. In the end it was decided that the peace delegation would consist of Alec and me.

'Be gentle with her,' said my wife who was picking her way through a pregnant woman's breakfast of cherries and cheese.

190

'I shall not only be gentle,' I said. 'I shall stand well back.'

'I shall be the interpreter,' said Alec, and we all laughed. His fondness for using French phrases in England had led us to believe that he would be in his element here but it hadn't turned out that way. Confronted by a language that he had only used in the unresponsive atmosphere of the classroom, he launched himself into extraordinary soliloquies and discovered to his chagrin that people who actually lived in France found him virtually incomprehensible.

'It's the accent,' he explained. 'People from Yorkshire can't understand the Cornish. I went to Glasgow once and couldn't make head nor tail of what they were on about.'

'I bought a French phrase book before we came,' said Kitty. 'God knows who'd use the phrases they suggested. We have lost our rucksacks. How long have you been like this? Get dressed again, please. I'd like to talk to the export manager. You're not going to understand the answers anyway.'

We spent a painfully expensive morning in Deauville's gleaming shops and after lunch Alec and I left for Honfleur. At his suggestion we went by bus. He thought it would be inadvisable to drive in case we drank, and a taxi would be too fast and too low for us to enjoy the scenery.

It was many years since I had been on a bus but I don't believe that public transport in England has anything to offer that would compare with the luxurious French experience. I half expected them to offer food and show a film. We sat back in comfortable, adjustable seats and peered round clean curtains at narrow country lanes that were barely wide enough to take a van.

Honfleur was half an hour up the coast towards Le Havre, and this was the scenic route. At Villerville we looked at old buildings that belonged to a village that had been hidden in the hills for centuries. Their steeply slanting roofs correctly told of incessant rain.

'There's a lot of bloody churches in France,' said Alec, taking a headmasterly interest in the local culture. I was more concerned about the reception awaiting us in Honfleur.

191

We arrived to discover that it was a beautiful port in which most of the buildings overlooked sea water in harbours and basins despite the fact that from the town you couldn't actually see the sea. It had trickled in somewhere and created an inward-facing port that had been in business for six hundred years. Normans had set off from here to colonize the others long before Britain went into the empire-building business; one of them founded Quebec in 1608.

Grey eight-storey buildings crowded the edge of the *vieux bassin* that was surrounded by lights and flags. The water was covered by white pleasure boats and the old buildings around it were all at ground level either restaurants or art galleries.

We walked beneath screeching gulls along a cobbled quay and eventually found the Hôtel du Cheval Blanc which had a stone picture of a white horse on its facade to help me with the translation.

'This seems to be the place,' I said as we approached. 'Cheval blanc means white horse.'

'I know that, Max,' said Alec sniffily. 'Well, three rounds with Judy the bruiser and we'll be off.' It was obvious that he did not relish the prospect of this part of our trip.

'It's a pretty place though,' I said.

'The grey buildings and the grey sky make it a little gloomy for my taste.'

Next to the Cheval Blanc is a brasserie and bar called the Café de Paris and glancing in I saw Judy Curtis sitting at the counter.

I grabbed Alec's sleeve. 'She's in there,' I said. 'Afternoon boozing! She's picked up some bad continental habits already.'

'Let's emulate them,' Alec said. 'We have to immerse ourselves in the local customs.'

We went in. Judy Curtis was sitting with her back to us and when we came up beside her she nearly jumped off her stool.

'*Bonjour,*' said Alec. '*Comment ça va?*'

192

'Christ!' said Judy. 'Where have you sprung from?'

'We're tourists,' I said.

'Is Laurie touring with you?'

'We left him at home.'

The news relaxed her. She was wearing old jeans and a blue denim shirt that made her look as if she belonged here. Her drink was Martini rouge. 'Well,' she said, but was too embarrassed to add anything to it.

'Is the beer good in here?' I asked.

She nodded to the barman. 'Ask Jean-Paul.'

He was a good-looking man in his mid-thirties, balding slightly but with friendly eyes. He had watched our arrival with wary concern.

'*Bière pression*,' Alec said, '*deux fois*.'

'A couple of draught beers?' said Jean-Paul. 'Certainly.'

'His English is better than my French,' said Alec.

'Whose isn't?' asked Judy, smiling at me. She sipped her drink. 'Now that you've found me, what can I do for you? And don't imagine that I'm coming back to the shack at Beuzeville.'

'We're not in the shack. We're in a luxury hotel.'

'Don't blame you. I am, too.'

I sat on the stool next to her. 'Would you say, Judy, that we are engaged on a forlorn mission?'

She smiled again. 'To answer that, Max, I would have to know what your mission is.'

'I think it's to persuade you to return to Laurie.'

Her laughter was unexpectedly joined by more from the other side of the counter. I had clearly amused Jean-Paul.

'It is not possible,' he said. 'She would sooner jump in the Seine at Rouen.'

Alec resented this intervention from the business side of the bar and moved slightly so that he gave Jean-Paul his back.

'And what about Helen?' he asked quietly.

The smile that the laughter had left on Judy's face faded at the mention of Helen's name.

193

'She's a woman now, Alec,' she said. 'Well, almost. And don't tell me that she needs me. For five years she hasn't taken a blind bit of notice of anything I've said.'

This did not seem to leave the diplomatic duo with much room for manoeuvre and I drank my beer thoughtfully and watched the other customers in the bar. Why do conversations in a foreign language always sound so interesting? I've overheard a thousand boring conversations in English, but directly someone starts up in Spanish or French it sounds fascinating, even important.

Judy said: 'This time next week your name could be on a tombstone.'

'I doubt whether stonemasons work that quickly,' I said, 'but I get your message.'

'I've been reading Henry James,' she said.

'A dangerous occupation at your age,' said Alec.

'He says live all you can. It doesn't matter what you do as long as you have your life. And he says: If you haven't had that, what *have* you had?'

I was beginning to feel that we had done our duty so far as the Curtis marriage was concerned, and that we would be better occupied seeing the alleged charm of Honfleur than getting engaged in a high moral discussion with Judy the bruiser that was evidently going to get us nowhere. But Alec's nose had caught the scent of academic debate and he gazed at the absconding wife as if she were an argumentative pupil in his school.

'I don't know what book that was in,' he said.

'*The Ambassadors*,' said Judy. 'As a matter of fact your wife lent it to me. We think the same way, you see. Two mothers disappointed with motherhood.'

'I imagine that they are words he put in a character's mouth, words with which he didn't necessarily agree. James was a very moral writer.'

'Alec,' said Judy, dismissing this, 'don't waste your time. Enjoy your holiday. Get back to your luxury hotel. What happened, anyway? Did the shack fall down?' She pushed her empty glass towards Jean-Paul and they exchanged lovers' smiles.

'I suppose,' I said doubtfully, 'that there's no message?'

'Drop dead springs to mind, but it doesn't sound quite right. Tell him to look after Helen.'

I looked at Alec who raised both eyebrows and shrugged. Our glasses were empty and I stood up.

'And that's it?' I said.

This time Judy shrugged. 'I expect I'll be in touch some time.'

We both kissed her cheek, wished her well and went out on to the quay. She seemed relieved to see us go.

'Laurie's going to be well chuffed,' I said. 'But I don't see what else we could have done.'

'She's made up her mind,' Alec said, 'and nothing we could say was going to change it.'

We decided to save time now by getting a taxi back and we roamed the quaint streets in search of one. But there is no taxi rank in Honfleur and Alec's attempts to track one down by interrogating the uncommunicative natives produced a series of blank stares, so in the end we found the tourist office in the Rue de la Ville. A girl made a telephone call on our behalf and said a taxi would arrive in five minutes. We went out to wait.

'A French five minutes is ten minutes shorter than a Spanish five minutes, but slightly longer than an English five minutes which is usually ten minutes,' said Alec.

This proved to be about right.

By Sunday morning the sad sight of defeated tourists wrestling with inside-out umbrellas had begun to pall; a man needs a summer holiday, but this rainswept, windswept coast was a curious place to take it.

The hostile weather seemed to have immobilized us. We hadn't seen the D-day beaches or the Bayeux Tapestry or the Abbey at Caen or Mont-Saint-Michel rising from the sea at the bottom of the Cotentin peninsula. We hadn't managed to get ourselves within viewing distance of the gothic steeple at Rouen.

But then the clouds, as vulnerable to wind as the rest of us, shifted out to the bay and something which Alec said he remembered was called the sun appeared overhead. Kitty said we should walk.

Annette, oddly, thought that a walk would suit her too, and so the five of us strolled through Deauville. We walked in a straight line through the town, past the statue of the Duc de Morny and found that we had left Deauville and reached a bridge over a river. Immediately on the other side of the bridge, not more than two or three hundred yards from our hotel, was Trouville. Deauville was posh, Trouville was French.

On the ground which ran along Trouville's side of the river was a big Sunday morning market and we wandered among the colourful stalls that sold cheeses, fruit, flowers, wallets and watches, perfumes and *pantalons*. The men eyed these products suspiciously, but the women spent. Annette was soon carrying an embroidered white tablecloth and Kitty was laden with fruit.

By the time we came out at the other end of the market the talk was of lunch. But first we had a look at the shops which, with a fine continental disregard for Britain's absurd laws, were open.

I found out afterwards that Trouville was the fashionable place when Deauville was just a street and a café. The man who owned Maxims in Paris built a huge casino on the seafront, which was still there, but Trouville put up his rent and so he built another in Deauville and made it famous. Trouville stopped being poncey and became French again. On the whole I preferred it.

We ate *fruits de mer* in a crowded brasserie on the front where the service was so fast that you felt they resented the loan of the table. An enormous silver tray of seafood was placed before us – crab, shrimps, crayfish, whelks, oysters, prawns, langoustines, mussels, clams and winkles – and we sat there for more than an hour.

196

Laurie, whose reaction to our news from Honfleur had caused him to ignore food for the more certain satisfactions of strong liquid, perked up at this feast and ignored the wine that came with it.

'Was there no message?' he had asked when Alec and I called on him in his hotel room. He was lying on his bed watching satellite television which had added to the horrors of abroad by giving you the news in English when you were in France.

'She said to look after Helen,' I told him.

'I can't believe she'd desert her daughter,' he said, covering his face with his hands. 'Normal women don't behave like that.'

'She's in the grip of a passion that only time will abate,' said Alec, in his best headmaster's manner. 'It can happen to women of a certain age and they'll sacrifice anything for it.'

'You wait till she starts knocking him about,' Laurie said, cheering up a little. 'He'll dump her on the next boat.'

He obviously thought that Judy hit men generally, that there was nothing personal about it. The possibility that she would find no reason to attack Jean-Paul just didn't occur to him.

'Perhaps he's a masochist,' suggested Alec. 'Her teeth fit his wound.'

'In that case, mate, he's struck oil,' said Laurie.

But over the oysters and crab at Trouville it was the welfare of Helen rather than the sexual prospects of Jean-Paul that concerned the female guests.

'What are you going to do about her?' Kitty asked. 'It's a serious matter, Laurie. She needs a woman around at this stage of her life.'

'I could always get married again,' said Laurie cheerfully. 'Some face-lifted fifty-five-year-old with false teeth and elastic stockings.'

'I should be careful if you're looking for a wife,' Alec told him solemnly. 'It's not like when we were young. These days

197

women accuse you of mental rape if you look at them and of being homosexual if you don't. It's a minefield for the healthy male out there.'

Kitty Benson laughed immoderately at this, and the picture of Alec as woman hunter made the rest of us smile. There were many stereotypes into which he haplessly fell – the pedant, the docile husband, the incompetent father – but womanizer was not one of them.

Alec was hurt. He pushed his glasses up his nose and announced: 'When I was wooing Mavis Jones she had a lot of competition.'

'What were they after?' Kitty asked, still laughing. 'Your body or your money?'

'My mind,' said Alec.

'Did they find it?' asked Laurie.

This banter irritated Annette who felt there were serious questions to discuss. 'You must get a housekeeper, Laurie,' she said. 'Somebody who can keep an eye on Helen.'

'You make me sound geriatric, Annette. I'm forty-two, for God's sake. If there's going to be a woman in my house she'll share my bed.'

'It might be easier to find a housekeeper,' said my wife unkindly.

That evening we walked through the tunnel that linked the hotel with the casino. You might have thought that a casino would be the first casualty of a recession but there were obviously plenty of people around that recessions didn't reach. They crowded round the French roulette table placing chips that cost as much as our holiday, and wearing clothes that probably cost more.

Our party had lost whatever pretensions to prosperity it ever had. Even Laurie, who had found himself paying the Bensons' hotel bill, was reluctant to risk more than a pound or two on the capricious spins of a wheel, and when ten pounds of mine had vanished beneath the croupier's rake my dreams of a quick killing vanished with them.

We watched the wealthy at play, winning and losing a

year's average wages in a matter of minutes with a nonchalance that seemed unreal.

'This is not moral,' said Alec. 'That money could save lives.'

'It could feed people,' said Kitty.

'It all ends up in a bank which lends it to a third world country that loses it,' I said. 'You idealists don't understand the real world.'

'Let's go on the fruit machines,' said Annette. 'I understand them.'

There was a battery of machines flashing gaudily and we got some change and went over. Our syndicate never looked like making money, but the women enjoyed it. Personally I thought that there was something horribly familiar about the one-armed bandits. You stood around hopefully, summoned up your reserves of optimism, spent money you couldn't afford, and waited for the prize that never came.

It was just like life.

PART THREE

· A game ·

Life is a game at which
everybody loses.

Leo Sarkadi-Schuller
Within Four Walls

13

De profundis

There was a formidable pile of mail waiting for me on the mat when we reached home. Most of it had arrived in brown envelopes with little windows that betrayed the unfriendliness of their contents. Sometimes, to obliterate doubt, they were printed in red, so I left them until the following day.

The important letter stood out from the rest of this unwanted stuff because on one corner of the envelope was a red French 2.30 franc stamp. For a moment I thought that it must be from the promiscuous Mrs Curtis, but then I recognized the writing.

I opened the envelope with a knife and started to read. I started to read standing up, but then I sat down. Then I stopped reading for a while as I paused to find the courage to read on.

> Garth Hadfield 12891
> Maison d'Arrêt de Bayonne
> 44 Rue Charles Floquet
> Boîte Postale 718
> 64107 Bayonne
> Cedex
> France

Dear Mum and Dad,

I hope you are both well and that Mum had a lovely

203

birthday. I thought of you on the day and wished I was there. How was the holiday in France? I hope you both managed to duck the Curtis family's flying plates!

Guess what? I'm in prison. I was arrested on July 15 and will not be considered for bail because I don't have residence in France.

What happened was this. A friend of mine called Bernard came down to Madrid on holiday with his wife and I went to see him. He had driven down from London in a Range Rover.

While they were in Madrid his wife fell ill with a stomach complaint and wanted to see her own doctor urgently. They had to fly home immediately, and Bernard said he would pay me to drive the Range Rover back to London, and give me an air ticket back to Spain.

At the Spanish-French border I was stopped by customs and they found thirty kilos of cannabis in the petrol tank. Apparently the tank had been altered so that only the bottom half held petrol. I had wondered why I had to keep stopping for gas.

Anyway, I'm stuck here now and God knows what is going to happen.

Time is not passing quickly which is not surprising as I am confined to the same small area for a minimum of 21 hours a day or on a bad day 22½. When you get out in ultra limited space for one and a half hours everybody walks aimlessly back and forth and not talking much because of all the different languages.

God knows when there will be a trial. One man has been here 16 months without getting to court, but it is the same in Britain. I read of a man in England who was found not guilty after being held in jail for two years. Legendary British justice is now an international joke.

Could you get a copy of 'A Guide to the French Criminal Justice System' from Prisoners Abroad in London? Their address is 82 Rosebery Avenue EC1.

I have made a written request for a solicitor which will

apparently cost an initial fee of £500. I am told that I will have to pay a hefty customs fine if I am convicted, and if it isn't paid two years is added to my sentence.

I share this cell with a Pole, a Portuguese and a Frenchman. There's not a lot of conversation.

What I urgently need at the moment, Dad, is money – 1000 francs a month for food, tobacco (I've started to smoke), toilet things and washing powder. It's £115 or £120 a month depending on the exchange rate. The rule is simple – no money and you have nothing. The money I had was confiscated on my arrest. Please don't send more than 1000 francs a month because they confiscate that too.

Life without money is not pleasant. I can't wash my clothes, shampoo my hair, and there is no tea or proper food. I get a tin of almost warm coffee and a bread stick at 7.15 a.m.

The social worker has written to a Catholic charity for the poor suggesting a donation for me. I am having to borrow pen, paper, envelopes and postage.

Do not bother to try to visit me. The paperwork is a nightmare. You fill in forms, send photocopies of your passport and have to get permission from the judge. And you are still not certain to be allowed to visit me. Some people have travelled across Europe and been refused at the door. The police can hold you up for hours and still say No.

I've got to stop now as I have no more paper. Please write soon.

Love,
Garth

For a while I sat with my head in my hands, unable to move. Slowly the horror sank in. My son in prison! The golden boy locked up in the company of villains! I waited a long time before reading the letter again, and just sat there imagining his squalid conditions. When I finally read it I wanted to talk about it and I went up to wake Annette.

She was deeply asleep as usual at this time of day, but she stirred when I sat on the bed.

'Where is it?' she said when she opened her eyes.

'What?'

'My cup of tea.'

'I haven't made any yet,' I said. 'You'd better read this.'

She pulled herself up and issued her first morning yawn.

'I wish we were still in the hotel,' she said. 'The service in France was much better.'

'It's bad news, Annette. You've got to read it.'

My tone alerted her and her eyes opened quite a lot as she looked at me.

'What is it?'

'Read it.'

She adjusted her pillow to lean back on and took the letter. As she read it I studied her face, curious about what I would see. Anger? Misery? What I actually saw was my wife age. She muttered a few phrases – 'Oh, no' and 'Oh my God' – but what really moved me as she read every word was that she seemed to age about five years in five minutes.

When she had finished reading she put the letter on the bed in front of her and stared at me. There were no tears.

'How could somebody do that to him?' I asked.

'Nobody did it to him, you bloody fool. He's lying.'

'What do you mean?' I asked, confused. (The honest man always misses the lie.)

Annette looked at me as if I were a backward child.

'Well, you've seen the Range Rover for a start. He's trying out his defence because the people at the prison will read this letter before they post it.'

'You mean he *is* a drug smuggler?'

'Where do you think all the money came from? He's never paid a debt as quickly as that five hundred pounds he gave back to you. Why was he in Seville one day and Barcelona the next? He was obviously delivering the stuff which got to be dangerous when he had to cross borders and deal with customs men.'

I stood up and walked out of the room, muttering some imprecation or another. I was in a bit of a daze. Downstairs I found that I did not want breakfast or even a cup of tea. I needed peace and fresh air. I walked out of the house and down the road and carried on walking, thinking about Garth, his happy past, his terrible present and his uncertain future, and I didn't see anything very much.

Some time that morning I arrived at Alec's.

People are full of surprises. I had expected to find Alec browsing over end of term papers or constructing rosters for his reluctant band of teachers. Instead he was slumped in his greenhouse with a bottle of gin.

It wasn't a greenhouse really. It was a small but extraordinary conservatory that he had built on to the back of their house. The temperature, the humidity and the plants gave you the impression that you were in a jungle.

It was filled mostly with ferns, but there were orchids, geraniums, polyanthus and begonias sprinkled around in its small space. The focal point was a fish pond in one corner above which Alec had built during the long school holidays an elaborate waterfall which consisted of three or four ledges a foot apart with water dropping on a time switch from one to the next and thence into the pond. On each ledge things were growing: mosses, ferns, water buttercups and water chestnuts which I had previously only seen in a Chinese restaurant.

The conservatory was double glazed and its heat, controlled by a thermostat, was provided by three aluminium heating tubes. A humidifier controlled the balance between the humidity level and the temperature, and a large silver fan was attached to the ceiling to circulate the air. The rest of the ceiling was covered with a grape vine which clung to wires tied to the dark brown rafters.

Alec sat in a rattan sofa staring at the fish.

'Nice place you've got here,' I said when I had burst in on him. There had been no reply to my knock on the door and I had wandered round to the back of the house on the off chance that he was in the garden.

'This is a rare pleasure,' he said, not getting up. 'You've stumbled across my hiding place. This is where I sit to contemplate the debris of my life.'

'What's that?' I asked, pointing at a plant on a shelf.

'A cheese plant. See the way the roots have come all the way to the ground looking for moisture?' He looked round. 'There's a toad in here somewhere. The gardener's friend.'

'What's the gin for?'

'That's the gardener's friend as well.'

He had mentioned the conservatory from time to time, but I had found the subject so boring that I hadn't encouraged him to go on. But now I was in the place I could see that this was where he was really happy. He sipped his gin and leaned forward to flick a switch that started the gentle waterfall.

'I made that,' he said proudly. 'I'm not just a defeated pedagogue.' He looked up at me and it suddenly occurred to him to ask why I was here. 'Is this just a social call or what?' he asked.

'I've had some bad news and I've been walking around,' I said. 'I seemed to end up here.'

'Oh dear, Max. What is it?'

'Garth is in prison.'

He put down his drink and stood up. 'In prison?'

'In France.'

'My God, I'm wittering on about cheese plants and waterfalls and your son's in prison. Sit down. Tell me.'

There was plenty of room for the two of us on the rattan sofa and we sat side by side and gazed gloomily at the fish which gazed gloomily back at us. Imprisonment and restriction was probably at the forefront of their minds too.

I told Alec the story which I had gone through a hundred times on my long walk. He looked as if he scarcely believed it.

'And Annette thinks he really did it?' he asked when I had finished.

208

'She's certain of it.'

'You'd better have some gin.'

He poured me a glass which I drank as if it were water. 'Annette's right. He's obviously guilty. It didn't even occur to me when I first read his letter. You assume your son is innocent. You've had some experience of that.'

'Yes,' he said. 'And we thought Garth was the good one.'

This painful reminder of our previous positions was not welcome.

'Easy money,' I said. 'Something happened to him and he suddenly had a big thing about money. He didn't mean a miserly cheque after five days' hard work, either.'

Alec topped up my glass. 'What are you going to do? Fly out?'

'He says not to. All he wants is money. Money for soap, money for food, money for a lawyer. It couldn't have happened at a worse time. Money has become a major problem for me now.'

'It's certainly not something I can help you with,' said Alec. 'Money and the Bensons are complete strangers.'

'Where's Kitty?'

'At some council committee meeting. If she wanted to work herself stupid, why couldn't she find a job that paid wages?'

I nodded sympathetically and we drank the gin. The financial consequences of Garth's imprisonment were only now dawning on me. What I had been thinking about was his loss of freedom, his awful living conditions and the slice of his young life that he was about to forfeit. I could send him a hundred pounds a month, but how was I going to pay for a lawyer? In Britain you had to remortgage your house if one of that breed so much as said hallo to you, and if you set foot in their office you had to delay your retirement.

I finished the drink and looked at my watch. It was one o'clock.

'I'd better go,' I said, before Alec could refill my glass. 'Annette will be wondering where the hell I am.'

209

I stood up. A young man had come round the side of the house and was knocking on the back door.

'You have a visitor,' I said.

Alec got up, opened the door of the conservatory and called 'Hallo?'

The young man waved and smiled and set off in our direction. He was about Garth's age, thin and pale which seemed to be the fashionable look among young people today, and had a lot of black curly hair.

'Hi!' he said when he reached the door of the conservatory. 'Would one of you gentlemen be Mr Alec Benson?'

He addressed this remark to me as if I had been selected for the honour.

'One of us would be,' I said, 'but I wouldn't.'

The young man turned with a huge smile to Alec who seemed suspicious to find such enthusiasm in a visitor.

'What can I do for you?' he said. 'I'm Alec Benson.'

'How do you do, sir?' said the young man, offering his hand. He certainly didn't lack confidence which wasn't always the case with kids of his age. 'I'm Warren Jones. Son of Mavis.'

The name created a *frisson* which ran round the conservatory.

'Really?' said Alec and sat down. It looked to me as if the sitting down was an involuntary act caused by a problem with his legs, rather than a carefully considered piece of social rearrangement.

'I just had to meet you,' said Warren Jones. He seemed genuinely thrilled to have met Alec which certainly marked him out from the common herd. But Alec, for his part, was staring at the intruder with a strange expression that combined the trepidation of a rabbit being formally greeted by a snake, and the stunned joy of a child finding Father Christmas on his bed in the middle of the night.

'How is Mavis?' Alec asked eventually.

'She's fine, sir. We're staying in the Willow Hotel by the river on a little holiday.'

The news that Mavis Jones was staying in the Comedy Hotel revived my sagging interest in the world.

'She'd be really pleased if you'd join us for a drink this evening. That's what she asked me to say.'

The prospect of this reunion overwhelmed Alec. He covered his face with his hands and muttered: 'I can't believe it.'

'She'd be really pleased,' Warren Jones repeated. 'I hope you can make it, sir?'

There was something transatlantic about this repetition of 'sir' and I was trying to place his accent.

'For a drink?' said Alec. 'That would be nice.'

'Shall we say seven o'clock?'

Alec stood up. He looked thoroughly bemused and was no longer entirely with us in the conservatory.

'Seven o'clock,' he said, trying to concentrate. 'I'll be there.'

Warren Jones shook his hand again and then nodded to me, the unnamed spectator at this meeting. He walked across the lawn with all the brisk energy of youth, and then gave us a final wave as he disappeared round the side of the house.

'Well,' said Alec.

'Well,' I repeated. 'Kitty is going to be thrilled.'

'I was thinking of not telling Kitty,' said Alec. 'Usual visit to the Comedy Hotel, game of pool, that sort of thing.'

'It might be best,' I said. 'What the heart doesn't see, the eye doesn't grieve about.'

Alec sniffed. 'I think you've got that the wrong way round. We've drunk too much gin.'

'What time did he say?'

'Seven o'clock. You're not going to be there, are you?'

'I'll be there,' I said. I certainly didn't intend to miss it. When Alec had managed to get to his feet to bid his young visitor goodbye, I had noticed that they had the same black curly hair.

Annette was not happy. 'Where the hell have you been?' she asked when I got back.

'Walking and thinking,' I said.

'Well, while you've been walking and thinking I've been

211

doing something, apart from taking your phone calls.'

I sat down. Midday gin was a bad idea.

'Who called?'

'Two of your shops, one of your banks.'

She handed me a sheet of paper with the names on. None was likely to be the bearer of glad tidings.

'I phoned the Foreign Office,' said Annette. 'The man responsible for that part of the world is a British Consul whose proper job is a bank manager in Biarritz. They promise that he will be helpful if you ring him. Here's his name and number.'

She gave me another sheet of paper.

'Ring him,' she said.

'He'll be having his lunch,' I stalled.

'No, he won't. They're an hour ahead of us.'

I went out to the hall where the phone sat on a small desk that I could write at, and dialled the number; and the wonderful world of British Telecom that has difficulty in connecting you to your next door neighbour, provided the Consul loud and clear in less than a minute. I gathered that with a prison near the Spanish border on his patch, this was the sort of call that he was quite used to.

'Send the money to me at the bank each month, Mr Hadfield, and I'll see your son gets it,' he said.

'Are there many British in that prison?' I asked.

'About twenty at the moment, but they don't necessarily meet up. Anyway I'll drop in next week to see your son and make sure he is okay.'

'One more thing,' I said, conscious of who was paying for this call, 'have you any idea what sort of sentence he might get if they convict him?'

'Don't quote me, but it usually works out at about a month a kilo.'

'Two and a half years?' said Annette, looking pale, when I returned from the phone.

'Four and a half if we can't afford to pay the customs fine,' I said. I could see that the hardness with which she had

212

greeted this morning's post had collapsed in my absence and she had been weeping alone. My own mood had shifted the other way and I was now quietly furious at my son's greed and stupidity and the hopeless expense that it was going to subject me to.

'We'd better write to him,' I said. 'I mean both of us.' I couldn't remember Annette writing a letter in five years and I could see that my suggestion was a bit of a shock. The people with whom she wished to communicate were usually at the end of a phone. I found her a writing pad and she settled down on the sofa with the pad on her knee and the pen, when I left her, poised thoughtfully in her mouth.

I went up to my office, sat at my desk and found some sheets of paper. I made a false start, forgetting that it was necessary to play his own deceitful game and appear to accept his pretence of innocent victim, cruelly misled by a supposed friend. This letter, too, would be scrutinized for evidence that could be used against him.

But I think that I managed to convey my disappointment even if the blame I threw at him only concentrated on his choice of friends. I promised to support him financially, do what I could for him from Britain, and I hoped that soon it would be possible for me to fly down to see him. It was a restrained letter of sadness and withheld love and it depressed me to write it.

When I went downstairs I discovered that Annette's effort by comparison was a cauldron of emotion, a scream of pain at her jailed son and his lost freedom. She ended by promising the most excruciating physical violence on the owner of the Range Rover who only a few hours earlier she had assured me did not exist.

'You should write more often,' I said. 'It really sings.'

'Post them,' she said sadly. 'Then you'd better go to the bank and arrange the money for France.'

'Talking about banks,' I said, 'what did Mr Fleming want?'

'A talk.'

*

The Comedy Hotel on a sunny August evening made travelling to more exotic locations quite unnecessary. There were tables and chairs outside now where customers could admire the roses, honeysuckle and buttercups, or watch the boats on the river while they supped their evening refreshments and fought off the gnats.

I was not one for the alfresco tipple myself and I arrived early and headed for the bar. Sober, but still tingling with alcohol from the lunchtime gin, I had every hope that the complications in other people's lives would temporarily distract me from my own.

Alec sat at the bar like a boy on a date. He had washed his hair and put on a bright yellow sweater I had never seen before but which seemed to knock a few years off his age.

'Where is she?' I asked.

'We're early. It's not yet seven.'

He was drinking gin again, as if his customary lager would not sustain him during the trauma of this reunion. I waited for him to offer me something but his head was full of other things.

'Mavis Jones,' he said. 'The name still creates a mild tumescence.'

'She isn't twenty any more,' I said, beckoning John the barman and ordering a pint.

Strangers came to the Comedy Hotel in the summer, seeking a rural respite from the daily grind, and there were lots of people in the bar I didn't know. But even in the restrained atmosphere of the cocktail bar, where customers were obliged to sit in armchairs and wait for a flunkey to take their orders, it was quite clear which men were here to soothe their spouses and which had booked in furtively for an illicit jump. In his new yellow sweater even Alec looked like a man who believed that a little extramarital activity was an idea whose time had come.

'We had a weekend in the Mendips once,' he said, pushing his empty glass across the counter. 'Ever been to the Mendips?'

214

'Heard of them,' I said.

'Of course we were young and couldn't afford a hotel like this, but we found a bed and breakfast place on a farm in the country. It was a magical weekend.'

'Is passionate a word that springs to mind?'

'Amorous, erotic, wanton, fervent, impulsive,' he said. 'What was your word?'

'It doesn't matter,' I said. 'You seem to have enough of your own.'

'She had a way with a man's body that I have never encountered since,' he said.

'Which way was that?'

'She sort of drained it like a Hoover.'

'And that was good, was it? Being drained by a Hoover?'

His new gin arrived and he put it to his lips. 'It was quite extraordinary.'

I drank some lager and looked at my watch. It was five past seven.

'Why did this lustful liaison come to an end?' I asked. 'The Hoover pack up?'

'Mavis got a job in Belgium. She was on the way up in the cosmetic business and pretty ambitious. I didn't hear from her and then I met Kitty.'

'Those were the days,' I said. 'Drop one woman, pick up the next.'

'Kitty laughs, but I was a very sexual person.'

'It's surprising,' I said. 'I always thought that you were to sexuality what the tortoise is to the London Marathon.'

He grinned at my cruel little joke. 'Alec the stud,' he said. 'It's a difficult concept for you to grasp, but I only had to kiss their cheek and they were a month late.'

At that moment Warren Jones came in. With him was a very smart lady, short and shapely, in a green linen dress with blue sandals and a matching shoulder bag, none of which had come from my shops. Her blonde hair had been handled by a skilled *coiffeuse* and her discreetly applied make-up suggested a career in cosmetics.

215

'Hallo Alec,' she said briskly. 'You've lost weight. Are you dieting or dying?'

'Mavis,' he said, standing to kiss the cheek that she offered. 'You look wonderful.' He turned to introduce me and I shook her hand and asked what she would drink.

While I was getting her a pink gin and Warren a lager Alec suggested a move to a table where the seating was more comfortable. I preferred the bar myself where the next drink was only an arm's length away, but I didn't want to miss this moving scene and I hurried over with their drinks.

'I wasn't fat at twenty,' Alec was saying. 'Why do you think I've lost weight?'

'I caught a glimpse of you in London a few years ago and I thought you were looking pudgy.'

'You should have stopped me for a chat,' Alec said, hurt.

'You were with a lady I assumed was your wife,' said Mavis Jones. She turned to Warren who was drinking his lager. 'Darling, I've left my cigarettes in the room.'

'I'll get them,' said Warren.

She turned to Alec when her son had gone.

'What do you think of him?'

'He's a fine chap,' said Alec, 'and so well mannered.'

'He was born in Brussels,' said Mavis Jones, looking at Alec.

'Twenty-four years ago.'

The significance of this missed Alec by a few million light years. 'Doesn't that make him Belgian?' he asked.

'Well, McEnroe was born in Wiesbaden, but I've never heard of him referred to as a German tennis player,' said Mavis Jones. 'Warren plays tennis, by the way. You should see his topspin backhand.'

'Twenty-four years ago?' said Alec.

Mavis Jones turned to me. 'Do you hear the sound of pennies dropping?' she asked.

'What are you telling me, Mavis?' said Alec.

'I'm not telling you anything, Alec,' said Mavis Jones, producing a packet of long, filter cigarettes from her shoulder

216

bag. She delved into the bag again and found a slim, gold lighter.

'I thought you'd left your cigarettes upstairs?' Alec said.

'There'll be the sound of more pennies dropping in a minute,' I said. 'It's just a question of waiting.'

'My God!' said Alec. 'Why didn't you tell me?'

'I didn't know I was pregnant until I'd been in Belgium for two months and by that time, my friends told me, you had a new girl called Kitty.'

'I could have helped,' said Alec.

'You were a trainee teacher, Alec. I was already earning two and a half times more than you. I thought I could have the baby and keep my career and that's what I did. It worked out very well. We spent a couple of years in America and he went to school there. He learned more there than he did in twelve years here.'

This dig at the work that Alec had devoted his life to did not help to revive his numbed persona.

'Does he know?' he whispered eventually.

Mavis Jones exhaled smoke through delicately pursed lips. 'You're dead,' she said. 'It was very sad. You passed on when he was only a few months old.'

Alec didn't like the sound of this. His face was a picture of pain.

'As a matter of interest,' he said, 'what did I die of?'

'A pig fell on you,' she said. 'From a balcony. Broken neck, I'm afraid. I got it from a Graham Greene short story.'

Alec looked seriously upset at this news; it was, one gathered, not the way he was hoping to go.

'You could have thought of something kinder,' he suggested.

'Like what?' said Mavis Jones. 'Leukaemia? Psittacosis? Cholera? I was trying to cheer the boy up. He'd lost his daddy.'

'What happened to the pig?' I asked.

'Unscathed,' Mavis Jones replied promptly. 'Its fall was fortunately cushioned by Warren's father. It got up and ran away.'

'Neat,' I said.

'It was necessary because "What happened to the pig?" was Warren's first question. Children identify with animals.'

'I'm glad the pig made it,' said Alec irritably, 'but it's hard to spot the humorous aspects of your own death.'

'So who does Warren think Alec is?' I asked.

Mavis Jones smiled. 'An old flame. He's curious about my romantic past.'

'You never married?'

'No, but we kept some pigs for a while when Warren was a kid. He sort of got interested in them.'

'I'd have thought he'd have developed an antipathy,' said Alec, 'seeing as how they wiped out his father.' Taking second place to a herd of swine was not improving his mood.

'And what about your surname?' I asked.

'Ah, that's one of life's coincidences. My maiden name was Jones and so was my late husband's.'

'You have it all worked out,' I said. 'Can I ask one more question?'

'Surely.'

'What was a pig doing on a balcony?'

'It happened in Calcutta,' said Mavis Jones, which evidently explained it. She had finished her drink and Alec got up to fetch us more. 'Is Alec still teaching?' she asked me.

I nodded. 'He's a headmaster now.'

'I should hope so,' said Mavis Jones. She was an attractive woman whose appearance was more than enough to rekindle the sexual ambitions of her old flame. By the time he returned with the drinks he had obviously put his setback with the pig from his mind.

'You're still beautiful, Mavis,' he said, handing her a drink. '*Nulli secundus*.'

Mavis's assurance, which I was beginning to admire, wavered in the face of this direct praise and she blushed girlishly.

'We had our moments, didn't we, Alec?' she said.

He smiled distantly. 'Do you remember the Mendips?'

I thought I was about to endure a guided tour of their old mating grounds but Warren now appeared through the drinkers and reclaimed his chair.

'I couldn't find them,' he announced.

'I'm sorry, darling. They were in my bag after all.'

'Fine,' he said, and grinned. He was more outgoing than Alec and I was able to ponder the age-old question of heredity versus environment. How different would he be if Alec had been at his side during the last twenty-four years?

Alec seemed unable to take his eyes off the boy now that he had returned.

'I have the feeling that you have been discussing me,' said Warren uneasily.

'We've been hearing about your topspin backhand,' I said. 'What else do you play?'

'I play pool,' he said. 'I see there's a table in the hotel.'

'I recognize a challenge,' I said, standing up. It seemed a good idea to rescue him from Alec's relentless scrutiny; I also thought the old lovers might appreciate time alone.

'Have you any children, Mr Hadfield?' Warren asked as I set the balls up on the table.

'I have a son about your age,' I said. 'He's in prison.'

14

The bald vulture

Mr Fleming's greeting the following morning fell some way short of what my dejected spirit required. A sick man confronted by an undertaker with a tape measure would have managed a more effusive welcome.

'I'm worried about your wife,' he said.

'*You're* worried about her,' I said. 'We should form a club.'

He sat upright at his desk, both hands laid flat on the folder in front of him. His tall bald head made me think of a vicar, but Mr Fleming was not a purveyor of spiritual balm nor any other kind of comfort.

'The Thames-side mansion,' he said. 'The home that you had valued at £800,000 and we have now valued at £450,000.'

'Oh, *that* home,' I said.

'We have a dilemma in the banking world when a home is used as security against an overdraft. It occurs, as in your case, when the account is in one name but the house is jointly owned. It's a question of banking confidentiality.'

I smiled. 'Now we know that banks launder money for the drugs trade and help dictators to loot their national treasures, I thought ethics were out of the window,' I said.

'That was one bank, Mr Hadfield. We do things differently here. The problem is that as your wife is not a joint holder of the bank account she is not entitled to information about the

220

account under law, and that includes that your house is at risk. Our hands are tied by the confidentiality rule.'

'I see,' I said.

'Legally, we could still force a sale of the house if the business fails, but forget the legalities. It all comes down to the moral obligations. Is your wife aware of our arrangement?'

'I don't believe she is. I don't like to worry her. She's pregnant.'

'Ah,' said Mr Fleming. 'We tend to assume that husbands have told their wives. Customers should talk to their partners first, and she should know about the risk to the house if the bank calls in the loan.'

'My wife has never shown any great interest in my business,' I said. 'She's not even one of my customers. Consequently the friendly little chats about cash flow and financial targets that you imagine us having don't actually take place.'

Mr Fleming raised one hand to massage the side of his nose. 'A bank would find it difficult to get possession if the wife has not signed a charge,' he said. 'No judge would evict the wife if the husband hadn't told her of the situation.'

I doubted this. There was no iniquity that I would put beyond a British judge. But I said nothing. Why should I help Mr Fleming into a position where he could grab my house? He was beginning to display the irascibility of a tired five-year-old and I wondered whether he was about to roll round on the carpet. His demeanour hardly encouraged warmth and friendship, and I remembered thinking once before that on the rare occasions when he did people favours it was with such ill grace that he never received the gratitude he was due.

'Let's look on the bright side, Mr Fleming,' I said. 'It was optimism that launched my business.'

'It was optimism that launched the *Titanic*, Mr Hadfield. What grounds are there for optimism now? I'm told that summer is not living up to retailers' hopes.'

He had obviously read a Confederation of British Industry survey of the distributive trades which reported that high street sales were 'bumping along the bottom'. On the whole this was information that I had hoped he had missed.

'According to Treasury officials,' I said, 'economic recovery will come in the second half of this year.'

'Treasury officials,' said Mr Fleming. 'That's a bigger guessing game than the weather forecast. The current fall in spending on consumer durables is the longest on record.'

'So improvement is overdue,' I said. 'The night is darkest just before the dawn.'

'Not according to your own people. The British Chambers of Commerce predict no recovery until next year.'

'I don't have to rely on predictions,' I said. 'I get the truth from my tills every day.'

Mr Fleming looked interested for the first time. 'And what do they tell you?'

'A marginal improvement. Of course, in the summer women have to buy summer clothes. They go on holiday. They need togs for the beach.'

'But what do they need to buy in September or October or November?' asked Mr Fleming in a tone that I wasn't very happy about. He had lost the vicar image now and assumed the role of a pitiless vulture who was circling over my head, waiting impatiently to pick up the pieces.

'We'll have a full autumn range,' I told him.

'But will the public have any money to buy it?' he asked. 'You must understand that there is a limit to how long we can go on supporting you, and our best information is that people just don't have the money. Belts are being pulled in. Extravagance is out.'

He looked at my expensive Charles Jourdan black suedes with distaste. When I got up to leave I felt strangely weakened as if Mr Fleming and I had exchanged something more punishing than words – a few body punches, perhaps, with the odd club to the side of the head to break the monotony.

He, on the other hand, looked like somebody who had had

222

a good work-out and felt all the better for an hour in a gym. He jumped up and crossed the room to open the door for me.

'No doubt I'll see you soon,' I said.

'For sure,' said Mr Fleming. 'In the meantime, have a word with your wife, will you?'

Annette had a visitor when I got home. I could hear her talking in the sitting room. I was slightly surprised because the presence of visitors was normally announced by a car in the drive and the drive was empty. This small mystery was explained when I stuck my head round the door to say hallo.

Annette was sitting on the sofa with Helen who looked up at me and then looked away again as if I hadn't really appeared.

'You're early,' said Annette, almost accusingly. Her tone told me that I was no more welcome here than I had been in the bank and so I told her that I had work to do upstairs. I probably had, but I didn't feel like doing it. Instead I sat at my desk and let my thoughts wander. At first I thought about Garth. This subject did not produce the desired state of peace and contentment and I began to think instead about Mr Fleming. It seemed to me that if I omitted to tell Annette that our house now stood as security against a growing debt, Mr Fleming's ability to sell it over our heads would be seriously impaired.

But this, too, was not a line of thought that induced serenity and what I thought about in the end was being forty, a continuing source of wonder and despair. The great pleasure of being forty, I had imagined before the momentous date crept up on me, was that I would be able to sit back and contemplate the failures and mistakes of my contemporaries. There had been ample time for them to see their ambitions crash, their marriages falter, and their expectations and aspirations, once so boundless, reduced suddenly to meagre and prosaic proportions. The reality of middle age had marched in with boots on and tossed youth's dream through the window.

The marriages had faltered all right. An astonishing number of men had left their wives and children and started fresh families with women they would never marry. The wives carried on, bringing up the first family with a sort of brave cheerfulness that might even have included an element of relief. Some marital break-ups were so friendly and civilized that you wondered how they happened, and why. Others occurred amid spectacular scenes of violence, cracked ribs, broken teeth, after which bruised wives and bitter husbands went off to consider a less dramatic existence.

Professionally, the twenty-odd years since school had provided plenty of time for disasters too, as my reunion lunch at the Waterside had shown. Hopes had been dashed, goals had been missed, illusions had been shattered and fantasies had been exposed for what they were. The solicitors had never quite become solicitors, the racing drivers had donned the overalls of a mechanic, the foreign correspondents still covered the flower show, the actors sat at a desk and the men who would never now become Members of Parliament were reduced to fomenting discontent in some odious office block.

There was something unpleasantly pleasant about the cock-ups that other people had made with their lives so long as you were viewing it from the warmth and security of your own unchallenged success.

But I wasn't. My business was heading for the rocks, my wife was mysteriously pregnant, and my only son was in prison. There was not much leeway for gloating here and when I heard the front door slam I went downstairs.

'What did Helen want?' I asked. 'Or are you the mother substitute now that Judy has gone?'

Annette looked grim. She had pulled two fillet steaks from the fridge and was preparing to grill them. New potatoes, freshly scraped, were bubbling on the cooker and I was glad to see that she had not allowed Helen's appearance to hold up her preparations for dinner.

'She has a problem,' said Annette. 'I don't know what to do about it.'

'Why is it your job to do anything about it?' I asked. 'Has she been stealing again?'

'She's pregnant,' said Annette. 'She's expecting a baby.'

'I know what pregnant means,' I said. 'Does Laurie know?'

'Not likely,' said Annette. 'He'd probably kill her. The tragedy is that Judy isn't here. If Helen ever needed her mother it's now.'

I took a bottle of red wine from the rack and set about opening it. 'Why did Helen come round to tell you?' I asked.

'It's obvious, isn't it? I'm pregnant.' She turned to me. 'What the hell am I to do?'

'There's a device called a telephone. You can talk to people in France on it.'

'That's it, Max. I knew you weren't entirely brain dead. Can you try to get the number while I prepare this banquet?'

I removed the cork from my Vina Real and went out to the phone. All our calls seemed to be to France these days; the bill should be fun. It took only ten minutes to get the number of the Cheval Blanc in Honfleur and I wrote it down and took it through to Annette.

'Dinner's ready,' she said. 'I'll call her when we've eaten.'

'If she's still in the hotel,' I said. 'I'd have thought she'd have moved into Jean-Paul's cosy *appartement* by now. You can see where the daughter gets it from.'

Fillet steak and Spanish wine is just about my favourite meal and for a while it had all my attention. I was thinking, anyway, that I had heard quite enough about the ways our young friends found to ruin their lives. The latest disastrous episode in the Curtis family saga suggested that their capacity for trouble was inexhaustible. A question arrived in my head.

'Did Helen happen to tell you,' I asked, 'who the father of the baby is?'

'Yes,' said Annette. 'Steven.'

'My God, that'll just about finish Alec off.'

'That's what I thought. You don't think it happened the night she stayed here?'

This idea had to be resisted. There were enough burdens on my shoulders.

'If they did it here they were probably doing it all over the place,' I said. 'They're like rabbits at that age if they're doing it at all.'

'I don't remember that,' said Annette.

'A selective memory is a great asset,' I said.

When she had finished eating I brought her the phone and then sat in silence while her finger danced through ten digits. She was soon in trouble with some fast-talking receptionist who didn't realize that the caller was in England. Annette spoke in slow English, lobbing in the occasional French word to keep her listener on her toes. Eventually she covered the phone with her hand and told me: 'They're getting someone who can speak English.'

She took her hand away. '*Oui. Madame Curtis*'. Then she frowned and said '*Merci*' and put the phone down.

'She moved out a week ago.'

'She must have sent Laurie her phone number,' I said, 'in case anything happened.'

'You mean you fancy a drink in the Comedy Hotel?'

'What a good idea,' I said.

Laurie was sitting at the bar discussing what the rain had done to his delphiniums with John the barman when I went in. Somewhere, in the early days of his regained bachelor-hood, he had lost his drab brown suits and replaced them with brightly coloured short-sleeve shirts that would have been less conspicuous in Hawaii.

He seemed pleased to see me as we hadn't met since he returned wifeless from France.

'Where have you been?' I asked.

'Busy, busy, busy,' he said with a smile. He wasn't wearing the distraught expression of the deserted husband. He had a carefree air and almost looked younger. 'I've been changing my will, altering various legal documents like the deeds of the

226

house, changing bank accounts, restructuring my insurance policies.'

'I see,' I said.

'I've also got a new money-making idea which is taking a bit of organizing.'

'Tell me.'

'Aerial pictures of towns. Taken from a helicopter. Printed as colour posters with the town's name at the bottom. What do you think?'

'Wonderful,' I said.

'Sell about four thousand in each town at two quid. Projected profit: five thousand per town.'

'What a fund of ideas you are,' I said. 'Have you ever thought of buying a drink?'

He laughed and bought me a lager. 'The single life has got a lot going for it. I used to drink with a glass in one hand and a stopwatch, as it were, in the other. Now I carry on drinking until I've had enough.'

'It's called alcoholism,' I told him. 'Have you heard from Judy?'

He pulled a postcard from his pocket. On one side was a picture of Rouen. I turned it over. It said: 'We live in Rouen. My phone number only to be used in an extreme emergency is 514091. Judy.'

I wondered whether I could write the number down without arousing his suspicions, but then I saw that it was a number that I could actually remember: the year of my birth, my age and this year. Of course, whether I would have it in the right order when I got home remained to be seen.

'Not the most informative card I've seen,' I said. 'But no suggestion that the French adventure is beginning to pall.'

'I should hope not,' said Laurie, but the truth was that he had been drinking and his true feelings were hard to guess.

'How's Helen taking it?' I asked.

Laurie stopped to think about this. 'I wish I knew. She's impossible to fathom. She was moody before and she's moody now. To that extent it hasn't made any difference. I don't seem able to get close to her at the moment.'

'Perhaps she needs her mother.'

'I've decided it's a phase girls go through. I try to be nice to her. I never mention the shoplifting, for instance. But she doesn't exactly throw her arms round my neck.'

On the way to the hotel I had tried to imagine how the news of Helen's pregnancy would be greeted by the four prospective grandparents but even my fevered imagination baulked at the horror of it. Alec would probably take to his bed again, but Kitty's reaction was impossible to predict. Laurie, already disillusioned with the daughter he once worshipped, would probably break things, finding no words to express his anger. Judy's response was difficult to forecast: she would hardly arrive at the family inquest as an innocent party herself.

I was left with a picture of a baby in a cot who didn't know that both its parents were on probation, a baby who could not rely on the traditional devotion of the grand-parents.

'What have I missed?' Laurie asked, lighting a cigar.

I spent some time updating him on the news – the imprison-ment of Garth, the appearance of Mavis Jones – and wondered whether I had a duty to tell him about the condition of his daughter. I decided that he would hear about it soon enough.

'Mind-boggling,' said Laurie. 'And we thought you had the good kid.'

'Don't rub it in,' I said irritably.

'Instead of which you've got the expensive one.'

'Don't celebrate too soon. Helen could cost you a few pennies yet.'

He shook his head. 'Not Helen. Spending money has never interested her.'

I resisted the temptation to say that this was a characteristic that I had myself noticed, particularly when she was in one of my shops. Instead I looked innocently round the bar and saw Kitty Benson marching in. She came over, clutching for some reason a yellow umbrella.

'Good evening, councillor,' said Laurie. 'Shall I buy you an orange juice?'

'Tonic water,' said Kitty, smiling at me. 'This is where the male cabal licks its wounds?'

It was unusual to see her in here at all, let alone without her husband. She was wearing slacks and a green woolly jumper, and the bright eyes behind her funny spectacles looked this way and that as if this was a scene she would like to remember.

'Now I'm on the council I have to take an interest in the lives of my voters,' she said. 'It even brings me to a place like this.'

'Where's Alec?' I asked. 'Talking about male cabals.'

'That's why I'm here really. He's away for the night. He says it's a teachers' conference, but I suspect he has a woman.'

'What makes you think that?' I asked, alarmed.

'A very interesting fact,' said Kitty. 'He took his toothbrush and not his Steradent tablets.'

This observation would have amused me more if I had not just seen Alec and Mavis Jones coming through the door.

'Not Alec,' said Laurie. 'He's not the womanizing sort.'

'I don't know what you're implying, Laurie,' said Kitty. 'He's the father of my son. It's something I can be quite sure about.'

'That's not womanizing, that's marriage,' said Laurie.

'The toothbrush is the clue,' said Kitty. 'It's the role of women to be lied to. It's all in my book. I'll never forget those beautiful Iraqi women sitting trustingly beside their cheap transistor radios listening to the lies of Saddam Hussein.'

'I saw men listening to that,' I said. 'Forget about the sex war, Kitty, and concentrate on the loggerhead turtle.'

Alec had now stopped near the door, frozen in fear at the sight of his wife. He said something to Mavis Jones who obviously shared his alarm and the two of them turned and left the room at a speed which attracted the attention of those nearest to them. But neither Kitty nor Laurie noticed.

I was beginning to feel that the pestilential gods who amuse themselves by heaping misfortunes on us were not, after all, picking on me. They were being quite open-handed with the calamities and there was nothing personal about the way that they were quietly unravelling my life. Kitty's teenage son was about to become a father and her husband had sneaked off for a little reproductive activity himself. Laurie had a pregnant daughter and a wife who had deserted him in favour of a randy Frenchman. My own situation was hardly enviable, but at least I wasn't alone.

I addressed my fellow victims: 'You two seem to have been a little careless with your consorts. You're supposed to keep an eye on them in case they stray.'

Kitty sipped her tonic water. 'I wonder what the balance sheet is on sex – the proportion of misery to joy that it's brought to people?'

I didn't like to tell her that the balance was about to be tipped firmly in the direction of misery when Steven got round to announcing his premature rendezvous with fatherhood.

An etiolated youth had put his half-full pint glass down on the counter at about twenty-five degrees, and the tilt was fascinating the whole bar. 'You just have to find the point of balance,' he said.

We lost Laurie to this scientific phenomenon and his departure produced in our new county councillor a more intimate approach to our conversation.

'Do you think Alec has a woman?' she asked.

'It's hard to imagine,' I replied with painstaking honesty.

'Only *you* know that it's my second marriage,' she said. 'You learn to be more tolerant the second time around.'

I was surprised to hear her say this. If Alec was discovered in bed with Mavis Jones I would have expected Kitty to throw him to one of her threatened species, like the crocodile. But the explanation was on the way.

'The pot can't call the kettle black,' said Kitty, giving me a funny grin.

'What do you mean, Kitty?' I asked. 'I can't believe that you –'

'Oliver,' said Kitty.

'Oliver?' I asked.

'What a stud that man is. A real sex machine.'

'Good God,' I said. 'I never realized.'

'It's true what they say about black men.'

'What saying is that?'

'I reckon they really do tie a brick on it as kids to make it bigger.'

This was far more than I wanted to know and I reached for my lager, trying to obliterate the psychological discomfort that Kitty had caused me.

'Have I shocked you?' she asked.

'Stunned me,' I said. 'I thought your mind was on higher things.'

'Even Mrs Thatcher had children.'

There were several answers to this, some of them rather amusing, but I didn't give any. Who was I to make moral judgements, even if I was drowning in a sea of promiscuity?

'Did Alec suspect anything?' I asked.

'Alec? Don't be silly. I could have it off with an elephant in the sitting room and he wouldn't notice.'

Imagining the scene upstairs, I realized that Alec's misfortune was that he had been blessed with a more vigilant partner.

In bed that night I told Annette: 'Kitty had an affair with Oliver.'

'The treacherous cow,' she exclaimed with a force that surprised me.

'Why do you say that?' I asked.

'Well,' she said, quietening down a little, 'Alec is such a nice man.'

'But not a sex machine like Oliver, evidently.'

231

'Is that what she called Oliver?'

'That and a stud.'

My wife lay on her back after many weeks searching for the position that discomforted her least. Her hair spread out on the pillow was more gold than auburn in the light above the bed.

'It's kicking,' she said.

I put my hand on her warm tummy and felt a small limb protesting from within. Stay where you are, I thought. It's hard out here.

In the eighth month of her pregnancy, Annette had become obsessed with oranges and crosswords and spent a lot of her time peeling fruit and consulting dictionaries. I circled the miracle nervously, unable to imagine what being pregnant could possibly feel like. She seemed more worried than she had been when she was carrying Garth, more withdrawn and less communicative. I attributed this to her age and her concern about how it might affect the baby, but I also thought that she might be worried about what had happened to her first child.

'The worst part of being eight months pregnant is the difficulty you have in cutting your toenails,' she said.

I was wondering whether to tell her that Alec, too, had strayed across those strict boundaries of marital rectitude which, we are led to believe, are so important to conventional suburban housewives, but she was beginning to look as if she might sleep and when the internal disturbance subsided she did.

In the morning she was awake before me, her body's present turbulent condition having frustrated her desire for a lie-in.

'I forgot to ask you last night about Judy's phone number,' she said when I opened one eye.

'Five one four oh nine one,' I said. 'She's in Rouen.'

She was surprised. 'How did you remember that? You can't remember your own number half the time.'

'I've been working on my memory,' I said.

232

'Why didn't you give me the number last night?'

'I forgot.'

She decided to ring early in case Judy went out, and as soon as she had a cup of tea and I had installed myself on the extension she dialled the number.

'*Allô*,' said Judy, after a surprisingly short wait.

'Judy Curtis, *s'il vous plaît*,' said Annette, not recognizing the new Frenchified Mrs Curtis.

'Is that Annette? It's me, you daft tart,' said Judy, laughing.

'So it is,' said Annette. 'How are you?'

'We're fine. Is this a social call?'

'Not exactly. I have news. Not very good news, I'm afraid.'

A nervous silence drifted across the channel.

'What is it, Annette?' said Judy's voice which had suddenly become quieter.

'It's Helen.'

'Helen?' said Judy quickly. 'What's the matter with Helen?'

'Nothing, Judy. She's fine. But she came to see me. I'm afraid she's expecting a baby, and I thought you ought to know.'

'Oh, Jesus,' said Judy Curtis and the line fell silent.

'Judy?' said Annette. 'Are you still there?'

'Are you sure about this?' Judy said after a moment. 'It's not some problem with her period?'

'Well, I haven't examined her, but she says a doctor has.'

There was another silence as Judy absorbed this information.

'I can hardly believe this,' she said finally. 'I wasn't expecting sex to be a problem quite so quickly.'

'I believe they mature quicker today,' said my wife, passing time.

'And she came to see you? Why did she do that?'

'Well, you weren't here, Judy, and I've always got on well with the girl. There's also the fact that I'm pregnant and she wanted to know about it.'

'You've hit me for six, Annette. I don't really know what to do.'

Standing in the hall with the extension to my ear I wanted to join the conversation at this stage and tell Judy to abandon the joys of adultery and fly home now. But I felt like an eavesdropper and would have been slightly ashamed to make a late appearance in this woman-to-woman chat. My wife, however, was free to speak.

'You've got to get home, Judy. The girl needs help.'

How unwelcome this suggestion was became clear from the long, expensive silence that came down the line from France.

'And what about Jean-Paul?' Judy asked. 'He'll think I'm leaving him. You don't know what the French are like with their women.'

'I'm not sure I want to, Judy. Get on the plane as quickly as possible is my advice.'

'What about Laurie?' Judy stalled. 'Does he know?'

'I gather he doesn't.'

'He'll go bananas. I'd better come back.'

'I think so,' said Annette. 'Pronto.'

'Could you ask Max to let Laurie know I'm coming? I wouldn't want to walk in unexpected. I'll try to get a flight tomorrow morning.'

'I'm sorry about this, Judy,' said Annette.

'Not half as sorry as I am,' came the distant reply.

It was a long time since I had visited Laurie in his country cottage. We seemed to see each other often enough in the Comedy Hotel.

All those money-making ideas had evidently yielded some dividend, because he had four acres out in the country five or six miles from my own plush homestead, with a stream running down through his grounds to a small lake where about a hundred trout awaited a date with his barbecue.

On the high ground in one corner he had built since I last visited him a gigantic wooden stable block with a dovecote on the top. It looked like part of the set for one of those western films they shoot in Spain and it had been built, so he

234

told me, to house the cars he had planned to buy for some money idea that he never quite carried out. It was designed like a stable block to enhance the property's value if he ever wanted to sell.

Surrounded by so much land, Glen Cottage itself seemed a tiny place to live. It was four hundred years old, but a new dining room had been built on one end, and Laurie had also built himself a small office at the other. It was to this room that he led me with plentiful warnings about low beams when I had threaded my way through the chickens that ran loose through his grounds.

'I didn't realize you were quite so rustic,' I said.

'I love it,' he replied enthusiastically. 'We get six deer through here every morning. Foxes, badgers, but no snakes because we're on clay. It beats living in London mate.'

His office, with a newish desk and two phones, was tiny but active. A fax machine was chattering in a corner, and Baron, his labrador, was licking his private parts in another.

Laurie paused by a ziggurat of wines and removed the pyramid's top bottle which he promptly opened.

'I should have been a farmer,' he said, pouring me a glass. 'Europe paid a farmer sixty thousand pounds the other day for not growing crops on his land. Well, I could not grow crops on my land.'

'There is a downside,' I said. 'Did you know that six farmers are killed by cows every year, and they've got one of the highest suicide rates in the country?'

'Perhaps I'll give agriculture a miss.' He sat at his desk which was strewn with brown folders, each bearing the name of one of his ventures. I read AIR PICTURES on one. 'Why aren't you at work, anyway?' he asked.

'Why aren't you?' I countered. I wasn't looking forward to delivering my news.

'I had a lot of phone calls to make. I'm selling the house in Beuzeville. Bloody French. *Sur votre bicyclette.*' He drank some more wine which was French. 'Have you noticed how many marriages break up when the kids reach sixteen? It's quite common, I'm told.'

'I know. Duty done, knackered parents stagger off in search of a little enjoyment before it's too late.'

'Like my wife.'

'It's about your wife that I'm calling.' He stopped drinking and looked at me. I had noticed when I arrived that he had put a new sticker on the rear window of his Shogun. It said: MY WIFE'S CAR IS A BROOMSTICK.

'Annette has talked to her and she's coming home tomorrow,' I said.

Laurie put his glass down on his desk.

'Forgive me if I conceal my exuberance,' he said. 'Why has Annette taken it upon herself to arrange this?'

'It's complicated,' I said. 'Any more wine available?' He filled my glass and I took a few sips. 'Where's Helen?'

'Swimming with Steven Benson, I understand. Why do you ask?'

'She came to see Annette,' I said. 'She's expecting a baby.'

'I know that, Max,' said Laurie. 'I've already congratulated you.'

'Not Annette,' I said. 'Helen.'

'Helen is expecting a baby?'

I nodded. 'That's why Annette rang Judy. She thought the mother ought to know.'

Laurie looked at me for a long time as if he thought this was a poor joke. But the news sank in slowly and then he leaned forward with his elbows on his desk and buried his face in his hands. 'Jesus Christ Almighty,' he said, and then 'Oh God.' I thought he was going to cry.

'I'm sorry, Laurie,' I said, to break a painful silence. For a full minute this produced no response, but finally he took his hands from his face and said: 'That poor little girl.'

'Judy's in a state of shock,' I said.

'Well she might be,' Laurie said, trying to pull himself together. 'The kid's done no more than imitate her mother.'

It occurred to me that the two kids had done no more than imitate all four parents, but this was not the moment to air such antisocial views. Laurie's compassionate reaction had surprised and encouraged me; the anger that I expected hadn't appeared. I didn't suppose the Bensons would display similar tenderness at the news of their coming promotion to the rank of grandparents.

'There's one more thing you ought to know,' I said. Laurie now was sitting motionless and staring at or through his desk.

'Go on,' he muttered.

'The father-to-be is Steven.'

He shook his head disbelievingly. 'Does Alec know?'

'It doesn't look as if Steven has told his parents yet.'

Laurie banged his fist on the desk.

'Well, I'll tell them,' he said. 'I'll tell them, then I'll geld the little bastard.'

15

A brief renascence

It was some time since I had given work the attention that it deserved and that afternoon I sat in one of my shops and drank a cup of tea. These little cells, the faulty hearts of my collapsing empire, had suddenly become sanctuaries from the drama that the world was directing at me elsewhere.

I sat and watched Charlotte dealing with a married couple who wanted to buy their four-year-old daughter a cheap summer dress. The girl was rejecting each dress that her parents offered, naming various friends who had quite different dresses, and the fat father sat there looking lost, like a bull who is getting the worst in a *corrida*. He seemed to me to be wondering why an aberrant and long-forgotten leg-over had confronted him with this noisy little tyrant. But the world, I supposed, was full of reluctant fathers because when a man makes love to a woman the last thing on his mind is becoming a parent.

They left without spending and as Charlotte returned a dozen dresses to their hangers she said: 'It's not even easy selling to kids now.'

'Who was it who said "I like kids but I couldn't eat a whole one"?'

She turned to me proudly so that the profile of her magnificent breasts was lost.

'As a matter of fact, I'm having one,' she said.

238

'Good lord,' I exclaimed, remembering the painful saga of her mobile love life. 'I thought you were waiting to conceive in the channel tunnel.'

'Close. It was on a channel ferry.'

'Well, congratulations,' I said.

'David was getting desperate. We were going to try it next in a hot-air balloon.'

I assumed that David was her college lecturer husband, and I was relieved for his sake that he had been spared the draughty problems of copulating at two thousand feet in the basket of a balloon.

'I thought you should know early because I'll have to leave the shop.'

'That isn't a problem, Charlotte,' I said. 'The way things are going there won't be a shop for you to leave. We're only hanging on now through the kindness of the bank who are waiting for things to improve.'

'If anything,' said Charlotte, 'they're getting worse.'

A lady came in now in search of a shawl, and I went through to the office at the back. I don't know why I referred to the kindness of the bank. That morning I had received a letter from one of Mr Fleming's robotic minions:

Regarding the security deposited for your account, we wish to advise you that we will be debiting the above account with the amounts specified below.

Bank fee	£180
Local search fee	£45
Registration fee	£30
Office copies fee	£12
Questionnaire fee	£40
Total debited to account	£307

It was surprising that the banks didn't charge you a 'fee' when you blew your nose on their premises, but it was a wonderful example of how the poor get poorer. Bills like this were unknown to people who had money.

For a while I went through the accounts of the shop and not liking their doleful message switched across to the order book in the hope of finding a line that was still meeting popular acclaim. Charlotte came in evincing an almost childish pleasure at having made a sale. It was a sign of how bad things were that the staff could get excited when they had persuaded somebody to buy a shawl.

'How's your friend the shoplifter?' she asked.

'As a matter of fact, she's expecting a baby too,' I said.

'My God, she's only sixteen.'

'Old enough to become pregnant, I understand.'

'It doesn't seem right, does it?' said Charlotte. 'We try for years to have a baby and a sixteen-year-old falls for one straight away.'

'Nothing seems right these days,' I told her.

Depression is a contagious disease and Charlotte hurried away from this to busy herself in the shop. Having nothing better to do I picked up the newspaper she had bought and flicked through it.

They knew how to make money in China:

> The usual Chinese form of execution is a rifle shot in the base of the skull, a method which gives doctors a good chance of retrieving such useful organs as kidneys.
>
> But human rights observers say executions are so carefully planned that if eyes are needed, prisoners are shot in the back.
>
> The authorities also ensure that those facing execution are not tortured in such a way that their organs are damaged.

Reading this I began to feel queasy and it was a relief to hear the phone ring. I picked it up.

'You're quite easy to get hold of really,' said the husky

240

voice of Sadie Beck. 'It's just a question of ringing a dozen shops.'

'Hallo,' I said, feeling vaguely guilty.

'I've been waiting to hear the result of your test. After all, I was a partner in the enterprise. I rang before to find out but they said you were in France.'

'Indeed I was. How are you, Sadie?'

'Working too hard for a girl of my tender years. Tell me about the test.'

I looked round the corner of the office to see how near Charlotte was, but she was as far away as she could be, rearranging a display in the window.

'The test said I'm still sterile and the vasectomy is sound,' I told her.

'Doesn't that cast a strange light on your wife's pregnancy?' she asked.

'It's only one of several worries I have at the moment,' I said. 'The spectre of personal bankruptcy looms and my son's in prison in France.'

'What a dramatic life you lead, Max. What did your son do?'

'He's accused of drug smuggling. God knows when the trial will be.'

Sadie Beck fell silent at this news and I was reminded of the fact that some people regard drug smuggling, even cannabis, as much worse than rape. But no judgements were about to be passed by my sexy caller. Instead she said: 'I think you need cheering up. It's a role I was born to.'

There was nothing I would have liked better than an evening with Sadie Beck but my head was filled these days with dark visions of the future which, if I had taken them to Strawberry Hill, would have destroyed Sadie's high spirits. I was becoming the sort of person whom people should stay away from.

'I'd love to,' I said, 'but just at this moment –'

'I know,' she said, retreating. 'Your life sounds like pretty good hell to me. What are you going to do about the baby?'

241

'Doctor Mortimer suggested waiting for the birth and then arranging some blood tests.'

'A bit coldhearted,' Sadie murmured. 'A little clinical.'

'Doctors are clinical,' I said. 'That's what they're for.'

'Well, I do hope that we're going to keep in touch. I would hate to think that you are going to drift out of my life.'

'I'll ring you,' I promised.

A prurient curiosity about the fate of Mavis Jones took me early that evening to the Comedy Hotel. I had hoped to find the reunited couple enjoying a trip down memory lane over cocktails, but instead Warren Jones sat alone at the bar discussing the collapse of Communism with John the barman.

'It was a pure laboratory test,' he was saying. 'Take a country that's on the floor, destroyed by war and utterly broke, cut it in half and give one half Communism and the other half capitalism. Stir gently, then come back in forty years and see which has worked better.'

'Germany,' said John.

'Exactly. There couldn't have been a fairer test of the two conflicting political claims, and it killed Communism stone dead for ever.'

'Have you heard of China?' I said, taking the next stool. 'They still shoot people, having tortured them first. I've just been reading about it.'

He turned to me. 'Good evening, Mr Hadfield,' he said politely. 'China? China is living in the eighteenth century.'

I ordered a lager.

'I wish I were,' I said. 'The twentieth century is a bit fast for me.'

He looked at me but didn't say anything. I wasn't feeling that chatty myself and was happy to drink in silence. What I really needed now was a restful holiday, free from the dramas of Deauville, with a warm beach and a swarm of waiters. But what I could afford was a seat in the back of a coach owned by a firm with a name like Poxy Tours, that pottered through

242

the rainswept south-west with a group of what they now called senior citizens, stopping occasionally to queue at a Wimpy or pee in a hedge.

This bleak prospect depressed me even more than my other pressing reasons for despondency and when Warren Jones spoke I was, after all, glad to be taken away from myself.

'I'd like to ask you a question, sir,' he said in that courteous transatlantic manner, 'about Alec Benson.'

'Where is Alec?' I asked.

'He's in Windsor with my mother. I'm expecting them back here soon.' He picked up his glass which appeared to hold cider and started turning it round almost nervously. 'I have my suspicions about that man.'

'Alec?'

'What does he do?'

'He's a headmaster,' I said.

'Is he, by God! Well, I've noticed that he has black curly hair. I have black curly hair. Then again, he last met my mother about twenty-four years ago. I'm twenty-four.'

'I catch your drift,' I said.

'My mother gave me a ludicrous story about my father being killed by a pig, but I never believed it. I suspect that my real father is Mr Benson.'

'It's an interesting idea,' I said. 'Have you talked to your mother about it?'

'I haven't seen much of her since Alec Benson appeared, and I haven't seen her at all since I had the idea.' He drank some cider and turned to me. 'What sort of man is he?'

'Rather serious,' I said. 'Conscientious, honest. A bit of a pedant, occasionally melancholy. He has often mentioned your mother over the years. Their romance, if that's what it was, has stuck in his mind.'

My somewhat comprehensive reply seemed to please Warren Jones. His thin, pale face broke into a grin as he tried to picture the tender affair all those years ago that, he now guessed, resulted in him.

'What's going to happen to them?' I asked. 'Are they

reliving old times, or are they about to pick up where they left off?'

'Oh, there's no room in my mother's life for a man now. She's got herself a perfect existence. She earns a hundred K for a start.'

'Does that mean a hundred thousand pounds a year?' I asked, surprised.

'It sure does. The cosmetics business is a goldmine and she's very high up in it. One week she's in Paris, the next in Rome. She flies to the States at least twelve times a year.'

I could see that this was not the sort of lifestyle that would suit Alec; he was slightly put out when Kitty won her part-time job on the council.

'Alec lives at a more modest level,' I said. 'If he travels to London he gets overexcited.'

'That's life,' said Warren Jones enigmatically. 'The worthwhile job pays the least because there will always be worthwhile people prepared to do it. I mean, what's the moral justification for a cosmetics industry?'

I realized that he had now convinced himself that he was Alec's son and had promptly assumed certain filial duties to do with defending him. I had to admire his adaptability.

'What do you do, Warren?' I asked.

'College. Studying politics and economics.'

'Then what?'

'Journalism, the House of Commons, 10 Downing Street.'

'Worthwhile jobs pay the least,' I said.

'Money's never going to be a problem with what my mother's saving. I'm her financial adviser. We grow the stuff in Jersey. What *was* going to be a problem was parentage. I have nightmares about the future, with headlines in *The Sun* saying "Pig Fell on Premier's Dad". It's not exactly image building.'

'But a headmaster as a dad would be good for your image?'

'Perfect.'

He beamed at me happily and was distracted by someone

244

approaching him from behind. It was Alec and Mavis Jones who arrived at the bar if not exactly hand in hand, at the very least looking like a couple who knew things that the rest of the world did not.

'Hi,' said Alec, giving me a nod. 'We've just been spending money in one of your shops.'

'That makes you a very rare species,' I said, standing up and offering my stool to Mavis Jones. She did not dress like a lady who used the Max Hadfield chain, but it emerged that her attention had been caught by a pair of orange jeans in the window at Windsor.

She sat down and opened her bag.

'Let me buy you all a drink,' she said, producing a ten-pound note.

There was a time when I would have politely refused this offer and insisted on buying the drinks myself, but now that I knew her salary I was quite happy to let her buy a hogshead of lager with no help from me.

In her company Alec seemed to have experienced some sort of renascence. The smile had never been a potent weapon in his social armoury, but now he couldn't get rid of it. He no longer crept into the bar as if he was moving from one defeat to the next, but strode in boyishly and used greetings like 'Hi'.

This new Alec unnerved me a little, accentuating my own deepening gloom, but my conversation with Warren Jones had convinced me that this romantic interlude was going to be a very brief Indian summer and I would soon have the standard Alec back.

'Alec has been showing me the pastoral life,' said Mavis Jones, lighting a cigarette. 'It's a long time since I saw a lamb without mint sauce on it.'

'Did you notice the cows?' I asked. 'That's where we get our milk from.'

'I remember that from school,' Mavis Jones said. 'In trains and planes and boardrooms you sort of forget about cows, except the ones you're dealing with across a desk.'

'We know about pigs, though,' Warren Jones said, 'don't we, Mum?'

'Don't mention pigs,' said his mother.

Warren Jones had been watching Alec with rather more absorption than was polite, and I wondered whether his reference to pigs meant that he was planning to raise the subject of his father's identity. But I was to be denied this titillating prospect by the emergence of a better one.

Kitty Benson arrived in the bar at that moment, and strode grim-faced in our direction. She reached us before anybody could move and gazed at Mavis Jones through her big glasses.

'This is Councillor Benson,' I said lightly. 'Of the Environmental Veggie Burger Party.'

'Ignore Max,' said Kitty. 'He's got a hole in his ozone layer.'

'This is Mavis Jones, Kitty,' said Alec uneasily.

'I thought it might be,' said Kitty. 'You used to know my husband when he was a man.'

'He was just a youth, Kitty,' said Mavis Jones who was so completely unruffled that I could suddenly see why she was worth her salary. 'May I buy you a drink?'

'A moonraker,' said Kitty. 'It's a non-alcoholic cocktail I have discovered.'

'I know,' said Mavis Jones, an old hand of the cocktail circuit. 'Tonic water, lemon juice, lime juice and grenadine.'

I avoided looking at anybody now, scared of catching a glance that would place the wrong expression on my face; I diligently drank my lager and tried to pretend that this was not an abnormal situation. At the same time I felt that as a non-participant in the little drama I was best placed to lead the conversation, but I couldn't summon a single plausible topic from my head.

The moonraker was ordered in silence. It was not a drink that arrived quickly, and while John was mixing it Kitty spoke up.

'I didn't mean to interrupt a tête-à-tête,' she said, 'but we have a crisis at home, Alec, and I think you should be there.'

246

'What crisis?' asked Alec, who looked as if he had all the crises he could handle here in the bar.

'It concerns our son,' said Kitty, taking the drink from Mavis Jones.

'Have you got a son, Mr Benson?' asked Warren Jones.

Alec looked at him in hopeless confusion. 'Er, yes, Warren,' he said. He turned to Kitty. 'What's he done now?'

Kitty drank her non-alcoholic cocktail while she considered what to say. 'I don't think it's something we want to air in here,' she said. 'It's something that requires a family conference.'

Alec finished his drink and then looked at Mavis Jones.

'I'll have to go,' he said. He shrugged and began to look like the helpless old Alec that I knew so well. When Kitty had finished her drink, she took him by the arm and with one 'Goodbye' to us all, led him from the room.

The next morning there was a letter from Garth. It was two weeks since he had written – his first letter had spent a week on our doormat while we were in France. The new one, written before he had heard from us, made sad reading and as I passed it sheet by sheet to Annette in bed I saw tears in her eyes.

He was sharing a cell with, among others, a man accused of armed kidnapping and forging nine million dollars.

'What will it do to him, mixing with people like that?' said Annette. 'He should be at university now, mingling with the future Cabinet.'

'He probably is mingling with the future Cabinet,' I said.

I was more concerned about his food.

'We are fed twice a day on a diet which, if you eat it at all, meets the minimum intake requirement,' he wrote.

School dinners were à la carte by comparison. They rely on the fact that by providing a food-ordering service, for which you pay, most prisoners ignore the basic requirements. But if you have no money the basic is what you have to eat.

247

You can have a cooked meal every Saturday evening – chicken and chips or steak and chips, but it costs between fifty and seventy francs. The price of everything is extortionate, but they do have a captive audience. I am down to sixty kilos. That's about nine and a half stone, isn't it?

The picture in my mind created the need for a large whisky, but it was too early in the day. I read on, without help.

It is getting to be a nightmare now because I can't see the end of it. You can be locked up here for more than a year before you even get to court and there doesn't seem to be any logic, let alone justice, in the sentences that are passed.

The trial system seems to be a farce. Four or five of you go up at once. You see the judge several times before the case so he has all the evidence he wants before the hearing. In court your solicitor delivers a five-minute plea, the prosecutor asks for the sentence he wants, and the customs ask for their fine or the term of imprisonment to be served if the fine isn't paid. Then you all stand in a line and the judge delivers his sentence. They get through half a dozen cases in an hour. If the prosecutor doesn't get the sentence he wants he has six weeks to appeal. If you want to appeal, you have ten days. Everybody leaves court terrified that the prosecution will appeal for a longer sentence because their requests are always granted.

You can apply for parole when you have served half your sentence but with remission for good behaviour and sometimes for passing exams I could be a lot less than halfway through it. Also Mitterrand usually announces some sort of amnesty, like ten days per month served, on Bastille Day. This could cut a five-year sentence down to two providing I have three things. One is a permanent address in England, two is a formal job offer on headed notepaper, and three is a certificate from customs saying I have paid the fine which could be as high as £20,000. If I

248

don't pay the fine I have to do an extra two years – plus I
lose all remission on the original sentence.

'He'd probably do an extra five years if we can't find
twenty thousand,' I said to Annette.

'I know. I read it. We've got to pay it.'

'I don't have twenty thousand,' I said.

'Sell the house, Max. We can't let him rot for five years.'

How could I tell her that it was no longer our house to
sell?

A routine check at the clinic that afternoon took her mind
off Garth for a few hours but did little to lift my own spirits. If
the paraphernalia of babyhood – cots, prams, dolls and potties
– was about to re-enter my life I would have liked the
certainty of a personal involvement. The compounded aroma
of the clinic was not to my taste either: you were never
quite sure what you were smelling.

I drove Annette home as she talked proudly about her
blood pressure, and I decided that once I had dropped her off
I would pay a visit to Alec who on all available evidence
must by now have a story to tell. It was no use waiting to
meet him in the Comedy Hotel where either Warren or Mavis
Jones would impede the free flow of information.

To my astonishment I found him in exultant mood. The
exam results had been released that morning and his school
had achieved greater success than ever before. Helen had
taken ten O level subjects and passed in all of them. Steven
had scored nine out of nine. I kept to myself my own sceptical
suspicion that the government, nervous at public outrage
over educational standards, had lowered the benchmark to
appease the crowds.

Alec sat at a garden table in the middle of the lawn,
surrounded by papers.

'Look at this!' he said blissfully. 'People talk about Britain's
aggressive, xenophobic youngsters, but here's the proof that
they're not daft! Here's a kid with four Bs and an A. To meet

him you wouldn't think he could walk and talk at the same time.'

'Very impressive,' I said.

'Steven with nine O levels! I didn't get that many myself.'

'Nor did I,' I said, feeling sour.

'The governors are going to be pleased,' said Alec, gathering up the sheets and trying to get them into a folder.

'That's the important thing,' I said.

'I think this calls for a drink.'

'I'll second that,' I said fervently.

He led me not to the house but to the conservatory where among the ferns he had left his bottle of gin and two glasses.

'We can talk better in here,' he said, ushering me to the rattan sofa. 'Kitty's indoors, doing her book.'

'How is Kitty?' I asked. 'I thought she behaved very well last night, all things considered.'

'I thought Mavis did,' said Alec. 'I thought she handled it superbly.'

I drank some gin. 'What's going to happen?' I asked. I hadn't come here to discuss the academic achievements of Alec's wilful youngsters.

'Happen?' said Alec. 'How do you mean?'

'You and Mavis,' I said. 'Not to mention Warren who, I may tell you, believes you're his father.'

'How do you know that?'

'He told me last night. He said he has his suspicions about you based on black curly hair and a twenty-four-year time span.'

Alec shook his head. 'Mavis didn't want him to know.'

'She couldn't expect him to believe the saga of the pig for ever.'

'Do you think I should talk to him?'

'Certainly. He's very happy to have a headmaster for a father instead of somebody who came second to a pig. What about Mavis? Did you have a good time?'

The waterfall in the corner of the fish pond splashed from one ledge to the next.

'You're a bloody gossip, Max,' Alec said. 'But since you ask, nothing happened.'

'No hoovering?'

'Certainly not. The whole thing was very decorous, quite apart from the fact that Warren had an adjacent bedroom.'

'I can see that that would put a dampener on things,' I said.

'We decided to behave like responsible adults. Well, Mavis decided to. I suspect that she has a man in New York.'

I felt a little cheated at this, having come here for an animated first-hand account of passionate reunions and uncontrollable lust on the carpet. Twenty-four years might be no more than a cosmic blink, but it was long enough between jumps to create an appetite.

'Responsible adults?' I said. 'I thought you were a very sexual person?'

'*Was* a very sexual person, Max. When I was twenty. I'm forty-four now. More gin?'

I held out my glass and allowed him to half fill it. 'So what's going to happen? Is Mavis about to vanish for another twenty-four years?'

'She flies to Geneva at the weekend and then on to Rome. She's a very busy lady.'

'Clearly.'

'We're not about to renew our romance, if that's what you're asking. I have Kitty and Steven. I have responsibilities.'

I looked at him while he made this solemn speech and then his face broke into the broadest of smiles. 'But it was magic to see her again!'

I nodded understandingly at this touching admission. 'The discovery of a son must have been fairly spellbinding, too,' I suggested. The smile faded at the mention of Warren.

'If you're a young father the child can be seen to be an interruption of your life, and this is reflected later in the relationship. I've found that with Steven. But to have a son you didn't know about appear fully grown is even more difficult. What can I say to him?'

251

'Tell him there's good news about the pig.'

Alec gave this the contempt it deserved and sipped his gin. I was trying to remember what the other item of gossip was that I had come here to dig out, but so many things seemed to be happening to so many people that I was beginning to lose track.

Alec said: 'I have one son who is apparently heading for the House of Commons, and another who is on probation. What does that tell us about genetics and heredity?'

I wasn't feeling sufficiently acerbic to suggest that Warren's great advantage was that he hadn't gone to Alec's school, and today's surprising exam results would probably have spoilt my joke. Instead, I said: 'I would have expected Kitty's offspring to be the political animal.'

'Oh, Steven's political,' said Alec. 'He's steeped in the stuff.'

'Breaking my windows was a political act, was it?' I asked.

'As a matter of fact, it was. He's a radical, you see.'

'Ah, that explains it,' I said.

In what tortuous metaphysical abyss this conversation might eventually have deposited us we were not destined to discover because there was now a tapping at the window and I could see Kitty heading for our door. She was wearing old corduroy trousers, a pink jumper and a harassed expression.

She opened the door. 'We've got visitors,' she said. 'Good afternoon, Max.'

'Hallo, Kitty,' I said. 'Tell the visitors to go away and get on with your book.'

'It's Laurie and Judy.'

'Judy?' said Alec. 'Return of the renegade.'

We both got up and followed Kitty out of the conservatory. As we walked across the lawn towards the Bensons' chilly house I remembered what it was that I had wanted to ask Alec. What 'crisis at home' had provoked Kitty's unexpected appearance in the Comedy Hotel the previous evening? I assumed that they had discovered that Helen was pregnant, but this was evidently not something that Alec had wanted to discuss with me or he would have brought the subject up himself.

But now, with the arrival of Mr and Mrs Curtis, the subject was due to be ventilated. I followed Alec and Kitty into the house, the odd man out in this inter-family conference, but determined not to leave unless I was asked.

Judy and Laurie were sitting side by side on the sofa like a couple who had never been apart. Judy's appearance had been improved by her French adventure: her plentiful blonde hair had been restyled in a way that made her look younger, and her snazzy suit had come from one of Deauville's expensive boutiques. She looked completely composed. Laurie looked like a man who had lost his grip on things, uneasy with Judy, uneasy to be here. The brown suit was back again, but looked rumpled; the moustache drooped.

'Hallo, Alec,' he said, ignoring me. 'This is an unhappy business.'

I kissed Judy on the cheek and she smiled ruefully. 'Thank Annette for ringing,' she said.

We all sat down feeling slightly embarrassed. It was like a meeting that has discovered there is no chairman.

'I don't think Max knows why we're here,' Alec said. I had the impression that he felt I should have done the decent thing and slipped away.

'He knows,' said Laurie. 'He told me.'

'How this thing happened I'll never know,' said Judy.

'The usual way, I imagine,' said Kitty. 'Kids grow up fast.'

'I thought Helen was still into dolls and kittens,' Judy said. 'It came as quite a shock, I can tell you.'

'What we have to decide,' said Alec, 'is what we're going to do about it.'

'For a start I should be horsewhipping your son,' said Laurie.

'Don't be too quick to attribute blame,' said Kitty. 'Given Steven's naivety it is just as likely that he was led on by Helen.'

'Led on by Helen?' said Judy. 'She's a sixteen-year-old schoolgirl, not a vamp.'

'Like most parents, you didn't notice them growing up,' I

253

said. Having had the misfortune to overhear this couple of young innocents struggling towards sexual satisfaction in my spare room, I could only marvel at the loving blindness of parents who thought a sixteen-year-old was still twelve, and a twelve-year-old was still eight.

'What are the options?' said Alec in his best headmasterly manner, and then he counted them off on his fingers. 'Marriage, adoption, abortion.'

'Marriage?' said Judy. 'Well, you can count that out for a start.'

'Has anyone thought to consult the couple concerned?' asked Kitty.

'It isn't a couple that's concerned,' said Judy. 'It's a sixteen-year-old girl. It's not Steven's future that will be blighted, Kitty.'

'I can see that,' said Kitty. 'But I don't think he should be excluded from the discussion.'

'Where are they, anyway?' I asked. 'Shouldn't they appear before the Star Chamber?'

'They're meeting friends in some coffee bar to congratulate each other on their O level results,' said Laurie. 'Helen got ten out of ten.'

'They both did brilliantly,' Kitty said, 'which is why we've got to get them out of this mess.'

'It would be difficult to pass your A levels when you've been up all night feeding the baby,' said Judy. 'There will have to be an abortion.'

The ugly word hung in the room and nobody wanted to touch it.

'What was the other option?' Laurie asked.

'Adoption.'

'I don't like the sound of that,' said Laurie. 'What about a fourth possibility – that she has the baby, but they don't marry?'

'That's what they do these days,' said Alec. 'And the kid has both parents' surnames. A double-barrelled surname used to mean you were posh. Now it means you're a bastard.'

'Don't be bloody stupid, Laurie,' said Judy. 'An unmarried mother at seventeen would be a great start in life, wouldn't it?'

'I think I'll make some tea,' said Kitty, standing up.

When she had gone, a strange silence fell on the room which, given the garrulous nature of the trio I was with, lent a dreamlike feeling to the occasion. They sat freeze-framed in their chairs, thoughtful but mute, and I guessed that quite a lot of mutual antipathy was destroying the prospect of conversation. What the situation was between Laurie and Judy didn't bear thinking about, and neither would be feeling very fond of Alec, the father of the boy who had ruined their daughter.

I asked: 'What does Helen say about it?'

'She had a bizarre idea,' said Judy, 'which she greeted me with when I got home.'

'What was that?' asked Laurie. 'She didn't say anything to me.'

'That she has the baby and we pass if off as her sister or brother. We pretend that I had the baby.'

'I think that's rather nice,' I said.

'Well, if you think it's so nice, you pretend that you had it,' said Judy. 'Bringing up a child was never my idea of fun.'

'It would solve a lot of problems, though,' said Laurie.

'Not as many as it would create,' said Judy. 'Particularly for me.'

'So it's one vote for abortion then,' said Alec. 'But not mine.'

'You don't have a vote, Alec,' said Judy. 'We're talking about my daughter here.'

'Suppose my son wants to marry your daughter?' said Alec.

'We'll consider his offer in ten years' time,' said Judy.

When Kitty returned with the tea, a fresh silence had descended, but people stirred at the sight of refreshments.

'What have you all decided?' Kitty asked as she filled the cups.

255

'Judy has decided on an abortion,' Alec said.

'I'm sorry to hear that, Judy,' said Kitty.

'There are no happy solutions to this problem, Kitty,' Judy said. 'It's a mess that ends in tears whichever way you go.'

'Some ways lead to more tears than others,' said Kitty. 'Have you mentioned abortion to Helen?'

'I doubt whether she knows what it is.'

'You doubted whether she knew what sexual intercourse was,' said Kitty. 'Stop underestimating the girl. She's got ten O levels.'

'I'll worry about Helen, you worry about Steven,' said Judy, slightly nettled.

'There's no blame in this house, Judy,' said Kitty. 'Boys will be boys and girls will be girls. I'm not going to stand in the way of the march of history.'

'That's the trouble with our society,' said Judy. 'Nobody blames anybody for anything and everybody does as they like.'

'Well, I must say that's a bit rich coming from somebody who's just crawled out of a French barman's bed,' said Kitty.

'If the conversation's sinking to that level I'm going home,' said Judy.

'Wherever that is,' said Kitty. 'You'd never make a councillor if you're that thin skinned.'

'I don't want to make a councillor,' said Judy, 'and at the moment I am more concerned about not making a grandmother.'

'Well, you seem to have scotched that possibility,' said Kitty. 'I only hope you bear in mind the long-term psychological damage to Helen.'

'That is what I'm bearing in mind,' said Judy, standing up. She looked down at her husband, who looked as unhappy as I had ever seen him.

'Are you coming?' she asked.

'Yep.' He got to his feet and turned to Alec as his wife headed for the door. 'Sorry it's ended like this,' he said.

'Don't worry about it,' said Alec, remaining firmly seated.

'Well,' said Kitty when they had gone, 'what's going to happen?'

'I wish I knew,' I said. 'Is there any more tea?'

On Sunday afternoon when the world paused for breath I sat on the patio watching the fitful progress of oarsmen on the Thames. To my mind it was the most uncomfortable method of transport ever devised, with the possible exception of brachiation.

On the table in front of me was a writing pad on which, in a sudden surge of verbal productivity, I had inscribed the words 'Dear Garth'. I owed my son a letter and could see him waiting helplessly for it in his cell, but the restrictions on what I could say meant that I could not write honestly and the letter was going to have an unreal air.

'It is the usual dull Sunday afternoon here and the usual dull Sunday afternoon television,' I wrote.

> Nigel Mansell throwing his driving gloves in disgust to the crowd, and an old black and white film featuring long-dead stars, something which I always find a depressing reminder of my own mortality.
>
> We found your letter depressing as well. I am sending the hundred pounds a month that you asked for and hope that by now it is reaching you and you can lash out on steak and chips on Saturday evenings. Your weight is alarming, but you were never fat. What worries me most is the customs fine that you will have to pay if they convict you. I no longer have that sort of money. I'm living with a growing debt. The shops are having a very bad time and I can't kid myself any longer that they are going to survive the recession.

I didn't know what I could say to him and spent the next quarter of an hour watching a garden warbler that would soon be off to Africa for the winter. He was a rare visitor to our garden and I began to envy him. Perhaps I could follow his example and find somewhere suitably obscure to escape to myself. Burkina-Faso sounded obscure enough.

Annette came out with some tea.

'What are you saying to him?' she asked.

'That I'm worried about how the customs fine will be paid.'

'Why don't you suggest that the man who got him to drive the Range Rover should pay it?'

'He doesn't exist.'

'I know he doesn't exist, but it will look good for Garth when the authorities read the letter.'

I took her advice and my letter moved into sheer fantasy.

'Can you give me the name and address of the man who asked you to drive his Range Rover back to London?' I wrote. 'I will go round and see him with some heavy friends of mine and perhaps he will become quite keen to pay your fine. It shouldn't be too difficult. With cannabis in his vehicle he would be vulnerable to threats, and I know men in London that you wouldn't want to meet on a dark night.'

The frustration of my son at realizing that I didn't understand the situation at all would be intense, but that was the position that he had brought us all to. I scribbled on, keen to give him something else to think about – Helen's pregnancy, Judy's romantic interlude, Alec's discovery of another son. In prison there is a lot of time to think.

'Send him my love and tell him that I think about him all the time,' said Annette, whose previous letter seemed to have exhausted her literary capacities for the time being.

I looked across to her to nod, and saw that there were tears in her eyes again.

'He won't be here for the baby,' she said. 'That's the saddest thing of all.'

Not necessarily, I thought. It could be a good event to miss.

But I didn't reply. Searching for words I found myself looking round for the garden warbler again, but the Hadfield family's dismal mood had obviously persuaded him to fly south.

16

Charcoal grilled

I can see that my life is disintegrating around me, but I can't see where I have gone wrong. I have plotted a boringly conventional route through life's little hazards, but the pitfalls and the pratfalls must have been concealed in the folds of my map.

My reaction to the multiplying disasters has been to start smoking again, further proof no doubt of the weakness that is presumably at the core of my problems. It was either that or refuge in religion – shuffling along Oxford Street in a bed sheet with my head brutally shaved, or joining the burgeoning groups of happy clappies who howl to God from converted warehouses, with insane smiles on their faces.

I was encouraged by the fact that experts, who once told you that cigarettes would kill you stone dead, had now decided that nicotine improved intellectual functions. The *British Medical Journal* has published a report that shows that smoking protects you against dementia. The risk of Alzheimer's is three times higher in non-smokers, and regular doses of nicotine stimulate the neurotransmitters to provide some protection against Parkinson's. Of course, when I was younger milk and exercise were thought to be good for you. Now we are told something quite different.

When I last smoked cigarettes they cost almost one pound for twenty. In the Comedy Hotel the notice says: 'This machine now vends at £2' and when it finally surrenders its precious packet you are lucky to find seventeen cigarettes inside.

I have not heard lately from Mr Fleming, my regrettably depilated financial tormentor, but I know he's out there somewhere, plotting my downfall. I'm living on borrowed time, and the interest rates apply there too. One of these days a depressingly formal letter will bounce erratically through my front door like a Scud missile.

I take my mind off these problems by listening to those of other people in the Comedy Hotel. The nickname that once applied to the quality of the jokes heard on its premises was still appropriate although to my mind it now meant something different. Most of us were comedians, joke figures presiding with equal incompetence over personal disasters that we seemed helpless to reverse.

This shift of emphasis struck me a couple of nights later when I arrived in the bar to find Laurie nursing a gin and a black eye. The visible signs of his domestic wounds were something I had come to ignore, but as this one had arrived since Judy's return from France it was too interesting to overlook.

'Everything okay at home?' I asked when I had lit my cigarette.

Laurie's one eye rolled skywards in a gesture of resignation.

'Describing her as a vindictive cow may have been a tactical error because she hit me with a hairbrush and for twenty minutes I couldn't see properly.'

'She hasn't lost her touch,' I said. 'They say the last thing a boxer loses is his punch.'

'What's the first?'

'Legs.'

'She's still got her legs. She moves very quickly.'

'Oh good,' I said. 'Can you see well enough to beat me at pool?'

'I don't need two eyes for that,' he replied.

We went through to the pool room and he started to cheer up. 'I've had a new money idea,' he said. 'Ads in all the tabloids asking men whether they are certain they are the fathers of their wives' children? A new survey says that one in ten fathers in England have a child that isn't theirs, and they don't know. So they send me twenty pounds and a hair from their head and one from their child's. I tell them in confidence whether they're the real father.'

'What's the matter with blood tests?' I asked, feeling that this idea was a little close to home.

'Use your imagination, mate. How do you think the wife reacts if you say "I'm just taking the boy down to the clinic for a blood test"? My way is easy and trouble-free.'

'Can you tell from hair?' I asked, interested.

'I've no idea,' said Laurie. 'What's that got to do with it?'

'The recession is edging you towards dishonesty,' I said.

'What the hell – there's a crime committed in England and Wales every seven seconds.' He squinted the length of his cue. He was quite wrong to suppose that he could beat me with one eye; judging distance was beyond him and often the cue ball didn't even reach its target. We abandoned the game and returned to the bar.

Sitting at the counter now were Alec and Warren Jones, closeted together like a couple of chess players. They seemed so preoccupied with their conversation that we thought it only polite to leave them in peace. We sat some way down the counter and I ordered drinks.

'How's your fecund daughter?' I asked Laurie.

'She's gone to stay with an aunt, Judy's sister in Bexhill,' he said, fingering his eye. 'The matter has been taken out of my hands.'

'I thought it might be,' I said. 'Judy has told you that men don't understand.'

'Something like that.'

'And what's Judy going to do? Is she staying or going?'

'Staying. Apparently Jean-Paul told her that if she went she needn't bother to come back.'

'What did Judy say?'

'What do you think? She walloped him. Said he was a bastard and of course she had to see her pregnant daughter. She broke his nose with a wine bottle.'

'My God, she's fighting her way across Europe. Where was she in 1944 when we needed her?'

'Actually she's calmed down a lot. The Helen business knocked her back. I blame myself for the black eye.'

'Very chivalrous of you,' I said, as he lit a cigar with some difficulty. He was having the same distance problem as he had had on the pool table.

We were interrupted now by Giles, the absentee owner of this watering hole, who was sporting his usual dark tan.

'Hotel owner visits England,' I said. 'You didn't get that tan beside the Thames.'

'How very true,' said Giles in his beautiful upper-class accent. 'I got it on Tahiti beach in Saint-Tropez. It's more fun there.'

'All right for some,' said Laurie.

'You can afford it, old boy,' said Giles. 'Stop behaving as if you are going to live for ever. There's a number to the days you have left.'

'Don't I know it, mate,' said Laurie.

'Well get out and enjoy yourself then,' said Giles sternly.

Laurie looked irritable, and I found Giles fairly trying myself. He was so smooth and his life was so totally devoted to pleasure that it could hardly fail to rile the rest of us who lacked his freedom and resources. His presence in his own hotel was an irrelevance: it ran perfectly well without him. And so he appeared and disappeared in the world's exotic spots, dropping into Britain now and again to check the till.

At one time I had hoped that my own business would afford me this luxury. After all, I didn't actually deal with the customers. But the recession had hit me in a way that the Comedy Hotel had avoided, and I felt obliged to stay in touch and keep one finger on the faltering pulse.

'Why don't you buy us a drink,' I said, 'like a proper proprietor?'

'I'll gladly do that,' said Giles. 'John, fill these gentlemen's glasses.' When the drinks had arrived, Giles announced that he was holding a big barbecue on Saturday evening and would be delighted if we were there.

'I saw the notice on the door,' I said. 'You're one of that growing band of people who think there's a Q in barbecue.'

'If I could spell I wouldn't be running a hotel, Max,' he said. 'Will you both come?'

'Of course,' said Laurie. 'But will you? Or will you have skipped off to Bermuda or somewhere?'

'I'll be here,' said Giles. 'It's my thirtieth birthday.'

'I used to be thirty,' I said. 'About twenty years ago.'

I pulled out a cigarette to cheer myself up and Giles was immediately beside me with a large gold lighter that said VENEZIA on one side.

When Laurie had departed for dinner and Giles had wandered off to inspect his kitchens, I eased my way down the bar in the direction of Alec and Warren Jones. I didn't want to disturb their conference, but I wanted them to know that my company was available. In the event they ignored me, but my sideways shuffle brought me within earshot of their intimate chat.

'It's been a shock for both of us,' Alec was saying, 'but the young can withstand these things better.'

'I don't know about that,' Warren said. 'Finding a father at twenty-four is a pretty big thing if you have spent your life not knowing that you've got one.'

'The important thing now is for us to stay in touch,' Alec said.

'We will,' Warren said, and I noticed that he had now dropped the 'sir' from his conversation. 'It will be nice to have a sort of unseen audience. It will give my work a point.'

'Well, I hope I'm not going to be *that* unseen,' Alec said. 'I'd like to think that we're going to meet up regularly.'

'I'd certainly like to meet my brother,' Warren said. 'My half brother.'

Alec looked glum. 'He's a barrel of trouble, I'm afraid.'

This news seemed to perk Warren up. 'Really? In what way?'

'He's a vandal. He's also got a girl pregnant, and he's only seventeen.'

'Who are we blaming for that?' Warren asked immediately.

'Blaming?' said Alec, temporarily at a loss. 'We're blaming him.'

'It's not that easy,' said Warren soberly. 'Up north now the teenagers are doing something they call ram-raiding – driving a stolen car into a shop window and looting the goods. Well, boys from Eton don't do that.'

'What's your point?' asked Alec uneasily.

'If the ram-raider had gone to Eton he wouldn't be a ram-raider. But it's not his fault that he didn't go to Eton.'

'Quite a lot of boys who didn't go to Eton have managed to get along without smashing shop windows.'

'Well, I did a survey on juvenile delinquency at college and I have to tell you that I didn't find a single example where I could unreservedly blame the boy. They had all been let down in some way by life's support systems, parents, teachers or just the local amenities.'

'It's difficult for the parent to blame the teacher when the parent is the teacher,' said Alec, looking far from happy with this conversation.

'I can see that,' said Warren briskly, 'but no teacher should have his own child at his own school. It gives the kid an unbalanced position.'

All in all, I thought Alec was taking these veiled rebukes rather well. He picked up his drink, a colourless short that could have been gin or vodka, and nodded slowly as if he were a pupil under instruction himself.

'I have a suggestion,' Warren said now. 'If you are agreeable.'

'What's that?'

'I should like to meet Steven. To talk to him alone.'

'At the moment he's not even aware of your existence.'

264

'I think he should be,' Warren said in a tone of voice that did not invite dissent. 'I think I could be helpful.'

Alec considered this proposal, its problems and its possible ramifications, and then started nodding again. 'Let's do that,' he said. 'Of course, I'll have to talk to Kitty first.'

'Fine,' said Warren. 'Now let me buy you a drink.'

As they turned to catch John's attention they both saw me.

'Max! How long have you been there?'

'Years.'

'We've been having a chat.'

'I gathered.'

'Warren has got this idea that he ought to talk to Steven.'

'A very good one,' I said. 'Warren is the sort of person Steven will listen to.'

'Do you think so?' Alec seemed gratified that I gave my approval to this suggestion, as if he was no longer willing to trust his own judgement in family matters.

'A brother will fill a void,' I said. 'The mutual interest in politics will be a great help, and if he looks up to Warren he'll listen to what he says.'

This optimistic scenario lifted a burden from Alec's back: the responsibility of Steven had been passed to other more enthusiastic hands.

'Have you seen Laurie?' he asked, happy to turn his attention to other subjects.

'He was in here just now.'

'How is he? I don't want to fall out with him over the Helen business.'

'He's fine,' I said, 'apart from a black eye.'

'Oh good. Everything's back to normal again.'

Warren bought me a drink, too, and the three of us sat at the bar while he treated us to his youthful view of the world, its economy and its prospects. It was infinitely more sanguine than anything that had ever been expressed on that subject by either Alec or me but, as he had paid for the drinks, we gave him our rapt attention.

*

265

Annette was groaning in bed when I got home and for a moment I thought she was about to give birth. The possibility of a tiny person appearing without the attention of professionals frightened the life out of me and the cheering effect of a few drinks evaporated on the spot.

'Are you okay?' I asked, ready to panic.

'I'm as okay as you can get if you're eight months pregnant,' she said. 'I don't think these are contractions.'

She lay on her back and looked up at me as I sat on the edge of the bed.

'What are we going to call this scrap?' she asked.

'I don't know,' I said. 'Have you any ideas?'

'I thought that if we called him Harrison Richard it would give him the initials H.R.H.'

'It's going to be a boy?'

'Boys are what I have.'

'Well, let's suppose she's a girl, as the scan suggested. How about an exotic name like Tamara?'

Annette shook her head at this suggestion. 'It sounds like a barrow boy trying to say tomorrow. Tamara never comes.'

'Naomi,' I said.

'He's a boy, Max. A future footballer by the feel of it.'

'Well, you decide,' I said, standing up. 'I must eat.'

'I was going to cook you dinner, but you're a little late. Put a lasagne in the microwave.'

'I'm afraid things got a little interesting in the Comedy Hotel. Judy has got to stay with Laurie because she broke the Frenchman's nose. Alec has been talking to his new-found son who seems to think he can straighten Steven out.'

'I suppose it helps to take your mind off your own disasters.'

'It certainly does that,' I said.

Downstairs I found that lasagne wasn't quite what my stomach wanted and made myself a ham omelette instead. I turned on the television without sound and switched to the news on teletext. A meteorite from beyond Mars had landed in a hedge in Kent, and down among the peaceful glades of the New Forest a thirty-stone wild pig had been terrorizing the visitors by stealing their food and biting them. There were probably more important events occurring on the world stage but these days I could only cope with the minutiae.

Annette's groans had disconcerted me. The coming birth had been a distant problem among several others, but tonight had made me realize that it was almost upon us. I would have to be ready at a moment's notice to drive her to the hospital, and could never be too far away.

I was quite used to driving her, of course. I was practically her chauffeur, a role I gladly fulfilled to stop her jumping into expensive taxis.

Annette's driving was so bad that she no longer wanted a car. When I first met her she had a Volkswagen Beetle and on one of our first dates she was driving me slowly through the crowded streets of a town on the south coast when she noticed, somewhat belatedly in my opinion, that an old lady with a shopping basket was sitting on her bonnet.

'How did she get there?' she asked.

'You scooped her up at the last pedestrian crossing,' I told her. 'I thought it was some sort of trick.'

'Christ Almighty,' said Annette, braking violently.

'Do you mean you don't know her?' I asked. 'I thought she was your granny or something, and you gave her lifts.'

The old lady disembarked, as it were, and we hurried off without explanation. But I could see that my life would be less anxious if I could consign Annette to the passenger seat and after a mild collision with a bus a year or two later in which only five people were slightly hurt she seemed to take the same view.

Kitty Benson turned up a couple or mornings later. I was washing the breakfast things while Annette slept on, and hearing a car in the drive I looked out and saw her Viva. This was so unusual that I hurried to the front door. She stood on the front step, holding an envelope and beaming up at me like a child who has been promised a long-wanted toy.

'I've had a letter,' she said. 'I just had to stop off and show you before I wend my way to the joys of the amenities committee.'

'Come in,' I said. 'Have a cup of tea.'

She followed me into the kitchen and cast an approving eye at my domestic chore. 'It's so nice to see a man wash up. Is Annette in bed?'

I nodded and held out my hand for the letter.

'It's from a publisher,' she said. 'I sent them the first chapter of *God is a Woman* to see what they thought. I didn't want to waste a year of my life writing something that nobody would want.'

In the envelope was the letter and a publisher's catalogue. The letter said: 'Dear Mrs Benson, Thank you for sending us the first chapter of your book. It is really very promising, and we can only urge you to continue with your project. If you can maintain this level of interest for eighty thousand words we would love to read the finished manuscript.'

'That's nice,' I said.

'I knew you'd be interested. You're one of the few people who are actually interested in other people. That's why you're such a gossip.'

'What did Alec say?'

'He said, "They haven't made you an offer then?" '

I flipped through the catalogue. The first title I noticed was *The Cognitive Revolution in Western Culture*.

'Heavy stuff,' I said, pouring her a cup of tea.

'A serious subject for a serious publisher,' said Kitty, still smiling. She sat down and drank her tea. 'The best thing is I shall have time to get on with it now.'

'Why's that?' I asked, pouring myself more tea. Any excuse to delay going to work was grabbed eagerly now.

'We've solved the Steven problem. Or Warren has.'

'Warren?'

'They spent yesterday together, strolling round the safari park, and it worked out rather well. Warren has persuaded my troublesome son that he should go to a sixth-form boarding college and concentrate on his A levels away from the girls. Luckily, Steven took a shine to him, thrilled to find a big brother. If Warren had told him to jump out of the window he would have jumped. Instead he outlined a glittering future but he had to get his A levels first.'

'Boarding?' I said.

'Exactly. No Steven for weeks on end. The only thing that stands between me and fame is Alec, and I am counting on you to entertain him at the Comedy Hotel.'

I looked at my watch and imagined my shops opening and being ignored.

'I'll do my best,' I said. 'What's the news on Helen?'

'She's having an abortion today. Sad, but I'm sure now it's for the best. Did you see those figures in the paper? One in three children are born out of wedlock, illegitimate births have trebled, schoolgirl pregnancies at a new high?'

'I don't have much time to read papers.'

'The number of illegitimate children is rising eight times faster than those born in wedlock.'

'Does it matter?' I asked.

'Of course it matters. What do you think is going to happen to all these kids being raised without fathers?'

'They've got fathers,' I said. 'They just don't think the marriage laws are too kind on men. Anyway, when I look at what happened to a few kids round here who did have fathers, I can't believe that the new lot will be any worse off.'

Kitty blithely ignored this condemnation of us all. 'A lot of them haven't got fathers and, as a councillor, I could tell you what the public bill is, but I don't want to frighten you.'

'It won't frighten me, Kitty. I don't have money any more. Bills are what other people pay.'

She laughed gaily as if I were joking and stood up. 'The odd thing is that Steven says he's going to marry Helen one day when he's got the money. He called her "really nice". He even called her "mega". Another ten years and marriage will be back in fashion.' She picked up the letter and catalogue and put them back in the envelope.

269

As we walked to the front door she said: 'If I ever finish this book I'm thinking of dedicating it to Oliver. Do you think Alec would mind?'

'I should think he'd be thoroughly pissed off,' I said. 'I'd leave Oliver well out of it.'

She gave me a funny look. 'It wasn't adultery, Max, you know. I wasn't married then.'

'So you weren't,' I said, remembering.

'It was the last fling of a single woman, although of course my first husband was still alive.'

'I think I've followed that,' I said, as we went out. 'Good luck with the book.'

She opened the door of her car and got in. 'It'll be a bestseller, God willing.'

'You'll be all right,' I said. 'God is a woman.'

It had been the wettest June since Noah built his ark and the driest August for half a century but now, in September, the weather had forsaken excess and settled down to produce the sort of days that a man can enjoy.

On the night of the barbecue at the Comedy Hotel a warm sun sat in a cloudless sky and the summer clothes that had been in and out of the wardrobe for months were produced with relish for a final airing.

With the resources of the hotel behind him, Giles had produced a more lavish barbecue than most of his guests were accustomed to, and the forty or so visitors who stood or sat on the hotel's huge patio overlooking the Thames were assailed by a tantalizing mixture of smells from three separate grills that were covered with everything from trout to duck.

As usual, I knew few of the people who had come here ostensibly to celebrate Giles completing thirty years on this quarrelsome planet. Some were friends of his from distant parts, others were customers of the Comedy Hotel with whom I had never mixed. They gathered in groups, sitting or standing, chatting endlessly in what sometimes seemed to be a competitive fashion. It always surprised me how much people

270

have got to talk about until I overhear them and discover that they haven't.

My wife and Councillor Benson, reluctant veterans of the social whirl, had found themselves a table overlooking the river where they sat with fruit juices waiting for the charcoal to surrender its feast, and I found myself in the company of a bizarre couple, foisted on me by our host, whose conversation didn't seem to meet at any point. She was discussing hypoallergenic cosmetics and he was trying to talk about the Hang Seng index in Hong Kong. She was one of those snotty bitches who don't thank you when you light their cigarette (non-smokers never encounter these little incivilities) and the thick lipstick on her mouth, so far from making her seem kissable, looked as if it might have the same deflective effect as the Vaseline on a boxer's eyebrows.

I tried to dent her hauteur when a gap appeared briefly in the conversation by saying 'You've just wasted five minutes of my life' but she was transmitting and not receiving and my little dig vanished into the balmy evening air. I was drinking lager which was no doubt a social gaffe among this champagne-swilling horde.

In one corner of the patio was a white piano which a young man in a white suit now began to play in a gentle rather sad sort of way. Drusilla, the blonde who had once rejected my sexual offer, was draped over the piano as if posing for a picture. There was no sign of her bookmaker husband.

Alec emerged through the throng in the company of Judy the bruiser. Their champagne glasses were nearly empty.

'Where's the food?' he asked.

'The soufflé never waits for the guests. The guests wait for the soufflé,' I said.

'Birthdays, birthdays,' said Alec. 'It's Kitty's next week. What can I buy her to make her happy?'

'Why don't you buy her a divorce?' asked Judy.

'I don't need her to be that happy.'

A boat on the river sounded its raucous hooter in acknowledgement of our celebration.

271

'What news of the contraband king?' Judy asked. They liked to remind me that my son too had fallen from grace.

'No news,' I said. 'We just have to wait for the trial date.'

'Kids,' said Judy. 'Helen had the abortion on Thursday.'

'How is she?'

'Fine, actually. She's here somewhere. We thought we'd expose her to some civilized company.'

'You call this civilized?' said Alec. 'Your average savage would take to the hills.'

He put his arm round her and I could see that he was engaged on some diplomatic repair work.

'Why don't we go and get some champagne?' Judy asked. 'It will be a terrible advert for Giles if we die of thirst on his premises.'

Laurie was sitting on a white plastic chair on the edge of all this and I went over to keep him company. He had a glass of champagne in one hand, a Hamlet cigar in the other, and seemed deep in thought.

'How many O levels did Garth get?' he asked.

'I don't know. Four, I think.'

'And you must have spent about twenty thousand on his education. Helen got ten and it didn't cost me a thing.'

'Thanks for reminding me,' I said.

'But she was a nightmare once. She couldn't do her sums as a kid and used to cry all the time. Then she couldn't spell. She used to dodge school by any means available. She'd put a hot flannel on her forehead and then ask her mum to feel it. Or put baby powder on her face to look pale. Or go to the loo and make noises that were supposed to convince us that she was being sick.'

'And then she got ten O levels.'

His remarks about Garth certainly gave me a jolt. When Steven and Helen had their examination results it never occurred to me to think back to Garth's expensive failures. How much better would it have been if I had left him to find his own way through one of our overcrowded state schools?

Helen suddenly arrived between us and for once she was

272

smiling. She was wearing a short pink dress and looked the picture of innocence. The only discordant note was some punk decoration on her ears – a hoop hanging on one, and a cross on the other. She was a pretty girl and this, I thought, was an awful blemish, like a satellite dish on the Taj Mahal.

'Hallo, Mr Hadfield,' she said politely. Recent events seemed to have matured her.

'Hallo, Helen. I haven't seen you in my shops lately.'

'I've given all that up, you'll be glad to hear.'

'Talking about hearing, what's that on your ears?'

'It's the fashion,' she said with a grin.

'They numb the ears with ice, apply surgical spirit and then use a piercing stud,' said Laurie. 'It's horrible. There's a popping noise like treading on a snail.' But he smiled proudly at his reformed daughter who had mastered the gruesome intricacies of post-modern jewellery.

'Where's Steven?' I asked.

'It turns out that he has a half brother who has taken him to a football match,' said Helen with a little grimace.

'That's nice,' I said.

'It isn't. It's totally boring.'

I looked round and saw that waiters were now producing food along with cutlery wrapped in paper serviettes. The food was not confined to the product of the grills. Other little delicacies were laid out on a table. I made my way across the patio to where Annette and Kitty were laughing together about something. The conversation died when I arrived and I had the usual impression in that situation that they had been talking about me.

When Giles came to our table to make certain that his guests were happy with the food, he received such doting attention from my table companions that I could see that with his good looks life was going to provide him with all the women he could handle.

'What do you think of your life so far?' Kitty asked him. She was wearing a new green trouser suit to match her political beliefs.

'I can't see how it could get any better,' Giles said almost apologetically, as if the grand total of his own happiness necessarily reduced the amount available for someone else. I watched him enviously, and such was my misanthropic mood that I began to wonder, as I ate my steak, whether he could be the father of Annette's baby. A handsome bachelor in our part of the world should be a prime suspect and I asked myself why I hadn't thought of it before. But my mind rolled on and I soon found myself wondering why, with my black hair and Annette's auburn glory, Garth was blond. Insecurity was beginning to gnaw away at the pillars of my life, like acid.

Alec arrived now carrying a plate of cold food. 'I've escaped from Mrs Jenkins,' he said. 'Her conversation is rumoured to boost the sales of ear plugs.'

'She seems to have more face on one side of her nose than the other,' said Kitty, but Alec was too concerned about the contents of his vol-au-vents to answer this.

I was nominated, apparently on the grounds of my grumpiness, to refill glasses and I found a tray and headed for the bar that had been created at the far corner of this suburban saturnalia. John, who had been shifted to outdoor duties for the evening, greeted me with a drunken grin. The restraint that he was obliged to show in the hotel was evidently not required at Giles's party, and the glass he was holding was not a customer's but his own.

'Knickerdropper Glory?' he asked.

'Just the usual,' I said. 'The others seem to be drinking this champagne stuff.'

'Well-fed philistines boring the arses off each other,' said John, including the entire party with one sweep of his hand.

'Blimey,' I said. 'You're not that caustic when you're indoors.'

'It's my night off, isn't it? The mask has slipped.' He filled my pint mug before wrestling with the cork of another bottle of champagne. 'You take that tart over there. Everything up front. Nothing left to the imagination. Subtle as a brick. And as for the two-faced little snot rag she calls her husband, I've never seen him smile except at someone else's misfortune.'

'It must take no little self-control to be polite to these people every day,' I said, surprised at the venom he had concealed. 'Why don't you concentrate on the goats' cheese?'

'There's a recession.'

'Tell me about it,' I said, picking up my drinks.

The pianist was playing 'Sweet Caroline', a selection which impelled some couples to gyrate woozily in what cramped space was available, and my progress with the tray was hindered by their valiant efforts. Some people dance naturally, some learn to dance, and others have dancing thrust upon them, and a fair proportion of the participants here seemed to belong to the last category.

I stood there in the evening sunshine, watching the public at play. It pleased me to wonder what personal disasters they were, like me, trying to hide – or, like John, what surprising hatreds. But they danced beside the Thames with an unambiguous determination to enjoy themselves, and their bland expressions suggested no awful secrets.

There was a chill in the air now, and the unique scent of autumn. They were both clear signals that this ominous summer was drawing towards its close.

PART FOUR

· A mystery ·

Life is a mystery and it's an
unsolvable one. You just simply
live it through and as you draw
your last breath you say 'What
was that all about?'

Marlon Brando

17

A sodality of sods

Talleyrand was so devious that when he died someone asked: 'I wonder why he has decided to do that?' The deviousness of my own son brought back the memory of that quotation, the scheming, evasive and deceitful way in which he had been earning his living.

I know all about the drugs business now although I didn't know it while we were waiting, hopeless and helpless, for Garth to be taken to court.

The drugs – hashish, cocaine and heroin – come into Spain (and Europe) from the north African coast by any means that are available. One way they do it is for a man to swim out from the Moroccan coast with the cargo strapped in watertight bags to his body. A mile or two out to sea he is met by men in a speedboat who take the drugs and dash back to the Spanish coast, avoiding the police boats which are usually slower.

The drugs are then delivered round Europe – Paris, Amsterdam, London – by young men like Garth who risk their freedom for huge piles of tax-free money, paid invariably in new French franc notes. On other occasions the drivers are involved in what they call the milk run, delivering small quantities of their goods to certain often famous people staying at luxurious hotels on the Iberian peninsula.

Once the people who paid Garth did a weapons-for-drugs

deal with the terrorists of ETA, and he had to drive a Talbot Express packed with Browning 303s and Russian Kalashnikovs, plus eight crates of ammunition, up into mountains near Valladolid.

Two men from ETA, wearing berets and fatigues, drove up in a Pegaso truck. They had brought with them cocaine worth more than a million pounds on the street.

When Garth got out of his vehicle to unlock the back, he found himself face to face with a bear that was nearly as big as he was. He hurled himself back into the driver's seat and slammed the door.

An ETA man called: '*Guardia?*'

Garth shook his head and drew their attention to the bear. And then for more than two hours they sat in their respective vehicles while the bear ambled round both, curious about what was going on. It must have made a pretty picture.

On another occasion, I now know, Garth went out with another man in the boat to meet the swimmer and returned to find a police boat waiting for them. They turned and fled – Garth's speedboat could do 70 knots, the police launch only 50 – but the police managed to get several shots off. Garth and his friend were at sea for thirty hours before coming ashore in the middle of the night north of Alicante.

I write these facts down in a state of stupefaction. Was it for this that I paid thousands of pounds every year to give him the best start in life? How could that education, designed to give him the qualifications that would provide a rich and fulfilling life, bring him so swiftly to such sordid depths where he is fired at by Spanish policemen and locked up by French ones? And, if my theory that it is always the parents who are to blame is correct, where did I go wrong?

He wrote this week: 'The funny thing is that the quality of my life would improve if I was convicted. I would be able to apply to transfer to another prison nearer Britain. I would get work and not be locked up for twenty-two hours a day. I could have two phone calls a month and easier visiting. In France you are guilty until you are proved innocent. I'm sorry if I sound morbid. I'm in a state of permanent confusion now. I hear nothing from the judge, and my solicitor never comes to see me. I'm left in the dark, and the days are long.'

The days are long here, too, and in the slow grey hours I imagine a helicopter dropping into the courtyard of a French prison and plucking my son from his captors.

Because I am the person who could straighten him out and try once more to set him off on the only intelligent path in life. One of my growing fears is that the brutal environment in which he now languishes will harden, embitter and finally corrupt him, turning him into the criminal that he never was.

Because it had become impossible for me to sleep through the night, my wife came up with the unsociable suggestion that we have separate bedrooms. I had always been able to banish my worries when my head touched the pillow but as I dispensed with one problem these days another was ready to fill the void. My mind crawled from thoughts of the imminent baby to a French prison and on to Mr Fleming's office in the city, and when it had completed one circuit, it set off on another. I twisted and turned in bed and sometimes even sat up. This was no use to Annette who had disturbances of her own. Perhaps if we had been able to synchronize our disruptions we could have lived with it, but either she was waking me up or I was waking her.

I can't complain about the new accommodation. Our main guest room with its four-poster bed, silk duvet and en suite bathroom would be the pride of a top-class hotel, and I installed a television set at the foot of the bed to help me through the nocturnal marathon.

I lie in bed and think about my impounded offspring and the steep learning curve he is now engaged upon, and I wonder what signs I missed, what clues I overlooked, as the golden boy was growing into a man.

Nearly two years ago he was on the dole (they have a fancier phrase for it now) and I remember that although he was willing to take the money, he was reluctant to get a job. However, a condition of accepting the dole was that you were prepared to take work if it was offered, and when he was given a job card and told to go round for an interview he would phone the firm first and pretend to be an official at the Labour Exchange. 'I'm sending round a chap called Garth Hadfield. I wouldn't recommend him or blame you if you turn him down, but we're duty bound to send him.' Thus he preserved his freedom while retaining his lucre, and although I laughed when he related the story I wonder now in the small hours whether this wasn't one of those signs that I missed.

I lie in bed and think about his school reports, and I wonder how truthful they were with their muted praise and hints of hope. What school wants to drive away a paying pupil? Was I getting a blurred message?

And then I sit up, light a cigarette which is permissible now that I have my own room, and turn on the television. I watch programmes that could only escape while the world sleeps.

I learn that the average human sneeze travels faster than a bullet, that the kilt was designed to allow armies to defecate on the move, and that the Chinese lifespan is a thousand full moons.

I reflect that the world's trouble spots, which once had familiar and pronounceable names like Ethiopia and Afghanistan, have shifted to more mysterious venues, like Bosnia-Hercegovina and Nagorno-Karabakh.

I discover with no surprise whatsoever that suicide among men has risen by thirty per cent in ten years and, in my own age group, by forty-six per cent, although among women of the same age it has declined.

I marvel at the insomniacs' diet that the television companies have produced for us: rock videos, American college football, Chinese cookery and an Italian film on the Roman persecution of the Christians, with English sub-titles.

And then I kill an hour or two by trawling through the

pages of teletext – not the holidays and horoscopes, or the recipes and religion, but the sport. Every sport that you are interested in and quite a few that you are not are here to help ease you towards the dawn: ice hockey (Sunday's results), tennis (Becker's back problem), cricket (Australia B versus Zimbabwe), boxing (two in hospital), badminton (the Canadian Open in Montreal), rallying (why are all the drivers Finnish?), speedway (the Sunbrite league tables – Milton Keynes are bottom), golf (teams for the Ryder Cup), motorcycling (the world champion has broken a thigh bone and three ribs), football (a £2.5 million transfer), rugby (who will win the World Cup?), table tennis (the European Masters in Bonn), snooker (the Asian Open), yachting (in Torbay), bowls (in Carlisle).

Sometimes I doze and then waken to the flickering rectangle at the end of my bed, and my thoughts turn from Garth in his cell to the malevolent pilgarlic who sits behind a desk in the city. Norman Alfred I believe Mr Fleming's Christian names are: it makes a suitable acronym.

In the lonely hours of the night I see him as mine own executioner, a gleaming axe propped against his desk while his secretary tries to find a moment in his crowded itinerary when he will have the time to wield it. There will be many calls on his attention now as firms collapse exponentially, leaving his bank with the debris and the debts of the enterprise years. My cries of pain will be scarcely heard as corporations tumble with liabilities that would build a score of hospitals, and snarling shareholders search vainly for their precious life savings.

It is a train of thought that carries me nowhere and soon I am thinking of the lady who is struggling bravely towards sleep in the next room. What thoughts disturb her quest for repose? Do women begin to wonder at this stage whether another baby was such a good idea? Whether a sixteen-year commitment is what their lives really need? Annette's thoughts will be darker than most, but she doesn't know that I know that.

I abandon the television. I twist and I turn. Finally I get up in the middle of the night, go through to the bathroom and fart for twenty minutes. Consternation and constipation, hand in hand.

Mr Fleming's secretary rang me as I was having my breakfast (a bowel-directed mixture of fruit and bran).

'I'm sorry to ring you at home this early but you're a difficult man to find, Mr Hadfield,' she said in a tone of voice more suited to the boudoir. 'Mr Fleming wondered whether you could find time to drop in this morning?'

I ignored the superfluous apology: the bank had never had any compunction about ringing me at home at any hour. 'Drop in what?' I asked, but humour was not on the agenda.

'He'd like to see you,' she responded sweetly. 'I believe it's quite urgent.'

'I bet it is,' I said. 'Eleven o'clock?'

'That would be fine, Mr Hadfield. See you then.'

I returned to my medicinal diet with a reduced appetite, and opened the morning paper at the financial pages in the pitiable hope of discovering some good news. The pound had gained a sixth of a pfennig against the Deutschmark, but that hardly seemed cause to hang out bunting. As I got out the Rover and headed for the motorway I told myself that the car was a luxury that I would shortly have to forgo.

I parked at Hammersmith and got a District line train to Mr Fleming's cavern in the city. He greeted me with all the rampant bonhomie of a chaplain at a hanging.

'Sit down, Mr Hadfield,' he said. 'Things are not good.'

I sat in the comfortable leather chair that was placed in front of his desk to accommodate prospective victims, and tried in vain to dream up some soothing, placatory remark that would restore the warmth of human kindness to his waxen features.

'In the first place there was a sharp drop in consumer sales in August after the tiny rise in July,' he said. 'A sharp drop.'

I nodded at this. The optimism that had been my sole

weapon in this room would no longer do.

'In the second place, your wife has failed to sign the necessary documents, so the collateral that we thought we had for your debts, your house, isn't actually in our possession.'

He looked at me as if I were a small boy who had failed to produce the necessary homework.

'Yes, I never got round to that,' I admitted.

'I did warn you of its importance, Mr Hadfield. I imagined that it had been done. Without her signature the bank has no claim on the house at all and no security for your debt which, I have to say, is growing and not shrinking. And the slump in high street sales makes it quite clear now that the situation is not going to improve.'

What was quite clear to me was that if Annette had signed the bank's documents they would now be taking our house. I congratulated myself on my prevarication. Whatever disasters were about to rain down on the Hadfield family, they would still have a roof over their heads.

Mr Fleming was consulting an impressive array of documents that were strewn over his desk.

'The Business Development Loan was a five-year affair and has another year to run,' he said. 'But the overdraft is a different matter.'

'Indeed,' I said.

'It has to be repaid, Mr Hadfield. I tell you frankly.'

'You know my problem as well as I do,' I said. 'People aren't buying clothes, never mind shops. If I could get rid of half a dozen shops, I would.'

'It's not an attractive scenario,' said Mr Fleming, who was still studying the papers in front of him. 'Our Corporate Insolvency Department is worried to death.'

'What department?' I asked, not liking the sound of this title.

'Corporate Insolvency Department. It's our busiest department these days, I'm afraid.'

I found myself lighting a cigarette, a move that did not meet with Mr Fleming's approval. He stood up and went across the room to open a window.

'I didn't know you smoked,' he said.

'Events have driven me to it,' I told him.

'That's not my idea of an economy.'

I ignored this reproach. Mr Fleming was tetchy enough without any help from me. He returned to his desk, shuffled through the papers for a final time and then fixed me with the basilisk gaze of a deranged seagull.

'What I am going to have to do,' he said, 'is write you a formal letter demanding repayment of the overdraft. After that, I'm afraid, it's out of my hands.'

I realized with a chill that the meeting was over. I was so accustomed to sitting in this room and exchanging nebulous waffle about lights at ends of tunnels that I had imagined there was still some mileage left in this painful conversation. But the shutter had come down.

Mr Fleming was now standing up in a way that meant he was about to show somebody off the premises.

'You'll get my letter in the morning, Mr Hadfield,' he said as we walked to the door.

'You've got more faith in the post office than I have,' I muttered.

'Faith is what you need in this business,' he replied, 'but sometimes it's misplaced.'

This parting jab hurt almost as much as what had gone before and by the time I reached the street I fancied that I could feel the bruises.

The chalked message on the wall opposite said God Gave His Only Sony.

In this prosperous square mile Mammon ruled, and I suddenly felt quite remote from this sodality of sods with their usurious interest rates and mercenary coups, their golden handshakes and their Corporate Insolvency Departments.

I checked my wallet and went into a wine bar for a couple of glasses of Côtes-du-Rhône with a few normal people.

The mail that hit the mat next morning sounded like a domestic accident – a dropped carrier bag or a collapsed shelf

286

– but when I had sifted my way through the dross (the mass of bills, the invitations to subscribe to arcane magazines, the twinkling declarations that I had won a million dollars or, just possibly, an alarm clock) there were only two letters.

One, an unwelcome vindication of Mr Fleming's faith in the post office, was from the bank. The other was from Garth, a brief note by his standards and dispatched in a hurry.

Contrary to all our expectations of endless months in prison waiting for a hearing, with its remotely connected hope of an acquittal, he had been given a date for his trial. In a valiant attempt to clear a backlog in the French judicial system, extra courts were sitting this autumn. Garth would face his accusers in another ten days from the date of his letter, which was three days from now.

This seemed to have given him new life and, no doubt for the benefit of the hidden censor, he rehearsed his defence and discussed the near certainty of his being in England soon, in time for the birth.

Perhaps most implausibly of all, he told us of his career plans for his return to this country. He had decided that the only way to make real money today was to start your own little business, build it up until the accounts looked good and then sell it for 'a telephone number figure'. I suppose the recession was a little regarded phenomenon among the inmates of French prisons.

The business he had in mind was producing greeting cards, birthday cards and anniversary cards. There was also, he believed, a considerable market for 'rude' cards, tied to no particular event.

He attached a postscript to his letter, urging me to forget any idea I might have about attending the trial, which would be in French and over in ten minutes. However, in the event of a miscarriage of justice, it would be nice to see me afterwards.

I took this letter up to my wife, along with a cup of tea. She was now in that delicate stage of her pregnancy when

287

the baby could arrive at any time although the scan had given us a date that was still more than a week away.

She sat up in bed and read the letter wearily, as if events were gradually becoming too much for her.

'What do you think, Max?' she asked. 'What's going to happen?'

I sat on the bed. 'I don't know any more than you do,' I said. 'I suppose there's an outside chance of an acquittal.'

'I imagine they've heard that friend's car story a few hundred times before.'

'But can they prove it?' I asked. I suddenly saw it as my duty to try to cheer her up, to paint a brighter picture than the one that she was seeing.

But she was seeing the real picture clearly enough. 'In France you're guilty until you're proved innocent. The burden of proof is on him, not them. Where is the owner of the Range Rover?' She put the letter down on the bed. 'I don't think I could stand it if they locked him up.'

It worried me that she was carrying this burden into the final days of her pregnancy and I got up and gave her a kiss. 'You've got to be strong, kid. It's a nightmare, I know, but nightmares end.'

'The one who has to be strong is Garth.'

'Well he is,' I said. 'He gets it from his mother.'

She smiled at that and picked up the cup of tea. 'I think I'll try to get up in a minute,' she said.

I went downstairs, conscious of some unfinished business. The morning paper lay unread on the table but I could see that for the fortieth time in fifty days there was a picture of Princess Diana on the front page. The overexposure was so insane that I presumed the paper was relying on market research conducted in a mental home.

And then I saw the letter from the bank and remembered what it was that I had left undone. It took a conscious effort of will to slit the envelope open and extract its noisome message.

N. A. Fleming, when he got down to the scribbling business, was brutal but brief.

'In view of the circumstances outlined in our conversation this morning, we are obliged to request an immediate repayment of your overdraft,' he wrote. 'We look forward to hearing from you about this matter.'

I sat down at the kitchen table and folded the letter into a plane which hurtled Concorde-like across the kitchen. I lit a cigarette and inhaled deeply, imagining my lungs as a bladder and not a sponge. The people who smoked seemed to be more human. (N. A. Fleming didn't smoke.)

After a while I opened the other post and was mildly surprised at the number of people who were anxious to separate me from my money. The bills came from all corners of the country, sent with an optimistic flourish by organizations who were unaware of my circumstances and who imagined ingenuously that a cheque with their name on would be winging its way towards them by return.

I went to the sink and began the washing up. One of these days, I thought, I could be doing this for a living, or had the dish-washing machine replaced the humble washer-up? A lot of humble workers had been replaced by machines and if the immediate future was going to find me looking for a job the soaring unemployment figures suggested that it could be a long hunt.

I shouted goodbye to Annette and went out to call on June at Burnham, Mrs Spalding at Windsor, Charlotte at Maidenhead, tense Hannah, Mrs Tibbott and the rest of my devoted team who didn't realize that future fixtures were about to be cancelled.

When I got home it was clear to even my unobservant eye that Annette had been crying. She was sitting on the sofa watching the early evening news – starvation in Albania, looting in Zaire, chaos in Bucharest – but I knew that this standard fare wasn't responsible for her red-rimmed eyes.

I assumed that she had been fretting about her son and I sat beside her and stared with token interest at the day's bad news on the box. I had had a trying day myself, attempting to assuage the anxieties of my staff while at the same time warning them that their jobs were no longer secure. I couldn't say with certainty that the end was near but I used phrases like 'terminal decline' which didn't noticeably perk anybody up. I had no doubt that at least half of them would by now have made a few inquiries about alternative employment.

I was thinking about this rather than the news when Annette picked up the remote control and with one swift jab of her finger quenched the sound.

'I found the letter on the floor,' she said, turning to me.

'The letter?'

'The letter that you had made a plane out of.'

'Ah, Mr Fleming's little billet-doux.'

'I don't know which worried me more, his message or the fact that you made a plane out of it. Why didn't you show me it?'

'I think you've got enough to worry about,' I said.

She put her hand on my knee. 'We're broke, aren't we?'

'More or less,' I agreed.

'What are we going to do?'

'It's more a question of what they're going to do. There's not a lot that I *can* do.'

'Well, I suppose you could take his letter seriously, and not make a plane out of it.'

'My making a plane out of it did not mean that I didn't take it seriously,' I said. 'I just fancied making a plane.'

'Are we going to lose the house?'

'I think the house is about the only thing we won't lose,' I said grimly. 'How much money have you got in the bank these days?'

With the monthly standing order that shifted money from my private account to hers, she could have quite a hoard stashed away if she had spent less time in shops, and I was curious about how much it was.

'A few thousand,' she said noncommittally, and I decided not to press it. 'What does it mean, Max? Will you have to shut the shops?'

'I won't. The bank might. It's what banks do. They lend billions to hopeless causes and screw the small businessman. They lend you money when you don't want it, and ask for it back when you haven't got it. It's the dirty world of finance. Don't bother your head with it.'

'Why would they lend it when you don't want it?'

'Bank managers' pay depends to some extent on the profits of the branch. If they can lend some sucker two hundred thousand, they're making more than two thousand a month in interest. Well, the bank manager gets some of that.'

This was much more than she wanted to know and I could see her interest switching off, although the mournful expression lingered on.

'It's a fine time to go broke,' she said, getting up. 'One child in prison needing money, and a baby on the way.'

'There isn't a good time to go broke,' I said.

She turned to me in the middle of the room.

'What are we going to do?'

I seemed to have spent most of the year developing a formidable talent for shutting out reality.

'You're going to prepare a wonderful dinner for us, and I'm sneaking out for a swift drink,' I said.

Alec was drunk on whisky when I reached the bar.

'Welcome to the slurps and burps of the Comedy Hotel,' he said, 'where men whose marriages lie in ruins about their feet sustain themselves with dreams induced by alcohol.'

'What is he chuntering about?' I asked Laurie who was sitting next to him on one of the high stools. I was glad to see that the two of them had resolved their little differences.

'I think it's a mid-life crisis, mate,' Laurie said. 'He's trying to be trendy.'

John, his sedate, sober self again, produced my lager and Alec insisted on paying for it.

'He's in rebellion against his stereotype,' I said. 'Headmasters don't get pissed.'

'*Au contraire*,' said Alec, drunkenly waving a finger. 'The

291

first teachers were priests and they were permanently plastered. I'm coping with a tradition here.'

'You're handling it very well,' I said. 'Don't fall off your stool. Is this a celebration or a lament?'

'Perhaps he's just thirsty,' said Laurie. 'It could be a dehydration problem.'

'I'm mourning a death,' said Alec.

Laurie paused. 'Have I dropped a clanger?' he asked. 'I only open my mouth to change feet.'

'The death of a dream,' said Alec stoically.

'Ah,' said Laurie.

'I'm just no good,' said Alec, cradling his whisky.

'At what?' I asked.

'Anything. Father. No good. Husband. No good. Teacher. No good.'

'And your pool isn't all that hot,' said Laurie.

'It's a terrible truth to have to reconcile yourself to,' said Alec. 'I'm forty-four years old and I'm no bloody good at anything.'

'What brought this on?' I asked. 'Apart from your general uselessness and ineptitude.'

'Everything. The new term. My wife who has no time for me. My son who despises me. Even my newly discovered son doesn't seem to think that I amount to much, and Mavis was obviously relieved at her lucky escape.'

'Such concern for your image!' I said. 'Who gives a toss what they think? After all, nobody gives a toss what you think.'

'You're a great consolation, Max,' said Alec. 'At least, I think you are.'

'You have a wonderful wife and a secure career,' said Laurie, struggling to identify some auspicious points in the disintegrating fabric of Alec's life. 'I have a wife who jumps into bed with Frenchmen, and a dodgy future. If we're after sympathy, mate, get me in the queue.'

'I won't even discuss my problems,' I said. 'Your tears would embarrass me.'

'You gentlemen are hucksters,' Alec said. 'You must submit to the demands of the market place. I'm a scholar, an intellectual, and the world rewards me with ridicule. You don't know how painful it can be. We don't have the huckster's thick skin.'

'Jesus,' I said. 'I'd better have another drink.'

The beautiful Drusilla was ordering something complicated down the bar and so I had time to finish my drink and order a pint instead of the half I had planned. I left Alec out, but bought Laurie a vodka.

'What's the difference between light and hard?' he said, as I gave him his glass. He was obviously as keen as I was to cut short Alec's plaintive soliloquy. I shrugged.

'You can go to sleep with a light on,' he said. I failed to laugh at this and so he became serious. 'What *are* your problems? You look sort of grim.'

Talking is release and I barely paused. I told him about my financial situation and then I told him about the letter from the bank. I had never before discussed my affairs so frankly in the Comedy Hotel but I had at the back of my mind the idea that Laurie might be of some help. I had never been able to guess what his personal wealth was as he wasn't an extravagant person. The baubles weren't there to give you a clue. He bought himself a Shogun because it was comfortable to drive and a house in France because he wanted one, but neither the vehicle nor the home were luxurious because he wasn't that sort of person. The cautious way that he disposed of his cash led me to believe that there was plenty to protect because his caution would have allowed it to accumulate. There was certainly an offshore nest egg in the Channel Islands earning tax-free interest, but how big is a nest egg? I began to imagine untold wealth and, in a hopeful burst of candour, filled out the picture of my financial collapse with details that I hoped would have him reaching tearfully for his cheque book.

'In short,' I finished, 'I'm dangling over the abyss.'

Laurie looked at me as if a recent unspecified event had somewhat diminished his regard for me.

293

'I'm sorry to hear that, Max,' he said. 'You're well stuffed.'

'Well, thanks,' I said. 'It's good to have the situation clarified by an expert.'

'What are you going to do?'

'What *can* I do?'

'Do a deal,' said Laurie instantly. 'Offer them forty grand in a full and final settlement. The banks do deals. They have to these days.'

'I haven't got forty grand, Laurie,' I said.

'Nor have I, Max, in case you wondered. Almost all my spare cash has been invested in various pathetic ventures. The printers want money up front these days, but you wait for what you're owed. The helicopter's costing me a fortune.'

'I didn't know you had a helicopter,' I said accusingly.

'I haven't, you daft sod. I'm hiring one to take aerial pictures. At the moment my attempts to make money aren't much more successful than yours, but at least I haven't got your debts. Debt in a recession equals death.'

'Well, thanks Laurie,' I said. 'You know how to cheer a chap up.'

Our drunken companion sought to rejoin the company at this stage but gave no sign that he had been following the conversation that had taken place.

'You haven't got any bruises, Laurie,' he said. 'What's going on?'

Laurie smiled proudly. 'Judy's a changed person, I'm glad to say. I think she's grateful I had her back.'

'I was surprised you did,' I said frankly.

'Oh, we mumble about it into our beer, but if you get a wife like Judy you hang on to her.'

I listened to this with some astonishment. 'You mean she understands your tastes? The way you like a smack in the mouth?'

'We've stopped all that. From now on it's peace and love.'

But I didn't want to talk about it. I had darker thoughts of my own, thoughts that were not helped by Laurie's casual dismissal of my financial crisis, nor by the fact that the drunken headmaster was too absorbed in his abundant shortcomings to care very much if I keeled over and died at his feet.

What you found in the end was that nobody really cared what happened to you or what sort of mess you were in; the purpose of your misfortunes was to supply an engrossing topic of conversation for other people, a service I would shortly be providing in spades.

What I didn't know as I stood there with my lager and my hopeless vision of the future was that this was the last time that I would drink in the Comedy Hotel and enjoy its relaxing moments, its mordant jokes, its games and its drinks. I had spent so much time and a fair amount of money easing my way through life in its agreeable company, that it would have contributed unbearably to my suffering had I known that I would not be stepping into this room again. There was always a ring of people around you here whose jokes seemed funny and whose asides on the world we live in could pass, after a few drinks, for wisdom.

As it happened, my last evening in these pleasant surroundings was to end, appropriately, in farce, because a short while later there was a thud and we saw that Alec and his stool had both fallen backwards to the floor. He was obviously unconscious but still sat on the stool, although horizontally now rather than vertically.

John was leaning forward, peering over the counter.

'I wondered where he'd gone,' he said. 'Is he all right?'

'He's all right as a newt,' said Laurie. 'He's not really a whisky drinker.'

'Could have fooled me,' said John. 'He seemed quite an expert.'

Laurie bent down and with a hand in each armpit yanked him to a sitting position with his back against the bar. However, both eyes were still shut.

'We'll have to take him home,' he said. 'It'll take two of us to carry him upstairs.'

We ignored the recumbent headmaster while we finished

our drinks at our own good pace and then Laurie, with no little panache, swung Alec's inert torso over one shoulder and carried him from the bar. Our departure was greeted with stares and the silence of disapproval.

'Heavy bastard,' said Laurie, unlocking his Shogun. We strapped Alec into the front seat, and then I went to get the Rover and followed Laurie through the country lanes.

Kitty was in, engaged apparently on the study of some council minutes, and the manner of our arrival was a source of considerable displeasure.

'Egregiously drunk,' she said briskly, looking into the Shogun.

'I can't fault your diagnosis, councillor,' I said.

'Nor can I,' said Laurie. 'He's pissed as a rat.'

'What is it with you men?' she asked. 'Isn't the world interesting enough for you without drugs?'

'He said he wasn't any good at anything,' I told her lamely.

'Has he only just discovered that?'

Laurie and I hoisted Mr Benson from the vehicle and, with Kitty leading the way, carried him upstairs to a bedroom. The angry wife gazed down at this somnolent bundle of flesh with which she was currently legally entangled and her expression looked very like distaste.

She came downstairs to see us off, but couldn't quite bring herself to say thanks, seeing us perhaps as guilty partners in the debacle.

I waved her goodbye and drove off sadly into the night.

18

In the guano

The phone call from France four days later disturbed my breakfast preparations at ten to eight. I remember the time because it was at that moment on the early morning radio programme when some tedious dog-collared lunatic tries to link a topical news item with a belief in God, all in three and a half minutes: 'Thought for the day' it is called.

I picked up the phone with certain premonitory feelings that did not help my pulse rate. This was a little early in the morning even for the dawn calls that routinely ruined my day.

'Mr Hadfield?' said a voice that I half remembered. 'I'm sorry that I couldn't ring you last night. I had a dinner party.'

It was the British Consul in Biarritz where, of course, it was nearly nine o'clock.

'There's good news and bad news,' he said.

'Tell me.'

'Garth went to court yesterday. They gave him three years.'

I sat down. 'What's the good news?'

'Well, frankly, he could have got a lot more. There's a real purge going on down here against the whole business. I thought three years was very fair in the circumstances.'

'Fair? You expected two and a half.'

'That was a guess, Mr Hadfield. But there was no defence,

297

only the usual story about somebody else's vehicle. Well, they all trot that one out.'

'Good God,' I said. 'Three years.'

'It sounds a lot,' said the British Consul soothingly.

'It is a lot,' I said.

'Most get more, Mr Hadfield. I think they took his youth into account. I also think they felt he wasn't, as it were, a major player. And there are plenty of opportunities for remission down here. They can even get a month knocked off their sentence for every exam that they pass.'

Garth's performance in various examinations did not automatically categorize this as the good news which the British Consul evidently thought it was.

'How is he?' I asked.

'Fine, in the circumstances. You have a strong boy there. I talked to him briefly after the case. He was only concerned that I should ring you and let you know what happened.'

I didn't know what to say. I kept thinking: *three years!* I suppose that, despite all the evidence, I had been clinging to the hope that the case against him would be thrown out and that he would arrive on the doorstep one of these days, chastened but free. Now he would reach manhood in a cell, and carry a different set of attitudes, talents and beliefs into the long, unforgiving haul of adulthood.

The British Consul said: 'They can apply for parole at the halfway mark. It's a bit of a lottery. The prisoner keeping out of trouble is a big part of it.'

Even after all that had happened it grated to hear my son described as the prisoner.

'What about the customs fine business?' I asked.

'That was twenty thousand pounds,' said our man in France as if we were talking about a couple of fivers. 'But nobody ever pays the full amount. You make them an offer.'

'And if it's not paid?'

'Ah then he does an extra two years with no remission. The sentence would be five and he'd have to serve it all.'

Receiving no reply from me, the smooth voice continued:

'What people do if they haven't got the money is go to the bank or get a second mortgage on their house. The customs fine is almost always paid because once the man is out of prison he can start earning and pay it back.'

'I see,' I said. I wasn't about to discuss banks, mortgages and my son's earning capacity with the British Consul in Biarritz who had a quite unreliable picture of my finances from the thousand francs I was sending him every month for Garth.

'I gather you have some shops,' he said now. 'So it won't be a problem.'

I resisted the temptation to disabuse him of this idea, and merely told him: 'Shops are not exactly a goldmine at the moment.'

'Well, I have to tell you that Garth didn't seem to think that the fine would pose a problem. I'm only telling you so that you know what he's expecting.'

'Thanks,' I said. 'Where is he?'

'He's still in Bayonne, but he'll be moved to another prison now that he's been sentenced. I should wait until you hear from him.'

'I'd like to visit him.'

'Of course, and I can help you arrange that. The red tape is terrible.'

I reached for my cigarettes and lit one. I absolutely never smoke before breakfast. As I paused to light it, I could hear Annette coming downstairs, another first for this time of the day.

'What happened?' she asked.

I held up three fingers and said to the telephone: 'I'd be glad of any help you can give me. I'll come down as soon as possible.'

As I put down the phone I could hear my wife weeping behind me. But when I turned I found that I was unable to comfort her. I went across to the kitchen table and sat down to hide my own tears.

*

It was a morning that I would never forget because an hour or so later – an hour in which Annette and I had sat side by side on the sofa in doleful silence, assimilating the news and then attempting, with no visible signs of success, to convince each other that things could somehow be worse – the phone rang again with news that stripped the last vestige of hope from my collapsing facade.

'I won't equivocate,' said Mr Fleming. 'We waited for your reply but haven't heard from you, so the bank has today appointed a receiver.'

'A receiver?' I said inanely.

'There was no alternative, Mr Hadfield, I'm afraid. Our Corporate Insolvency Department took a dim view . . .'

I could hear him going on about my 'attenuated prospects' and my 'carefree style of management' but I wasn't fully taking it in. The crisis was now a disaster, and I had lost control of my own business.

I replaced the phone and made myself a coffee. Annette was upstairs dressing, which was a relief. After the strain that she had endured this morning, the news that the Max Hadfield shops were in receivership could be one trauma too many for the delicate processes that were working their way towards a climax in her busy little body.

I was feeling fairly dazed myself in the wake of this torrent of bad news and for some time I sat sipping coffee and staring blankly at the kitchen wall.

What I finally decided to do was go to see my accountant.

I have an accountant called Eric. He has an office in Aldgate where he acts as a sort of middleman between people like me, the adventurous self-employed, and the shadowy agents of the government who make an annual raid on what they perceive to be your profits.

Once a year we meet for lunch in London's oldest restaurant in Covent Garden, and we discuss profits and taxes, expenses and investment, over food which he tells me whether I can afford. In a good year, I pay; more recently Eric has been picking up the bill.

300

'You're in the guano,' he said when I rang and explained my situation. 'I don't think it will be lunch at Rules today.'

Instead we ate tough steaks in a dusty East End bistro and consoled ourselves with two bottles of cheap wine. Eric was not a stranger to financial disasters but even he blanched at my litany of misfortunes.

He was a bright young man, younger than me, with prematurely greying hair and thick hornrim glasses. His little firm had grown since I was first introduced to him and there were now a dozen underlings poring over ledgers in the offices that he rented over a warehouse in Aldgate.

He said: 'This is terrible, Max.'

Of course he was losing a client, but I like to think that his unhappiness ran deeper than that.

'Tell me what will happen,' I said. 'I haven't dealt with a receiver before.'

'Sort of chap you want to avoid,' said Eric, 'but it's too late now. You should have provided the collateral that the bank wanted.'

'And then I would have lost my house as well as my business.'

'Probably,' said Eric, searching for some lean meat on his steak. 'What happens? Well, the receiver now controls your shops. They'll have guys in each one telling the staff to carry on working. Effectively you've lost ownership. You can't write cheques or do anything else for that matter. Initially, they'll try to find a buyer.'

'Fat chance,' I said.

'That so? Well, in that case they'll move to Plan B. They'll bring in a valuer to assess the assets, the stock, the leases on the shops.'

'My car.'

'Is that on the firm? Well, you can say goodbye to that. In the meantime, the receiver will be trying to get in all the money that you are owed by customers or whoever.'

'Good luck to him,' I said.

'Receivers work quite hard because they'll get the first

forty thousand they can lay their hands on. That'll be their fee.'

I finished, or rather left, my meal and drank some wine.

'This is a grim story, Eric,' I said.

'Grim? That was the nice bit. Let me tell you what happens next. If when they've disposed of everything the money falls short of your overdraft, on which you have a personal unlimited guarantee, the bank will go for personal bankruptcy. They'll look for any assets you have, hidden accounts that they think you're not disclosing, anything they think you own that they can turn into money. And if you lie, you go to jail.'

He drank some wine. 'The figures you've given me suggest a six-figure shortfall.'

I didn't say anything.

'At this stage you might try to do a deal. The bank may feel that making you bankrupt isn't going to produce anything like the amount of money that they are owed, and will settle for less on the grounds that at least it's something.'

'I don't have anything to deal with,' I said. 'Everything I had was in the business.'

'In that case the bank may think it a waste of time and money to go for bankruptcy. It's a question of what they believe. You'll have to convince them that you're seriously poor.'

'That shouldn't be difficult,' I said.

'I think this lunch is on me,' said Eric.

As I cruised down the motorway, wishing that I was the man who invented the traffic cone, I felt like someone who wondered where his next hot dinner was coming from. The financial catastrophe which had seemed to be at one remove when it involved my shops, had moved appreciably nearer over my lunch with Eric and I could now feel the bank's hand in my pocket.

How much money did I have? There had been a time when Laurie urged me to start dumping cash offshore, but I had never got around to doing it. He even devised a wonderful scheme which involved me selling all the shops to a mysterious firm in Liechtenstein or the Cayman Islands, a mysterious firm of which I was the owner, but I never quite understood how I was to benefit from this complex manoeuvre. But then it is my fiscal naivety that had brought me to my current straits.

I tried to list in my head what I took to be my assets and a pretty unimpressive inventory it made. Instead of portfolios of shares and cellars of wine, it included items like camcorders and lawnmowers.

And then, as we all ground to a halt while somewhere ahead the police disentangled the battered components of an everyday motorway pile-up, I remembered with glee a small paternal programme of generosity that I had instituted many years ago when Garth was young and I was not old. I had opened a building society account in Windsor with a fistful of fivers soon after his birth, and vowed to add to it when there was money to spare. And several times over the years I had. In the good times, when the shops were producing a cheerful return, I would drop cheques into the building society's gloomy offices and wander off thinking how fortunate Garth was with his choice of parents.

The plan, conceived in the first flurry of fatherhood, had been to present Garth with this treasure trove on his twenty-first birthday. In the meantime, of course, somebody somewhere had decided that adulthood now arrived at eighteen, but I stuck to my original schedule, partly so that there would be more money for Garth when he got it, and partly because at eighteen he would have blown the lot. And now I was glad that I did: I was broke and Garth was in prison.

As we began to inch forward slowly on the motorway, all struggling irritably for the single lane that it had become, I decided to get to the building society's office as quickly as possible and reclaim my son's birthday present. Any cheques I wrote now were likely to ricochet, and what I needed was a fat wallet.

303

There was a nervous moment when I parked the car and suddenly wondered whether this account was in Garth's name, but then I remembered that the relevant documents were in my briefcase and I pulled them out to reassure myself. The only thing left to wonder as I hurried down the High Street was how much money was quietly fructifying in this forgotten account.

I suppose at one time it would have taken three men, four phone calls and a couple of hours to answer this question, but today one girl and her computer can provide the figure before you've finished asking.

'Nine thousand two hundred and seventy one, with the updated interest,' she said sweetly. She looked like the girl in a building society's television advertisement and I beamed back. It was more than I had dared hope.

'I want to withdraw it all,' I said.

She looked slightly hurt. 'Do you mean you want to close the account?' she asked.

'Afraid so,' I said. There are some accounts these days for which you have to give quite a lot of notice before taking this sort of drastic action, but I had opened this one before they started that nonsense. 'I would also like cash,' I said, trying not to feel embarrassed. How many people asked for cash these days unless there was something shifty about their activities?

'It's usually a money order,' the girl said doubtfully.

I didn't feel like explaining to her that if I paid it into a bank I would never see it again.

'I don't have a bank account,' I told her.

'I'll see if we can do that much,' she said, and left her desk while I stood there trying to look like the sort of person who had never had a bank account.

It took some time to find that much in folding money and I studied the posters on the wall, all showing good-looking young couples with beautiful homes, an acquisition which evidently arrived fairly quickly once you started bringing your spare cash to this modest office.

304

The people who were doing just that gave me furtive sideways looks when the girl reappeared with two handfuls of plastic envelopes which, she assured me, contained £9271. I stuffed it into several pockets and hurried out into the street.

Sitting in the car that would soon no longer be mine, I toyed with the idea of dropping in to one of my shops, but then I shied away from it. The encounter with my staff would be too painful, and a chat with the receiver seemed unlikely to improve my mood.

There was nothing left to do but drive home and after sitting in the car for ten minutes and enjoying a cigarette I did.

Annette was not comfortable when I reached home.

'I think it's going to be today,' she said.

'Three days early? Here's a child who wants to get on with things.'

She was sitting on the sofa trying to read a magazine and I sat beside her and felt her stomach. A small person moved beneath my hand.

'Should I phone the hospital?' I asked, but she shook her head.

'Not yet. I don't want to be in there any longer than I can help. What you can do is make some tea.'

I went out to the kitchen and switched on the kettle. My mind was in turmoil and I was operating on some sort of automatic pilot. It seemed to me that Annette ought to know that I no longer had a business, but in her present condition it could be dangerous to mention it. And so, desperate to talk, I kept it to myself.

I was in constant dread of the phone ringing then, with an unknown, hostile caller asking for my car or anything else that might be in this house belonging to the Max Hadfield chain of shops. A phone call now was something that Annette would overhear.

I took the tea in and sat down.

'Any phone calls?' I asked.

'None. Were you expecting any?'

'I never expect them but they keep coming.'

'How's the business?'

'Don't let's even talk about it.'

And we sat there not talking about anything and Annette went back to her magazine. It would have been natural for us to discuss Garth now, but I was frightened of upsetting her; and obviously she didn't want to be reminded of the subject. There was very little we could do with this day except sit and wait, and so we sat and waited.

Upstairs her case was packed with nighties, toiletries, a dressing gown and slippers. There were baby clothes and even nappies which the hospital had asked her to bring in as our vaunted health service buckled at the knees. All this, plus a camera, was packed ready for the mad dash to the midwife.

The mother-to-be had a light salad in mid-afternoon and then went upstairs and tried to sleep. I would like to have slept myself but my mind wouldn't entertain the idea. Instead I watched afternoon television which seemed to consist largely of cartoons for children. This was just what my head wanted and I sat engrossed.

In the early evening Annette came down and talked about contractions. We rang the hospital but after Annette had described what was happening to her they said there was no need to leave home yet.

Neither of us felt like eating and we stared mindlessly at the television, taking in very little. I made myself a coffee but Annette, now in visible discomfort, didn't want one.

Along towards midnight the picture disappeared to free us from our trance.

'You'd better ring the hospital again,' Annette said. 'They're getting more frequent.'

This time the hospital suggested that we come in and I rushed upstairs to get Annette's case and then helped her, in a subdued panic, into the back seat of the Rover.

And so we hurtled through the night towards the dramatic parturition.

19

A child is born

Hospitals are not places that I enjoy. They are full of people who groan, vomit and expire with a sublime disregard for the feelings of others and I prefer to be elsewhere. But from the early hours of that morning I was a prisoner in their aseptic corridors.

Annette's arrival had not provoked the drama I expected. Staff did not rush out with stretchers or wheelchairs; in fact no staff appeared at all. Brand new human beings were being produced here on a conveyor belt basis, and one more arrival wasn't going to excite anybody. Apathy reigned.

An elderly nurse appeared eventually when we had walked in, and she suggested that Annette take a warm bath. I had a strong feeling that the nurse thought that this was an unsociable hour to arrive.

It was clear from early on that my role didn't exist and my presence was unnecessary. My contribution, if it was my contribution, had been made a long time ago. I sat in uncomfortable chairs, stared at chilly green walls, counted squares on the tiled floor and read, in scrupulous detail, wall posters telling me what to do in the event of fire.

Annette lay in the bath for over an hour with only her swollen belly breaking the surface of the water, and then the nurse reappeared and told her to get out. When she had dried and donned some sort of smock, the three of us walked a few yards to the delivery room, but I soon gathered that this did not mean that the baby was imminent. Annette lay on a tall bed in the middle of the small room and two o'clock turned to three o'clock and then four. Across the country people slept in warm beds, unaware of the slow, painful passage of time. I sat and then stood and sometimes went outside to stroll the length of the dreary corridor, peering for signs of dawn through the hospital's grimy windows.

Annette had a succession of visitors. The doctor who was presiding over this event was a small busy man with a clipboard which suggested to me that other births were expected in other rooms. He had short, dark hair and his handsome face was deeply tanned. He was very young and looked more like a county cricketer than an overworked doctor. The nurse referred to him as 'the obstetrician'.

The nurse went in and out and other doctors sauntered in from time to time as if the main problem here was killing the long hours of the nightshift.

I found a seat and, luckily, beside it an old newspaper, and for more than an hour I struggled with an impossibly difficult crossword.

One or other of the visitors had wired Annette up to a machine which measured the size and frequency of her contractions. Its message appeared in a graph which spun out over reels of paper that ended up on the floor. The doctor on his frequent visits didn't have to talk to anybody but only consult the paper. At five o'clock another machine was installed to monitor the baby's heartbeats.

'God, this is hurting, Max,' Annette said at one stage. But I could see that for myself, not just from her face but from the story of pain revealed by the graph on the floor.

'Is it too late for an epidural?' I asked the doctor on his next visit.

'I'm afraid it is,' he said. 'The anaesthetist is off duty now. You have to give him a bit of notice.' He turned to Annette. 'It won't be long now. The baby's fine.'

I went back to my crossword: Blind obstinacy characteristic

of the Minotaur (14); I wished that a more downmarket rag had been left for my perusal, but eventually I thought of 'bullheadedness' and went out to find a toilet. The sign on the door said EN LEMEN which only confused me briefly. Spotting the missing letters was a simple task after an hour with a crossword.

There were sounds of activity in the hospital now. These were not places where you could enjoy a lie-in. The early-morning staff were hurrying to their posts, trolleys were being wheeled down corridors, lifts were in action and I could hear the clink of distant crockery. Soon reluctant patients would be woken and offered food when they were quite certain that what they really wanted was another couple of hours' sleep.

I walked uneasily to Annette's room. A hospital, I realized, is no place for somebody with my hypochondriacal tendencies; not for me the tomorrow-we-die insouciance of a Bolivian peasant – I fret and anguish over every pain.

When I got back a degree of animation had been brought to the scene. There were now two doctors and two nurses, none of whom seemed to be on the usual fleeting visit, but were here for business.

'We think your wife is ready,' said the nurse.

I looked at Annette. Her eyes were closed but the grimaces of pain were more frequent.

I am not convinced that the Great Designer in the Sky was entirely sober when he devised the means by which we propagate. The eccentric process that he came up with starts in farce, ends in pain and is messy, uncomfortable and danger-ous. Unfortunately there was nobody there to take him firmly by the elbow and whisper in his ear: 'Back to the drawing board on this one, Sunshine.' And so we are saddled with the discomforts of childbirth which had provided an agonizing night for Annette and a harrowing one for me.

The nurse was talking to Annette now, and the doctor was waiting expectantly between her legs. The nurse was saying 'Push', and I came round to the side of the bed to talk

310

to Annette, if she wanted to talk. Her pain was upsetting me and seemed unjust. But she didn't want to talk – what energy she had left was devoted to pushing.

'It's coming,' said the nurse, who had taken up a position alongside the doctor. The other doctor and nurse stood beside them, reserves who might never be used.

'Here comes the head,' said the nurse, but from where I was standing I couldn't see it.

'Push,' said the nurse. 'Push!'

And suddenly the baby appeared, shouting and covered with blood. The doctor, more rugby player than cricketer now, caught it in a towel.

'It's a girl,' he said, giving me a funny look that I only understood later.

'It's a girl, darling,' I said. 'Isn't that wonderful?'

'Wonderful,' she whispered and closed her eyes.

I looked across at the baby's scrunched-up face. The doctor was checking the hands, feet, mouth and nose.

'Well,' said the nurse, looking at me, and suddenly I realized that something was wrong.

I left the side of the bed and walked round to take a closer look at the new arrival. The doctor and nurse looked at me and looked at the baby. I looked at the baby, too. She was black. It was hard to tell at first because of the mess that covered her, but this was definitely not the pink model that had been my first sight of Garth. I cleared my throat.

'Is this baby black?' I asked.

The doctor was embarrassed.

'It looks that way to me,' he said quietly.

'The baby is black, Annette,' I said.

But she lay there with her eyes closed and a smile on her face and I didn't even know whether she had heard.

I looked at the baby again and then I looked at the dumpy redhead on the bed as if I had never seen her before and then I pushed past the bewildered obstetrician and made for the door.

*

They chose the site for Stonehenge five thousand years ago, but it was two thousand years later that work began in earnest. I suppose the project got bogged down in the squabbles of a Bronze Age planning committee for a couple of thousand years, but eventually permission came through and the local unemployment figures dramatically dropped.

The largest stones were brought about twenty miles, dragged by teams of five hundred men who used sledges and rollers, but the bluestones were brought 240 miles from Wales. They were carried by raft along the Welsh coast and then by boat up river, and finally overland on sledges and rollers. The thing was pretty well up two thousand years before Christ, and now it was the finest Bronze Age sanctuary in Europe although, like many more recent constructions, nobody knows why it was built.

It is stuff like this that gives you perspective, I thought as I drove past it later that morning. I didn't know where I was going – I was just driving and by lunchtime I was in the heart of Wessex.

I had paused only briefly at home to throw a few things into a bag – toothbrush, razor, shirts – and then I put my foot down. In England the scenery gets better the further west you go, but hunger eventually caused me to ease up and in the early afternoon, after cruising aimlessly through picturesquely named villages and dramatic hills, I arrived in the city of Salisbury. I found a hotel in the centre, with an imposing Georgian stone portico, and booked in.

I ordered sandwiches and ate them in my room and then I went out and walked. My strategy here was to find something else to think about. Salisbury, with its medieval buildings, dinky streets and endless history, was well equipped to distract me. Everybody had stopped here, I soon learned, from Charles II and Oliver Cromwell to Dr Johnson and George Frederick Handel, and so it was worth a day or two of my life.

I wandered along streets with strange names like Oatmeal Row and Ox Row, and noted happily the plentiful supply of public houses. They had strange names, too: the Haunch of Venison, the Wig and Quill, the Cloisters. The River Avon and streams that ran off it seemed to lace the town and for a long time I stood outside Culpeper the Herbalist's and watched languid ducks, motionless in the fast-moving water, staring resentfully at discarded supermarket trolleys.

There was a street market in the Square which, we tourists soon learned, had been held here since 1219, and I passed among the stalls spending nothing. There was a tea dance in the Guildhall and an exhibition on cats in the museum, but in the late afternoon I made my way back to the hotel and had a bath before dinner. My fellow guests seemed to be appreciably older than me and, judging by the car park, had mostly arrived in coaches.

It was now around thirty-six hours since I had slept or, at any rate, laid on a bed and I went down to dinner worried that I would fall asleep in my soup. The most surprising thing to me was that I hadn't had a drink all day; tiredness or events had made my stomach deeply unreceptive to the idea, and I didn't even want wine with my food. My appetite had been adversely affected by recent developments, too, and I didn't really do justice to the chef at the White Hart, as I now discovered my hotel was called.

Two books had been left in my room by somebody, providing me with a choice of reading: the Regency England of Jane Austen or the extraordinary tightrope act of Mikhail Sergeyevich Gorbachev, but before I could cast a vote on this subject I was asleep.

I awoke at ten the following morning feeling almost normal. At any rate the thought of alcoholic nourishment was no longer repellent, and after a light, late breakfast, I stepped out into Salisbury's ancient streets in search of the drink that cheers.

Bored men played spoof in a darkened corner of my first pub, while wrestling, I romantically imagined, with a firkin of scrumpy. I opted for bitter myself and sat at the counter on an upholstered stool feeling finally able to consider my situation. I could see now why Annette had seemed so worried during the later stages of her pregnancy. She was clinging to the forlorn hope that I was the baby's father while fearing that the proud daddy was somebody quite different and that his role would be difficult to disguise once the child appeared.

I remembered interrupting a conversation between Annette and Kitty Benson at Giles's barbecue which had stopped abruptly when I arrived. At the time I thought that they had been discussing me, but I was certain now that they had been exchanging fond memories of Oliver and his generous ways with his prodigious sexuality.

'What a stud that man is,' Kitty had said to me once. 'A real sex machine.' Annette had said 'The treacherous cow' about Kitty when I told her about Mrs Benson's dalliance with the energetic professor from Sierre Leone. At the time I had thought she intended Alec as the victim of this treachery but now I realized that she was thinking of herself.

I had another pint and moved on. The bars were cosy and hospitable, and the beer was good. The problems that I thought I had – a son in jail, a business collapse with the concomitant joys of probable bankruptcy – were only sour memories now as I contemplated this new development in my life. And once I had dispensed with the remorse there was the delicate matter of how I should react to it.

I could only stay awake after serious lunchtime drinking by walking (if I could still walk) and I decided that no visit to Salisbury would be complete without at least a glimpse at the cathedral. It had been there for nearly eight hundred years and its spire made it the tallest cathedral in Britain. I walked through the High Street Gate which had been built in the fourteenth century to separate the clerics in the Close from the heathens in the town and could still see the groove for the portcullis. The Close was full of some old and wonderful houses where famous men had lived. The only famous man who lived there today, in a large grey house with tall black gates, was a former Prime Minister who retired with

314

his piano to sulk in the shadow of the cathedral. (So far as I am concerned, the last Prime Minister who looked like a Prime Minister was Harold Macmillan. Perhaps it is because I have grown older, but all his successors have seemed to me to have arrived at 10 Downing Street like wartime evacuees who have been parked in more luxurious accommodation than they had expected. So they keep dashing out of that sombre doorway and waving gratefully to us for our unexpected generosity, and we stare back thinking that a semi-detached in Chigwell would have been quite adequate.)

The cathedral's spire was adorned with scaffolding and an appeal for the cost of repairs had raised three and a half million pounds. This was a million and a half short of what was required. It cost £27,000 to build the cathedral and £5 million to repair the spire, the ultimate anecdote about inflation. Luckily nobody approached me for a contribution and I wandered over to a seat under a tree and sat down. I had intended to go in – the oldest working clock in England, built in 1386, was in the nave – but there was an admission fee to this particular house of God, and I had other things to think about.

After a while I found to my surprise that I was talking to myself. I don't know whether it was the stress or the alcohol but I suddenly discovered that I was listening to my own voice.

I despise racism more than most people, I heard myself say. *My problem is how can I possibly persuade the world that I am the baby's father?*

Talking to yourself isn't a sign of madness, I thought. It's just showing that you are choosy about who you talk to. But the possibility that men in uniforms might appear to restrain the gabbling drunkard under the tree and drag him off to one of the medieval cellars that presumably abounded in these hallowed grounds caused me to get a grip on myself and think without moving my lips.

I wondered if Annette had received any visitors in her private ward and, if so, how they had reacted to the sight of her baby. Would politeness inhibit them from referring to her dusky skin? I could well imagine how Annette would behave. She would ignore the baby's colour entirely and allow her visitors to fester in their own unease.

And what of the father, the proud progenitor of this little diamond? Was he even now winging his way towards Europe on some discounted air ticket to join in the celebrations? Or was he already the father of more children than he could count, and unmoved by the arrival of another? A more likely possibility was that he was happily unaware of the dramatic consequences of a forgotten jump last Christmas, helped along as it no doubt was by intemperate incursions into the Hadfield family's liquor reserves. Somewhere out there in the sunshine he went about his noble business, unbothered by the prospect of dirty nappies and interrupted sleep.

My thoughts turned to the baby then, the bright-eyed little creature who was now enjoying her second sleepy day on this earth. What did the future hold for her? A loving mother, I hoped, who was now prepared to pay the price for her infidelity. A father who would provide money even if he couldn't provide himself. My final humiliating thought on this unnamed mite was what a bright girl she was going to grow up to be! Her daddy was a professor and not a bankrupt failure who used to sell knickers.

Rain that had threatened all day now began to dampen the Close and I got up and walked slowly back to the hotel. This time I picked up Jane Austen. It was *Northanger Abbey* and for a couple of hours it took me away from my own insoluble problems and dropped me into a simpler world.

Hunger stopped my reading. After a few days in a hotel the food tastes the same no matter what you order but I ate whatever the dinner was and began to feel more like my normal self.

At the next table a couple were having a fearful barney about the conduct of their errant four-year-old. With his glasses and his big forehead you could see exactly what he would look like at forty, but it was the parents that I felt sorry for now. What letdowns and setbacks awaited them as they heroically steered this unresponsive urchin towards manhood?

Only a few months ago my sympathy would have been with the boy, misguided and badly led by parents who had no idea how to raise a child. Only a few months ago I was prepared to blame parents for every failing in their children, but the sad events since have caused me to broaden my view. Parents were children once, and the truth that I now see is this: people don't have a chance because they were brought up by people.

After dinner I went into the hotel's Spires Bar and ordered a pint of lager. My fellow guests, I gathered, were going to a service at the cathedral and I attracted some disapproving glances when it became clear that I was not going to join them but rely instead on the more certain solace of my pint.

Two days without conversation, bills or phone calls had cleared my mind, and after a couple of drinks I began to wonder why I was hiding in an obscure hotel. I went to the girl on reception and told her that I would be leaving in the morning.

In the event I overslept again as my body was still searching for the sleep it had missed, and it was eleven o'clock before I went downstairs to settle my bill. I sat in the lounge and had a coffee while the hotel's computer decided how much it would like.

October approached but the sky was blue and I drove home in weak sunshine. I stopped in Andover for a cold lunch and then wove a leisurely route to the motorway.

A strange nervousness gripped me as I approached the empty house. The world was full of people I didn't want to see. An emissary from my wife, perhaps Kitty Benson, could be hovering in the hedges, or an anguished employee with bills that she could no longer pay. Men in suits could be waiting to confiscate my Rover, or remove the television.

But there was no sign of life as I pulled up at the front door with its white row of milk bottles, and once I had pushed it open against the pile of mail and newspapers on the mat I was able to slip inside and separate myself from the cruel world.

Of course, once I'd summoned the nerve to confront the mail I discovered that I had locked several fragments of that world in with me. Bills, complaints, requests and invitations enjoyed only brief lives before facing the oblivion of the bin, and then I saw the familiar French stamp and realized that a letter from Garth had broken all previous records and reached me in three days. Perhaps the postal system worked more efficiently once you had been sentenced and letters weren't held up while censors looked for evidence that would convict.

I went into the kitchen to find the abandoned plates that had been left on our flight to hospital, and made myself a cup of tea, and then I took it and Garth's letter to the most comfortable armchair in the sitting room and reminded myself that real life had begun again.

> Garth Hadfield 13918
> Maison d'Arrêt de Pau
> Boîte Postale 1616,
> 64016 Pau
> Cedex
> France

Dear Mum and Dad,

This is one filthy hell-hole. I thought the world had dispensed with this level of incarceration. The other place was a palace by comparison. I am jammed in with ten others (no English) in very limited space. Honestly, I could never have imagined anything as bad as this. It is both a detention centre and central prison and holds three times as many people as Bayonne.

The accommodation is straight out of a Dickens workhouse, plaster falling off the walls which are covered with fungus, holes in the ceiling, 12 bunks in the cell piled three high, and one light.

It's a full house – five French, four Moroccans (complete

318

with prayer mats) and an old Dutchman who came direct from a heart bypass operation and can't climb on a bunk so has to sleep on foam rubber on the floor. He got twelve years but when he appealed they raised it to fifteen. The doctors say he has only a year to live.

I am ten feet from the ground and spend most of the time on a bunk six feet by 2 ft 6 in.

Anyway, note the new address.

I believe you have been told of my sentence – three years. The court case was a French farce. I had been given a woman solicitor who only came to see me the day before the hearing, and she had to bring an interpreter as she didn't speak English.

In court the prosecutor spoke for less than five minutes. He said, according to the interpreter they gave me, that there were doubts but he believed that I was guilty although not deeply involved in the drugs business. He was therefore only asking for a sentence of three years.

The customs solicitor spoke next and asked for a fine of twenty thousand pounds. Then my solicitor spoke for ten minutes and demanded my immediate freedom because of doubt about my guilt. I was then asked if I had anything to say and told the story about my friend asking me to take the vehicle back to London.

The judge retired and returned after ten minutes to say that I was guilty and should serve three years. He said that if you drive a car you must know the owner, and if there are illegal substances in the car you are associating with a person involved in illegal activities. Most of all, he said, you didn't check the car before leaving Spain. Two days later I was moved to this pigsty.

If I told you the things that happened here I doubt whether you would believe them. Violence is rife but I have only had one fight myself. Homosexuality is legal but they try to discourage it by never having less than three together at one time. Four days ago they actually had to use gas to separate two men. The act wasn't illegal, but

319

they hadn't asked for a condom which, with the Aids scare, is compulsory!

Since writing the last paragraph I have been taken to see the legal bod here whose job is to explain to prisoners what their situation is. My position is as follows. Having got a three-year sentence I can apply for parole after 18 months (the halfway mark) BUT with various remissions for good behaviour, passing exams, presidential decrees etc., my sentence of 36 months would normally get reduced to about twenty and I could therefore apply for parole after 10 months – that's in May as I was arrested in July.

So I could be out in the spring! All I need is (a) a job offer (b) an address in England (c) a certificate from the customs saying that I have paid the fine.

About the latter, the fines can be negotiated, and the legal eagle here says that they would certainly accept ten grand instead of twenty if I offered it. So all that stands between me and freedom in the spring is £10,000.

The bad thing is that if I don't pay the fine I not only lose all remission but also have to do an extra two years. That would mean I'm locked up now for another four years and nine months.

Well, Dad, it won't have escaped your notice that I don't have ten grand and given what you have spent on me over the years I can't tell you how bad I feel about asking for it. But the difference between sticking this out for another eight months or staying here for nearly five years is so huge that I've GOT to find the money somewhere. I can only promise to repay you bit by bit over the next few years. Please accept this as my I.O.U.

I hope you are both fit and that mum's pregnancy is going along all right. Please let me know as soon as possible whether I have a brother or a sister (or one of both!) It's sad that I won't be there but life is sad at the moment. I must stop now as I've run out of paper – again.

Love,

Garth

I read this letter twice and then fetched myself more tea and read it again. I was astonished by my son's apparent resilience, the easy-going way in which he could discuss his plight, but of course a letter can mislead you, lacking a facial expression and a tone of voice. I couldn't imagine writing so breezily myself in such a desperate situation, but who knew what tears were being shed in the endless hours on his grubby bunk?

When I finally put Garth's message to one side I wondered whether anybody since the first missive was inscribed on papyrus reeds had ever received a letter that was more difficult to answer. I wanted to head for my desk and get out my pen but the thought of what I had to say to him froze me in my chair.

It was impossible to guess how he would react to Annette's baby. Perhaps, in the relaxed manner of today's youth, he would see nothing amiss. But the news of my business collapse – the news that I did not have ten thousand pounds and that my ability to borrow had already been stretched beyond any limits known to the average bank manager – would come as a crushing blow, consigning him to years in prison, a lost youth, a wrecked future.

So I sat with my drink and did not venture to my writing desk. I sank into the deepest reverie, feeling that I was abandoning my son to his fate, and that, as a father, I had been exposed as worse than useless. In the last few months I had already covered every conceivable money-raising possibility in the search for funds that would save my shops.

I felt so low that when I heard a car pull up by the front door I didn't even bother to get up to see who it was. I heard a car door slam, the sound of female footsteps – louder and more importunate than a man's – and then the front door bell rang. I didn't move. There were people I wanted to see, but nobody I was able to face. The door bell rang again and curiosity eventually got me to my feet to peer unseen through the curtains.

A small blonde girl I didn't know stood patiently on the step and as I didn't know her I decided to open the door. Directly I did I realized that I did know her. It was Annabel Henderson, the beggar's daughter.

'Hallo, Mr Hadfield,' she said brightly. 'I wondered if we could have a chat?'

'Come in,' I said, glad now of company which would steer well clear of the painful subjects of Annette, the baby, the shops and the debts.

I showed her to a sofa where she sat down and crossed her legs. She still wore the panda-like eye make-up and funny T-shirts. The message on this one seemed to refer to a pop star I had not heard of. She hadn't put on any weight.

'It's about Garth, of course,' she said.

I nodded. 'I've been sitting here thinking about him myself,' I said. 'It's hard to believe what's happened when I think of him as a little boy.'

The idea made her smile. 'Was he a happy boy?' she asked.

'Very,' I told her.

'Good. Children usually remember the bad things about their childhood if there were any bad things.'

'Like what?'

'Oh, I don't know. The dog being run over. The Christmas present that never arrived.'

'He was happy,' I assured her.

She smiled broadly at this good news and then her face clouded over.

'He has written to me explaining the situation,' she said. 'I went up to London and talked to the people at Prisoners Abroad.'

'You went to London?' I asked, surprised.

'I wanted to get the exact position. You never know what the restrictions are on a letter that is written in prison.'

I felt both guilty and impressed by this; I had never contacted Prisoners Abroad myself although I remembered that Garth had mentioned the organization in one of his letters.

'What did you learn?' I asked.

'The facts are as he gave them to me. Ten thousand pounds will get him out of prison in the spring. The customs fine is the crucial thing.'

'Well,' I said, not knowing quite what to say on this subject, and she looked at me as if she was uncertain too. She was a fragile little creature who reminded me of a kitten that you were frightened of treading on, but she had her father's eyes which suggested intelligence and determination.

'The thing is,' she said finally, 'Garth thought that the recession is hitting you, that things aren't going too well.'

'You could say that,' I agreed cautiously.

'He's worried, to put it bluntly, that you might not be able to find ten thousand.'

'I might not,' I said. 'The shops have closed.'

This grim news cheered her enormously. 'Well, that's fine,' she said. 'You see, my father would like to pay the money.'

'Your father?'

'More for my sake than Garth's, of course. He knows how important it is to me. When I put the equation to him – ten thousand pounds against five years in a French prison – he said at once that he would pay it. If Garth can pay him back one day, fine. If not, not.'

I stared at her in amazement.

'He would do that?'

'It's no big deal. They're overpaid in the Foreign Office.'

'I don't know what to say.'

'You don't have to say anything, Mr Hadfield. I just wanted to make sure that we weren't both trying to pay the same bill.'

She stood up, her business done, and I walked with her to the door.

'Is it okay if I write to Garth to tell him?' she asked when we were outside. 'It would cheer him up.'

'Please do,' I said. 'I think I'll have to fly down there in the next day or two. I've got a few things to tell him myself.'

'Give him my love,' she said. 'My father sends you his regards, by the way.'

323

'Send him mine,' I said, feeling as stupid as I have ever done.

She got into her little car, gave me a wave and roared off down the drive, leaving me to contemplate the humbling fact that my son's freedom was to be bought by a beggar.

20

Strawberry Hill

By the time that Annette was released from hospital with her little friend, I was thirty thousand feet over Nantes or Bordeaux and heading south. I was surprised to learn that I could fly to Pau; before my son took up residence there I had never heard of the place. I had never heard of Air Littoral either, but I found that they provide a return flight from Gatwick for just under two hundred pounds and bought myself a ticket. Climbing through Britain's clouds and discovering that the sun is there all the time always gives me a lift and as the miles between the plane and England increased I began to feel quite cheerful in spite of the nature of my mission.

And Pau, despite its erstwhile obscurity, turned out to be a fine old town with castles and cathedrals and its very own river. Air Littoral recommended the Hôtel Continental and I took a taxi from the airport. (I also, I forgot to say, took a taxi *to* the airport back in England. A smart young man in a suit had arrived at my front door the previous evening and demanded the keys of the Rover which he drove off with a grin that verged on the malicious. But I am learning not to worry about events I can't influence. Pau, at the foot of France, is not far from Lourdes, but it is too late for miracles.)

I spent the first hour in my room at the hotel using the telephone and trying to establish when, or indeed whether, I would be allowed to visit Garth. There is more red tape attached to seeing somebody in a French prison than to almost any other human activity, but the British Consul had not been idle. The forms that I had sent to him along with photocopies of my passport had been forwarded to the relevant department and he now had my visitor's permit and a date two days hence for an 'open visit' of forty-five minutes. All I had to do was ring the prison to confirm that I would actually be appearing.

Once I had dealt with this essential business I felt free to go out for refreshment and a discreet look at French night life. Arabs smoked hookahs in the corner of the first bar that I visited, while chic French ladies, fatally flawed by hirsute armpits, gave me looks which convinced me that they were prepared to put their bodies at my disposal. It was tempting, but not tempting enough, and I spent my money on *filet mignon* instead. Then I went for a long walk along the Boulevard des Pyrénées where the lugubrious natives promenaded in twos and threes.

Garth was less than a mile away now and I wondered what he would be doing. I also wondered, for the hundredth time, whether it was greed, laziness or boredom that had dumped him in these unlikely surroundings. Perhaps there was a misguided spirit of adventure lurking beneath his placid exterior. I hoped it was that.

The following day I filled the time by taking a bus ride to the foothills of the Pyrenees, the mountain range that stretched for nearly three hundred miles from the Atlantic to the Mediterranean and provided one border that was beyond dispute in the world's council chambers. On the other side there were Spaniards getting brown, on this side there were Frenchmen getting wet, and I got wet with them and returned damply to my hotel early in the evening.

The Maison d'Arrêt de Pau, at which I presented myself the following morning, was a sinister-looking building with sinister-looking staff. I had bought at the airport half a dozen paperbacks for Garth to read but these were immediately taken from me as if an explosive device might be concealed among their turgid pages. An official in a blue suit wanted to see my visitor's permit and my passport, and then he gave me a box in which I was asked to leave everything I had with me: pen, lighter, cigarettes, keys, money. Next came a form that I had to read and sign. This said that I undertook not to pass anything to the prisoner, and listed the penalties I would suffer if I did. At worst, I could be locked up for three months myself.

I was now taken by a uniformed guard to a security check, similar to those used in airports, and when this failed to reveal anything subversive I was escorted to a waiting room where half a dozen people mostly women, sat in postures of abject misery.

After a few minutes we were invited to follow the guard out of the room. We went along one echoing corridor and then another. Suddenly I became aware of a row of cubicles with a man sitting in each. The other visitors, accustomed to the procedure, began to disappear into the cubicles and soon I was alone walking up and down and trying to see which one held Garth.

I didn't recognize him at first. The blond hair had been converted into a very short crew cut. The brown face was white and even thinner than before. He stood up but didn't smile, uncertain perhaps of what sort of greeting he was to receive.

'Hallo, Dad,' he said, and shook my hand. 'Thanks for coming.'

There was one fixed bench across the middle of the cubicle with a plastic chair either side. Above about two feet the walls were glass so that the guards could see what was going on inside. The smell was of cheap eau de cologne.

'My God,' I said. 'If this is an open visit, what's a closed one like?'

'It's like a confessional box with an unbreakable glass screen and a bit of mesh between you and the visitor,' Garth said. 'How are you?'

327

'Terrible. And you?'

'About the same.'

He was wearing a rather dirty shirt, track-suit bottoms and canvas shoes with no socks. The general picture was even worse than I had imagined.

'This is not where you are supposed to be,' I said. 'It wasn't part of the programme.'

'Things go wrong in the best-regulated circles, Dad, but first things first. Has Mum had the baby?'

I nodded. 'It was a girl.'

He looked at me. 'Great! You don't seem very pleased about it.'

'There was a complication,' I said.

'Oh no – not Down's Syndrome?'

'Not that, I'm glad to say. No, the baby was black, Garth. So, you see, I'm not the father.'

'Black?' He looked stunned.

'Definitely. I was present at the birth.'

'I don't understand.'

'I thought you might figure it out. You're nineteen.'

'Twenty, actually. I had a birthday last week.'

I felt a pang of remorse at this. My life had been so busy lately that for the first time I had forgotten my son's birthday.

'I'm sorry, Garth,' I said. 'I'll make it up to you.'

But he was thinking about the baby. 'Listen, who do you think the father is?'

'Oliver, obviously. That somewhat dark-skinned professor we entertained last Christmas.'

Garth nodded. 'Of course. I thought he was a nice chap.'

'So did Annette.'

He leaned forward on his plastic chair.

'What are you going to do?'

'Move out.'

'Do you have to?'

'Wouldn't you?'

'I suppose I would. Poor Mum.'

328

'I rather thought "Poor Dad" myself.'

'Well, yes, of course. Poor both of you. What a disaster. What does Mum say about it?'

'I don't know. I left when the baby arrived. Annette wasn't saying a lot. She'd been in labour all night.'

'Jesus,' said Garth and fell silent.

Looking at his pinched face I could only wonder what the last three months had been like for him, but kids are tough at twenty and he looked as if he was going to survive.

'I have other news,' I said. 'I'm afraid it's no better than the first item.'

'Blimey,' said Garth. 'I was hoping you'd cheer me up.'

'The news I've got, I should have stayed at home,' I admitted. 'But I wanted to see you. You don't look too bad. You'll survive and learn from your mistake.'

He scowled at this. A lecture was the last thing that he needed – he'd had plenty of time to reproach himself.

'What's the news?' he asked.

A guard appeared on his side of the cubicle and I realized that we were being watched from both sides. He stood there for a while looking at us, and then moved on.

'I've gone broke,' I said.

Garth looked at me as if I hadn't made sense.

'What do you mean exactly?'

'The shops are in the hands of a receiver. I've lost everything, including the Rover.'

'God, you *are* having a good year,' he said.

'But there is some good news.'

'I don't believe it.'

'I had a visit from your friend Annabel Henderson. She asked whether her father could pay your customs fine so that you could be out in the spring.'

'What did you say?' he asked nervously.

'I said that would be very kind of him. There's a letter for you from her in the post.'

The first genuine smile filled his face.

'That's terrific,' he said. 'I can start counting days.'

329

'I can't wait for you to get back to England,' I said. 'Of course, I don't know where I'll be.'

The smile faded. 'That's awful news about the baby, Dad. I can hardly believe it.'

'She's still your half sister,' I told him. 'Be kind to her.'

We talked then about how he spent his time and what he ate, and he told me a little about his depressing existence. He talked of wild-eyed psychopaths, violent, predatory youths, and the constant menace of perverts in search of a partner. The company he was keeping sounded less attractive than a knot of toads. Soon after that a bell rang to tell us that our time had expired, and a guard appeared on my side of the cubicle and said something which obviously meant that I should leave.

'I bought you some books,' I said, 'but they took them away.'

'They're like that,' said Garth briefly.

We both stood up and I gave him a hug, a proximity which seemed to alarm the guard who stepped forward and put his hand on my shoulder.

'Look after yourself,' I said fatuously. I was afraid that tears might appear in my eyes. My son had never looked more lost than he did standing alone in that cubicle waiting to be taken back to his cell. 'We'll have a holiday in the spring together.'

'We certainly will,' he said, and summoned up a smile from somewhere.

And then the guard busily ushered me and the other visitors back down the ill-lit corridors to a room where we were all searched. This took longer than I expected – they obviously thought that they were going to find something. But finally I was allowed to move on to another room where I collected my confiscated belongings.

I left the prison and walked thoughtfully back to my hotel to make a phone call.

Landing at London Gatwick Airport when you want to go to

330

London must, I thought, be like arriving in Britain by boat and being told that you have to disembark on the Isle of Wight. It was no inconvenience to me, of course. I knew the airport before they mysteriously added London to its name. But it won't surprise me if a few foreign tourists don't feel short-changed one of these days and start breaking noses.

I made the long walk from aircraft to baggage reclaim with a spring in my stride. I lifted my heavy case from the carousel as if it were empty, and I smiled at the group of surly customs officers who lurked in my path and defied them to challenge me.

Among the meeters and the greeters on the other side of the customs hall, Sadie Beck stood out like champagne on a tea trolley. And as soon as I had barged my way through the crowds I dumped my case and hugged her. The long kiss that followed pre-empted all conversation and moved eventually from her lips to her snub nose.

'Well, hallo,' said her husky voice when I let her go.

'Why aren't you at work?' I asked, picking up my case.

'I got a phone call from my favourite man. He was in France, apparently, and had nowhere to live.'

'How awful. Did you think of anywhere?'

'I have a flat that is big enough for four.'

I took her hand and we walked across the concourse to the short-stay car park where she had left a BMW which turned out to be hers. She was wearing very casual clothes, a loose yellow sweater and pale blue jeans, and her ponytail hung down her back. I was quite certain that she was as pleased to see me as I was to see her. When I rang the previous evening she had whooped with delight at my bad news.

'I'm always owed days off,' she said now, 'so I told them that I was taking one.'

'Wonderful,' I said, getting into her car. 'Strawberry Hill, please.'

Once we had got out of the car park and were on the London road, she said: 'So your wife had a black baby, your

331

son's in prison and your business has gone bust. Apart from that, how have things been?'

We both laughed. She wanted more details about the bare facts that I had given her on the phone, but with her as an audience a tragic recital of my misfortunes became a comedy show. She was a professional cheerer-upper.

'My future is bleak,' I concluded. 'On the other hand, I've always wanted to be a kept man.'

'I've always wanted to keep one,' she said, 'and he was always going to look like you.'

'I suppose you hoped that when he arrived he wouldn't be broke and demoralized?'

'They are both very temporary conditions.'

This upbeat approach to my manifold problems lifted me even further and by the time we reached Strawberry Hill I was beginning to think of the future rather than the past. It wasn't at all clear how it was going to develop, but Sadie's cheerful reaction to my situation began to convince me that it wouldn't be all black.

We stood in the lift in silence, perhaps in wonder at what we were doing, but she leapt into action once we were alone in her flat on the third floor and I watched fascinated as the successful television executive segued into domestic mode. Within half an hour my dirty shirts were in a washing machine and I was lying in her blue bath, drinking sherry.

'I'm taking you out to dinner tonight,' she called. 'It's a celebration.'

When I came out of the bathroom she refilled my glass and planted me in front of one of her television sets while she took a bath herself.

'Do you like television?' she asked.

'Love it. All those people talking to you and you don't have to answer.'

The flat was fairly luxurious, I realized when she disappeared. A professional lady with no commitments had money to spare on the very best furniture and fittings. The

332

paintings on the grey walls, mostly of northern Italy, looked as if they were investment as well as decoration.

I listened to the usual senseless atrocities on the news and tried to overcome my feeling of strangeness at being in this flat. When you are accustomed to your own place it takes some adjustment to feel at home in someone else's, but despite its immaculate condition this wasn't a showroom apartment. It had a lived-in feeling to it that allowed visitors to relax.

Sadie reappeared in a white silk housecoat with her hair pinned up.

'I could sell photographs of you,' I said.

She came up and kissed me.

'You're not going to be bored here, are you?'

'Bored? I've had all the excitement I can take. What you have here is an oasis of peace.'

She smiled at that and went off to dress. I wandered across the room to a group of framed photographs that stood on top of an ornate bookcase. There was one of Sadie at about seventeen in school uniform with a building that looked like Cheltenham Ladies' College in the background. Another showed her in what appeared to be Africa, surrounded by various animals who had been tamed by her charm. There were others that featured the accoutrements of a television studio, and were filled with well-known faces grinning jokily for an informal picture. These few clues to Sadie's past presented a portrait of a fulfilled life and unrelieved success. A similar selection of pictures from my own life would tell a less rapturous story.

The television news had been replaced by a game show of mind-numbing banality, but out of deference to my hostess's career I quelled the urge to turn it off. I didn't have to watch it, though. I returned to the bookcase and picked up a few volumes that stood in pristine condition on the polished shelves: Zola, Fielding, Melville, Flaubert, Joyce. They looked very like the sort of books that belong to people who don't read books.

When Sadie next appeared she was wearing a short red dress with a low neckline and some sort of black shawl.

'I'm ready,' she said.

'For what?'

'I thought we'd eat first.'

'Lead me to it,' I said. 'Airline food leaves a hole in your stomach.'

We got into the lift. Sadie said: 'I knew we'd get together in the end, you know. I knew it was only a question of patience.'

'How did you know that?' I asked.

She smiled at me. 'I'd made up my mind.'

In the end men are sadder than women because they start out wanting much more. Ambition is built into their genes, and for the unhappy majority there is a chastening disparity between their grasp and their reach.

I had plenty of time at Strawberry Hill to consider the perversity of life.

I had thought that it was Alec and Laurie who had reared delinquent children but it was the tarnished golden boy who was in prison.

I had imagined that neither of their marriages would survive as Alec eloped with the long-lost Mavis Jones, and Judy the bruiser found her rightful vocation of mistress in France. But it is my marriage that is over.

I had deluded myself that I had erected a bastion of financial security, while Alec slaved irritably for a pittance and Laurie involved himself in a series of increasingly uncertain money-making adventures. But I am the one who has been left penniless.

These were reverses enough to confine me to Sadie's flat for two full days while I pondered the enormity of my fall. I had no urge to go out. Nobody knew where I was and the shrill demands of the telephone had been mercifully removed from my life.

Newspapers arrived in copious quantities, a tax-deductible benefit of Sadie's career which required more than a minimal knowledge of world events. Their cross words and crosswords carried me through until lunch when I concocted something light in her white kitchen, confident of a feast later. The afternoons I divided between television and reading *Moby-Dick*. Call me Ishmael.

In my confused condition such uneventful days were a treat. It was the early retirement that I had planned, even if it had arrived without a pension. On the other hand I spent nothing and the money I had withdrawn from the building society, minus the costs of Salisbury and France, remained beautifully untouched in plastic envelopes in my suitcase.

Sadie kept erratic hours. There was nothing conventional about the world of television. She might arrive at four in the afternoon or eight o'clock in the evening. But she arrived bearing food and by the time she appeared I was ready for company. Our dinners were something to look forward to. The wine that we consumed in inordinate quantities was the only alcohol I touched all day.

After one gargantuan nosh she declared tipsily: 'I yearn for you with every fibre of my being.' And we skipped coffee and adjourned hastily to her bed. Her wide eyes looked up at me afterwards as if she couldn't believe her luck.

'I always expect to get home and find that you've gone,' she whispered.

'Gone?' I said. 'You'll need a court order to get me out of here.'

'I'd like a court order to keep you in here.' And she hung on to me as if there was a real danger that I would leave.

On the third day I went out to buy her a present. The world was still going on. The teeming hordes were still working to live or living for work – it wasn't clear which. The recession was still going on, too, I noticed. The 'sale' notices were on display in every other shop.

I went into a jeweller's and bought a brooch and some costume jewellery. I wanted to buy her a ring, but I would need her finger for that. The idea of buying her something helped to relieve the guilt that I felt at being a squatter in her fragrant home. My offer of rent had been sternly rejected, although my battered self-esteem would have benefited from the passing of money. I bought myself a few things in the toothpaste, shampoo and deodorant line, and drifted unthinkingly into a small pub.

Two other recession victims stood at the counter with pints of beer, discussing jobs they couldn't get. They were both ruddy-faced men in their thirties, once involved, I gathered, in the double-glazing business. I could never understand why people spent about six thousand pounds on double glazing to cut their heating bills. They would have to live a long time before their heating bills matched the cost of the double glazing.

'Anyway, I've been promoted at home,' one of the men said.

'Promoted at home, Geoff? How's that?'

'I've moved up in the hierarchy. One of the gerbils died.'

I finished my half pint and fled. Raw insights into other men's domestic pain was the last thing that I needed, and I set off briskly on the longish walk to Sadie's flat. Walking alone is the best time for thinking. There are no distractions, no newspapers, radio or television, no conversation. In fact thinking is all that you can do.

And it dawned on me as I walked back that I would have to visit Annette – not just to collect the rest of my wardrobe and any other little possessions that I had acquired in forty years and actually wanted to keep, but also to tie up the loose ends with my unfaithful wife.

I told Sadie this over dinner that evening and wondered how she would take it.

'Use the BMW,' she said. 'You can pack a lot of stuff in there.'

And so the following morning, feeling only slightly apprehensive, I drove north to Richmond and Kew, joined the M4 and headed west. After the majestic protection of my Rover I felt strangely vulnerable in a smaller car to the eccentricities of other drivers, but perhaps I was feeling vulnerable anyway.

What sort of reception did I expect? Annette's maxim, like many another battler, had always been that the best form of defence was attack, and I didn't plan to waste time looking for any contrition. Abuse was more likely to be my lot.

I pulled into the drive and looked at the house which had once been my pride and joy, visible proof of my success and an investment which, if all went wrong, would make me a rich man in a much smaller house. There was no clue about whether anybody was there.

But then I heard a baby cry. I unlocked the front door and went in. There was nobody there to greet me and I followed the sound of the crying baby into the sitting room.

Annette, in jeans and an old shirt, was kneeling on the floor changing a nappy. The naked baby lay on her back on a changing mat, kicking her legs and crying. I stood watching this cosy scene and said nothing. Annette looked up at me, went back to her nappy-changing duties, and said nothing.

I don't know why I was in any doubt at the hospital about whether the baby was black. She was very black indeed, despite having one white parent. She looked up at me as if I were intruding on her space. It was good to know that she already felt at home.

'Sophie,' said Annette.

'What?'

'Her name is Sophie.'

'Really?' I said. 'What's her surname?'

Annette gave me one of her looks which, over the years, had dispatched many a blundering recipient to social extinction, and didn't reply.

But when the nappy was fixed and the baby returned to a new cot in the corner of the room, she walked across to the sofa, sat down, and said: 'Are you back for good or is this just a visit?'

I sat down myself in an armchair that faced her.

'It's a visit,' I said. 'I've come to collect some things.'

She looked sad at that. 'I see,' she said.

'I take it you hoped the baby would be white?'

'Well,' she said with just the hint of a smile, 'there was a chance.'

'Not much of one. I had a vasectomy over two years ago, Annette.'

She thought about this and then frowned. 'You were waiting just in case the vasectomy had gone wrong?'

I nodded. 'The skin colour was a bit of a giveaway.'

'You deceitful bastard,' she said quietly.

For some reason I found this observation intensely gratifying: I felt that I was reaching her at last.

'Is Oliver flying over?' I asked.

'Oliver doesn't even know.'

'I think he ought to.'

'I may write.'

There was a silence then that threatened to become embarrassing, and I got up and went over to look at the baby. She was very pretty, with lovely features despite her age.

'You're moving out then?' Annette said.

'Today.'

'And I keep the house?'

'Of course.'

I returned to the armchair and looked at her. She seemed more relaxed now that she had the house.

'Have you got any money?' I asked.

She smiled.

'Quite a lot, actually.'

We had always kept separate bank accounts, an unusual arrangement these days apparently, but a necessary one because my own account sometimes became inextricably linked with the shops. A standing order every month transferred a generous amount to Annette's bank account. At the height of the shops' success it was two or three thousand a month. It didn't matter one way or the other to me at the time because I always expected that, in a pinch, we would share it.

'How much have you got?' I asked. 'It's no longer my business but I need to know.'

'I'm not sure. It must be between twenty and thirty thousand.'

'Good God, and I'm broke.'

She laughed. 'Well, don't ask me to help you, Max. I've got a big house to run and a child to raise.'

'It didn't seem to occur to you,' I said, 'to offer to pay Garth's fine and save him from spending five years in prison.'

'Of course it occurred to me,' she said indignantly. 'I was waiting to see whether you could find the money first. And now it looks as if I shall need every penny.'

The baby began to cry and she went over and picked her up.

'I've been to see him,' I said.

'See who?' she said, rocking the baby.

'Garth. You've got this son called Garth.'

'You went to see him? How is he?'

'Dreadful, but you needn't worry. The fine is being paid and he could be out in May.'

She returned the baby to the cot. 'I knew you had the money,' she said. 'When I heard that the shops had gone bust, I thought I bet he's got a fortune hidden away somewhere.'

'I have nothing,' I said. 'No job, no money, no home and no car.'

She stared at me coldly. 'Well, don't expect me to weep. It's you who's moving out.'

'Good God!' I said angrily. 'Did you expect me to stay?'

She looked at me then with genuine dislike. 'The trouble with you, Max, apart from the fact that you're unbelievably lazy and totally selfish, is that you're bloody pompous.'

'Pompous?'

'He asked pompously! Standing on your dignity like that when you haven't got any is a fruitless exercise.'

'Thanks,' I said, standing up. 'I'll just collect my things and be off then.'

'To see your doxie.'

'What?'

'Sadie Beck.'

I was thrown but I didn't show it. I didn't even bother to ask how she knew about Sadie. The lethal workings of the female network had always been a mystery to me.

My wife's green eyes half closed. 'Do you know what really pisses me off?' she asked. 'A woman gets caught with a baby, but a man just puts his trousers on and goes home.'

I could see her point, of course, but I wasn't here to negotiate. There are actions and there are consequences in this harsh world and a small black baby was sleeping happily in her cot.

'Having had a vasectomy,' I said.

This mild rejoinder seemed to infuriate her out of all proportion and it became necessary for her to stand up.

'That makes your adultery okay, does it?' she shouted. 'Your licence to screw! Well, screw you, Max. That thing in the wall over there is called a door.'

There was nothing more to be said. I went upstairs and spent half an hour collecting the things that I wanted to take with me, emptying drawers and filling bags and cases.

I carried my belongings out to the car, climbed in wearily and slammed the door.

As I drove for the last time through my elegant white gates I realized with a chill in my stomach that a very uncertain future stretched before me. Perhaps, when the recession is over, I shall make friends with a different bank manager and open a small shop that I shall run myself. Perhaps one day Sadie and I will move out of her flat and buy a big house in the country.

New interests will replace the old and then with time and the elusive commodity of luck I won't even miss the reassuring pleasures of the Comedy Hotel.

READ MORE IN PENGUIN

In every corner of the world, on every subject under the sun, Penguin represents quality and variety – the very best in publishing today.

For complete information about books available from Penguin – including Puffins, Penguin Classics and Arkana – and how to order them, write to us at the appropriate address below. Please note that for copyright reasons the selection of books varies from country to country.

In the United Kingdom: Please write to *Dept. JC, Penguin Books Ltd, FREEPOST, West Drayton, Middlesex UB7 OBR*

If you have any difficulty in obtaining a title, please send your order with the correct money, plus ten per cent for postage and packaging, to *PO Box No. 11, West Drayton, Middlesex UB7 OBR*

In the United States: Please write to *Penguin USA Inc., 375 Hudson Street, New York, NY 10014*

In Canada: Please write to *Penguin Books Canada Ltd, 10 Alcorn Avenue, Suite 300, Toronto, Ontario M4V 3B2*

In Australia: Please write to *Penguin Books Australia Ltd, 487 Maroondah Highway, Ringwood, Victoria 3134*

In New Zealand: Please write to *Penguin Books (NZ) Ltd, 182–190 Wairau Road, Private Bag, Takapuna, Auckland 9*

In India: Please write to *Penguin Books India Pvt Ltd, 706 Eros Apartments, 56 Nehru Place, New Delhi 110 019*

In the Netherlands: Please write to *Penguin Books Netherlands B.V., Keizersgracht 231 NL–1016 DV Amsterdam*

In Germany: Please write to *Penguin Books Deutschland GmbH, Friedrichstrasse 10–12, W–6000 Frankfurt/Main 1*

In Spain: Please write to *Penguin Books S. A., C. San Bernardo 117–6° E–28015 Madrid*

In Italy: Please write to *Penguin Italia s.r.l., Via Felice Casati 20, I–20124 Milano*

In France: Please write to *Penguin France S. A., 17 rue Lejeune, F–31000 Toulouse*

In Japan: Please write to *Penguin Books Japan, Ishikiribashi Building, 2–5–4, Suido, Tokyo 112*

In Greece: Please write to *Penguin Hellas Ltd, Dimocritou 3, GR–106 71 Athens*

In South Africa: Please write to *Longman Penguin Southern Africa (Pty) Ltd, Private Bag X08, Bertsham 2013*

BY THE SAME AUTHOR

A Village Called Sin

The idyllic village of Compton Sinbury – better known as Sin – has two types of citizen: the randy poor and the preoccupied rich. Paul Vanner, for example, can't make money *and* love, much to his wife's chagrin. But to the likes of Toby Beauchamp, in deep trouble for offering sweeteners to the planning office, money can get you in even *more* trouble than sex. Then there's Harry Grant, local journalist, hungry for news. The only trouble is that when a big story breaks, it's far too salacious to appear in print . . .

In the Midday Sun

On the sun-soaked Costa del Sol three fugitive brothers from England contemplate the female form and the shape of things to come.

Matthew has incurred the wrath of the Inland Revenue, Daniel has pulled the perfect bank job and Mark – well, Mark sings for his supper playing seventies hits on tourist bar pianos. But Matthew, Mark and Daniel have spent far too long in the midday sun. And for three volatile young Englishmen in Spain, that's a recipe for big trouble . . .

The Sinner's Congregation

Named after a trip to see *South Pacific*, the Bali Hotel stands not in the South Seas but in a remote corner of Southern England. Reluctantly owned by Martin Lomax, the Bali has a bar that provides refuge to residents and a group of eccentric locals including the sharp-tongued, gin-swilling Mrs Stapleton and her verbal sparring partner Adam.

One fateful day, however, the mirth and merriment of the Bali is clouded by the arrival of a spectre from Martin's past. His name is Edwin Catchpole and to say that he is a vicious brute would be flattery. To Martin, the opportunity to even the score is far too tempting to resist . . .

also published:

The Nudists
Secret Lemonade Drinker
The Tax Exile